THE WEIGHT OF CONVERSATION

Dialogues Across Time

JON NELSON

NELSHEIM
PRESS

Phoenix, Arizona
www.NelsheimPress.com

Copyright © 2026
JON NELSON
THE WEIGHT OF CONVERSATION
Dialogues Across Time
All rights reserved.

No part of this publication may be reproduced, distributed, or transmitted in any form or by any means, including photocopying, recording, or other electronic or mechanical methods, without the prior written permission of the author, except in the case of brief quotations embodied in critical reviews and certain other non-commercial uses permitted by copyright law.
This work may not be used, reproduced, ingested, or otherwise incorporated, in whole or in part, into any machine-learning dataset, generative AI system, or large language model without the author's express written permission.

JON NELSON
For permissions or inquiries, contact: Jon@NelsheimPress.com

Printed Worldwide
First Printing 2026
First Edition 2026

Library of Congress Control Number: 2025924817
ISBN 979-8-9936009-0-1 (Trade Paperback)
ISBN 979-8-9936009-1-8 (Deluxe Hardcover, Dust Jacket)
ISBN 979-8-9936009-2-5 (Hardcover, Case Laminate)
ISBN 979-8-9936009-3-2 (eBook)

10 9 8 7 6 5 4 3 2 1

This is a work of fiction. Names, characters, places, and incidents either are the product of the author's imagination or are used fictitiously. Any resemblance to actual persons, living or dead, events, or locales is entirely coincidental.

Interior Book Design by Walt's Book Design
www.waltsbookdesign.com

Where events from a living person's life are referenced, they reflect matters previously made public by that individual; no new factual allegations are asserted.
No person or estate has endorsed this work. All trademarks and quoted material remain the property of their respective owners and are used under applicable law.

Published by Nelsheim Press LLC

For My Mother

who taught me to love stories,
ask questions,
and listen with both ears.

Gone from this world, but always in the front row.

We are shaped by the conversations we survive.

Table of Contents

Preface 1
ACT I 3
    THE SHAPE OF THE SELF
Chapter 1 5
    Socrates – Jordan Peterson: *The Unexamined Life*
Chapter 2 21
    Sigmund Freud – Carl Jung: *Sight beyond Sight*
Chapter 3 37
    Simone Weil – Friedrich Nietzsche: *The Hunger of the Soul*
Chapter 4 53
    Jesus – Judas: *The Silver and the Silence*
ACT II 67
    FAITH, FIRE, AND THE FRINGE
Chapter 5 69
    Jesus – Bill Maher: *Faith Without Thunder*
Chapter 6 87
    Dalai Lama – Adolf Hitler: *The Sermon and the Swastika*
Chapter 7 105
    Mary Shelley – Galileo Galilei: *The Monster We Made*
Chapter 8 121
    Thomas Edison – Steve Jobs: *The Patent and the Pixel*
Chapter 9 137
    Helen Keller – Stephen Hawking: *Touch and the Edge of Space*
ACT III 151
    THE THEATER OF GENIUS
Chapter 10 153
    Oprah Winfrey – Marilyn Monroe: *The Spotlight and the Silence*
Chapter 11 173
    Fred Rogers – Robin Williams: *The Man Behind the Laughter*
Chapter 12 191
    Mark Twain – Oscar Wilde: *The Weight of Wit*
Chapter 13 211
    George Carlin – Hunter S. Thompson: *Fear and Laughter in America*

Chapter 14 233
    William Shakespeare – Lin-Manuel Miranda: *The Verse and the Flow*

Chapter 15 251
    Frida Kahlo – Pablo Picasso: *The Door and the Wall*

Chapter 16 269
    Ludwig van Beethoven – Wolfgang Amadeus Mozart: *The Phantom and the Prodigy*

ACT IV 283
    THE COST OF CROWNS

Chapter 17 285
    Cleopatra – Julius Caesar: *Love and Conquest*

Chapter 18 307
    George Washington – King George III: *The Crown and the Crossing*

Chapter 19 323
    Winston Churchill – Sitting Bull: *The Land and the Lion*

Chapter 20 339
    John F. Kennedy – Fidel Castro: *The Missile and the Mirror*

ACT V 357
    FIRE AND MEMORY

Chapter 21 359
    Maya Angelou – Harriet Tubman: *Still I Rise—Still We Run*

Chapter 22 373
    Martin Luther King Jr. – Abraham Lincoln: *The Long Arc*

Chapter 23 389
    Malcolm X – Nathan Bedford Forrest: *The Rifle and the Resolve*

Chapter 24 405
    James Baldwin – Anne Frank: *Echoes in the Silence*

Chapter 25 419
    Nelson Mandela – Princess Diana: *The Prison and the Palace*

Albert Einstein..435
    Closing Thoughts

Postscript 437

About the Author...439

PREFACE

History is not a timeline. It's a battleground of ideas echoing across generations. This book isn't a fantasy; it's a thought experiment that bites back.

Imagine a space where time collapses, language adapts, and impossible conversations happen with clarity, chaos, grace, and grit.

I didn't give these people scripts. I gave them voices, then stepped back and let each conversation take the shape it demanded: unpredictable, alive, untamed.

Some talks cut straight through. Others circle for a while before anything honest shows up.

What would happen if Jesus debated Bill Maher on faith?

If Socrates sparred with Jordan Peterson?

If Mandela helped Princess Diana reclaim her voice?

Or if Sitting Bull faced Winston Churchill across the table?

It all rests on one thing:

Conversations have weight. And when we listen to the past, we start hearing ourselves.

I didn't write this to teach history. I wrote it to argue with it.

Come for the legends or for the fight. Either way, you'll leave with the people, not the lecture. You'll see how raw, strange, brilliant, hilarious, and human these figures really were.

Here they speak for themselves.

You'll laugh.

You'll roll your eyes.

You might forget to breathe.

If Robin Williams brings you to tears, or Nathan Bedford Forrest incites rage, the experiment is working.

Welcome to *The Weight of Conversation*. Take a seat. Turn the page.

ACT I

THE SHAPE OF THE SELF

What happens when the soul looks in the mirror?

Before anyone was drawing borders or polishing crowns, people were already lying awake asking the same heavy questions. Who am I? Why am I here? This act starts there, not with a lecture, but with the kind of arguments that follow you into the shower, the commute, the sleepless 2 a.m. stare at the ceiling.

Socrates sits across from Jordan Peterson, two men constitutionally incapable of letting a question stay simple. One rattled ancient Athens, the other rattles modern culture, but both insist the unexamined life is a kind of death. Their conversation doesn't land on a slogan. It keeps coming back to a quieter question: is it really worth tearing your life open just to stop lying to yourself?

Freud and Jung return to the fight they never settled, not so much circling as pacing: two men who'd rather keep arguing than find out who they are without the feud. They still can't agree on what the mind even is: prison, chapel, or some half-lit stage full of shadows convinced they're running the show. Neither lets the last word go, because if the fight ever ended, they'd have to figure out what was left of them afterward.

Simone Weil confronts Nietzsche, hunger against will, fragility against force. Their meeting isn't fair. She brings emptiness and surrender; he brings swagger and a raised fist. Neither one backs off what they are. They don't fix the tension between them. They just sit in it and let it hurt.

And finally, Jesus and Judas: love and betrayal wrapped so tight around each other it's hard to say which one moved first. The coins haven't moved yet. Neither has the guilt. Two men looking at the same night from different angles, both half-afraid of how their story will be told long after they're gone.

Nothing settles down in this act. The soul prowls, pokes at itself, and keeps reopening the same old questions. These aren't clean origin stories; they're proof we've been fighting over meaning for as long as people have been brave enough, or bored enough, to ask why anything matters at all.

Chapter 1

Socrates – Jordan Peterson: *The Unexamined Life*

ACT I: The Shape of the Self

Socrates (c. 470–399 BCE)
Athenian stonemason-turned-teacher who taught by questions and left no books of his own. He embarrassed pretenders, stood his ground in court, and drank the hemlock rather than beg for exile. No slogans, no flattery. Just the examined life and the discipline to accept its costs. Through Plato he survives as a voice that corners lazy certainty and asks for definitions before applause. Not a saint, a citizen with stubborn courage, convinced freedom begins where pride yields to correction.

Dr. Jordan B. Peterson (1962–)
Canadian psychologist and professor whose classroom voice spilled online and turned into a global argument about responsibility. He answers emails at midnight, tells people to carry weight, and pays a public price for saying it out loud. Loved and loathed in equal measure, he frames meaning as practice, not mood: habits, honesty, small aims that stack. Jungian roots, clinical spine. Not a mascot; a clinician who thinks competence beats outrage and that careful speech is cheaper than regret.

Setting
Late afternoon in a stoa-meets-seminar room: stone walls and fluorescent light. A scarred oak table, a paperback of the *Republic* open by habit, a legal pad waiting for the next admission. One chair ergonomic, one

stubborn wood, angled for talk more than performance. Coffee cooling. The room remembers arguments and forgives them. It's a place you can be wrong out loud and not be thrown away. Call it fair ground, not safe ground. The stone hangs on to what's said, the light lets some of it fade, and the heat wears people down until honesty feels cheaper than performance.

Peterson dabs his forehead, sweating like a child sent to the principal's office. Socrates rolls his shoulders like he's removing a cloak of noise and hanging it where the air won't touch it. Begin.

Socrates

Jordan, people have carved your sentences into talismans and weapons. Before we inherit the worship or the anger, answer plainly. Why begin with order?

Peterson

Because chaos doesn't negotiate. When you're drowning you don't start a debate about swimming theory; you grab the first thing that feels solid. Order isn't a slogan. It's the difference between a day you can survive and a day that swallows you. I've watched the second happen too many times.

Socrates

Last year a magistrate's son kept quoting maxims about purpose. I walked him to the market with a drachma and a list: bread, olives, salt. "Left hand: coin. Right hand: list. First things first." He reached for the olives and forgot the bread. That night dinner was thin, but the point wasn't. Order feeds you eventually; it just doesn't bother flattering you on the way in.

Peterson

I had a student who'd "cleaned his room" and nothing changed. We wrote down one conversation he was avoiding: his sister. He made the call at lunch. The room stayed messy for a week; his life didn't.

Socrates

Order feeds, yes, but it wounds, too.

Peterson

You try to stop the bleeding and the questions keep coming, and eventually you realize the wound isn't just damage. It's the place you actually notice what hurts and what matters.

Socrates

We agree. A city will grant you a parade for a lie that flatters and a scaffold for a truth that doesn't. Keep the parade; the costume costs too much.

Peterson

That's familiar. The longer I've talked, the more I've been misunderstood. Sometimes on purpose, sometimes not. I've been a prophet, a monster, a father figure, a fraud, a meme. Some days before lunch.

Socrates

A meme is only a rumor with pictures. The question remains the same: are you willing to be useful even when the usefulness is ugly?

Peterson

So what do I do? Stop? Speak softer?

Socrates

Speak slower. Leave air inside the sentences so they cannot be hammered flat into slogans. Even fire needs oxygen or it just leaves smoke.

Peterson

I can try. The problem with speaking slowly is people fill the silence for you. But if I may pivot, do you ever wonder if your questions caused more harm than good? Honestly.

Socrates

Every day. I learned to love the wound that teaching leaves, but not all wounds heal straight. I have seen men use my questions like picks to dig tunnels under their duties. It is not the question's fault, but I do not absolve myself easily.

Peterson

Yeah. You know, sometimes I want to go silent for a year. Just vanish. Let the noise fall back to its natural level without me. Then I get an email from someone who made it one more day because something clicked. And… damn it, I'm back at the microphone.

Socrates

Once, a boy mistook my silence for approval. He went into the city and quoted me, reading my pause as consent. That laughter still rings in my ears: a reminder that silence can pass for agreement when it was only grief.

The ergonomic chair squeaks like it's negotiating a contract with gravity.

Peterson

This chair's going to break before my soul does.

Socrates

You say, "clean your room." I hear the city mumble: the poor have no rooms, only debts with walls. What then?

Peterson

Then you fight on two fronts. Start with the lever you can pull today: sleep, food, work, small aims. That's agency. But don't stop there. Bad rooms are built by bad incentives. So you vote, you sue, you organize. Broom in one hand, ballot, or lawsuit, in the other.

Socrates

So you do not despise the citizen who demands the city be just?

Peterson

No. I despise theatrical justice that never fixes a hinge. If protest doesn't change a policy or a person's next Thursday, it's a selfie with a slogan.

Socrates

Then let us speak to the weary: repair what is within reach while you learn how to reach further.

Peterson

And stop calling cynicism wisdom. That lie takes bright kids and turns them into very articulate ghosts.

Socrates

You have been placed on banners.

Peterson

Right, exactly. Hence people call me right-wing. Others insist I'm left until I offend their favorite fantasy. For the record: I come from a country with universal healthcare and I've argued for treatment over cages for addicts, and for protecting speech even when it offends. That doesn't fit into one American team jersey. I'm not a hashtag; I'm a human being. Teams want mascots. I'm not applying.

Socrates

A lion painted on a standard is not a lion. Your complaint is ancient. In my day I was "corruptor" or "saint," depending on who needed me to prove their point. Between those posters lived a person who could still misplace his sandals.

Peterson

Exactly. The brand eats the man. I'll take correction; I'm just not interested in spending the rest of my life as a logo on somebody's team jersey.

Socrates

You speak of being eaten. Let us speak of being carried. My companions carried my name forward, Plato most of all. In his telling I shone brighter than the man deserved. Xenophon set me at polite tables; Alcibiades dragged my questions into bed and into war. Survival changes the story; that is the price of being taught.

Peterson

I worry about that constantly. I say "responsibility," and some hear "domination." I say "tell the truth," and some take it as a license to be cruel. My audience skewed young and hungry. That's a blessing. It's also a risk. When you're starving, you don't ask too many questions about what's in the stew.

Socrates

Then you must teach them to chew.

Peterson

Okay, so, how?

Socrates

With pauses. With questions that do not flatter. With examples that excuse no one, including you. Plato preserved me with precision; Alcibiades converted me into a weapon. Both called themselves my students. You cannot choose your interpreters; you can choose your clarity.

Peterson

So I aim to be harder to misuse. Cut down the slogans and put some actual air back in the sentences.

Socrates

Yes. And sometimes, a warning printed on the label: "This medicine has side effects if taken without love."

Peterson

I could live with that.

Socrates

Tell me of your students. Not the enrolled, the listening.

Peterson

The letters I remember come from people who were nearly gone. "I was going to quit my job, my marriage, my life. I set one thing in order instead. It was small; it mattered." And then there are the ones who try to imitate my rough edges. It's easier to cosplay a tone than to build a soul.

Socrates

Children copy masks before faces. Be patient with their first attempts and ruthless with your own.

Peterson

Ruthless with my own?

Socrates

Your sentences are hammers. Learn where the nail belongs. And if a boy uses your hammer to break a window, do not pretend you never forged it. Teach him where the window ends and the structure begins.

Peterson

I'll try. The trouble is the scale. I can't sit with each kid and ask the dumb practicals: "Did you sleep? Who's your honest friend? What weight are you carrying this week?" That's where the change actually happens.

Socrates

Then say it again here. Call it your liturgy.

Peterson

I've watched three things change more young men in a couple of months than a thousand tweets ever will: regular sleep, one honest friend, and picking up something heavy three times a week. Sleep gives the brain a leash; the friend picks up the leash when you drop it; the weight teaches your body it isn't only a head. None of that is ideology. It's plumbing.

Socrates

Plumbers hold cities together while orators argue about fountains.

Peterson

That line should be embroidered on a towel.

Socrates

Add a footnote: sleep lets a man meet himself; only then can he meet another without disguise.

Peterson

Disguise is efficient until it isn't. I thought careful speech would save me from being misused. It helps. It also makes enemies of people who prefer simple villains.

Socrates

We have time for the gods.

Peterson

Careful.

Socrates

I am careful. You have said: act as if God exists. Your words have traveled far, and some have used them to build a ladder they refuse to climb.

Peterson

I say it because people want belief to descend like lightning. For most, belief grows through practice. Live as if the highest thing is watching and deserving of your best, and you become someone who could believe without embarrassment.

Socrates

I had a voice. Not a god with a biography, but a restraint I could feel. It did not tell me what to do. It warned me what not to do.

Peterson

More like a brake before the cliff than a map of the whole route.

Socrates

Yes. Your "as if" points direction; my "do not" keeps the cart from rolling into ditches. Together they make a passable road.

Peterson

In clinic, conscience feels like that: direction plus boundary. People ask for revelation; most days they need a guardrail.

Socrates

You have spoken much of suffering. We should make it explicit. Pain delivered me knowledge the way midwives deliver children: noisy, often bloody, never optional. The questions were the hands.

Peterson

I frame suffering as inevitable, not as punishment. If you carry it voluntarily, it becomes meaning; if you deny it, it becomes resentment. But I don't romanticize it. Some pain is senseless. We don't fix it by pretending it's a poem.

Socrates

We fix it by staying. Midwives do not flee because a birth is difficult.

Peterson

Staying is the whole trick. Sleep helps you stay. Friends help you stay. Lifting teaches your body you can push against resistance and not break. Then you can pick up moral weights without folding.

Socrates

And when a man says, "I have suffered; therefore, I am permitted," we must answer, "You are permitted to become gentle."

Peterson

Yes. I wish that line would travel.

Narrator (V.O.)

That sound you heard wasn't surrender. It was the human exhale: the kind you make when the point lands and you can finally unclench your jaw without losing your place. Socrates knows it. It feels like an opening to keep things simple.

Socrates

Jordan, say it plainly: do you believe your age is in moral decay?

Peterson

Yes. Falling birth rates, rising anxiety, tribal politics, endless dopamine chasing; discipline traded for outrage. We outsource meaning to hashtags and then medicate the emptiness. We're clever and lonely and dangerous all at once and… damn, these lamps are making me sweat like a televangelist.

He coughs, waves it off.

Peterson

Sorry. Point is: we're collapsing in slow motion.

Socrates

Define virtue for me without reciting a catechism.

Peterson

Responsibility. Discipline. Speaking truth even when it burns. Building families and strength. Muscle, yes, but character too. Keep your promises. Clean your mess. Aim at the good and act like it matters that you do.

Socrates

Has your truth burned you?

Peterson

Repeatedly. Publicly. I've lost health, friends, jobs. I've been misquoted so often I forget what I said. Most of us aren't afraid of the truth; we're afraid of hearing it phrased so clearly we can't pretend we misunderstood. But silence is worse. It doesn't explode, it just eats away at you. One day you're effectively gone and people are still waiting for a funeral that already took place.

Socrates

Then why persist? Conviction is a long road with short rations.

Peterson

Sure, well, yeah—because not speaking feels like betrayal. Betrayal of the people I've watched teeter at the edge, of my profession, of myself. There is a difference between suffering you choose and suffering that picks you. If I choose to carry some of this, maybe a few others lift their portion too. Maybe that's enough for now.

Socrates

And if, while you carry it, bystanders catch a spark?

Peterson

Then I repent and adjust. I don't dump the torch; I just try to be more careful where I swing it. It doesn't make me innocent. It just keeps me accountable.

Narrator (V.O.)

It isn't drama; it's a breath. The kind that follows a clean hit and lets two men admit they're not just symbols with quotes attached. If this were a play, somebody would cue a laugh right here. Peterson trips over one anyway, which is the honest kind.

Peterson

Children tidy their rooms.

Socrates

Children who tidy their rooms?

Peterson

That's—yeah, that's not what I meant. Great. Now I'm being trolled by a dead philosopher.

Socrates

A rare perk of dying is the leisure to troll. But if you wish to be precise, say it more precisely.

Peterson

Fine. Start where you stand. Make one thing you touch a little less hellish. Keep your word to one person. Expand from there. If your house is on fire, you don't start with a lecture on urban planning before you pick up a bucket.

Socrates

And if the city's aqueduct is cracked?

Peterson

You fix that, too. But you don't drown in theory while the kitchen burns.

Socrates

You have avoided one word: politics.

Peterson

Of course. Yeah, because I don't want to be in politics. I want to be in clinics. I want rooms with one person and one problem and enough time to tell the truth.

Socrates

The city decides what your room costs, whether the person inside is caged or treated, and what words are permitted in that room. You can say you're not "in politics," but politics still prices your work and locks or opens your doors. A city's just a clinic blown up to street size. If you pretend it isn't, the illness keeps walking past your laws while you argue over labels.

Peterson

We think we're arguing about politics, or God, or justice. Mostly we're arguing about which words get to count as real.

Socrates

Then choose carefully which ones you're willing to live by.

Peterson shifts and the chair groans. He presses his lips, not to stall but to choose. Socrates offers no way out. Just the challenge to speak plainly.

Peterson

Then I'll keep it simple. Start with the basics. Floors: no one should fall through one and not come back. Cages: use them when you have to keep people safe, not so you can pretend the problem's cured. And speech: if only the loyal get to talk, you don't have a city anymore; you've built a camp with better branding.

Socrates

If the names confuse the crowd, omit the names and keep the practices. But never omit the courage.

Peterson

I'll try to remember that on the days the emails pile up like snow.

Socrates

Snow's honest. It never pretends to be warm.

Peterson

You can be impossible.

Socrates

So can you. We continue.

Peterson

Do you ever think about what your students did with you after you were gone? Not philosophically, personally.

Socrates

Plato cleaned me up in his grief. He straightened the straps on my sandals and smoothed my rough answers. It was affection, and it was revision, and I suspect he thought they were the same act. Xenophon made me safe for dinner: tidied the edges, softened the questions, turned me into someone a household could quote. And Alcibiades. He made me thrilling. He wanted permission more than wisdom and sometimes took my questions as signatures. I left them all with burdens they chose themselves.

Peterson

That's what scares me about legacy. I don't fear being forgotten. I fear being remembered as a caricature that hurts people I wanted to help. "Be responsible" becomes a sneer. "Tell the truth" becomes a cudgel.

Socrates

Then make your last words instructions on how to read your first ones.

Peterson

How would that sound?

Socrates

Begin with mercy; proceed with discipline; end with apology where you failed. Place that at the door of your house. Let every visitor touch it as they enter.

Peterson

I could live with that, too.

Socrates

Now—death. Less drama than arithmetic, if you're honest. I chose mine; you've walked near yours. What, precisely, frightens you?

Peterson

Not the moment. The misreading after. That what I said becomes a costume someone wears to justify harm. That my children carry a burden that isn't theirs. That the people who needed help lose it in the noise.

Socrates

Then start ordering your death now, while you're still alive to do it. Leave instructions for your students and your enemies. For your children: tell them they are not you. For your enemies: tell them you are not theirs. For those you helped: tell them you did not save them; you showed them where their hands were.

Peterson

I can write that. As for my own fear, if there's anything left, I suppose it's irrelevance. Not to be important, but to have mattered in the place where I actually stood.

Socrates

You matter where you stand if the person beside you manages to find his feet.

Peterson

Right. Of course. That's a good measuring stick.

Socrates

My fear is simpler: that my questions become furniture: polished, admired, unused.

Peterson

We can fight that together: me by speaking slower, you by refusing to let the questions get comfortable.

Socrates

We can try.

Peterson taps the legal pad once, like a gavel, and leaves a small blot of ink. He grimaces, thumbs at it, then looks up.

Peterson

Okay. Let me ask the present-tense, unpoetic question. People are breaking. Families, institutions, young men especially: they're unraveling. If you were alive now, really alive, not visiting in a room that feels like history, what would you do tomorrow morning?

Socrates

I would ask them in public to account for one belief they hold without knowing why. Not to humiliate, though some would feel humiliated, but to make visible the hole where the foundation should be. Then I would stand there while they tried to patch it with slogans, and I would wait, and when the slogans failed, as they must, I would help them build something truer from the rubble.

Peterson

That would get you canceled by noon.

Socrates

Then perhaps the afternoon would be quiet enough for study.

Peterson

You're infuriating.

Socrates

And you are tired. We are both what we are advertised to be. Only more human and therefore less consistent.

Peterson

Yeah. That's accurate.

Socrates

There is something else. Many who suffer have been taught that their suffering is their identity. Ask them to put part of it down and they fear disappearance. I knew a boy once who wore his pain like a crest; when I asked him to set it on the table, he looked at his hands as if they'd vanish. We must see them first. Call them by name. Only then do we ask them to set anything aside.

Peterson

And if we miss?

Socrates

We are allowed to miss. One cannot examine a life one refuses to admit is error-prone.

Peterson

Say the line, then. The one everyone came for.

Socrates

If I say it for applause, it becomes less true. I'll try anyway.

Peterson

Don't make it a sermon. Just say it crooked, the way it actually lives.

Socrates

I am saying it crooked.

He rubs his temples, counting the words he won't use. Then he speaks.

Socrates

The unexamined life may not be worth living. And the unexamined conviction—no, wait—ah. The unexamined conviction may be what burns the world.

Peterson

That… yes. That lands. Maybe because you let it wobble first. And good. At least you didn't tell me to tidy my tomb.

Socrates

I don't tell anyone to tidy their tombs. Truth walks, it does not vault.

Peterson

I'll… keep walking. Keep asking. Try to be a worse idol and a better man. Try to leave room in the sentence for someone else to breathe.

Socrates

And I will keep listening. Even when I am gone. Perhaps especially then.

They don't shake hands. Peterson caps his pen and misses the clip. Socrates leaves his cup unemptied. Outside, a cart rattles past. Inside, they let the quiet stand.

Narrator (V.O.)

If you showed up for a winner and a loser, you picked the wrong room. What you get instead is two men leaving space in their sentences and then refusing to rush in and fill it. If you're going to steal anything, steal that.

Chapter 2

Sigmund Freud – Carl Jung: *Sight Beyond Sight*
ACT I: The Shape of the Self

Dr. Sigmund Freud (1856–1939)

Physician who gave the private life a clinic. With a couch, a clock, and relentless notes, he turned symptoms into sentences and insisted the unconscious be treated, not mythologized. His terms entered the language, including ego, id, and repression, because the method worked often enough to keep discipline honest. Critics call him reductionist; he called himself practical. He prized evidence, schedules, and limits, and mistrusted euphemism and theater. Read fairly, he taught a century to bring pain into daylight and to make confession a tool, not a pageant.

Dr. Carl Jung (1875–1961)

Freud's heir who wandered past the laboratory into symbol, myth, and memory older than one lifetime. He named archetypes, sketched mandalas, and argued that wholeness requires making peace with what we fear and disown. Too mystical for some, too clinical for others, he still gave artists and analysts a grammar for images that won't sit still. Individuation as pilgrimage, not pose. A room big enough for reason, ritual, and the stubborn dream that keeps returning.

Setting

Vienna, an office made for work. A warm lamp, a low couch, a rug that prefers symmetry. Case cards fanned like work, not decor. On one wall: a mandala; on another: the eye's cross-section. A pocket watch keeps ordinary time while two men try to name what hurts. Books lean in quiet rows; tobacco and cabinet polish share the air. Outside, tramlines; inside, a table where discipline meets symbol and neither is allowed to grandstand.

Freud taps ash that wasn't there and grimaces at his own habit. Jung's pencil makes a light groove on a blank card he doesn't mean to use, then he turns the card over as if to spare it from duty. They sit as men who have written each other letters they still know by heart and would not send again.

Freud

We should begin with a patient, not a preface. Thirty-two, married. She cries when touched—here, at the shoulder, never the wrist. Briefly, cleanly; her body keeps its own schedule. Then apologies, one after the other like coins counted. She hates the crying and hates the hating. That is the fact.

Jung

Before the fact: what visits her in that hour before the house remembers breakfast. Name one image and you'll move the hour; refuse the image and it will move you.

Freud

Don't cut my case into parable. The lever is childhood. Training toward usefulness. Tears punished by the silence that claims to be proud of you. We follow avoidance until it exposes wanting. The symptom is a lock; the work is the key. No prize for the lock.

Jung

If she brings me a figure: an old woman at the bedpost, a dog who refuses the door, that figure will do more work than an adjective. If she brings me nothing, I accept the nothing. It is evidence.

Freud

Evidence is what can be repeated. An "old woman at the bedpost" appears whenever metaphor is hungry.

Jung

Hunger usually points you to a kitchen, not a fantasy. If the image feeds, it remains. If it refuses to feed, I let it go. The rule is not poetry. The rule changes things.

The clock keeps time without asking for notice. Coal settles. They give the room a moment to find its rhythm.

Freud

You resisted me the day you decided meaning could be older than a body and still be medicine. I have no argument against age. I have an argument against fog.

Jung

Then let us keep the air clear. Your case card, my drawing, your watch. Three objects. No incense.

Freud rotates the case card once and leaves it open. The script is compact, disciplined. Across the room, the mandala sits where he can see it, patient as a diagram.

Freud

Second patient. A barrister, forty-six. He counts the brass tacks on his desk before leaving chambers. He calls it "quaint." He is tired of—

Freud glances down, misreads his own note.

—quiet. Tired of quaint.

Jung

Compulsion is a guard who still thinks he's on duty. Until you tell him otherwise, he keeps saluting ghosts.

Freud

I ask, "Who dies if you leave without counting?" He names what the ritual has kept from daylight. We move the counting here, to this room, and starve the superstition while teaching the hand not to panic. No pension. Retired all the same.

Jung

Our difference is not method in that case; it is tempo. You cut faster.

Freud

Cutting is sometimes mercy.

Jung

Agreed. And sometimes the wound will not close until it has been named by something older than technique. That is what your students call mysticism when they are tired and afraid.

Freud

They call it mysticism. I call it a bill: numbers, dates, results I can point at.

Jung

You trusted me until I stopped sounding like your echo.

Freud

I trusted you until you stopped sounding like a clinic. You brought a cathedral to my street and told me you had improved the lighting.

Jung

Lighting matters. But I accept the rebuke. I made a perimeter with ink in years when the floor tilted. I am not ashamed of the drawing; I am ashamed of how loudly I needed its order to keep from breaking.

Freud

You frightened yourself.

Jung

I did. And you frightened the room when you were afraid to lose it. But don't answer that yet. Let it sit.

Freud

I frightened the discipline into obedience. We're both guilty of saving our lives and calling it principle.

Freud closes the case card and places his hand on the pipe case without opening it. It is a habit, not a pose.

Freud

Third case: a nine-year-old won't sleep without a lamp—he's "busy with night."

Jung

Name the guard and retire him; then he sleeps.

Freud

He turns it to the wall, then off; agency teaches sleep.

Jung

Agency, yes. But meaning too. If he believes the room is on his side, he sleeps.

Freud

Rooms don't take sides; people do—well or badly.

They leave the boy in peace. The coal settles with that tired little sigh it makes at the end of its burn.

Freud

Fourth case: a seamstress who stops breathing when the thread knots. She says, "it's the machine."

Jung

Or the knot. Or a mother who taught that a mistake is a verdict.

Freud

I move the verdict here. We tangle the thread on purpose and time the panic. We name the judge and dismiss him when he goes off docket.

Jung

I ask her to draw the first dress she ever wanted and the dress she was allowed. If the second picture looks like a permission slip, we keep drawing until the hand remembers it's not a court.

Freud

And yet every verdict leaves paperwork. Even when the court is gone, the docket lingers. Our work is to decide which pages are evidence and which are only habit.

Jung

We should speak the difference plainly. You begin with drives. You ask desire what mask it wears. You cut where repression tightens the bandage.

Freud

I name the defense and remove it where possible. I mistrust the stories because stories can be trained to flatter the teller.

Jung

I begin with pattern. I ask whether the dream belongs to a grammar older than the patient and whether that grammar can be taught to the daylight without worship. If the figure becomes an idol, I break it.

Freud

We agree more than our students hope. They enjoy a schism. It excuses the work.

Jung

Students love a clean break. If the fathers never reconcile, they get to play the exiled heirs.

Freud

Religion. While we are naming differences. You smuggle it into medicine and insist it is psychology.

Jung

I smuggle nothing. I observe how human kneeling redistributes itself. If a god leaves, something else gets the kneeling—a schedule, a lover, a nation. I just name where the knees went. When the altar goes, people just pick a new place to kneel. Sometimes it's a lover. Sometimes it's a job. I name the kneeling so it can be bargained with, not worshiped blindly.

Freud

Piety is wish arranged into ceremony. I neutralize wish so the patient can work. Altars are for people who can afford not to change their mind.

Jung

And yet, some leave my room with a figure that kept them alive when your handle slipped. Others leave yours with a handle that kept them from drowning in a storm I would have watched too long. Between the handle you give them and the figure I give them, there's a person in the middle just trying to breathe.

Freud

As long as breathing does not become an excuse for never deciding.

Jung

We are agreed.

The pocket watch glints. Freud palms it and lets it be.

Freud

Let us risk the part that embarrasses us both. You accuse me of making everything sex.

Jung

I accuse you of answering that question twice. You taught Europe to confess, and then you kept the confessional open because you feared the doors would close to anything else.

Freud

I feared the mob. I have been called a corrupter of youth by men who had never looked inside their own shame. Method kept the room from becoming a trial.

Jung

And I made the room a chapel. Not to scold you. To survive. I needed a pattern that did not change with every face. I see now what I could not then: I wanted the pattern to bless me too.

Freud

So we come, as always, to transference. Patients bring us the fathers they could not argue with and the sons they could not keep.

Jung

How many sons does a theory insist on before it admits it's lonely?

Freud

Fewer than you think. More than I wanted. I said I was protecting a fragile discipline. I was. I was also protecting the part of me that believed I had earned the right to be right.

Jung

I wanted a father who could bless the part of me that did not look like him. When you could not, I called disagreement destiny and left.

Freud

I wanted a son who did not leave.

Narrator (V.O.)

They don't look at each other when the worst line lands. Men who've lived by discipline take pain without spectacle; too much attention would turn confession into a show. In the quiet between hand and object, each knows how he leaned on the other, not to worship or to wound, but to steady the work of making suffering less cruel.

Jung

We did not grieve in private. We argued in public with microphones tied to our throats. I prefer this room. And I… I must admit: I kept your first letter in a drawer that smelled like varnish. I told myself it was for the record. It was for the room we could not occupy at the same hour.

Freud

I marked your lectures with a pencil too hard for the paper. I told myself it was rigor. It was worry that the boy who admired me would not survive the man who disagreed with me.

Jung

We were wrong about what admiration must become.

Freud

And about what disagreement must forbid.

No hand reaches for the other. The instruments stay between them like witnesses not asked to swear. The room holds the admission and refuses to clap.

Freud

Applause confuses noise with consent. Coal heat persuades without witnesses.

Jung

I kept journals when the floor tilted. I drew so the words would stop performing. If the drawing looks like vanity to a street I do not blame the street. From inside, it was triage.

Freud

I made a clean room in a dirty century. You came in with muddy boots and I mistook your tracks for contempt. They were fear, not contempt.

Jung

And pride. I will not purify that sentence. I liked being called necessary. It kept me from admitting how often I felt like a patient with no analyst.

Freud

You have one now. He is older and less certain. He distrusts your most eloquent sentences and his own.

Jung

I hear his marginalia when I write. It used to slow me into cowardice. Now it slows me into care.

Freud

That is acceptable.

Outside, the tram drags the city past. Inside, the room refuses to become a museum. It insists on being a place where work still happens.

Freud

A veteran wakes at two. No images. Only the certainty that something essential has been forgotten. He drinks water, counts nothing, waits for sleep that does not honor him.

Jung

Certainty itself is the dream. I give it a shape so it will stop being a fog. A door in a barracks, a shed, a kitchen. He opens the same door each night until the room that keeps refusing him remembers his name. Then we walk it to daylight.

Freud

We reassign the alarm: breathing with numbers, drinking a glass of cold water, placing a hand on wood. If an image arrives, good. If not, we do not kneel to absence. The body learns alarm; it can learn refusal.

Jung

Some refusals are the only holy things we ever manage. Saying no to what keeps cutting you. That's as close as some people ever get to prayer.

Freud

Holy is your word. I will not correct it. I understand what you intend.

Jung

Thank you.

They are stingy with gratitude because they know it can be a bribe.

Freud

Another. A priest who no longer believes. Panic at the altar; relief at funerals because grief provides a script.

Jung

We remove the nouns from God until he can describe what love asks of him without props. If the picture won't make room for him to be decent, he leaves before it crushes him.

Freud

We treat the panic first. Then the lie. If he will not respect the role, he leaves. I will not stitch metaphysics to an ulcer.

Jung

He is not an ulcer. He is a man who loves a village he can no longer speak to without lying.

Freud

He is both. He will also need money. That is not cynicism. It is a case note.

Jung

Then we find him work that does not ask him to be divided.

Freud

That sentence meets standard.

Jung

We keep walking the same streets with different maps. You draw straight lines; I keep sketching trees in the margins. We still turn up at the same bridges, grumbling about direction, but neither of us walks away when the beams start to sag.

Freud

Bridges stay up because of bolts, not because somebody wished hard enough.

Jung

Wishes build nothing. But images can teach a hand what to lift when it forgets it is allowed to lift.

Freud

So we argue the same argument in cleaner sentences. That is progress.

Jung

Or rehearsal. Which is not an insult. Rehearsal's fine. Keeps the beams from sagging.

Freud

Legacy. I want a young doctor in a provincial town to open a book and not drown. I want lines that keep bridges standing when the river is high.

Jung

And I want the same doctor, once he can breathe, to remember that the patient is older than textbooks. That she arrives with a dream about a river she has never crossed and that the river is not a test but a guide. The scaffold should not block the view.

Freud

Reasonable.

Jung

We disagree on first principles. We are faithful to the same suffering.

Narrator (V.O.)

Let's not use the moment for a eulogy. Offer the long comfort to the person who'll need it, and use this room for what can still be made right.

Freud

There is a simpler confession I have avoided. I did not want to be surpassed. I wanted the room to obey me and call it gratitude. I tell you this now because the sentence is true and because my pride cannot use it to earn applause in this room.

Jung

I did not want a seat at your table. I wanted my own altar. I say it now because I am tired of smuggling sainthood in through the back door of theory.

Freud

Then we are even and indebted. That is an honest inventory.

Jung

It is.

Freud opens the pipe case and closes it again without touching the pipe. He sets the watch on the desk and does not wind it. Jung leans closer to the mandala and does not point.

Freud

One more case. A painter, thirty. Two exhibitions. Neither success nor failure. He says he is "resting his eye." He hates the late mornings and cannot lift a brush.

Jung

We paint one ugly picture no one will see. If joy returns to the hand, we follow. If not, we grieve the career and save the person.

Freud

We treat refusal disguised as fatigue. Who is he refusing? We find the name and place it where he can see it without pretending it is weather. The canvas returns or does not. Either outcome is cleaner than a lie.

Jung

You are kinder than rumor.

Freud

I am not a rumor, Jung. I'm a tired physician with charts and blood pressure readings, and I don't trust adjectives to do the work numbers can do.

Jung

And I am a physician who mistrusts emptiness when it arrives dressed as discipline.

Freud

That line will be popular.

Jung

I consent to popularity when it serves the work.

The fire dulls. The room drops the theater and just starts tallying what's left on the table and what's going to follow them into morning.

Jung

A question, and I will owe you silence afterward. What do we owe the wound beyond naming it?

Freud

A treatment plan. A schedule. Limits. The refusal to make the wound a credential.

Jung

And a story that lets the guard go home without calling him a fool. That is all I ever meant by symbol.

Freud

Then say "story" when you mean story. Leave "god" to men with different uniforms.

Jung

I will if the story agrees to be heavy enough to hold the weight I put on it. When a story starts to float, it stops being honest and starts turning into an idol. I would rather crack it than let a patient bow to it.

Freud

Good.

Narrator (V.O.)

Freud reaches for the watch and decides not to wind it. Jung caps his pencil and leaves the mark he didn't use. It isn't reconciliation. It's restraint: two men letting their hands do small work instead of turning the moment into a monument.

Jung

You once said disagreement is not a sacrament. You were right. It is our dialect.

Freud

A useful one. It prevents superstition and complacency in equal measure.

Jung

If we were other men, this is where we would pretend reconciliation.

Freud

We are not other men. We're technicians. Let's keep this a conversation, not a pageant.

Jung

No theater. Only the morning.

Freud

Bring a journal. I will not worship it. I will look at what chased you and failed.

Jung

Bring the notes from the woman who cries at a hand on the shoulder. I will see if your key cut too close to the skin.

Freud

Done.

Jung

Done.

Narrator (V.O.)

The corridor wants them single file. They don't oblige. No benediction, no curtain call. Just two tired men putting on coats after a long shift. Same honesty, less theater.

Chapter 3

Simone Weil – Friedrich Nietzsche: *The Hunger of the Soul*

ACT I: The Shape of the Self

Simone Weil (1909–1943)

French philosopher, factory worker, and ascetic who treated attention as a moral act and suffering as something to honor without romance. She starved in solidarity with occupied France, wrote with surgical clarity, and kept asking whether love meant making space so another could live. Suspicious of power and sentimentality, she tethered justice to hard truth. Dead at thirty-four, she left notebooks that read like dispatches from the front: fierce, spare, and allergic to self-flattery.

Friedrich Nietzsche (1844–1900)

Philologist-poet who wrote in lightning and paid for it with loneliness and illness. He smashed idols, warned against ressentiment, and asked whether we could will a clean "yes" to life without leaning on borrowed heavens. Misread often; useful when read carefully. Not a cartoon of cruelty, closer to a man begging for courage to tell the truth about power, art, and pain. His best pages demand strength without swagger and honesty without costume.

Setting

A plain refectory overlooking a working street. Long wooden table, heel of bread, chalk dust on a slate the cleaner missed. The window opens to bicycles and a street that works. A kettle keeps its small promise. Books and notebooks sit ready, margins wide enough for second thoughts. No flowers. The chairs are unkind to backs and kind to attention. Nothing here is romantic on purpose. It is a room where you could eat, argue, or pray, and none of it would need an announcement. Plain things that do not lie. A good place to test whether strength and surrender are enemies, or simply the same nerve reporting two ways.

Weil turns the slate toward Nietzsche. The chalk phrase reads: "Attend to what is." The word "Attend" is nearly gone, the others still intact. She sets the chalk beside it, then folds her hands.

Weil

Hunger is not a metaphor here. It's a witness that refuses to flatter us. It keeps count while the mind tries to turn things into poetry. Today we let it testify.

Nietzsche

Hunger testifies to weakness before it testifies to truth. It makes the saint proud and the coward obedient. Be careful what you enthrone.

Weil

I enthrone nothing. I place the crust where we can see it and ask whether the soul can be fed without stealing from the body that carries it.

Nietzsche

The body is not a courier; it is the first fact. Break it, and the soul plays funeral songs to prove it is still present.

Weil

I have starved. Not to perform, but to listen. I wished to hear truth without the noise of appetite. If I call that obedience, you will hear cowardice. I call it attention.

Weil

At the factory I learned the kind of attention that doesn't feel holy at all. Oil under the nails, a foreman who thinks shouting makes the belt run faster, a stopwatch that believes it is God. If you don't attend, the glove catches, the wrist pays, the day bleeds.

Attention wasn't a halo; it was counting screws, learning which sound means the press is about to jam, looking up when the new girl's face goes white. If I used a sacred word for that, forgive me. In kitchen language: attention means you keep people from getting hurt and you tell the truth about what hurt them.

Nietzsche

Attention cuts—but only where it should. When you starved, did you sever illusion or merely pierce your own heart and name the wound holy?

Weil

Both, at different hours. The honest answer isn't tidy. The poor taught me this: under affliction, truth visits briefly and without warning. If you're not watching, you miss it.

Nietzsche

Then write it on your slate and stop bleeding for it. This—

Nietzsche taps the walking stick with two fingers, its metal ring faint against the wood.

Nietzsche

—has been my tutor. Every step: economy. Every pain: a censor. I have no appetite for pieties that congratulate suffering for merely existing.

Weil

Nor do I. Affliction is not a sacrament. If any speech remains, it owes precision. I call that obedience: to what is, not to men, crowds, or doctrines.

The talk slows down. The bread stays where it is; the chalk waits its turn.

Nietzsche

You have chosen your tyrant well. Reality is a stricter master than any priest. I chose a rival instead: the will. My stubborn next step, a rope pulled hand over hand out of a ditch without asking the ditch for permission to be crossed.

Weil

And when the rope burned your hands, did the burning teach you anything gentler than victory?

Nietzsche

It taught me not to pretend gentleness is a method. Gentleness isn't a method; it's what shows up afterward, if it shows up at all. And it's usually late.

Weil moves the crust with two fingers toward the center of the table. Crumbs scatter like small admissions.

Weil

Not self-hatred.

Nietzsche

Not vanity in armor.

Weil

Decreation isn't self-hatred or disappearing so the cruel can breathe easier. It's setting down enough "I" for truth to make its own gravity. In kitchen words: make space so truth can walk in without tripping.

Nietzsche

Will isn't vanity in armor or swelling until the room breaks; it's choosing the next step when applause is unavailable.

Weil

Obedience: refusing to lie about what is in front of you.

Nietzsche

Strength: refusing to lie about what is inside you.

Weil

That hinge between us is just the strip of ground between our verbs.

Nietzsche

Bad roads, too many graves. Miss the signs and you're liable to end up in one of them.

Weil

Then let us name the difference without hatred. I submit the self to reality. You assert the self against it. Between those verbs the ground is hard.

Narrator (V.O.)

Even the fly makes an effort. We wave it off and let the room do its small, practical job: listen first, decide later.

Weil

When I refused bread, I did not believe bread was evil. I believed that hunger could teach me where my speech was corrupted by comfort. The body objected. It had reason.

Nietzsche

Reason's often just a guard at the gate of fear, making sure nothing too honest gets through. Yet I will not scold the body for shouting. Mine has shouted me into lucidity and madness by turns. There are mornings when the light itself is a whip.

Nietzsche

On those mornings I make a tent of my fingers and turn the lamp until the room is almost honest. Cloth on the eyes. Bitter drink. Steps counted from bed to desk like a man crossing a river in flood, touching only the sure stones.

When I say will, I mean the next stone. Not conquest, not flags. A plan no larger than one clean sentence, then another. If a trumpet ever sounds, it is far away and for someone else. My instrument is a walking stick and a rag over the light.

Weil

Then I ask forgiveness for making chastity of pain. It is a habit of mine. A bad habit in good clothing.

Nietzsche

That sentence is the first incense I trust. Self-suspicion's cleaner than any creed I know.

Nietzsche lifts the walking stick, balances it across his knees, and lets it rest there like a measure laid over unruly notes.

Weil

You wrote sentences that sounded like trumpets. I do not despise trumpets. But the poor do not own them. The poor own silence, and the little rhythm of a spoon against a tin bowl.

Nietzsche

Then keep the rhythm, and I will keep the blast. Between them, perhaps, we strike something like music.

Weil

We may. But only if we attend.

Weil touches the slate.

Weil

Attention is a slow instrument. It doesn't flatter the one who holds it.

Nietzsche

A blade dulls on purpose when it fears blood. Your attention refuses suspense, refuses theatre. That is its nobility. It is also its peril.

Weil

Because it tempts pride. Because it's easy to fall in love with austerity and mistake emptiness for wisdom. I know.

Nietzsche

And I know the opposite temptation: to gild appetite and baptize it genius. The soul, drunk on itself, will happily turn any craving into a principle if the room claps loud enough.

The crust stays unbroken. Not holy, just... not spoken for yet.

Weil

You wrote, once, about strength that did not need the permission of heaven. I have no quarrel with strength. I quarrel with the word "need." The strong often mistake their resolve for reality and break people against it.

Nietzsche

The weak mistake reality for law and call their surrender virtue. Both lies are efficient—and fashionable. I grew ill of them long before my spine learned to write its own letters in pain.

Weil

You speak of pain as a critic. I have known it as a censor. It crosses out entire paragraphs of thought and leaves only a single word: "Breathe."

Nietzsche

On certain days it leaves only, "Endure." On others it whispers nothing whatsoever and even makes the whisper seem theatrical.

He raises the walking stick, then rests it again. The click on the floor is sharp, like a tick of time.

Nietzsche

My pain isn't noble. It just shows up on time.

Weil writes one word on the slate: "Hunger." The chalk squeaks, then quiets. She rubs the tail of the "r" with her thumb until it blurs like weather on stone.

Weil

Hunger has taught me how little of me is necessary for love to act. If God exists, He uses small doors. The hinges complain a little, but they hold.

Nietzsche

If God exists, He keeps an insulting silence.

The words come in one long piece, steady, like they've been waiting behind his teeth for years.

Nietzsche

Still I have sometimes envied the creature who kneels with honest bewilderment and manages to rise again with the bewilderment intact and somehow bearable, because the very shape of kneeling seems to lengthen the lungs and let him carry one more hour without lying to himself that the hour was sweet.

Nietzsche breathes once and lets the sentence arrive unbroken.

Weil

Thank you. That is not mockery. It is the courage to admit longing without instructing it.

Nietzsche

Longing is stubborn. It sits at the edge of the bed like an old dog and refuses to learn tricks. I trained mine to bite rhetoric first.

Weil

Did it obey?

Nietzsche

Poorly. It prefers to bite at night when the room is darkest and my sentences have lost their posture.

Weil

Mine prefers morning. It wakes before me and steals my breath until I pray without words. I do not ask; I attend.

She nudges the crust his way. He studies it like a proposal that doesn't insist.

Nietzsche

If I eat, will it ruin your lesson?

Weil

It may rescue it. Take half. We will call it a grammar of mercy.

He splits the crust, a quick, clean break. Crumbs fall. He chews simply. Weil looks past him, watching the slate like it might speak.

Nietzsche

Mercy beats pity. Pity likes to be seen. Mercy just pays and goes home without leaving a trail.

Weil

Yes. Pity is just the strong admiring themselves. Mercy feels more like an apprenticeship between equals.

Nietzsche

Equality isn't sameness. It's just paying a soul what it's owed without slipping yourself a little tip for being so noble about it.

Weil

Write that on the slate if you like.

Nietzsche

No. Words harden when they enter chalk. Let yours remain soft long enough to be useful.

The walking stick leaves a faint crescent on the wall. In the window's light, it looks like an eyelid half-shut.

Weil

You have been used by the wicked and misunderstood by the lazy. That is not entirely your fault. But some sentences of yours carry knives in their pockets; men who love knives borrow pockets.

Nietzsche

I know. My sister stitched sheaths while I slept. Later, uniforms marched with quotations they did not deserve. It's a grief that doesn't age out. Years pass and it still hits like fresh shame when I see my sentences in their uniforms.

Weil

Then permit me a counter-reading. Your Übermensch, to my ear, is not a tyrant. It is a person who refuses to make others small in the bread line to feel large.

Nietzsche

I would sign that sentence without edits, gladly.

Weil

Then you see: obedience and will are not enemies if they report to the same truth. My obedience bows to reality, not to domination. Your will bows to creation, not to appetite.

Nietzsche

We're cousins, then, pulled apart by pride, shoved back under the same sky.

Weil writes a second word on the slate, below the first: "Attention." The dust gathers in the groove of the "t" as if even chalk could learn to pause.

Weil

Attention learns the difference between a poor man and a "problem."

Nietzsche

Unprofitable, yes. Hence rare.

Weil

Rarity does not absolve us.

Nietzsche

No. But it explains the news.

They let the window breathe. A cloud drifts by, slow and heavy.

Weil

You once placed your arms around a horse and wept. I will not interpret it for you. I will only honor it. There was no audience, and you were still real. That is more valuable to me than any book review.

Nietzsche

If I have one absolution, it lives in that mane. The world insists that the mind is the cleanest organ; the body keeps embarrassing the thesis. Good. Embarrassment is a decent pedagogue; it gets to the point faster than shame ever does.

Weil

Shame wastes time. Embarrassment just tells the truth and lets us move.

Nietzsche

Proceed, then. Ask the question you have been aiming at since you said "witness."

Weil

If the boy you were sat here, frightened of his own fervor, what would you place in his hands: this stick, this bread, or this chalk?

Nietzsche

The chalk. The stick is a memory of defeat; the bread spoils quickly. But chalk—

Nietzsche takes it between thumb and forefinger; white grit coats the half-moons of his nails.

Nietzsche

—chalk makes cheap vows. That's its mercy; you can write hard words and still wash them off when you realize you were wrong.

Weil

Write, then.

Nietzsche hesitates, then prints a small, exact word beneath hers: "Stay." The "S" is careful, the "y" almost shy. He returns the chalk like it might bruise.

Nietzsche

I left too many rooms before they learned how to keep me. Loneliness made a doctrine of my exits. It is time to contradict myself.

Weil

Contradiction can be a kind of sacrament, but only if it refuses vanity.

Nietzsche

Refuse mine for me. You have the hands for it.

Weil

I have only attention. But attention can move a stone if it is patient and the stone is tired of being admired.

Weil breaks her half of the crust and eats. The room stays calm. The walking stick slips; Nietzsche steadies it with practiced ease.

Nietzsche

Now your question to the girl you were.

Weil

I asked it already each time I declined a warm room. I would place the bread in her mouth and the slate in her lap. I would tell her to remain in the world long enough to love it without wanting to own it. I would forbid her from hiding in virtue.

Nietzsche

Forbidding the righteous from hiding in righteousness—

His mouth curves, not into mirth, but into accuracy.

Nietzsche

—this would be a new catechism worth failing, as long as we failed at it honestly.

Weil

I will fail at it before vespers.

Nietzsche

So will I. The stick and the habit will conspire; I will sound like myself and suspect myself too late.

He draws the stick closer, as if to remind it that it serves and does not command.

Weil

We have not spoken of death. Perhaps we need not. It will speak of us.

Nietzsche

Death is still the harshest critic, and it doesn't even bother to write. It just stands there. The pages fall in line. I have no new insults for it. Only this: it hasn't learned to read the margins.

Weil

Your margins carry more sentences than some men's books.

Nietzsche

Then, one more sentence for the center.

The next sentence arrives the same way: unbroken, measured, like he's reading a verdict he already knows.

Nietzsche

Live so that "again" isn't a threat. Pick a gesture you could bear to repeat: no crowd, no name on the door, just the world shrugging and moving on. If you can stomach that, keep it.

Narrator (V.O.)

You don't unhear a true sentence. You only decide how much of your old life has to burn to make room for it.

Weil

I accept that instruction because it honors smallness. The gesture I choose is washing a stranger's hands without speaking. Yours?

Nietzsche

Holding the head of the animal until the blows stop.

Weil

Then we have agreed on tenderness without agreeing on God.

Nietzsche

Which may be as much agreement as two honest throats can safely bear.

She wipes the slate clean with the heel of her hand, but leaves one word: "Stay." The rest becomes a pale cloud on the black surface, a season erased, not denied.

Weil

Attention wanders. We will not pretend otherwise. The word will help us call it back.

Nietzsche

A single imperative. Almost austere enough to please even you.

Weil

I am pleased only when a room is faithful to its use. Today, this room has kept us from lies. That is enough.

Nietzsche

Enough is a difficult portion to measure.

Weil

It is measured by what remains unspent after gratitude. If you can say "thank you" and still require trumpet calls, you have not said it yet.

Nietzsche

Then—thank you. Without choreography.

Weil

Received.

Nietzsche

You limited your questions. Let me burn one. Is your God a silence that listens or a presence that speaks?

Weil

He is reality visited without bargaining.

Nietzsche

Clever answer.

Weil

An exact one. Cleverness is the sin of people who don't want the weight.

Nietzsche

Then send me the weight. I'll carry it with whatever strength remains after this hour.

Weil

Carry it by not despising weakness, especially your own. Not to enthrone it. To honor it as the door through which help enters without shame.

Nietzsche

I will attempt it. Attempts are never as elegant as oaths, but they're more honest.

Weil

Attempts are the only kind of oath the poor can carry.

Narrator (V.O.)

When nobody's faking, the quiet stops feeling dangerous. Bread, chalk, a walking stick: plain tools doing what they're for, not holding a sermon. For a random Tuesday, that's plenty of theology.

Nietzsche

The world will ask for an ending.

Weil

Then let us refuse one that lies. We leave the bread remembered, not multiplied. We leave the word "Stay" where it can shame us later. We leave the walking stick upright, letting it stand on its own.

Nietzsche

I will give them a fragment, not a conclusion.

Weil

And I will give them quiet.

Nietzsche

Very well.

Nietzsche rises with care, fingers on the stick, and looks once at the slate.

Nietzsche

Endure cleanly, then.

Weil nods slightly. The window stays dim. The room holds its promise. When she speaks, it feels like permission to pause.

Weil

—

Nothing else. The bread is gone; the chalk rests; the stick leans; the quiet completes its small, exact work.

Narrator (V.O.)

They leave one word on the slate and a few crumbs on the table. No loaves multiplied, no halos. Just nothing wasted. Strength and obedience still don't quite shake hands, but at least they're not reaching for knives tonight. Some nights, that's as close to a miracle as you get.

Chapter 4

Jesus – Judas: *The Silver and the Silence*
ACT I: The Shape of the Self

Jesus of Nazareth (c. 4 BCE – c. 30 CE)
Galilean teacher and healer whose parables made holiness sound like neighbor duty and table manners for strangers. He comforted the broken, needled the proud, and preached a kingdom that reverses the pecking order. Betrayed by a friend, killed by a state, remembered for a kingdom you cannot map but can recognize by its bread. God to many, radical rabbi to others. Either way, his words keep bruising and mending consciences. Forgiveness as revolution, love as command, hope as a stubborn, living verb. Two millennia later his sayings still split rooms: blessed are the poor, love your enemies, forgive seventy times seven. Commands that feel like cliffs and wings.

Judas Iscariot (d. c. 30 CE)
Apostle remembered for a kiss that felt like a knife to history. Thirty silver pieces bought the moment; motives remain hazy, whether greed, disillusionment, or prophecy's machinery. Regret arrived faster than absolution; the money would not stay in his hands. He is remorse made human, the cautionary parable inside every trust. Theology asks whether mercy could stretch to him; literature keeps retelling the night. Defined by one act and its echo, he stands where betrayal and destiny argue about

agency and blame. Neither pure villain nor secret hero, just the terrible truth that love and calculation can live in one man too long.

Setting

Upstairs, away from the street where coins are louder than names. The table is a carpenter's table, not a prop, marked by knife cuts, oil, and a second life after labor. Bread sits with the dignity of work; a cup waits without ceremony. Open shutters frame a city that keeps happening whether you repent or not. A basin and towel rest against the leg of a stool, close enough to matter. On the shelf are a clay lamp, a bundle of figs, and a folded cloak that knows the weather. The room is honest about its size and stingy with places to hide. Near the door, a bent nail shows where people kept hanging hope anyway.

Jesus (V.O.)

I'm not here to reopen wounds. I'm here because friendship doesn't vanish with nails or ropes. Love doesn't stop because someone miscounted their courage the first time. The world told me to call him enemy, but I will not. I came back to the table because tables are where forgiveness breathes. You pass bread, you share wine, and somehow that's enough to remind you what a person is worth.

Jesus sits at the table, hands folded, waiting with the patience of someone who has already lived through the hardest silence a room can hold.

Narrator (V.O.)

Some know him as a teacher. Some as rebel. Some as Christ. But before all that, he was simply a man at a table with friends. One of them was Judas. They call him traitor. Jesus called him brother. The air in this room has no politics, only memory. The silence doesn't care what history wrote; it just waits for what love will say.

The stair creaks. Judas enters slowly, hesitant, like the air itself might accuse him. He doesn't look at the bread or the wine; he looks at the floor, then the wall, then finally at Jesus.

Jesus

The bread is still warm. Sit with me.

Judas

I… I didn't know where to put my hands. That's the truth. You kneel and the room turns sideways. I wanted to pull back, but I froze, because part of me liked being treated like I was worth the water. And part of me hated that I liked it.

Jesus

You think I did it to shame you?

Judas

Yes. Please tell me you weren't making an example of me. Just say it plain. Because I've replayed that moment a hundred times and I can't tell if you were loving me or warning me. Maybe both. I don't have words for it. Just your hands. And my shame.

Jesus

No, Judas. I did it to love you. Not to mock, not to expose. To say with my body that not a man at that table sat above another. Even me. You saw humiliation. I meant mercy.

A pause. Judas laughs, but there's no humor in it. Just memory.

I saw it in your eyes. You'd already made up your mind.

Judas

Not there. Not then. The seed wasn't a coin; it was a clock. I started counting: days, crowds, chances. I kept counting chances. Certain the next would break you open. Certain. Then ashamed.

Jesus

You thought heaven tearing open was the point. It wasn't.

Judas

I believed you were who you said you were, even when you never said it. That's why I pushed. Not for silver. For certainty. If Rome cornered you, you'd have to stop hiding your mercy behind riddles. No, that's not fair. Your mercy behind metaphors.

I told myself a forced hour would reveal you. Call it arrogance. I called it *love turned practical.* If a wound would wake the world, then let it cut me too. I wasn't selling you; I was daring you to be undeniable. And I know how that sounds. It sounded cleaner in my head.

Jesus

You wanted a crown. But crowns are just metal bent into circles. They don't make a man whole, they only mark him as a target. You wanted history to remember your choice; I wanted people to survive theirs.

Judas

I didn't want the noise of the crowds. I wanted the men who carve stories into stone. If they dragged you into their court, you'd have to answer without parable. Plain speech. No fig trees, no seeds. Just you and power in the same room.

Jesus

And you mistook silence for strategy.

Judas

You let them spit and I told myself it was tactics. I kept waiting for the moment you'd say one word and end the theater. It never came. And every hour that passed felt like I was failing you, so I pushed harder. That's the rot of it.

Jesus

Did you ever ask me if I wanted to win their theater?

Judas

I kept thinking, "Any minute now." I fell asleep telling myself that. Woke up telling myself that. Do you know how tired faith can get? It's not doubt; it's exhaustion with nothing to lift.

Jesus

Faith isn't some lever you haul on to move God. It's what steadies you when the ground tilts. You turned trust into strategy because strategy felt safer. You could measure it. But faith was never math; it's presence.

Judas

They felt the same once. What I called strategy was just trust with a calendar. What I called devotion was pressure with a deadline. That's the lie I kept buying.

Jesus

You call it strategy. I call it betrayal, even if you said a prayer over it.

Judas

Strategy wasn't enough. I wanted certainty. I wanted to corner you. To make heaven tear itself open. I thought I was helping.

Jesus

Strategy builds kingdoms that fall. I wasn't building that kind of kingdom.

Judas

You knew at Bethany. I could feel it. You could have named me. You didn't. That mercy felt like a dare. Like you were leaving the door open to see if I'd walk through it or turn around. I hated you for it and loved you for it.

Jesus

Sending you away wouldn't have healed you. Naming you would have branded you before you chose. So I left the door open. Even when it hurt.

Judas

Then hear me once more, and I'll try to be plain: no parables, no cleverness. I thought: If I force the moment, you'll have to stop hiding on purpose. Sorry, I don't mean hiding. Mercy can feel like hiding when men are bleeding.

I told myself crisis would show you unarguable. That once Rome touched you, you'd burn the doubt out of the world. I wasn't counting silver. I was counting chances. I told myself rushing was faith. I told myself pushing was care. Lies I wanted to believe. And saying it now, I hear the pride wheezing through it.

Jesus

You called it love. It was fear.

Judas

Maybe both. I was afraid your way would be swallowed by theirs.

The candle gutters, then steadies. Wax runs in thin, stubborn lines. Somewhere in the wall a board shifts with a small complaint, like an old man clearing his throat.

Judas

You said one of us would betray you. That night. You looked at all of us, but you never named me. Why?

Jesus

That night, I named the wound, not the man. I wouldn't strip you of the chance to choose, even if it broke mine.

Judas

The kiss was supposed to be code. It was habit by then: brothers greeting each other. I weaponized it. Then you said "friend," and I wanted you to call me traitor so I could live as the villain. "Friend" makes me live as a man.

Jesus

You were always stingy with your own.

Narrator (V.O.)

No thunder. Just that burned-match smell when a decision beats the announcement. Judas already decided who Jesus wasn't; the room is only now catching up to the truth everyone felt first.

Judas

I told myself I was walking you to the proof, not the pit. That's how I made the road bearable. I wasn't escorting you to death; I was escorting you to revelation. You see the problem.

Jesus

The kind who walks with them until the edge.

Judas looks at the bread. Doesn't take it. His jaw clenches like he's testing whether it still belongs to his face.

Jesus

This is my body.

Judas

Don't do that.

Jesus

Do what?

Judas

Offer forgiveness I haven't asked for.

Jesus

You never asked to be born, Judas. But even so, I gave it to you—freely.

Judas

That's different.

Jesus

Is it?

Jesus pours the wine into Judas' cup. Not as ceremony. As intimacy. Judas watches it fill, then doesn't drink.

Judas

What would you have done if I hadn't left that night?

Jesus

I still would've gone. Not because of your leaving, not because of your kiss. I was already walking toward it. The cross wasn't your idea; it was Rome's. You just hurried along what was already in motion.

Judas

And if I hadn't kissed you?

Jesus

Someone else would have. But it wouldn't have hurt as much.

The bread sits, torn. The wine waits. The candle leans, dripping wax that runs in uneven lines.

Judas

You know what I bought with the silver?

Jesus

I know what they gave you.

Judas

Thirty pieces. That's what they said a life was worth. I didn't count them. I couldn't. I carried them like a sickness and then I threw them where they belonged: on the floor, in their holy place, so they'd have to step over the price of me. Let them hear the clatter.

Jesus

And when you let it go?

Judas

I went to the field outside the city. You know the one. Where they bury strangers and thieves. I stood there with the rope in my hands. I thought maybe that would weigh more than what I'd done. It didn't.

Jesus

So you climbed the tree.

Judas

I did.

The silence that follows is brutal. Not from judgment. From knowing.

Jesus

I saw you there.

Judas

I thought you'd look away.

Jesus

I didn't.

Judas doesn't cry, but he's close. The edge of unraveling without the drama.

Judas

You carried mine too, didn't you?

Jesus

And theirs. And the ones still coming.

Judas

I didn't ask you to.

Jesus

I didn't wait for permission to carry what you couldn't. That's the burden of love: it doesn't ask first. If it waited, it wouldn't be love; it would be a contract. And what we carried together wasn't a contract, Judas. It was a wound, and wounds don't heal on paper.

Jesus sets the bread down. Judas' fingers flex against the table like he's trying to sandpaper the shame out of them.

Judas

I used to dream of being remembered. Not famous, just useful. A name that helped the world bend a degree closer to right. Moses has tablets. David has a city. I wanted a footnote that mattered. I wanted the story to remember me. Not just as a shadow at your table. I didn't mean to become a warning label.

Jesus

You wanted the kingdom, but shaped by your hands, not mine.

Judas

I wanted a world that made sense. Where Rome paid for what it did. Where Caesar bled. Where the poor weren't told to wait for heaven while starving in the dirt. A Messiah who refuses a crown leaves the throne empty, and empty thrones invite blood. So I chose a smaller wound to force a greater healing. If pain was coming either way, better the pain that wakes you.

Jesus

You're not the first man to mistake urgency for love. I watched you start counting outcomes the way other men count coins. And I've seen what real surrender looks like too: Bethany, the oil, the room going quiet because somebody finally stopped protecting their future. Mary didn't care what it cost. Maybe that was foolish. Or maybe that's the only kind of love that ever mattered.

Judas

Maybe I was stealing. Maybe I was telling myself I was efficient. I don't know anymore. When you stand near holiness, even your thrift feels crooked.

Judas

I hated how they looked at you. Like you were the answer to every ache. Simon, trying to be holy in public. James, pretending he always understood. Peter, acting like courage was a pose you could hold if you just stared hard enough. And me, counting things that didn't need counting.

Jesus

You didn't hate them. You were afraid you weren't them.

Judas

No, I needed you. That's not the same. I needed you to be more than you chose to be. Or maybe I needed myself to be less greedy for certainty. I can't tell anymore.

Jesus

Was it me you needed, or a king on your schedule?

Judas

I kept insisting you be more than you chose to be. I tried to put a crown on your day. That wasn't love. It was control.

Judas hears his own confession settle in the room. Control pretending to be care. A door where he begged for a wall. The next words aren't strategy; they're surrender.

Judas

Why didn't you stop me?

Jesus

I told you what you needed to know.

Judas

That's not an answer. But I know you don't do answers the way I want them. You do doors. And I keep looking for walls.

Jesus

If I had stopped you, would it have changed your heart?

Judas

When I kissed you in the garden… it was supposed to be simple. A sign. Then your eyes made it a sentence I have to serve. I still hear "friend" like a bell I can't unring.

Jesus

You were never outside my love.

Judas

That's the story I told to live with myself: the necessary wound, the shadow that saves a life by blocking a worse blow. It sounds clever until you say it out loud.

Jesus

It always sounds clever until you say it out loud.

Judas

So hear me one more time, and I'll try not to hide behind theories. After Bethany, I stood outside and swore I'd stop counting. I lasted a day. I told myself urgency was faith. I told myself pushing was care. Those lies tasted like truth to me. I kept thinking, *if I force the hinge, the door will admit the truth*. It was just arrogance, dressed like devotion. I meant love. I practiced control.

Jesus

Control can look like care when you're tired.

Judas

I was tired to the bone.

Jesus

So rest.

Judas

They say I hanged myself in a field. That the rope broke, that my body tore apart on the rocks. That I died alone, as I deserved. If history needed a villain, I volunteered. I thought I could carry it so the others could carry you.

I called it sacrifice. It was pride. And I liked how it looked. I wanted to control the part I played: down to the way the curtain fell. And still, even at the end, I kept waiting for thunder. All I got was a branch.

Jesus

You were wrong. There's a difference. Wrong is not damned. A sin is something you did. A curse is a sentence laid over you. One you confess. The other, I can rewrite.

Judas

Then why does every story end with me damned?

Jesus

Stories end when people close the page. Mercy keeps reading. You're sitting here because love doesn't care if the ink ran out.

Judas

Because it's easier to damn a man than to sit with what made him possible. If they make me a monster, they don't have to ask what kind of love would still call me "friend."

Jesus

Would you have taken you back?

Judas

I don't know how.

Jesus

I would have set another place at the table.

Judas

Washed my feet again?

Jesus

Yes.

Judas

You called me friend. Even when I kissed you.

Jesus

I wasn't lying. You were still my friend.

Judas

I broke everything.

Jesus

If you're still carrying the pieces, let me help hold them.

Judas

Why?

Jesus

It won't be tidy, and it won't erase what happened. But it's not beyond grace.

Judas

If you say yes, I don't know what to do with it. I don't know how to live inside a pardon. Teach me how to sit down again.

Jesus

You start by breathing. By letting the chair hold you. Pardon isn't a skill; it's just sitting in a seat you were sure you'd already lost. Judas, I forgive you. And the weight of what I call you will prove it. Because long after the coins are gone, long after the tree, your story will be remembered by this word: friend.

Judas

After—after all of it? You mean… even then?

Jesus

Especially after all of it.

Judas closes his eyes. He doesn't ask. Doesn't beg. He stands there while the candle ticks faintly in the quiet.

Jesus

You were never beyond my love, Judas. Not in the garden. Not under the tree. Not here.

A pause. The kind that holds its breath between verses.

Jesus

You walked away from the table once. But grace waits for those who return hungry.

Judas doesn't speak. Doesn't run. He walks into the shadow, neither proud nor broken. Mercy doesn't rewrite the past. It reclaims it.

Narrator (V.O.)

Somewhere there is always a room with bread and a place still open. The memory of a kiss, the weight of a word like friend, the stubborn light of a candle. Grace waits. Especially for the ones who come back hungry.

ACT II

FAITH, FIRE, AND THE FRINGE

Where conviction meets consequence

Faith almost never shows up cleaned and pressed. It sneaks in through jokes, horror stories, awkward silence at the bedside. This act isn't interested in hymns. It puts belief on the stand and asks it to answer hard questions without hiding behind stained glass.

Jesus sits across from Bill Maher, and the jokes land like cross-examination. Every tag line pokes at scripture, daring it to answer without thunder or special effects. It doesn't feel like pure mockery so much as someone shaking the foundations to see what actually holds.

The Dalai Lama faces Adolf Hitler: quiet, steady compassion across from industrialized brutality. No one "wins" a conversation like that. Even so, his calm doesn't turn into approval; it just sits there, refusing to hate him back, which might be the one thing Hitler never learned how to handle.

Mary Shelley sits with Galileo: her monsters, his stars. She's lived with the fear that what we make will outrun us. He's lived with the backlash that comes when evidence walks in and won't sit quietly in the corner of the old myths. They don't say it once and move on. They circle the same uneasy fact: knowledge doesn't calm us; half the time it just gives us better nightmares.

Thomas Edison and Steve Jobs don't argue theology; they argue legacy. Both obsessed with credit, both willing to steal, both convinced they alone carried the spark. When they argue, invention stops looking noble. It feels more like wanting something so badly you're willing to sign any document that gets you there.

And finally, Helen Keller and Stephen Hawking. Two voices history tried to silence, two minds that kept taking up more space than the world ever planned to give them. They make it hard to keep pretending genius lives only in perfect bodies. What they had wasn't physical perfection; it was the stubborn habit of refusing to shut their minds off.

The faith that walks through this act doesn't look confident. It's taken hits, been laughed at, gone quiet more than once. But it shows up anyway, even in rooms that were supposed to be done with God a long time ago.

CHAPTER 5

JESUS – BILL MAHER: *FAITH WITHOUT THUNDER*

ACT II: Faith, Fire, and the Fringe

Jesus of Nazareth (c. 4 BCE – c. 30 CE)

Galilean teacher and healer whose parables made holiness sound like neighbor duty and table manners for strangers. He comforted the broken, needled the proud, and preached a kingdom that reverses the pecking order. Betrayed by a friend, killed by a state, remembered for a kingdom you cannot map but can recognize by its bread. God to many, radical rabbi to others. Either way, his words keep bruising and mending consciences. Forgiveness as revolution, love as command, hope as a stubborn, living verb. Two millennia later his sayings still split rooms: blessed are the poor, love your enemies, forgive seventy times seven. Commands that feel like cliffs and wings.

Bill Maher (1956–)

Stand-up comic and TV host (Politically Incorrect; Real Time) who treats jokes like stress tests for sacred cows. Openly secular with libertarian streaks, he aims at religion, parties, and media groupthink, and expects pushback. Fans call it candor; critics hear contempt. He champions free speech, prefers competence over piety, and keeps booking the argument. Awards have followed, including an Emmy, and so have boycotts. Agree or not, he shows up with a mic and a case, insisting comedy can pressure-test ideas without wrapping them in bubble wrap.

Setting

A small soundstage after taping. House lights down, work lights up. Two stools face each other under a grid of lamps cooling with small clicks. Cue cards sit at the stage edge; tape marks cross the floor; a cable rests in one loop. A boom mic droops. An uncapped water bottle waits on a riser. The red tally is dark; the wall clock keeps time. The audience is gone by design. What is left is a room built for sentences instead of applause.

One rule: say it plain, or let the silence earn its paycheck. I'm good with either.

Maher

Thanks for showing up. I like rooms with laughs; this one feels like jury duty. So, let's start simple. Are you a story I'm arguing with, or a person I can interrupt?

Jesus

You can interrupt a person. Try it when you need to.

Maher

Cute. I'm asking about capes. Walking on water, dead-and-back. If you want me to buy the sequel, show me the special effects.

Jesus

I'm not a cape. I'm a man who brought food where there wasn't any and stayed when staying cost. If you start there, you'll know more about me than a headline carved in the sky.

Maher

You hear how that sounds like dodging?

Jesus

It's choosing the part that feeds people before the part that wins arguments.

Maher

Arguments pay my rent. Also: people staple your name to laws that make life worse for the same folks you fed. If you're real, doesn't that bother you?

Jesus

Every misuse of my name has a neighbor attached. I look for the neighbor.

Maher

You keep saying "neighbor" like it's a policy. I'm asking for proof, not casseroles.

Jesus

Proof mostly just gets people to fall in line. Presence is what actually gives them company. Bill, when your mother died, did the silence comfort you?

Narrator (V.O.)

He doesn't answer at first. The question lands somewhere deeper than he's prepared for. His jaw works once, like he's deciding whether to lie about it.

Maher

No. It mocked me. The silence was louder than anything. People sent flowers. Priests said she was in a "better place."

His voice catches, despite himself.

Maher

I sat there thinking: if there's a God, He sure as hell wasn't in that room. Just me, her, and a beep that stopped. I don't even know why I remember the beep more than the priest, but I do.

He tries to smirk, but it flickers instead of landing.

Maher

So yeah, maybe that's when I started yelling at the sky. Better than whispering to nothing.

Jesus

You didn't need faith to feel the absence. Only love could've made that silence hurt so much. Sometimes the loudest critics are disappointed believers.

Maher

Okay, yeah, you know—that's human. I expected incense.

Jesus

Incense doesn't carry a bag up the stairs.

Maher

Yeah, but upstairs isn't the problem. It's Congress. It's judges. It's school boards banning books because they think they've got you on speed dial. Slap your name on a bill and suddenly cruelty looks holy. That's the scam: make hate sound sacred.

Jesus

It's not new. Rome marched under eagles; priests marched under law. Even my friends argued about who got the best seat while I was talking about serving the least. Faith has always been easy to weaponize.

Maher

And it hasn't stopped. Prosperity preachers with jets. Bishops covering up abuse. Evangelicals cheering politicians who brag about assault and lie with every breath. That's your fan club. You don't get to shrug. It's in your name.

Jesus

And every time my name is used to wound, it wounds me too. Counterfeits don't erase the real.

Maher

Yeah? Then where the hell is the real? Where's the thunder? Look, if you're love, you're truth. Why let your message be this easy to hijack? If you did the big miracle every time we needed it, wouldn't that help?

Jesus

It would prove I can throw thunder. People already believe in thunder. I want them to believe in staying.

Maher

You see what you're doing? You're making faith sound like a group chat that actually checks in.

Jesus

That's not the worst definition.

Maher

And still, if you exist, you let kids die. Don't tell me presence is enough.

Jesus

No. Presence isn't enough. But it's where it starts. Without it, we lie about what comes next.

Maher

Which is?

Jesus

Whatever the cost. If it helps, you pay it.

Maher

And we're back to bills. We'll fight about who pays in a bit. Before we get there, one more: you aren't interested in proving yourself?

Jesus

Bill, I'm interested in the person who's hungry when this taping ends. If you want proof, come with me when we leave and carry something.

Maher

You're… you're insufferably practical.

Jesus

It keeps me from being imaginary.

Narrator (V.O.)

Thunder's easy; it hits everybody at once. Staying's the rude part. It gets very specific about who you are. It asks for names, and then it asks again.

The LEDs don't blink; they stare. The steadiness is a mercy.

Maher

Okay, let see. Institutions. Religion behaves like a corporation. Mission statement, logo, market expansion. Then the board starts protecting the brand at the expense of the human. I don't go after the nun at the clinic; I go after the board that pays lawyers to turn "welcome" into a waiver. Your name is the logo. How do you want me to play that?

Jesus

Aim at the boardroom. Don't hit the clinic.

Maher

I try. But the camera loves excess. The grifter with the jet trends. The person who stocks a pantry at 6 a.m. does not.

Jesus

Love doesn't trend. It lasts.

Maher

Lasting doesn't drive ratings.

Jesus

Ratings don't keep anyone warm. You have reach. Use it to make ordinary mercy impossible to ignore. Show the pantry more than the jet.

Maher

I do that and half my audience calls me soft.

Jesus

"Soft" is what people call you when paying attention scares them.

Maher

Good grief. No, I mean, you're not wrong, but let's move on. All right, Rabbi. Sermon, short and human. What would you put on the cue cards if you produced my monologue?

Jesus

Start with a story where nobody is a metaphor. Name the city. Name the bus line. Name the landlord who returned the deposit. Tell me who carried the second bag of groceries when the first one tore. Then say what the budget did to that street last month. No adjectives. End with a place people can stand tonight that turns a sentence into heat or food. If there's a joke, let it punch a door open, not a person.

Maher

You just gave me the format my producers beg me to use and I resist because outrage punchlines hit cleaner.

Bill leans in like he's asking for secrets.

Maher

So, Jesus, you mad at churches?

Jesus

I overturned tables in a temple. You can be mad at a house and still feed people on its porch. Some churches love power. Some love neighbors.

Maher

I do, but the worst examples make the best TV. That's not entirely my fault. That's the species.

Jesus

Then teach the species a better appetite.

Maher

You make that sound easy. It's not. Cynicism is cheap sugar. It spikes engagement.

Jesus

And leaves everyone tired. You're good enough to stop selling it.

Maher

You're good at telling other people what to do. How about this: give me your version of a creed that doesn't need stained glass.

Jesus

Love your neighbor, even the annoying ones. Feed first, argue if you must. Use whatever power you've got to carry, not to climb. Count the ones nobody else is counting. If you win, don't gloat; pay the bill. If you lose, don't sulk; show up tomorrow.

Maher

That's either beautifully clear or aggressively naïve. I'm with you on feeding people. It's the metaphysics that drives me nuts. If God is real, he's real. If he's not, the casserole isn't proof; it's lunch.

Jesus

Then start with lunch. If God shows up, you'll have company. If not, you still fed someone.

Maher

You… You are unfireable. You dodge and you don't. Infuriating combo.

Jesus

You invite me back?

Maher

I don't do bookings. I do regrets.

Jesus

We have that in common.

Narrator (V.O.)

The room exhales; even the microphones unclench. Regret is not a doctrine, but it hangs between them like one. Maher leans forward again, Jesus doesn't move, and for once the silence feels less like a standoff than a truce.

Maher

Your fans say "charity begins at home." I say that's code for "never leaves the driveway."

Jesus

Then say it on air and invite them out of the driveway. There's room in the car.

Maher

You know, you realize every time you answer like that, a bishop somewhere grinds his teeth and a Reddit thread calls you mid.

Jesus

Both groups can bring water to the cooling center. The heat won't ask for credentials.

Maher

See, there. Now you're specific. I trust you more when you're specific. Now… yeah, we're getting somewhere.

Jesus

Specific is where love stops pretending.

Maher

And institutions start panicking.

Jesus

Good. Panic moves money. Mercy spends it.

Maher

Sure, but say I buy your neighbor obsession. How do I avoid becoming the mascot for one side of the culture war?

Jesus

Stop being a mascot. Be a neighbor. Neighbors disappoint every side eventually.

Maher

That line's staying in. My staff will hate it. But anyway, you know what I want from religion? Not certainty—competence. If you're going to claim the moral high ground, run the soup line on time and keep the lights paid.

Jesus

Competence is love with a schedule.

Maher

Cute Jesus. But, okay, fine. Last question before I break from this topic. Your followers nailed you to wood while quoting scripture. If you walk back into a church now and see your name propping up cruelty, what do you do?

Jesus

I look for the person getting hurt and stand next to them until the room has to choose between its reputation and its neighbor. Then I set another table across the street.

Maher

You really are dreadfully reasonable.

Jesus

It keeps the room honest.

Maher

Oof. Honest, huh? I wish comedy rooms stayed that way. After a show goes sideways, I don't go to the party. I walk home too fast, then too slow. I open the fridge and stare like the food owes me an apology. That's my liturgy.

The clock forgets to click for one beat, then remembers. The room doesn't take sides. But it waits longer than either man wants.

Maher

Lightning round. Gay marriage?

Jesus

Love your neighbor.

Maher

Abortion?

Jesus

Love your neighbor.

Maher

Immigration?

Jesus

Love your neighbor.

Maher

You hear how that sounds like a non-answer?

Jesus

It only sounds like one if you've never tried it.

Maher

Oh, give me a break. I mean, okay sure, you're not wrong, but I said specifics help.

Bill clears his throat.

Maher

Let's try something different. Scenario one: midnight bus, families at the border, shelters full, voters furious. I'm the mayor. What do I do?

Jesus

Unlock empty buildings tonight: church basements, gyms, schools. Feed first, register second. Tomorrow, call the state: "Here's what we did. Match it."

Maher

And voters?

Jesus

Hungry children change more than angry voters.

Maher

Scenario two: book bans. State labels a science book on evolution as dangerous. Libraries take it off the shelves.

Jesus

Put the book back on the shelf. Knowledge isn't dangerous—fear of it is. Show them the difference.

Maher

Scenario three: prisons. Guy gets out with nothing but gravity pulling him back.

Jesus

Treat reentry as ER, not a sermon: ID, bed, phone, job. Day one. Mercy that plans beats mercy that weeps.

Maher

Scenario four: health care. Insulin or rent.

Jesus

Law and receipts. Cap prices. Fund clinics where people already stand in line. If a mother must choose between medicine and roof, the city has failed.

Maher

Scenario five: speech. My jokes bruise bystanders.

Jesus

Three questions before posting: Does it punch a door open? Are the weakest safer? Will you still own it tomorrow? If not, edit. Courage without accuracy is vandalism.

Maher

Dammit. Yeah, that's not wrong. Okay scenario—where was I? Scenario six: climate. Heatwave. Cooling centers only on paper.

Jesus

Everyone with keys moves. Churches, libraries, unions. Post signs, run buses with water. Treat it like what it is: survival.

The mics don't blink; they lean.

Maher

All right, Nazarene. Policy is safer than feelings. But the show I run is built on two currencies: outrage and grief. Outrage pays better. Grief doesn't trend; it leaks. I don't say this on TV, but I talk to the dead sometimes: on the walk home, in the aisle with the cereal, in a hotel mirror that looks like a witness with bad lighting.

I ask the same question every time: "Did I waste my hours on applause?" I can hear her say, "You were a kid. Be kind." I'm not good at that. I weaponize truth.

My mother used to laugh when I was mean to a person who deserved it, and then, after the show, she'd touch my arm and say, "Don't forget the ones who didn't." She's not here to touch my arm.

On bad nights I pick fights with God because picking fights with the void is worse. If you're real, you should know I don't have a prayer life. I have a noise life.

Jesus

Noise is honest when it doesn't pretend. You don't owe me incense. You owe your grief a chair and some water.

Bill, here is a small liturgy you can do without believing anything: When the house is too loud in your head, wash a dish by hand. Name one person you loved; say what you fed them. Send money to a clinic and don't tweet about it. Walk a block slower than the city wants. If you can, put your phone on a shelf for one hour where it can't vibrate like a trapped moth. Call someone you'd rather text. Tell a true story that doesn't make you the hero. If you need a word for this, call it prayer. If that tastes like metal, call it maintenance. Human things that keep a life from becoming weather.

Maher

Maintenance. That I understand. It's not holy, but it keeps the floor from eating you.

Jesus

Some floors are altars once you stop slipping.

Maher

Don't get poetic on me Jesus. Okay, well, actually, fine. A little. Here's my side of maintenance: I write. A lot. Jokes that don't air, letters I never send, lists I won't keep. I used to think the point of writing was audience. The last few years, it's survival. If I don't name the thing, it gets to be bigger than the room.

Jesus

Name it. And let someone else read it when you're brave enough. Companionship turns survival into living.

Maher

You keep pushing "we." I'm good at "I." "We" feels like a team jersey I didn't pick.

Jesus

Find a smaller we. Ten people you owe your time to and who owe you theirs. Cook, carry, sit, argue, forgive, repeat. "We" stops being a brand when it starts being a calendar.

Maher

Ok then, tell me something you regret. Not doctrine. An error.

Jesus

I wish I'd said more names out loud so the editors couldn't trim them later. I wish I'd stayed at one table longer that last week, even if the city burned faster. I wish I hadn't let fear teach my friends silence. I wish I'd taught them how to rest without feeling like traitors to the cause.

Maher

That last one hits. I don't rest because it feels like indulgence. The algorithm is a jealous god.

Jesus

Then betray it. Jealous gods deserve betrayal.

Maher

If I do, I pay in relevance.

Jesus

Relevance is just the loud way of saying "picked today." Love's the part that's still there when that changes tomorrow.

Maher

That's true. Yeah. You talk like someone who's been both worshiped and ignored.

Jesus

I have. Both are bad teachers.

Maher

I've been both worshiped and ignored too, except my altar was ratings. That's a lousy school, but it teaches you to hide what you need.

No one's checking the clock, except grief. It doesn't measure time. It measures returns.

Maher

Let me try something unusual for me: generosity. There are nights I want you to be true. Not the cape. The person who stayed. If you're only a story, it's a story I wish more people told without turning it into a weapon. If you're real, show up in ways that don't need cameras. I'll try to notice.

Jesus

I can work with that.

Maher

Bumper sticker edit before they yank the cord. If I say, "Offended? Good," you say…?

Jesus

"Offended? …Fine. But check where it hurts, and ask why." And then ask who pays when your joke lands a little off.

Maher

Fair. Your turn: "God is in control"?

Jesus

"God is with you." *Control* is a word leaders use. *With* is a word neighbors use.

Maher

Neighbors again. Fine. One promise, one dare, one thing I'll hate. Give me all three without poetry and flowers.

Jesus

Promise: If you try to carry more than your share, I'll tap your shoulder to set it down.

Dare: Invite someone you're paid to dunk on and ask them who they love. Start there; then argue.

Thing you'll hate: Take one night off when a trending fight begs you to stay up. Don't answer it. Answer a friend's text instead.

Maher

I already hate it. Which means I probably need it. Hmm. Okay. You want one from me?

Jesus

I'll take it.

Maher

I'll cut a monologue this month that ends with a place to stand, not a line to cheer. I'll show a pantry instead of a scandal. My producers will groan; my inbox will split; the pantry will fill. And, you know, we'll call that a win.

Jesus

It will be. Mercy doesn't trend, but it remembers. A casserole reheated at midnight tastes like loyalty, not leftovers. A call returned three days late still saves a person from quitting. Presence looks small until someone measures it against absence. I've seen men with armies lose to silence; I've seen widows with neighbors win against despair. If you want immortality, don't start with monuments. Put names in your phone and answer when they call. That outlives headlines.

Behind the glass, a hand flickers up: the slow, apologetic "one minute."

Maher

There's the hand. Last honest thing: I don't convert. I correct. That's my religion.

Jesus

Then keep correcting what hurts the hungry after the taping ends and leaves the powerful without a costume.

Maher

You just wrote my next episode and my next headache.

Maher takes a deep breath and slows to exhale as he gathers his thoughts.

Maher

Ok Jesus—would you—this is ridiculous. Would you stay a minute after the lights? Not for prayer. For soup scheduling.

Jesus

Yes.

Maher

God. I hate that I believe you. And I don't mean "God" like… ugh, you know what I mean. Don't smirk.

Jesus

I do.

Someone kills the LEDs with the tenderness reserved for night-lights. The room exhales its cables. On the table: two cups, a list that wasn't there an hour ago, and a pen that seems heavier after being used. Outside, a hallway forgets to be sacred and manages it anyway.

Maher

Oh geez, okay, let's not do the fake handshake.

Jesus

We can carry something instead.

Maher

The pantry's two blocks. I know the back door.

Jesus

Lead.

They stand. The studio forgets to be holy. Or maybe it remembers better than most places. The chairs give the little sigh of furniture that has done its job. The clock, useless and faithful, keeps clicking to no one in particular.

Maher

I'm going to regret this tomorrow.

Jesus

I'll still be here if you want to regret it with someone.

Maher

You and your lines. Don't... don't edit the silences out. Let them stay ugly.

Jesus

The silences are the point.

Maher

For once, yeah.

Narrator (V.O.)

Just a door and a plan. They walk toward a circled kitchen on a beat-up map: bus route, bad lighting, good neighbors. Presence goes where the map points and hands follow. Call that its prayer if you like. I do.

CHAPTER 6

Dalai Lama – Adolf Hitler: *The Sermon and the Swastika*

ACT II: Faith, Fire, and the Fringe

His Holiness the 14th Dalai Lama (Tenzin Gyatso, 1935–)
Recognized at two, enthroned at four, he inherited a nation and its exile. After the 1959 uprising, he fled to India and built a government-in-exile that runs on patience and paperwork. Nobel Peace Prize recipient in 1989. He meets power with a laugh that is not naïve and treats compassion as discipline: keep the person a person, even in conflict. He argues for dialogue that can survive propaganda and for mercy that is not sentimental, habits you practice daily rather than moods you admire once a year.

Chancellor Adolf Hitler (1889–1945)
Austrian-born Nazi leader who became Germany's chancellor in 1933 and dismantled democracy. He launched a war across Europe (1939) and directed the systematic murder of six million Jews and millions of others. Propaganda, law, and terror fused grievance into policy; camps and timetables made killing administrative. He ended in a bunker by suicide as the regime collapsed. He isn't remembered for "genius," but as a warning label: dehumanization, cults of purity, and leaders who turn cruelty into a tool the bureaucracy can use.

Setting

A bare room. One table, one lamp. In the light sit a child's shoe with a blue thread, a torn letter with a sentence rewritten above the tear, and a manifest listing three names, one spelled two ways. No banners, no insignia. Two chairs with space between them. The air is courthouse-quiet, built for hearing rather than performance. The objects are not symbols; they are evidence. The conversation keeps circling them on purpose.

The room does not pretend to be neutral. It was built to hold memory in plain sight so no one can say later they did not know what it looked like.

Narrator (V.O.)

Objects don't argue, but they remember. A shoe knotted by a mother's mouth, a crease where a hand pressed too hard, a page that carries two spellings of the same name. These are not props. They are evidence.

Dalai Lama

Look at the table. Three ordinary things. A shoe. A letter. A page with names. They are here because ordinariness is where truth holds still.

Hitler

Truth isn't what holds still. Truth is what prevails. Nations do not live by objects under a lamp. They live by will, by direction, by a map that does not apologize.

Dalai Lama

Maps are useful until they are used to step on people. Then they are only paper. Tell me your map without the words "destiny," "purity," or "will." Tell me what you did.

Hitler

I restored a broken people to unity. I gave them a meaning stronger than their wounds. I refused to let a defeated treaty write our future. I took a scattered voice and made it singular.

Dalai Lama

You made it singular by removing the mouths that would contradict it. You did not restore. You removed. Where did your trains go?

Hitler

Trains go where a government directs them. Order is how a nation survives. Disorder is how it dies.

Dalai Lama

When "order" starts eating people just to stay standing, no one in that country is safe. That's not order; that's a hunger that forgot it ever had a face.

Hitler

To where work was required and relocation necessary. To where the future could be secured against the enemies who would dissolve it.

Dalai Lama

Say the word you are avoiding. Camps. Say it and keep your voice steady.

Hitler

Harsh measures are not cruelty when a nation is at stake. They are surgery. The weak term it brutality because they fear the knife that saves the body.

Dalai Lama

No body is saved by carving out its heart. You did not heal your country. You taught it to live with a wound in the place where its neighbors had stood. And then you taught it to call that wound by a heroic name.

Hitler

I taught it to call weakness by its name and to choose against it. I taught it that a future requires exclusion. A border is mercy for those within it.

Dalai Lama

If your mercy needs a fence, call it what it is: comfort you buy with someone else's breath. Look again at the shoe.

Hitler

A sentiment.

Dalai Lama

A measurement. A child's foot, the knot made by a mother's mouth when she wetted the thread and pushed it through. You did not fight ideas. You fought that mouth. You starved it, shaved it, tagged it, and sent it into a room designed to remove breath from bodies.

Hitler

I did what history demands when it is written by the strong. We survived humiliation by refusing to carry it. We made law out of will. We made will into geometry: lines, columns, procedures. Weak nations apologize for their survival. Strong nations arrange it.

Narrator (V.O.)

He says "geometry" the way some men say "salvation," like straight lines could wash the blood off the hands that drew them.

Dalai Lama

You arranged trains, laws, columns. You arranged families into piles. You arranged names into numbers. Say it plainly: You tried to erase the Jews. You tried to eradicate Roma. You crushed those who did not fit your picture. The record is not shy. Gas chambers are not shy. Graves do not blush. Why should you?

Hitler

You list horrors and call it judgment. I faced a century of fractures: borders cut by other men, debts that strangled trade, enemies inside the walls who preached decay. A leader decides whether a people will continue. I decided.

Dalai Lama

You decided to use camps and trains and bullets and smoke. Decisions can be measured by their tools. Yours were not laws that protect; they were machines that erase.

Hitler

Laws are tools. Borders are tools. Removal is a tool. To me, history is carpentry, not prayer.

Dalai Lama

Then name your house. Not "Germany." Not "future." Name the house you built out of laws and borders and removal. What does it look like when the door opens?

Hitler

It looks like safety. It looks like a people no longer bent by shame. It looks like order that does not apologize for existing.

Dalai Lama

Safety that requires ovens is not safety. Order that needs numbers burned into skin is not order. A house that locks from the outside is not a home. It's a trap with curtains.

Narrator (V.O.)

The room doesn't move, but something in it changes. Even the lamplight seems to pull back, as if it refuses to warm the sentence hanging between them.

Hitler

Versailles humiliated us.

Dalai Lama

You answered by teaching crowds to chant louder than they could think. You taught them that a neighbor's death was a kind of medicine. Medicine for what? For the soreness in their pride?

Hitler

For national life. For continuity. For a future in which children would not grow up as I did, watching the country mocked, watching adults count humiliation like coins.

Dalai Lama

Those children watched smoke. They watched families split at gates. They watched a father grow smaller through slats until he was a dot and then nothing. That was your "continuity."

Hitler

War breeds cruelty. I didn't invent that. I disciplined it.

Dalai Lama

You industrialized it. You wrote schedules for it. You designed rooms so precise that murder could be repeated without a single variable left to conscience.

Hitler

Precision wins wars.

Dalai Lama

Precision also makes guilt legible. That is why your files still speak. That is why this page remembers where a hand pressed too hard. Your system left fingerprints. History keeps them.

Hitler

You want me to kneel. I will not. Conviction does not kneel to tears.

Dalai Lama

Conviction can kneel to truth. Try one truth: You targeted Jews as Jews. Say it. You attempted genocide. This is the word for removing a people because they are that people. If the word burns, it fits.

Hitler

I would do it again to save the state.

Dalai Lama

Then let the record keep that sentence beside the names you will not say.

Hitler

Do you think records frighten me?

Dalai Lama

No. They teach others to be braver than your fear dressed up as destiny.

Hitler

And yet here I am, still spoken of.

Dalai Lama

Spoken of, not honored. Remembered, not praised. That is the difference you could never keep in your head.

Hitler

Because I do not have to ask forgiveness for doing what a nation must. The audience that judged me has always been soft. They eat the fruit of order and call the tree cruel.

Dalai Lama

The audience here is not soft. The audience is a shoe, a letter, a page with three names. We will speak them, and then we will look at your words again and measure what they cost.

Dalai Lama

Leah. Mendel. Sara.

Say them.

Hitler

Names blur a policy. Policy prevents blurring. If you wish to survey tragedy, go to poets. I came to power to repair a world. Repair requires hardness.

Dalai Lama

A language that cannot say "Leah" unless it is stamped and filed? Hardness is not a virtue when it is blind.

Hitler

It is a language that avoided the confusion of sentiment. The times called for ranks, not lullabies.

Dalai Lama

Ranks delivered children to a door that sealed behind them. Call that what it is. Courage does not need smoke. Strategy does not need barbed wire. Survival does not need piles of shoes.

Hitler

You are a priest of softness who imagines kindness can weld a nation. It cannot. The century asked for iron.

Dalai Lama

Iron rusts. The hand that carries water lasts longer. Your iron cut the century into pieces and told the survivors to admire the edges.

Hitler

You mistake me. I did not offer admiration. I offered victory. For a time, I gave it.

Dalai Lama

At what price? Speak in coins if you like: "territory," "pride," "unity." Then open your palm. There are teeth in it.

Hitler

You want remorse. I will not give it. My language is purpose. Purpose does not cry.

Dalai Lama

I do not want your tears. I want your nouns to stand in the right rooms. Call the camps by their names. Call the trains by their destinations. Call the smoke by the people inside it.

Hitler

You are skilled in theatrics.

Dalai Lama

I am skilled in truth that will not leave quietly. The room is not a stage. It is a table. And on this table is proof. A knot. A crease. A rewritten line where a hand pressed so hard the page remembers pain.

Hitler

You recite paper like it's going to stand a border guard to attention. Borders answer to danger, not diaries.

Dalai Lama

Borders that cannot face a diary are already in danger. They are defended by people who refuse to read. That is how harm becomes efficient.

Hitler

Harm and defense are twins in politics. One grows when the other sleeps. I chose which one to feed.

Dalai Lama

You fed both. Defense that devours children is just harm wearing a badge.

Hitler

You keep returning to children, but policy is not a nursery. Nations are not raised on lullabies. They are raised on labor, discipline, sacrifice. I spoke to adults who understood the price of survival.

Dalai Lama

Adults who later stood beside pits. Adults who arrived at gates and learned a number they did not ask for. Adults who watched smoke and hoped it was only smoke. If you insist on adulthood, give them the dignity of a sentence that names what you did.

Hitler

I named enemies and kept my promise to confront them. I refused the theatre of apology for decisive action.

Dalai Lama

A promise that requires killing families is a promise no one had the right to make. A leader who makes it steals the future from everyone else and calls it destiny.

Hitler

You despise destiny because it speaks louder than consolation.

Dalai Lama

I despise destiny when it is used like a hammer and handed to a crowd who has not been taught to hold anything gently.

Hitler

Gentleness loses wars.

Dalai Lama

Gentleness loses fewer souls. Your arithmetic ignored them.

Hitler

History rewards those who act.

Dalai Lama

It remembers those who act. Reward is a different sentence. The remembering will not be kind to you, and it should not be.

Hitler

Remembering is a stage play written by victors. They gather their juries, polish their vocabulary, and rehearse outrage. I will not audition.

Dalai Lama

Memory is older than courts. It lives where a neighbor points to a gap at a table and says the name that should be there. That witness is not a victor. That witness is a person.

Hitler

Persons are persuaded by strength. I learned that truth on nights when crowds filled squares and the air carried my voice farther than any argument. They wanted a spine. I gave them one.

Dalai Lama

A spine does not need a fist. A spine needs a reason to stand that does not crush what is in front of it.

Hitler

Then say your reasons. Say how a nation humiliated, indebted, starved of work, flooded with ideology from the east, drowning in decadence at home, ought to have stood without a fist.

Dalai Lama

With work that remembers people rather than turning them into fuel. With law that refuses blood as a shortcut. With borders that protect without pretending purity. With leaders who can say "enough" before the victory becomes a funeral.

Hitler

Your "enough" is what weak men say when the strong are almost finished. I did not arrive in history to stop before the shape was clear.

Dalai Lama

Your shape is clear: camps, trains, mass graves. If clarity is what you wanted, you succeeded.

Hitler

I wanted permanence. I wanted a future that could not be mocked by yesterday's failures.

Dalai Lama

Permanence bought with murder collapses into ash and shame. That's not philosophy; that's physics.

Hitler

You moralize failure because you prefer sorrow to victory.

Dalai Lama

I prefer life to systems. That's the divide you never crossed. Systems make you feel safe. Life makes you answer questions.

Hitler

And what of your questions? Do they build factories? Roads? Armies?

Dalai Lama

Sometimes they keep a door open long enough for a person to pass through it alive. To me, that's what infrastructure really is.

Hitler

Rhetoric.

Dalai Lama

Practice. A stationmaster who buys ten minutes with a bent rule. That's all it takes sometimes.

Hitler

You celebrate disobedience because you have no taste for cost.

Dalai Lama

I count cost differently. I include the people your math discarded.

Hitler

We removed them.

Narrator (V.O.)

Two words. Cold as the tile floor. Heavy as the shoes on the table. They land without flourish: an invoice stamped in red ink, final, unsigned, still demanding payment. Not a battle, not a clash of ideas, but removal, stripped to its coldest verb. Rooms built to turn breath into smoke. Lists into numbers. Neighbors into cargo. A sentence carrying the weight of rails that hummed through villages, of doors that sealed, of ovens that left only ash. Silence doesn't soften it. Silence only makes it ring.

Dalai Lama

That sentence is the whole machine. "We removed them." Not a war, not a debate. Removal.

Hitler

You stand acting like I must submit to your altar. But your own country was taken. Your philosophy did not keep your borders. What did compassion purchase for Tibet?

Dalai Lama

It did not purchase safety. It preserved a face. We lost land. We did not build camps to keep the loss company. We did not turn the defeated into fuel. The world can argue with our politics. It cannot dig a field and find our ovens.

Hitler

So you accept that power speaks last.

Dalai Lama

Power speaks loud. It does not speak last. The last voice is the one that keeps returning when the banners are gone. A mother's instruction. A neighbor's hand. A name said right in a room that would prefer a number.

Hitler

You keep arranging your modest furniture: shoe, page, letter, wanting it to fend off steel.

Dalai Lama

No. No they cannot. People can. A stationmaster can confuse a route for an hour. A typist can notice a second spelling and insist on the first. A guard can count slowly. A supervisor can demand a signature that cannot be found. These are not grand gestures. They are human ones. Steel wins the day. People keep the night from learning the wrong lesson.

Hitler

You celebrate disobedience because you cannot bear the clean line of decision.

Dalai Lama

I bear it. I refuse it. Those are different verbs. When a "clean line" runs through a living person, it may be straight, but it is never clean.

Hitler

You ask for softness because it flatters your calling.

Dalai Lama

I ask for attention because it saves lives. Listen.

He lifts the letter and reads the one sentence that remained after the tear.

Dalai Lama

"I kept a little sugar for your birthday."

Dalai Lama

Feeling is not yet virtue. Ethics is what we do to other people when the crowd is singing. If a song makes a neighbor a "they," it is a bad song, even if it is beautiful. Compassion isn't softness; it is the discipline to keep a person a person when fear offers an easier category.

Dalai Lama

Sugar is not doctrine. It is a promise that a day will come with sweetness inside it. You built rooms to end days. That is the disagreement. Not empire, not treaty, not anthem. Days. Adolf, what happens if sweetness wastes the nation?

Hitler

Order keeps the stomach fed. Truth does not schedule trains. I will choose what binds many over what frees one, because a nation cannot wait for every conscience to finish its private work. The clerk is cleaner than the hero; the ledger outlives the poem. Call it cold if you like. Cold keeps shape.

Dalai Lama

A nation ought to be ashamed if it hands the bill to a child.

Hitler

You believe children are the measure of policy.

Dalai Lama

I believe policy that cannot face a child should not face a legislature.

Hitler

Enough. You mistake me for a man persuadable by stories.

Dalai Lama

I do not mistake you. I address the ones who might still be. The clerk. The captain. The neighbor who can stand one more minute at a door. The student who will hear a lazy joke and not laugh. None of this redeems the dead. It protects the living from becoming more of them.

Hitler

You end on warnings because you cannot end on victory.

Dalai Lama

No. I end on work. Naming. Pausing. Refusing. Work small enough to carry every day without ceremony. Work stubborn enough to survive the next order.

Hitler

Then write your names. I have said what I will.

Dalai Lama

You have. And the room has heard you. Now it will hear them.

Hitler

Proceed.

Dalai Lama

We proceed to the ordinary, where history either collapses into numbers or stands up as people. We proceed to kitchens and bus stops and stairwells. We proceed to a mother tying a knot with her teeth because there is work to be done and a child who wants to run. That is the world you tried to break. It is still walking.

Hitler

Your ending is a sermon.

Dalai Lama

No. A measurement.

Hitler

Conclude.

Dalai Lama

Not yet. You keep circling the same altar: names, children, kitchens. You say nations are not built from kitchens.

Hitler

They are not.

Dalai Lama

They fall apart without them. You cannot build a future that survives the death of its mothers.

Hitler

Mothers send sons to war. They understand cost.

Dalai Lama

They do. They do not understand why a government would harvest children like wheat. That is not war. That is policy feeding on the people it claims to protect.

Hitler

Policy requires hard arithmetic.

Dalai Lama

Then do this arithmetic with me: If one train is full of names and one order is written to remove them, which number is the nation proudest of? The answer tells you whether you have a country or a machine.

Hitler

Pride is a poor instrument.

Dalai Lama

So is fear, and you used it more. You frightened crowds with fantasies of purity and with real punishments for doubt. You offered belonging and charged the price of someone else's life.

Hitler

Belonging without price is sentiment.

Dalai Lama

Belonging that demands a corpse is a cult.

Hitler

Your mercy would have left Germany small.

Dalai Lama

Small is better than stained. A nation that can't bear to be small will be made small by its crimes.

Hitler

You keep turning back to the page hoping the paper will judge me.

Dalai Lama

Paper does not judge. It remembers. It is the smallest grave that can still speak. This one speaks through a second spelling and the shallow bruise left by a hand that hesitated under pressure. Someone tried to get the name right. That is the kind of country I believe in. One that still tries to get a name right.

Hitler

And if the name is wrong?

Dalai Lama

Then you ask. Then you slow down. Then you act like a person in a room with another person. That is the work after this book is closed.

Hitler

I do not accept your work.

Dalai Lama

You don't have to. It isn't for you. It's for the reader who might hold a list and decide what it becomes. It's for anyone offered a story that feels efficient but tastes like a lie.

Hitler

You think they will resist?

Dalai Lama

Enough of them. Enough is what history asks for.

Hitler

Now conclude.

Dalai Lama

We will conclude with a practice. Leah. Mendel. Sara.

To anyone reading: say three names you know from a list that tried to hide them. Say them again if your mouth tries to hurry. If you cannot remember any, go find one. Then another. Then do the smallest honest thing your hand can do to keep them in the world.

Narrator (V.O.)

What's left on the table isn't paper or thread. It's the work of saying names until someone answers back. Records don't close themselves; they wait. If the silence feels heavy, that's because it's asking for your mouth to move. Say a name. That's the ending, and it's yours now.

CHAPTER 7

MARY SHELLEY – GALILEO GALILEI: *THE MONSTER WE MADE*

ACT II: Faith, Fire, and the Fringe

Mary Shelley (1797–1851)
Daughter of Mary Wollstonecraft and William Godwin, she eloped with Percy Shelley as a teen. At eighteen to nineteen she drafted *Frankenstein* after the stormy summer at Lake Geneva and published it in 1818. She buried children, then her husband; she kept writing anyway. The novel is not about a monster so much as responsibility, what we owe what we make and the lives we exile. She edited Percy's work, managed debts, and built a career a culture tried to footnote. She argued grief could be honest and still produce work.

Galileo Galilei (1564–1642)
Tuscan scientist who improved the telescope and let it correct authority. In 1610 he published Jupiter's moons, sunspots, and Venus's phases; the data undercut comfortable doctrine. Tried in 1633, forced to recant, and kept under house arrest. Devout in his way and stubborn in method, he insisted observation earns the right to speak. His legacy is procedural courage: measure, repeat, revise, then tell the truth even when a court prefers incense. The heavens did not move for him; he moved our stance toward them.

Setting

An observatory tucked under old beams. A telescope aimed through a slit of sky. A violin case lies open, a phonograph idles beside a coil of wire. Sketches share a shelf, craters and stitched anatomy side by side. A kettle clicks; the dome groans. On the table sit a telescope cap, a quill, and a loose screw. It is a room built for simple work: look, note, assemble. Tonight, two minds try to agree on what still qualifies as wonder.

Shelley

This room keeps both science and ghosts.

Galileo

Then it will feel at home with us.

Narrator (V.O.)

The monster-maker and the star-watcher. One taught lightning to speak; the other made the sky answer. Tonight they share a room where order feels temporary and the noise costs nothing. The place sounds like it wants to sing but keeps choking on dust. In the corner, a record skips: less a metaphor than a reminder that neat patterns always give way to static.

Shelley

You bent the heavens into numbers, Signor Galilei, and called it harmony. Yet what is harmony without rupture? My monster would tell you that creation sounds more like a broken chord.

Galileo

And yet it's still music. The cosmos is counterpoint: planets take notes, orbits keep time. The brass is cold, his knuckles aching, his breath smearing the lens. It's off-key and still playing. That's the only reason he trusts it.

Shelley

Tell that to a mother burying her infant. I tried three times before one child lived long enough to call me mother. No resolution came. Only graves and silence. Do not speak to me of harmony unless you admit it is sometimes deaf.

Galileo

My daughter Virginia, the one who prayed for me, died behind convent walls. I still feel the crease of her last letter in my palm. When her voice stopped, the heavens kept turning, indifferent. The cosmos has structure; it offers no consolation.

Shelley

Then we agree. Creation doesn't really soothe; it unsettles. You looked through glass and saw orbits; I looked at grief and saw a monster. Both were warnings dressed as revelations.

Galileo

Warnings? I gave mankind truth. The earth moves. The stars don't care for our myths. That isn't a warning; it's liberation.

Shelley

Liberation? My creature was liberated from death itself, and what did freedom give him? Misery. Isolation. Murder. Sometimes knowledge does not liberate; it estranges. Like a violin played in the wrong room.

Galileo

You turned rupture into art. An out-of-tune violin still makes music, because it insists on being heard.

Shelley

Do you hear it now, the phonograph coughing up madrigals? The voices are warped, but they try. That is closer to creation than your neat orbits. Broken voices, straining against dust.

Galileo

Then say it plainly: you prefer fracture to order.

Shelley

I prefer truth. And truth is often fracture. Ask the families who saw your telescope pointed at the heavens while the plague prowled their streets. Did the moons of Jupiter save them?

Galileo

No more than your fiction saved yours. We both escaped into our instruments. Yours was ink, mine was glass. Should I apologize for the tool I chose?

He scratches the desk with his nail, like a quill run dry. She taps the violin, not playing, just testing whether wood still vibrates. Two artists, neither calling themselves artists, circling blame while the record skips on the same bar until the needle jumps forward.

Shelley

Your Church silenced you, yet you still spoke of divine harmony. How can you praise the same heavens that blinded you?

Galileo

Blindness taught me what sight could not. I lost the stars and learned the weight of voices. My daughter's letters, ink pressed hard, edges softened from folding, were the only scripture I believed. If meaning exists, it's because those pages still sound when I open them.

Shelley

Letters as scripture. Then you understand. *Frankenstein* was my letter to the world. A letter no one asked for, but one I could not stop writing. Each page was a chord struck against silence, begging someone to hear grief as more than background noise.

Galileo

Her letters smelled of wax and kitchen smoke. The seal sometimes crooked. She was always in a hurry. She'd tuck in a scrap of cloth, a list of small requests, and once a folded recipe in the margin because she knew I forgot to eat when the sky was clear. I kept them under a ribbon, then under a hand, then under my pillow when the coughing got worse.

Shelley

People think grief is thunder. Most of the time it's housekeeping. Ribbons and scraps and the way paper softens from being opened too much.

Galileo

Exactly. When sight left me, I traced her handwriting with my thumb until the ink felt like thread. I tell myself it was prayer. Perhaps it was just proof she existed where my eyes could no longer go. And they did. They still do. Your monster walks in classrooms and theatres while my moons orbit unnoticed in most minds. Perhaps you succeeded more than I did.

Shelley

Success? My book was confession, not triumph. Do you measure confession by applause?

Galileo

Sometimes. When the applause is the only sound left after the Inquisition's silence. I remember standing, forced to recant, muttering under my breath that the earth moves still. The words were music only I could hear. Bitter, but mine.

Shelley

And when you whispered, did you not feel the weight of cowardice?

Galileo

I felt the weight of survival. Cowardice keeps the throat alive, at least long enough to whisper again. Would you rather I had burned? I have polished lenses with fingers that shook. Not from courage. Shame. The first thing I saw clearly was my own fear.

Shelley

Sometimes burning clarifies. My mother died giving me life. Fire is both monster and midwife. You swallowed the truth to save your skin; I wrote to set mine aflame. Which of us is braver? If I'm honest, bravery was the word I used when I wanted my grief to sit still.

Galileo

Perhaps bravery is just a word audiences clap for. I did what I could. You did what you could. History entered us in the same catalog.

Galileo

I named them for a patron first. The Medicean stars. That's what I called Jupiter's four lights. Truth needs time, and time needs money. I wasn't buying favor; I was buying days to keep looking.

Shelley

And you paid with the name.

Galileo

Names are the way men bargain with power. I wrote their dance as carefully as a prayer. Then tied a ribbon around the title so the door would open. Later the scholars renamed them one by one. That was fine. I only needed the nights.

Shelley

My creature never had a name. I thought that protected him from the world. It only made it easier for people to decide what he was.

Galileo

Then we both learned it the hard way. A name doesn't pull anyone out of the grave. But saying nothing shoves them in faster.

Shelley

I wonder sometimes whether my creature was really the monster. Or whether I was. A young widow, mother, orphan—scraping grief into prose. He is my shadow given breath.

Galileo

Then he is no different than my telescope. A shadow given glass. Each of us built a mirror to reveal what we could not face in daylight.

Shelley

And yet yours pointed outward, mine inward. Tell me, Signor, did you ever doubt your stars? Did you ever think perhaps the heavens should be left as mystery, not dissected into orbits?

Galileo

As a boy, I lay in the grass outside Pisa, the sky wide and unsliced. Stars pulsed like fires no hand could touch. I almost miss that version of them. Before lenses made them numbers.

For a moment he's just a child again, lying in the dark, counting stars with his fingers. Back then wonder was something that pressed on his ribs, not a column of numbers. Losing that feels like being sent away from your own house.

Galileo

To answer your question: every night. Mystery is sweeter than mathematics. But I could not stop looking. The moons betrayed me by existing. They demanded I tell the truth of their dance. Even when I feared I'd lose everything, I could not stop.

Shelley

That is the cruelty of creation. The work demands itself. My monster demanded pages. Your moons demanded sketches. We obeyed, not out of pride, but because silence was heavier.

Galileo

Yes. The Church tried. Your critics tried. But the thing that really wins is the quiet when no one's listening. That's the one that guts you.

He pauses, not for drama. Just to let the sentence land. The telescope waits like an answer that won't volunteer itself.

Galileo

Here. Take the eyepiece. Slow breath. Don't chase the stars; let them come to you.

Shelley

I only see blur, and that's familiar. The quiet does it too. It smears everything until you doubt your own eyes.

Galileo

Good. Then you already know what it costs to make truth hold still. Turn the barrel the width of a fingernail. Yes. Now hold still.

Shelley

Four dots. They look pinned there.

Galileo

Wait. Watch for the smallest shift. Jupiter drags them, night by night. Tomorrow they will not be where they are now.

Shelley

They're moving.

Galileo

Everything is. That was the heresy: that movement can be measured and mystery can survive it. That's parallax.

Shelley

It feels like the first time my son tried to breathe. A tiny rise, and then another, and then I couldn't pretend the world hadn't changed.

Galileo

Yes. Once you see it move, you can't say it stands still.

Shelley

And so we broke it. You with glass, I with ink. And look what it made of us: you—trial, blindness, exile; me—widow, mythmaker, outcast.

Galileo

I kept the sky. They could not confiscate that.

A rare grin from Galileo slips.

Galileo

Do you regret it?

Shelley

Every day. And not once.

The phonograph skips; voices catch in static. The stumble is more honest than the song.

Galileo

When they sentenced me, I thought I'd been stripped of everything: light, freedom, dignity. The bench bit splinters into my palms. Darkness moved in behind my eyes, and still the orbits spun.

House arrest sounds gentle until you start counting nights. In Arcetri there was an evening when the guards forgot to close the shutter all the way. A thin triangle of sky sat over the cypresses like a coin left on a table. I could barely make out the stars—my eyes were already failing. But I knew where Jupiter would be from habit.

I sat with my fingers in the groove of the sill, tracing an orbit in dust while the friars whispered prayers in the next room. Every footstep in the corridor sounded like a verdict checking whether I was properly repentant. I wasn't. I was tired, ashamed, and still measuring angles in my head, like the math could keep me honest when the world wouldn't.

Shelley

And yet you bent. You recanted. They tell stories about brave whispers after the fact. Did you feel brave, or just small?

Galileo

I bent because I was frail, and I was old. Don't mistake bending for silence. They say I muttered it; I only remember my jaw tight and my tongue against my tooth. Whether that story's true or not, the earth still moves.

Shelley

Whispers haunt more than screams. My book was a whisper mistaken for thunder. They saw spectacle; it was mourning.

Galileo

What did you mourn?

Shelley

My children. Three gone before they could speak their first words. Percy drowned. My husband, swept under like some myth punished by Poseidon. I remember one boy in the garden, chasing at nothing, laughing as though the air itself had played with him. He was gone by morning. The grass stayed damp where he had fallen. My mother gone before I drew breath.

She left me a silhouette above the stair and sentences that did not know they were bequeathing a daughter. I learned my mother out of margins: a note at the side of a page, a complaint about a publisher, a half-finished argument about women written in a hand that stopped mid-thought. As a girl I would stand on the third step to be level with her painted gaze and report my day to oil and varnish. It was a ridiculous ritual and I never stopped. You bury enough people and you start talking to furniture.

Every page I wrote was an elegy disguised as fiction.

Galileo

Then your monster was grief with stitches.

Shelley

Of course he was. And your telescope was your fear screwed into glass and pointed at heaven, pretending it was faith.

Galileo

Faith? They accused me of heresy.

Shelley

And yet you clung to pattern, to a cosmos you insisted was ordered. That is faith. To keep tracing lines even after your vision failed.

Galileo

Maybe. Or maybe it was obsession. When I lost my sight, I hummed psalms off-key. The friars winced, but I needed it. Singing badly was still proof I was alive.

Shelley

And to write badly is still to insist on being remembered. Half my sentences were fragments of desperation. Some I dashed off without thought, others I bled over. Readers cannot tell the difference. They think all of it was lightning.

Galileo

Do you resent them for that?

Shelley

No. But I envy their ignorance. They read triumph where I wrote lament.

Galileo's hands twitch as they hold a quill. Shelley fiddles with the violin bow but does not raise it. The phonograph drags, the madrigal's voices slowing into something that sounds more like groaning than song. The room feels suspended, like two beats that will never resolve into measure.

Galileo

You once wrote that the monster wanted a companion: someone to share his exile. Did you write him that companion, or did you abandon him too?

Shelley

I abandoned him: out of fear, exhaustion, cowardice. Easier to leave him in the snow than confess I shared his loneliness.

Narrator (V.O.)

This was not fiction: it was the oldest fear: shoes left under a bed, a door locked from the outside.

Galileo

Then we are alike. I abandoned Virginia to her convent walls. She begged me in letters to be freed, to live beside me, but I told her it was safer there. I convinced myself it was protection, but it was cowardice. I left her in silence, and silence buried her.

Shelley

And yet you call yourself father of astronomy.

Galileo

Titles are given by others. Fathers do most of their failing in private.

Shelley

Mothers too. After Percy drowned, they pulled his coat from the sea. I kept it beside me for weeks, salt stiff in the fabric. Ink stained the cuffs where I gripped it at night. That was my relic, more holy than any altar. I survived, and my children did not. What kind of mother survives her children?

Galileo

The kind who keeps writing. The kind who does not let absence win.

Shelley

And the kind who invents a monster to scream what she cannot.

Galileo

Then we are both guilty. Both afraid and confessor. Both teacher and deserter.

The song falters, replaced by the soft hiss of the groove. In the dome, the silence, imagined or real, holds its own breath too.

Shelley

You speak of hush as though it were the enemy, but you clung to it when it suited you. You hid behind banners, behind whispers. That is not bravery, Signor, that is retreat.

Galileo

You call me coward because it makes you taller.

Shelley

I call you coward because you abandoned faces for formulas. You stared at moons to avoid staring at your daughter behind convent walls.

Galileo

And you stared at paper to avoid your children's graves. We both hid. Do not pretend your ink absolves you.

Shelley

I never pretended. My book is confession. Yours is excuse.

Galileo

And yet your monster killed in rage. What do you confess then? That creation in grief breeds destruction?

Shelley

Yes. And that pretending otherwise is a lie. You wrapped your stars in divine order, but you refused to admit they did not care whether your daughter prayed or your neighbors starved.

Galileo

And you refused to admit your monster was you.

Shelley

I admitted it on every page. Readers just lacked the courage to see it.

The violin bow slips and clatters to the floor. Neither moves. The phonograph sputters back into tune, almost mocking them.

Galileo

Tell me, Mary—do you regret it? Writing him into being?

Shelley

He is my son, my ghost, my punishment. He reminds me I am alive.

Galileo

Then I envy you. My moons will never speak back. They orbit indifferent, eternal, deaf to my pleas. At least your monster answered.

Shelley

He answered with rage.

Galileo

Better rage than nothing.

Shelley

Careful. That logic made tyrants. Rage mistaken for creation births nothing but graves.

Galileo

Then you condemn us both.

Shelley

Yes.

The dome creaks, like the building itself wants to interrupt. But nothing does. Just their words, hanging in the air, raw and unfinished. The room waits for a verdict that never comes.

Galileo

If I am coward, so are you. If I am betrayer, so are you.

Shelley

Then what are we to the world? Heroes? Monsters? Footnotes?

Galileo

We're a mess, Mary. They'll grind us down into parables and hang what's left on classroom walls like we meant it that way.

Shelley

And the parables will be lies.

Galileo

Perhaps. But sometimes lies are the only way listeners can stand the story.

Their words have worn the air thin. The bow stays on the floor, the record wheezes, and neither adds another strike. What's left is two people breathing harder than they should be, no victor, no verdict. Just the ache of still being here.

Shelley

You still cling to the idea of order. Even after blindness, trial, death. You still imagine the universe cares to arrange itself.

Galileo

And you still cling to grief. Every page you wrote, every metaphor. It was mourning in disguise.

Shelley

Because mourning is honest. Order is the mask.

Galileo

And yet both survive. Even the mask makes sound.

Shelley

So which one do we leave them? Order or lament?

Galileo

Both. Because creation is both. Even a scream counts as sound if the ear is desperate enough. A sob is rhythm if the heart listens.

Shelley

You sound like my monster begging for a companion.

Galileo

And you sound like me, whispering to the stars after my sight was gone.

Shelley

Perhaps that is why we are here. To admit we were both lonely.

Galileo

Yes.

Not harmony, not heresy: loneliness. The kind of note everyone recognizes and nobody knows how to finish. The phonograph sputters and dies. Quiet. The dome makes every breath louder than it should be. Shelley lifts the violin bow, presses it against the string. One note. Raw, imperfect, aching. It cuts the air.

Shelley

Then let them hear this. Not perfection, not resolution. Just the sound of two voices unwilling to vanish.

Galileo

That is the truest accord of all.

Shelley

And the truest lament.

Galileo

Both.

Shelley

Both.

Narrator (V.O.)

They do not shake hands. They do not argue further. The duet ends without applause, without tidy conclusion.

The night creaks on, the telescope stares blindly at the heavens, and the violin hums its last vibration. Perhaps that was the point all along.

The room exhales, not sure if it heard music or noise. That feels right.

CHAPTER 8

Thomas Edison – Steve Jobs: *The Patent and the Pixel*
ACT II: Faith, Fire, and the Fringe

Thomas Edison (1847–1931)
Inventor-operator who turned tinkering into a system. Menlo Park built the template: teams, testing, and a pipeline from sketch to market. He brought sound to cylinders, light to streets, and standardization to power. Holder of over a thousand U.S. patents, he could be harsh, litigious, and effective. He prized iteration, scale, and ownership. Get it working, get it everywhere, keep the bill honest. The devices mattered, but the real invention was the factory for inventions.

Steve Jobs (1955–2011)
Co-founded Apple, was fired, built NeXT, helped launch Pixar, then returned in 1997 to refocus the company. He made design non-optional: tight hardware-software integration, ruthless feature cuts, and storytelling that taught ordinary users to want fewer, better things. iMac, iPod, iPhone, iPad. Products that hid complexity without dumbing it down. Demanding to the point of cruelty, but right often enough to change habits. Legacy: taste enforced at scale.

Setting
A shared workbench, Menlo Park meets Cupertino. Oak top scarred by prototypes; a steady bulb; a chalkboard with a filament sketch beside rounded rectangles. A drawer of glass, a blackened soldering iron, and one

handset parked on a clean cloth. Coffee rings, patent numbers, a power strip underfoot. No shrine, no mystique, just a bench that rewards what ships.

Narrator (V.O.)

Most minds meet on paper; these two meet over a scarred bench. The fight isn't mystique; it's responsibility. One man worships reliability you can live with. The other chases a kind of delight you don't have to apologize for later.

Edison

See that glow? It's not romance. It's work that refused to quit. I don't sell miracles. I sell nights that don't burn houses.

Jobs

It's still hot glass that explodes if you get sloppy. We didn't invent light; we just taught it not to bite. Iteration beats scripture, most days.

Edison

Scripture is for poets. I ran a factory. I worked nights and paid for it. Ten thousand failures, then a lamp a mother could trust.

Jobs

Trust is design that doesn't ask permission every five minutes. The hand should feel welcome. The eye should feel understood.

Edison

I kept books like I kept bulbs, until they stayed lit.

He flips a page.

Edison

People think a patent is a trophy. It's a receipt.

Jobs

Receipts are for parts. People don't come with line items. You think focus is about ideas; half the time it's about who can stand each other at 2 a.m. I've fired the right person the wrong way and watched a great team turn average for six months. I've kept the wrong person because the room liked him and paid for it in bugs you could feel in your pocket. Delight costs real money—and attention. If you ignore it, people feel it.

There's a guy whose name I still won't say on stage. I fired him, and he packed his box in silence while I pretended the meeting next door was urgent. Years later I held a phone that still carried lines of his code and wondered what his kids thought I did for a living that day. Focus is easy to preach when you're not the one driving home with a box on your lap.

Narrator (V.O.)

He skips the man's name on purpose. The story isn't about a legend getting fired; it's about a stranger driving home with a cardboard box and kids who will never know their father's code is still lighting up the world in their hands.

Edison

You talk like I never watched a man carry his work out past the gate. They just didn't put my halls on magazine covers. Build systems big enough and the public only sees the glow. You don't wire cities without breaking a few circuits that had names and rent due.

Jobs

Focus is a work roster too. Say no to a hundred good ideas so one great thing can walk on stage without tripping over cousins. Keep the backbeat simple so the melody shows up.

Edison

You made theatres out of glass. Nice work. But a crowd doesn't fix a street. Wires do. Wires and the habit of reliability.

Jobs

I made objects that taught people the world could be careful. Mercy looks like a switch that's gentle, a hinge that doesn't pinch, a screen that wakes without a jolt.

Edison

Screens are polite until they take over a room. My switch bows once, then minds its business.

Jobs

Then give me business that bows without groveling. A seam can be honest and still be kind.

Edison closes the ledger and leaves a black thumb on the margin. He rubs at it, makes it worse, then leaves it be. The patent book bears the weight without comment.

Edison

You and seams. I like a screw you can see. If a thing breaks, a man should fix it without a priest.

Jobs

Some priests are engineers in better turtlenecks. I sealed doors to keep junk from crawling in and gnawing at trust. It isn't secrecy. It's stewardship.

Edison

Stewardship that charges tolls.

Jobs

Sometimes, yes. And sometimes the toll pays the guy sweeping the bridge so families don't slip. I've seen what "open" turns into when nobody owns the mess: five remotes on a coffee table and a house that feels like a lab.

Edison

I know a gate when I see one.

Jobs

Tickets pay for bridges. Bridges bring the future to people who can't cross on their own each morning.

The bulb ticks. Hot metal meeting air. Edison likes the honesty of it.

Jobs

I'll forgive the switch—

Edison

—I dragged a kid into court once because his connector made mine look slow. He couldn't afford the train to the hearing. I slept fine and told myself I was defending standards. The part of that sentence that's true doesn't help the rest.

Jobs clears his throat and lets the last word land. He lifts the phone, then sets it back like a kept promise.

Jobs

I'll forgive the switch. I won't forgive ugliness that excuses itself with longevity. The object can work and still respect your hand.

Edison

You talk about respect. Respect looks like a night shift that knows when it ends. Respect looks like wages that show up even if the investor doesn't. I fed furnaces so strangers could read.

Jobs

I know the cost. Factories. Hours. Nets on windows. The story of speed written on other bodies. I didn't like the ending. I changed what I could, late and not enough. The room doesn't clap. Silence isn't romance; it's testing. If a room stays quiet, the idea still works without applause.

Edison

Good. Applause doesn't pay my machine shop.

Jobs

You counted patents like points. I counted delight.

Edison

Delight doesn't keep a night crew fed.

Jobs

Yeah, okay, Tom, but it kept them coming back. Same thing, different currency.

Edison pauses to find his words.

Edison

Very well. My record isn't innocent either. I ran men past their knees and called it progress. I buried competitors in paperwork. I told myself families slept safer because I won. Some of that is true. The part that isn't still visits.

Jobs

We both took the same fire. You protected it with patents; I put it in people's hands. Different methods. Same heat.

He nods toward the patent book. Edison opens to a page that remembers a courtroom's cough.

Edison

Names and claims: the only way I knew to keep people from forgetting who did the work. Patents paid wages; without them, good ideas starved.

Jobs

And with it, some good names went missing. The public remembers the last man to sign. The first man to spark goes hungry in the footnotes.

Edison

The last man had to ship. Shipping makes decent men look ruthless and ruthless men look ordinary. I can live with that arithmetic.

Jobs

I lived with a different math. One device right, not twenty mediocre. One line that feels inevitable when you hear it. Fewer words, sharper edges.

Edison

You love inevitability. I love reliability. You called your launches magic. I called my demonstrations proof. Underneath, both of us wanted obedience, from machines, from men, from failure.

Jobs

Obedience to a standard that honors the human. Not to taste that bullies. Not to a spec sheet that wins a race no one asked to run.

Edison

Taste doesn't wire a block.

Jobs

Taste decides whether the block feels like home.

The ledger is closed again. The prototype sits in the middle like it belongs there.

Edison

Let's say it. You visited a lab. You walked out with the future under your coat and called it a product. They called that theft. You called it care.

Jobs

They filed a report; I got it into people's hands. Potential is a polite word for neglect. The work isn't finished until a customer can use it.

Edison

I protected the work with paperwork; you evangelized it with glass. We both told stories about mercy while we counted.

Jobs

Counting is a form of care when it protects the person at the end of the line. The line gets long. The care gets thin. I failed often.

Edison

I failed long, rooms and wrong turns, until one door opened and stayed open.

Jobs

Mine: remove the unnecessary until the necessary breathes. Elegance is just honesty that learned some manners.

He talks in one clean ribbon, measured and steady, filing the edge as he speaks.

Jobs

I wanted the object in your hand to say, without speaking, that someone thought about you when you weren't in the room. I thought about your thumb, and your pocket, and the moment between need and relief. That the care would repeat tomorrow without scolding you for not reading a manual somebody wrote to show off.

There was a guy on the line in Elk Grove who kept a tiny cloth in his pocket. Not company issue. His. He wiped the edge of every third unit like the person who'd open that box might be his sister. No one asked him. No metric caught it. He did it because the work felt like a promise he'd signed. When we sealed more of the device, he kept the cloth. That's the user I picture when I argue for closed doors: his habit, not my marketing.

Edison

That sermon would get a foreman fired for wasting daylight. But I hear the heart in it. I'm not deaf. The poor like beauty too. They just hate when beauty raises the price and then calls itself virtue. I mistook ugliness for honesty more than once. That wasn't frugality; it was a blind spot.

Jobs

Then build beauty that pays its own way. I tried; sometimes the math worked, and sometimes it bought me applause and sent the bill to someone else.

The chalkboard is ready for another line. No one gives it. The bulb sticks to its job: repeat, don't pose.

Edison

We've treated each other politely enough. You called me a patent bully. I called you a priest. There's truth in both insults. I stiff-armed names. You fenced gardens. We both wanted a monopoly on gratitude.

Jobs

Gratitude looks cleaner on your grid. Mine smudges with fingerprints. Different dirt. Same hands.

Edison

I chased control because chaos breaks machines.

Jobs

And I chased it because chaos breaks people. I wanted glass and light to say *welcome home*.

Edison

I wanted wire and heat to say *still working*.

Jobs

Both are prayers. We just aimed them at different gods.

Edison

Let's talk wounds, not polish. My phonograph was a joke to men with soft chairs, until their children kept their dead fathers in kitchens and learned lullabies by memory instead of myth.

I saw one once—little house, bad wallpaper. The kid had the horn propped on a crate, standing there in socks, listening to a younger version of his father telling a bedtime story. The man in the chair was older, thinner, already dying. The record did the talking. Nobody laughed in that room.

I took the laughing personal. I fought mean with AC because I was scared of fires and of losing. The elephant did not deserve that lesson. Neither did the public. Fear, dressed as safety, bites everyone.

Jobs

I went home from my own company with a box and a story about vision no one wanted to hear. The badge stopped working before the box got heavy; the walk across the parking lot felt longer than some product cycles. I kept telling myself I was the one who understood, but the only thing listening was the cardboard digging into my fingers.

I built another house and taught myself to knock before entering. Then I came back with manners mean enough to win. I burned teams in the name of care. I wish I'd learned sooner that care without mercy is theatre.

Edison

Theatre persuades senators. I played some, poorly and loud. The grid still got built. The country still read at midnight without candles, and streets stopped acting like alleys. I'll take the ugliness I earned if the night stays civilized.

Jobs

I'll take the ugliness I earned if the hand stays unafraid. The first wake of a screen in the morning shouldn't feel like a barked order. It should feel like a nod.

Edison

What is invention to you: birth or adoption that refuses to fail?

Jobs

Birth without adoption is vanity. Adoption without birth is theft with better shoes. Invention is custody that's supposed to keep its promises. I didn't always.

Edison

Custody needs lawyers. I brought mine.

Jobs

Custody also needs taste. I brought mine.

Edison

We'll split the bill and pretend we didn't.

The heat moves. The room smells like rain after a long day. The bulb keeps the air honest.

Edison

You talk a lot about love. You love a curve and a corner. Does the seam teach, or does it punish?

Jobs

Teach. The seam whispers, *Not here. Try there.* It refuses clumsiness without calling you stupid. It makes you better without leaving a bruise.

Edison

My seams bleed and then stop. People learn quicker when the lesson stings. That's factory pedagogy.

Jobs

I wanted the lesson without blood. The world supplies blood without my help. I tried to reduce the tax.

Edison lets out one laugh: the kind you give a promise you'd never write down.

Edison

There's a difference between a priest and a foreman that matters less at midnight. Both want a room to behave. One prays, one shouts. The bulb doesn't care which voice bought its supper.

Jobs

Then define the difference between taste and tyranny. A grid can bully. So can a brand.

Edison

A brand dies when the room gets bored. A grid dies when you forget to tighten bolts. Boredom is kinder than fire.

Jobs

Attention burns fast. I built products for it and told myself they were tools. Sometimes they were. Sometimes they were just better toys.

He touches the tablet without waking it, a father who knows when to let a child sleep.

Edison

You want absolution?

Jobs

No. A better sentence. Fewer knives hidden in kindness. More doors that open without debt.

Edison

Doors cost. Hinges squeak truth. Someone oils them. Someone pays. I wrote names next to chores. I enforced them. I was proud of the enforcement.

Jobs

I wrote names next to dreams. I enforced them too. Pride looks cleaner in a keynote. It still bruises.

The bulb dips, then comes back. Edison leans on the workbench; it's used to him.

Edison

You were adopted. You built belonging with devices. Crowds gave it back because they were hungry for a room that called them by their first name.

Jobs

Yes. The stage was a substitute for a family tree I already had and still wanted to redraw. The applause was borrowed. It didn't pass to my kids. They learned early that their father owned rooms full of strangers better than he owned a Tuesday night at home. I could fill a theatre and still miss a bedtime. The applause went dark when the lights did. The look on my kids' faces when I was late—that stayed.

Edison

Children need light to do algebra without squinting. The inheritance I like is a habit: the switch is where the hand remembers. It clicks the same way on bad days. That's design. You can keep the word. I'll keep the click.

Jobs

Keep it. The click is respect. I tuned the feel. You built the foundation.

Edison

Tell me what you'd have changed before the fruit ripened and the bill got itemized.

Jobs

More patience in rooms without cameras. More sleep that belonged to my children. Fewer righteous firings. More righteous forgiveness. Still the same insistence on care in small things: the corner, the hinge, the box that opens like a welcome and not a chore.

Edison

I'd have said no quicker. Left a rival alive twice a year to keep my blood honest. Paid one genius sooner. Trusted one lie later. Standards turn into cages when you stop letting them change.

Jobs

Then call that a shared errata. Not a truce. A correction.

Edison

Noted. Back to the ledger. We're drifting toward poetry and that breaks machines.

Pages turn. The bulb stamps a bright coin on the ledger's dates. The phone shows a thin, borrowed moon.

Edison

People will say you bewitched me. They say that when a man with soft hands wins. I'll enjoy their discomfort and keep my bolts tight.

Jobs

They'll say you were a troll with lawyers instead of teeth. I'll enjoy their discomfort and keep my corners exact.

Edison

You got thrown out of your own house and then got handed the keys back. That's not common.

Jobs

Exile taught me to visit. Return taught me to own. Death taught me to shut up sometimes and let the room be more important than my certainty.

Edison

Death taught me nothing; it just kept the clock honest. Deadlines make standards behave.

Jobs

Deadlines make taste braver. Keep the curve; keep the seam honest. Even I learned to listen.

The bulb holds. The room cools the way iron does: slow and sure. Edison slides the ledger aside; Jobs squares the device.

Edison

You wanted to define invention. Here: it's the part of pride that learned a schedule. It shows up. It repeats. It forgives bad weather by working anyway.

Jobs

And here: it's the part of beauty that refuses to be decoration. It works, and in working it makes the person feel like they matter.

Edison

Our definitions fight without knives. That's an upgrade.

Jobs

It is.

They meet at the line where workbench becomes show. The bulb hums on, the chalkboard holds still, the prototype keeps its stare.

Edison

You used to ask the world to gasp on cue. I used to ask it to stop setting things on fire. Both requests were sincere. Both got granted sometimes.

Jobs

The gasp helped me. The fire hurt other people. I learned slower than I like.

Edison

Learning is slow. Shipping is fast. That's the oldest fight in any building. We both chose fast more often than we should have. The world lived through it and sometimes because of it.

Jobs

Then let's leave the world with two sentences it can use without us.

Edison

You first.

Jobs

I usually do.

Edison

Make yours short. Mine will be shorter.

Jobs

Fine.

Edison turns the bulb a fraction, just enough to feel the thread take. He doesn't show off. He never did, not successfully.

Edison

Get it working. Get it everywhere. Keep the bill honest.

Jobs

Build it like you love the hand that holds it, and the life around that hand.

Narrator (V.O.)

The bulb keeps its heat, the aluminum its smudge. Edison leaves another page of ownership; Jobs leaves another argument for care. What lingers is not ordinary at all: the suspicion that progress needs both men, the ruthless foreman and the restless designer. The room doesn't resolve the fight, but it remembers, every time a kid does homework under a cheap lamp or scrolls a cracked screen that still wakes up on the first touch.

CHAPTER 9

HELEN KELLER – STEPHEN HAWKING: *TOUCH AND THE EDGE OF SPACE*

ACT II: Faith, Fire, and the Fringe

Helen Keller (1880–1968)

Deafblind since infancy, she learned language through Anne Sullivan's hand and refused to stop there. First deafblind person to earn a B.A. (Radcliffe, 1904), she wrote, lectured worldwide, and campaigned for disability rights, women's suffrage, labor, and free speech. A founding member of the ACLU, she raised funds for vision care and pushed access as infrastructure, not charity. Fame tried to fix her as a miracle; she answered with policy, craft, and a lifetime of work, capped by the Presidential Medal of Freedom (1964).

Dr. Stephen Hawking (1942–2018)

Cosmologist who mapped the early universe while ALS narrowed his body. Lucasian Professor at Cambridge; proposed Hawking radiation; helped prove key singularity theorems. *A Brief History of Time* made cosmology a household subject. A wheelchair, a synthetic voice, and a dry joke became part of the message: limits can still do first-rate science. Honors include the U.S. Presidential Medal of Freedom (2009), but he preferred clarity over ceremony. Curiosity as a public good.

Setting

A planetarium in daylight. A narrow slit of sky makes dust visible. A wheelchair waits at a thinking angle. Braille pages stack on a low table; a child's solar system hangs steady from fine threads. The projector sleeps; a handrail holds the last tour's warmth. Somewhere, a chair leg ticks the floor. Touch is allowed; apology isn't needed. The room doesn't demand silence. It already listens.

Narrator (V.O.)

They arrive as the world imagines them: icons. She made language out of dark and silence; he let his mind slip past gravity to peek at the beginning of time. But imagine them instead as two human beings with errands, with laundry in baskets, with socks that never come out of the dryer matched. Imagine them as nervous. Because everyone is, a little, when the talk matters.

Keller

Stephen, before we begin, can I say something ordinary? This chair is tilted like a boat with a bad keel and I love it already because it reminds me I'm not furniture either. I have been polished so many times by people's expectations that I forget I can creak. If I'm creaking tonight, forgive me.

Hawking

Creaking is data. The universe creaks; that's half of cosmology. And thank you for the chair warning. I've learned to avoid surprises, except the good kind. We can keep the good surprises.

Keller

When I was a child, the world had no edges. There was only touch, hunger, and this endless pushing against what felt like water. Then the pump, the rush of cold, the word in my hand. It wasn't a miracle with trumpets. More like a door clicking unlocked that had never been a door at all. I have lived a long time with the knowledge that the ordinary is the only magic we can trust.

Hawking

I disliked magic until equations began doing it. I was told I had two years. Those two years stretched like old elastic until eventually they held a whole life and some extra. I found out that when you think you are running out of time, you become greedy for questions that do not care whether you have legs. It's a relief, really, to talk to curiosities that don't pity you.

Keller

Did you feel it? The first time you knew your body had betrayed you? I do not mean the headline version. I mean the small treasons. The fork you cannot grip on a tired day. The way a stranger speaks too slowly, like slowness were kindness. I forgive big things faster than small ones; the small ones scratch like a crow tonight.

Hawking

The small treasons are the biography no one writes. The first time my hand would not pour a cup of tea I almost laughed because the moment felt staged, like a character beat from a film about someone else. It took longer to admit it was me. Later, when the machine gave me a voice, I found myself missing the pointless noises of speech. The wasted words. The ums and stray metaphors. The machine hated waste. It streamlined me until I became an outline of myself.

Narrator (V.O.)

If this were staged with two chairs, a dome, and a sky, you would hear the motor and think it metaphorical. Which is not wrong.

Keller

People like to say that I triumphed over silence. I did not. I domesticated it. Silence is a wild animal that never really tames. Some days it sits at your feet and lets you scratch its head; some nights it breaks the door and sleeps on your chest so you can't breathe. It still loves me, even when I am tired of it.

Hawking

I warned the world about artificial intelligence not because I fear intelligence, but because I fear our appetite to outsource responsibility. A machine without empathy worries me. A human who chooses not to feel? That's catastrophic. We like to imagine harm as an external force. Most of the time, harm is the concierge we tipped on the way in without reading the name tag.

Keller

You say "empathy" and heads nod; it's a word that has grown shiny with overuse. But I remember the first time I understood another person's mind—not the idea of it, the texture of it. Anne's hand in mine, spelling, and suddenly I felt the temperature of her attention. I do not know if machines will ever have hands that warm. I am not sure some people do.

Hawking

I don't require warmth.

That is a lie. Or perhaps a defense.

Hawking

What I require is time. Enough to finish a thought before it dissolves.

Keller

You speak of time like a profession. I have held time the way a person holds a stone to the tongue to see if it is salt. I have counted time by the seasons of other people's lives. Their faces shifting when my hand finds their cheek, the way a voice I can't hear moves the body underneath it. I have never been alone in time, not truly, which is another kind of miracle the world keeps pretending isn't one.

Hawking

Do you want the science answer about time or the human one? The science one is cleaner and wrong in the way clean answers often are. The human one is messy, but it's the only version that makes my children's faces make sense.

Keller

Both, but begin with the wrong one. I like to hear the elegant error first; it makes me braver about my clumsy truths.

Hawking

Very well. Time curves with mass and energy. It is elastic at scale. At the beginning of the universe it may have been different in a way we cannot properly imagine because imagination, like physics, has boundary conditions. Black holes are holes in our confidence about what reality can endure. That is the clean answer and it is useful when one needs to win an argument or a grant.

Keller

And the messy one?

Hawking

I mourn the kind of time that lets you be impulsive. The uncalculated afternoon. The decision to go to a bad film with a friend and argue about it afterward. ALS did not take my curiosity. It took spontaneity, and spontaneity is the combustion engine of intimacy. I adapted. I found new ways to be present. But I won't pretend that loss was noble. It was just loss.

Keller

There is a sentence I do not love, but people pin on me anyway: "You overcame." They send it to me like a compliment and I send it back unopened. I did not *overcame*. I *became*. There is a difference, and it took me a lifetime to insist on it. Half my public speeches I dashed off on trains; others I sweated over like laundry on a washboard. The ones people quote are not always the ones that cost me blood. I try not to take it personally when the easy lines get the applause.

Hawking

That is uncomfortably familiar. Some of my best-known lines were conveniences—a way to answer a complicated question in an airport corridor before the attendant wheeled me away. People prefer the sentence you can print on a mug. I kept the complex conversation for the papers hardly anyone reads. That is not bitterness.

It is a little bitterness.

Keller

You may have it; you earned it. I keep a little bitterness for the way people speak to me like a child at a petting zoo. *"What a marvelous goat," they say, "and look at her tricks."* Forgive me. Humor is my immune system when politeness fails.

Hawking

Humor is physics for feelings. It releases pressure. I once made a joke about time travel at a party to which I invited time travelers a week after it happened. No one came. It is not the worst result for a party.

Keller

If we are confessing, I will admit: sometimes I could not bear the pity. It felt like being wrapped in the wrong blanket: warm but suffocating. I wanted to be cold and honest instead. I wanted to be allowed to be unremarkable for an afternoon. To drop the mantle of inspiration and just be a tired woman who wants her tea, who will complain about this chair one more time because the left leg really is shorter. Tonight I'm perched like a bird with bad balance.

Narrator (V.O.)

There is a relief in watching the heroic dab at irritation the way the rest of us do. The room shrinks to human size. The stars lean in. Somewhere a moth is having a theological argument with the light.

Hawking

Do you believe in souls, Helen? Not the word; the thing.

Keller

I believe in the part of us that persists in wanting meaning even after proof refuses to shake our hand. Call that soul. I believe in the stubborn insistence that love is not an illusion even when we cannot evidence it like a theorem. I also believe some people use the word to excuse bad behavior while pretending to be profound. Humanity contains multitudes; multitudes contain a lot of nonsense.

Hawking

I do not believe in souls as substances that float when the body stops. But I have felt the sacred. It happens when a solution clicks, or when I watch my children trying not to laugh at a joke they know they should not encourage. If machines can have that, this sudden coherence that feels larger than us, then perhaps the word "soul" is just our first bad draft of a better definition.

Keller

You're letting in more light than you did at the beginning of that sentence. I appreciate it. My faith is not the faith of tidy miracles. It is closer to a willingness to keep speaking into a room where you are not sure anyone will answer. Which is to say, it is a lot like your work.

Hawking

Touché. And you are braver than I am to say it out loud. I hide my reverence behind math because math does not pity. That is the attraction. It lets me be exact without apology. But yes, there are nights when exactness feels like a small blanket for a very large cold.

Keller

When you close your eyes—truly close them—what do you see?

Hawking

Structure. Not void. A quiet grid. A universe whispering in code waiting to be solved. I see my children's laughter before the machine. I sometimes see a version of myself that did not get sick, and I am surprised to feel relief that I am who I am. Regret is a worse physicist than gratitude; gratitude actually tests more possible realities.

Keller

I see hands. Always hands. Hands spelling into my palm. Hands that smell of soap and ink. Hands that are clumsy because love is clumsy. I also see nothing, in the truest sense, and I have made peace with that. The mind can paint in the dark if it must.

Narrator (V.O.)

We have reached the section of the night where comfort gives way to unease. The questions are no longer safe. Even the dome motor is polite enough to quiet down to a hum you notice only when it stops.

Hawking

Do you ever think your courage has been used against you? That people brandish your story to make others behave?

Keller

Yes, and it angers me. Do not borrow my body for your lecture on gratitude. Do not cite my life to avoid spending money to make someone else's life bearable. I'm not a coupon for the human spirit.

Hawking

I love that line. May I borrow it for my enemies?

Keller

You may borrow it for your friends. Enemies will misquote it and sell it back to you as wisdom.

Hawking

Fair point. Then let me admit something that does not travel well as a slogan: I chose logic because it would not pity me. The convenience of indifference. Equations did not ask me how I felt when I could not move my hand to scratch an itch. They offered me work instead. Work is the opposite of despair because it asks for a next step. Even if the next step is tiny and performed by someone else's hands on your behalf.

Keller

Work saved me, too. There is a way people look at you when you are disabled, like they are waiting for your meaning to arrive in the room behind you. Work says, "I arrived myself." Work says, "I'll decide what I add up to."

Hawking

Then perhaps our disagreement is smaller than it appears. I have been accused of being a priest for reason. But I do not worship reason. I use it the way a sailor uses wind. It gets you somewhere if you remember the water is the point.

Keller

I will still argue that there is warmth necessary to live that you cannot find in equations. Your work explains the sky; love explains why we look up at all. And some nights, some nights, Stephen, I don't think the universe is indifferent; it's quiet—waiting for us to bring warmth to it, the way a hand warms a stone.

Hawking

We can coexist, warmth and math. Even I admit hot tea is superior to cold elegance at three in the morning.

Keller

Now you're preaching.

Narrator (V.O.)

If this were a novel, the author would underline that the room itself is rotating gently, which is admittedly a bit on-the-nose but also true.

Hawking

I am going to ask a selfish question: If your mind could outlive your body, uploaded, preserved, would you choose it?

Keller

No. Not as a copy. Not as a ghost of logic floating in circuitry. What makes consciousness human is limitation. Death gives shape to life. The clock is not cruel. It's sacred. I would rather fade as a whole person than persist as a fragment of one.

Hawking

We agree. People assume I would be first in line for that experiment. I would not. A self with no constraints is just a model with no calibration. It stops telling you anything real. Also, I suspect eternity would make me unbearably lazy.

Keller

You? Lazy?

Hawking

Theoretical laziness. A thought experiment. I would get around to things "eventually." "Eventually" is the enemy of tenderness, at least for me.

Keller

You are smuggling a poem into your science, Doctor, and I approve. Sometimes tenderness is the only thing that keeps us from becoming efficient monsters.

Hawking

Efficient monsters, that is very good. It describes more institutions than we can name without losing our venue.

Keller

You'll get us thrown out of the observatory and I will write the letter of complaint with a quill that scratches like a crow tonight. There, I have ruined the metaphor and now we can move on with clean consciences.

Hawking

I like when you miss. It gives the rest of us permission.

Keller

I miss often; I just learned to do it with authority. Here is a worse one: grief is a room with carpeting. See? No good. It deadens everything, even itself.

Hawking

Allow me one in exchange: black holes are the universe's way of filing what it can't deal with. Also bad. We are even.

Keller

We are even. And now that the metaphor quota has been fulfilled poorly, we may proceed to truth with our sleeves rolled up.

Hawking

Truth, then: I am afraid of a future where we are clever enough to destroy ourselves before we are wise enough to stop it. The math of extinction is elegant. The math of restraint is a lot harder.

Keller

Restraint is a human art. It requires feeling. Which brings us back to your fear, not of machines, but of us. A human who refuses to feel is the most dangerous machine of all.

Hawking

Yes. I have watched people turn off empathy like it were a light that wasted electricity. The bill always comes due. Usually for someone who cannot pay it.

Keller

Without tenderness we floor the gas and call it progress; most of the time it just ends in a collision.

Hawking

Put that on a road sign, not a mug.

Keller

Done. Now, before we run out of time, and yes, I hear the irony, tell me the kindest thing anyone ever did for you when they didn't have to.

Hawking

My wife once sat beside me after a night of fighting the ventilator and whispered, "*You are still you. That's what I married.*" She did not say it to cheer me. She said it because I had forgotten. Kindness restores you to yourself.

Keller

Anne did that. Many times. When I grew exhausted with being inspirational, she let me be ordinary and angry and uncombed. She did not decorate me with virtue. She brushed my hair and told me to eat something and then told me to keep going, not because I was a symbol, but because I was a person.

Hawking

Symbols are dangerous when they replace people. I tried to remember that when my face was on the cover of a magazine. I was still a man who needed help adjusting a blanket at 3 a.m. The blanket did not care about the cover. The blanket wanted physics of a very practical sort.

Keller

There's the title of your memoir: "*Blanket Physics.*"

Hawking

Too domestic. The publisher would insist on "*Time's Edge*" or some such. But yes, the truth is in the blanket at 3 a.m., not in the headline.

Keller

Then let us arrive where we both must. Stephen, if tonight were your final breath, what truth would you want whispered into the dark?

Hawking

That we were never alone. That life, brief, broken, astonished, mattered. Not because it changed the cosmos but because it looked up at the stars and refused to blink.

Keller

Then I will say mine: that meaning is not discovered like a coin in the street; it is built like a ramp you actually use. I want the last voice in my mind to say, "You did enough." And the last touch to be a hand squeezing my palm, like a conversation we didn't finish and won't regret ending.

Narrator (V.O.)

This is the quiet part. Nobody moves. Even the motor seems to wait. Science and faith stop at the same ledge and, for once, agree: we're better climbers than jumpers. That works for me.

Hawking

Helen, if you could go back and speak to the child at the pump, would you?

Keller

Yes, for the simplest reason. I would tell her, "You are not your diagnosis. You are not the eyes that pity you. You are thought, and when thought refuses to die, it becomes light." Then I would hug her, because all our theories lose to a good hug.

Hawking

I would tell my younger self the same, in different words.

He likes her version better.

Hawking

And then I would ask him to be kinder sooner. I spent too long being clever. Clever makes rooms feel smaller. Kindness makes them larger.

Keller

That sounds like the beginning of wisdom, which is inconveniently late for most of us. But late wisdom is still wisdom. Even the stars are late; their light arrives when they are already changed.

Hawking

You are doing astronomy better than the astronomer. I should be offended.

Keller

Please be. It will sell tickets for the rematch.

Hawking

Very well. Final disagreement of the night: does the universe care?

Keller

No. But we do, and that is enough to change how it feels to live in it. The universe is the stage. We are the ones who decide to clap.

Hawking

I can live with that. And die with it, which is a rarer compliment.

Keller

Then let us close as the observatory prefers: quietly, with a whir. The dome will swing shut and the night will go on not needing us. But someone will leave here and talk to a stranger with more patience, and someone else will forgive the small treason of a body that needs help, and that will be our contribution to the expansion of the universe.

Hawking

Not the heat death I expected, but a warming I prefer.

Keller

I'm stealing that for the program notes.

Hawking

Take it. The equations will survive the theft.

Narrator (V.O.)

They do not rise for ceremony. Rising is complicated, and anyway ceremony is only one kind of answer. Instead they sit for a minute in the settling quiet, two humans cooling like kettles, steam finishing its sentence. Someone opens the outer door. Night unrolls like a fabric you can lay your head on. The chairs creak. The room remembers to breathe again.

Keller

Stephen, would you like tea?

Hawking

Very much. And if there are biscuits—

Keller

There are always biscuits. The universe is indifferent, but the kitchen is not.

Hawking

A comforting cosmology.

Keller

One cup at a time.

Narrator (V.O.)

Out under the dome, the telescope is parked, lens cap on, waiting like a big animal that has done its trick for the night and now wants only to be quiet. Above the slit of roof, the stars do what they always do: pretend they are not impressed. Down here, two minds who have carried more than their share hand off the weight to cups, to breath, to small talk that means more because it means nothing. It is a good ending. The human kind.

ACT III

THE THEATER OF GENIUS

When brilliance performs, mocks, or spirals into spectacle

Genius rarely sits quietly in the corner. It hogs the mic, chases applause, and sometimes lights the curtains on fire. Act III is the night you stuff wit, comedy, invention, and obsession onto the same cramped stage and hope the sprinklers are working.

Oprah Winfrey and Marilyn Monroe sit under the spotlight, two icons caught between worship and loneliness. One built an empire on confession, the other became a symbol of desire she could never escape. Their dialogue doesn't solve the riddle of fame; it just keeps circling the bruise, showing how the same spotlight can feel like a hug one night and an autopsy lamp the next.

Fred Rogers and Robin Williams strip away performance until kindness and chaos touch raw nerves. Laughter hides pain; gentleness hides fear. By the time they're done, the person under the act is showing: makeup half-wiped, cardigan crooked, punchline hanging in the air a second too long for anybody to pretend it didn't hurt.

Mark Twain and Oscar Wilde duel with words, their wit sharp enough to wound. They weaponize the joke and then pretend it's nothing, because if either of them lets the silence hang for more than a beat, the room might see that all that wit is mostly armor.

George Carlin and Hunter S. Thompson corner America in a dirty Vegas motel, mixing rage with punchlines until the flag looks less like a symbol and more like something somebody spilled beer on. One used comedy as rebellion, the other journalism as provocation. Together they drag out a version of the country where the truth doesn't show up in press conferences. It shows up high, hoarse from swearing, and not entirely sure if the safety's on.

William Shakespeare and Lin-Manuel Miranda spar across centuries, the bard of pentameter against the modern master of rhyme. One wrote for wooden stages and candlelight, the other for mics and turntables; two men quietly betting their lines would outlive the buildings they were spoken in. They keep glancing past the footlights, wondering who's still stuck outside the theater and how much work it really is to build a wider doorway instead of just a higher stage.

Frida Kahlo and Pablo Picasso face off in a studio of smoke, scars, and splintered vision. She insists on painting pain without disguise; he fractures form until perspective shatters. Stay in that studio long enough and whatever we call 'genius' starts to smell like turpentine and cold coffee instead of destiny. It looks like someone arguing with a canvas at 3 a.m., scraping paint back off with a knife because whatever's on the canvas still looks too polite for what actually happened.

And then Beethoven and Mozart: thunder and elegance colliding in harmony and rivalry. One carved symphonies with fury, the other danced with genius so fluid it seemed effortless. Their duet doesn't settle anything. It sounds like a waltz that can't stop tripping over its own feet, lullaby in one hand, war drum in the other, every bar carrying more strain than harmony.

This isn't a hall of statues. It's a packed little theater where the lights flicker, geniuses trip over their own props, and every spark tries to hog the view.

CHAPTER 10

OPRAH WINFREY – MARILYN MONROE: *THE SPOTLIGHT AND THE SILENCE*

ACT III: The Theater of Genius

Oprah Winfrey (1954–)

Born in Mississippi and raised across tough rooms that didn't expect much, she started reading news at 19 and turned a local job into a global microphone. *The Oprah Winfrey Show* (1986–2011) made confession a civic ritual; Harpo built the empire that followed. She opened a girls' school in South Africa, launched a book club that moved markets, and kept shifting lanes: producer, actor, philanthropist. Honors include the Jean Hersholt Humanitarian Award and the Presidential Medal of Freedom. Underneath the brand is the recurring theme: survive, then build rooms where others can too.

Marilyn Monroe (1926–1962)

Born Norma Jeane, shuttled through foster homes, married at 16, she remade herself with grit and studio lighting, then fought for better work than the lighting allowed. She formed her own production company, studied at the Actors Studio, and turned "bombshell" into a mask she tried to control. *Some Like It Hot* earned her a Golden Globe; fame earned her little sleep. The vulnerability wasn't an act; the ambition wasn't either. She remains America's uneasy icon: desire, agency, punishment, and the cost of being seen before being understood.

Setting

A simple soundstage: white cyclorama wall, two chairs, a glass of water, makeup table off to the side. Nothing fancy, everything exposed. It's a room that forces eye contact, not spectacle, built for a conversation that can't hide behind props. Marks on the floor do the directing; the air feels like last takes and first truths. Cameras sleep until they don't. When the light warms, you hear the kind of quiet that makes people honest, or makes them leave.

Narrator (V.O.)

One woman survived by telling stories. The other by becoming one. Two women shaped by the camera One woman survived by telling stories. The other by becoming one. Two women shaped by the camera, one who built the stage, one who was buried beneath it. If you've ever sat under buzzing lights, office, classroom, exam room, and felt your throat tighten for no good reason, you already know this set. Your body remembers before your brain does.

Oprah

Take a breath. You're not being watched tonight. You're being heard.

Marilyn

Then I don't know what to do with myself. I've only ever known how to be watched.

Oprah

Then we'll start where being watched can't help you, before the myth, before the photograph, before anyone told you who to be.

Marilyn

Norma Jeane.

Oprah

Tell me about her.

Marilyn

She was passed around like junk mail. Eleven foster homes before I could vote. Bars on the windows once—they said to keep people out, but I knew it was to keep me in. I used to whisper before bed, *somebody remember me*. Not famous. Just remembered.

Oprah

That kind of loneliness settles in the body. I know it.

Marilyn

You do?

Oprah

Molested at nine. Pregnant at fourteen. I lost a son and kept working because silence felt safer than the truth. I hid for twenty years behind a smile big enough to sell anything.

Marilyn

You carried a child. And silence.

Oprah

They weighed nearly the same.

Narrator (V.O.)

Some pauses are selfish, meant to gather power. Others are generous; they give the other person a place to put their breath. This one is generous.

Marilyn

I married at sixteen. He was kind, and there was a door that locked from the inside. That felt like love to a girl who'd never had either. Nobody writes about that marriage. The famous ones are easier to frame.

Oprah

Joe and Arthur.

Marilyn

Joe wanted to save me, provided I behaved. He hated the sway, the smile, the white dress over the grate. The very things that paid for dinner were the things that made him look away at dessert. Arthur wanted an idea—a clean muse he could annotate. I miscarried and found his journal a month later. He'd written that I embarrassed him. Childish. Diminishing. It was like reading a review of myself while I was still bleeding.

Oprah

That isn't love. That's someone rewriting you and calling it a marriage.

Marilyn

I kept smiling on cue. It was a skill, and it was a sentence.

Oprah

I know that sentence. Five tapings in a day. Then home. Fried chicken in the dark. Crying while the credits rolled. People saw the weight, not the reason for it.

Marilyn

Uppers to start. Downers to end. The studio called it managing nerves. I called it permission to keep working.

Oprah

And the world applauded the performance.

Marilyn

Or stared. I miscarried once—blood in the backseat of a limo, towel between my knees—and the next morning the papers ran, Marilyn Radiant.

Oprah

Jesus.

Marilyn

I was dying gently and they said I was glowing.

Oprah

That's the trick the culture plays. It turns suffering into spectacle.

Marilyn

And calls cruelty gossip.

The room settles, like a stage crew you can't see has finished moving the heavy set pieces. Nothing flashy, just the scene finally where it belongs.

Narrator (V.O.)

Somewhere in your past there's a mirror you remember too clearly, the one where you learned which angles were lovable and which were "fixable." That mirror's here too. Doesn't matter that no one hung it.

Oprah

Let's talk about the body.

Marilyn

The product, you mean. Measurements before lines. Hips penciled, waist cinched until breath got priced by the inch. I learned to pose before I learned to answer questions. Once they put me in the ocean in December because the shot needed honest light. My dress was soaked, clinging, lips blue. They called it luminous. Luminous! My teeth were chattering so hard the sound guy thought the mic was broken.

Oprah

I starved before shoots and binged after. People called it a storyline. I called it a war. My body never belonged to me when the camera did.

Marilyn

They told me beauty was a vault. It was a door. The more they wanted me, the more they acted like the key was theirs.

Oprah

Wanting and owning often get mistaken for the same thing by people who don't know how to love.

Marilyn

I tried to quit the pills. Flushed them. Fired a doctor who kept prescribing sleep like it was candy. Two weeks awake. Shaking. The studio told me, *"you're not Marilyn without sparkle."*

Oprah

When I stopped signing diet contracts, someone said, *"but your brand is the struggle."* Apparently healing made me unrelatable.

Marilyn

Healing is messy. It ruins takes. It misses its mark and cries between takes.

Oprah

It doesn't test well in syndication.

Marilyn

I don't want to be remembered for the way I died.

Oprah

Then we'll remember you for the ways you lived, and the ways you tried.

Marilyn

Tried is the right word. I wanted to be whole. Not iconic. Not tragic. Whole.

Oprah

Say her name again.

Marilyn

Norma Jeane.

Oprah

Say it like it belongs to you.

Marilyn

It does.

Narrator (V.O.)

There are moments in therapy, call this therapy with better lighting, when a person says their own name like a key and you hear, faintly, an old lock turn.

Oprah

Tell me something you've never said out loud.

Marilyn

I don't know how to answer. But tonight feels... less like acting. More like a room without an audience. Do you know how rare that is for me?

Oprah

Rare for both of us.

Marilyn

I used to rehearse my laugh in the mirror. The tilt of the head. The bit of the lip that said hungry without saying hungry. I could calibrate desire down to the millimeter and still go home alone.

Oprah

I rehearsed gratitude. Pivot from tears to a book recommendation in fifteen seconds. Vulnerability with a commercial break. If I brought my full self, they called it too much. If I brought less, they called it phony. There's a narrow slice of what counts as an "acceptable woman," and I kept missing it by being real.

Marilyn

There is no acceptable slice. There's only the woman who pays for the slice with her life.

Oprah

And the cost shows up in the headlines later.

Marilyn

Do you know how many times they asked me if I was pregnant when I was bloated from pills, from grief, from doing my job while my body tried to quit me?

Oprah

I know that question. It's a scalpel asked like a compliment.

Marilyn

I lost three. Two miscarriages. One ectopic pregnancy. Everyone blamed the pills, the schedule, my hysteria, as though grief were a career choice. No one asked what it was like to see a nursery in a dream and then wake up empty.

Oprah

When they asked me why I never had children, I wanted to scream because I did, and he died. But I was busy being inspirational. I was busy selling the version of pain that made other people comfortable.

Marilyn

I tried to sell comfort too. It never fit.

Oprah

What did fit?

Marilyn

Comedy. People forget I was funny. Timing is a kind of warfare. I could hear where the laugh would land and aim for it like a safe house. The tragedy is that I needed the laugh to survive the room I was in.

Oprah

Humor as oxygen.

Marilyn

Exactly. But the oxygen tank got branded. Breathtaking Bombshell. You hear the joke? They branded my breath.

Oprah

I hear it.

Marilyn

I wasn't anyone's fantasy. I was a mirror. People looked at me and saw their ache and named it beauty. When they cracked, they blamed the glass. I wasn't fragile. I was exhausted. I wasn't shallow. I was silenced. I wasn't a cautionary tale. I was a novel nobody finished reading.

Oprah

I've believed the quiet version of that lie. That if I were smaller, softer, some man would stay. But I wasn't made to shrink. And neither were you.

Oprah reaches across the small country between chairs and rests a hand over Marilyn's. If there's a god of studios, he's finally decided to let them talk without interruptions.

Oprah

Let's open the door you never got to walk through. Producing. If they'd handed you the slate, what films would you have made?

Marilyn

No one ever asked me that.

Oprah

I'm asking now.

Marilyn

Stories where the women are allowed to fail without becoming punchlines or corpses. A woman who cheats and doesn't get flattened into a moral fable for it. A mother who wants work more than worship and doesn't apologize at the altar of public opinion.

Oprah

That's the story they were afraid of.

Marilyn

A comedienne whose joke doesn't have to end in an apology tour. I wanted roles with mess and mortgages and morning breath. I wanted the camera to admit that women wake up human before they wake up beautiful.

Oprah

You were a decade early, and half a century, too. I fought for survivors on daytime TV and they told me it wasn't women's interest. I learned the only way to protect the story was to own the studio.

Marilyn

I never owned my name. They took that too. Try building a life when the door has your face on it but someone else owns the lock.

Oprah

I've been escorted out of rooms I paid for. There are always ten men at the table who think your seat is provisional. Until you build your own table.

Marilyn

I tried to build one. Hired a teacher to help me act, not just smile. Started a company to develop scripts for me instead of waiting to be chosen. Every time I showed backbone, they called it a breakdown. Every no I said turned into the headline they wanted anyway.

Oprah

The punishment for a woman's boundary is a rumor about her sanity.

Marilyn

And the rumor works because it's economical. It absolves everyone at once. They don't have to ask what they did. They just point to what you are, crazy, and the math looks neat.

Oprah

Say it plain.

Marilyn

They wanted me obedient. When I tried to be an equal, they put me in a padded room and called it help.

Oprah

How did you get out?

Marilyn

I screamed until someone who still remembered my billing overrode someone who remembered my bruises. Fame can feel like a key until you realize someone else owns the lock. Oprah, the lock was inside, the one labeled *enough*.

Oprah

When did you last feel it?

Marilyn

It's going to sound small. A day on set when I made a grip laugh so hard he dropped a sandbag. Not the director or the producer, the guy sweating, keeping the lights from killing us. He laughed and said, "*You're trouble, Monroe.*" Not like a threat. Like I was a person who could cause delight. That felt like enough for five minutes.

Oprah

And after five minutes?

Marilyn

The key went missing, and the door remembered its job. How about you? Enough?

Oprah

A girl in line for a book signing once told me she hadn't killed herself because she wanted to finish the chapter we were talking about on air. I went home and sat in the dark and realized a show can be a shelter if you build the roof right. That didn't fix me. It just gave my work a door I could stand behind when everything else was loud.

Marilyn

A door is a miracle when your whole life has been windows.

Oprah

We'll make one here then. With your name on it. No one else's.

Marilyn

Spell it right.

Oprah

Norma Jeane.

Marilyn

Thank you.

Oprah

What do you want them to remember? Not the myth. Not the men. You.

Marilyn

That I kept trying to tell the truth and every time I got close, they turned up the lights. That I wasn't a candle to be watched but a woman who wanted to warm a room from the inside. That my life was not a postcard. It was a house under renovation I never got to finish.

Oprah

Say the hard part, too.

Marilyn

Fine. I wanted love to save me. It didn't. I wanted work to prove me. It couldn't. I wanted fame to feed me. It ate me. But not all of me. Enough of me walked out to sit here with you.

Oprah

I'm glad she did.

Marilyn

Me too.

Oprah

You're not unfinished. You're not a myth. You're not what they sold.

Marilyn

Then what am I?

Oprah

You're real. And that's enough.

Narrator (V.O.)

If this were a daytime segment, someone off-camera would be gesturing for a break, counting backward with fingers. No fingers here. Just time, finally behaving.

Oprah

We haven't laughed enough.

Marilyn

We can fix that. The press used to call me late because I refused to walk fast in heels. I'd hide a pair of flats under the chair on set and swap them in like a magician. A producer once told me I ruined continuity. I told him continuity had never met my arches.

Oprah

I once taped an episode in a dress so tight I couldn't hug the guest without both of us getting a lawsuit. When we cut to commercial, I split the seam and did the second half in a blazer over a prayer.

Marilyn

We improvise or we die.

Oprah

Both is an option some days.

Marilyn

Today feels like neither.

Oprah

That's progress.

Marilyn

Oprah?

Oprah

Mm?

Marilyn

Thank you for asking if I was okay.

Oprah

Are you?

Marilyn

Not always. Better, though. Better than being loved for the wrong thing. Better than being watched and never seen. Better than silence.

Oprah

Better counts.

Marilyn

Write that on a mug.

Oprah

I'll write it in a book and pretend it was always yours.

Marilyn

That's the only kind of theft I allow.

Oprah

Anything you want to say to the girl you were? The one counting windows?

Marilyn

Yes. Don't sell yourself for shelter. You can be wanted without being wounded. Love is not a transaction. It's a return. Wait for the return.

Oprah

I wish someone had told me that, too.

Marilyn

We're telling them now.

Oprah

We are.

Somewhere outside, a stagehand kills the last of the hum. The room goes honest-quiet. You can hear their breath. No audience. No applause. Just two women who outlasted the version of themselves the world preferred.

Oprah

I want to ask about the beginning-beginning. Not the studio. The little girl who read anything with a spine because the house didn't have one.

Marilyn

There was a library near one of the houses. I used to take home more than they allowed by tucking paperbacks under my sweater. That's an awful confession. But I kept the books perfect. Returned them without a dog-ear. I liked the weight of them against my ribs. It made me feel… held.

Oprah

Books are the first rooms I owned. I learned that words could widen a day that had no windows.

Marilyn

I wanted to widen my days too. That's why I went to the Actors Studio in New York. People thought I just wanted to be looked at. I wanted to learn how to look back, with skill. Lee and Paula Strasberg didn't fix me, but they gave me tools. Sometimes a tool is enough. It's a little dignity you can keep in your pocket when everything else empties your purse.

Oprah

A pocket dignity. I know that one. When I got told I wasn't the right look for Baltimore news, I took a job that was supposed to be smaller just to keep a paycheck. Then I learned to build a bigger room than they'd ever imagined. Sometimes the job that feels like a demotion ends up being the runway.

Marilyn

I wish I'd had a runway that didn't end in a wall. I tried to renegotiate my contract once. Asked for fewer pin-up obligations, more control of scripts. They smiled, changed my call time, and sent flowers to my dressing room. You can drown in bouquets.

Oprah

Yes, you can. The apologies come with ribbons when they want you to keep quiet.

Marilyn

Do you think we teach people how to treat us?

Oprah

In small ways. But institutions teach faster. They have training manuals, budgets, and lawyers. A woman's lesson can get erased by a line item.

Marilyn

That's what happened. The men in the room had lines on the budget. I had a line on the call sheet.

Oprah

You were the reason there was a set, and they still made you act grateful for entry.

Marilyn

Gratitude is a beautiful thing. Twist it, and gratitude turns into a leash.

Oprah

Say that again, slower for the men in the back.

Marilyn

Gratitude is a beautiful thing. Weaponized gratitude is a leash.

Oprah

There it is. Not a slogan—an alarm.

Marilyn

A small religion. I could keep that.

Oprah

Keep it.

They both reach for their glasses at the same time, then laugh when the clink sounds like a bad toast at a wedding neither of them wanted to attend.

Marilyn

There's a story about me and a jazz club. People tell it like a fable now. Some of it's true. The part I keep isn't the glamour. It's the call I made, asking a man to take a chance on a woman who should have been headlining already. I wasn't saving anyone. I was paying a debt to the version of me who kept being told, later.

Oprah

I've made those calls. The ones where you can hear a door open for someone else and your younger self sighs with relief.

Marilyn

Exactly. It felt like a tiny crack in a big wall. Not a revolution. A draft through the bricks. Sometimes that's enough to keep breathing.

Oprah

Breathing is underrated.

Marilyn

Coming from a woman who built an empire on book clubs and breath work.

Oprah

Touché.

Marilyn

I used to mark my scripts up with questions. Page margins full of why would she say this, and what's the truth under this joke. People assumed I didn't read. I read all the time, just not always what they wanted me to read. Manuals on lighting. Sloppy paperbacks. A cookbook I never cooked from. Recipes feel like a promise: do these steps, get cake. Life never gave me cake for following directions.

Oprah

So you changed the recipe.

Marilyn

Or burned the pan.

Narrator (V.O.)

Your brain wants to bolt for something lighter, a joke, a distraction, anything. Let it fidget and then let it stay. They stay with what hurts and what helps, and the point isn't to impress anyone; it's to say the real thing while it still matters.

Oprah

Tell me something you're not proud of.

Marilyn

I knew you were going to ask Oprah. The truth—I used people. Used charm like a crowbar. I told myself I was surviving. Sometimes I was just lazy with the truth. It was easier to be adorable than to be honest. I'm not proud of that.

Oprah

I used my platform to fix holes in me that therapy should have touched first. Put the work on an audience that didn't owe me my healing. I regret the times I made other people responsible for my peace.

Marilyn

Look at us. Two women with words for our guilt. Now we need mercy without the campaign.

Oprah

Granted. And ongoing.

Oprah

We're circling the ending and I hate neat endings. Let's end like life ends a day, mid-sentence, with laundry in the dryer.

Marilyn

There's a slip in my bag that isn't mine. Wardrobe sent it. It scratches like it wants credit. That's how tonight feels, like I'm wearing something from someone else's life but finally tailoring it.

Oprah

Take a seam in where you want.

Marilyn

Here: I forgive the girl who thought attention was love. She used the tools she had. I forgive the men who shrank in my shadow. Not for them, for me. I forgive the audience who wanted a myth. I forgive the studio that called grief glow. I don't forgive the system that made the myth profitable. But I can stop auditioning for it.

Oprah

That's a benediction and a boundary.

Marilyn

I'll take both.

Narrator (V.O.)

Applause would ruin this. Violins would embarrass it. Let the words work without decoration; the whole point was to stop performing. If the ending feels quiet, good. Quiet is where decisions get made.

Oprah

Before we close: one request. Give me a line you'd want printed under your picture if you finally got to choose the caption.

Marilyn

No aphorisms, right?

Oprah

No bumper stickers. Just breath.

Marilyn

Let me be a person.

Oprah

That's the whole thing, isn't it?

Marilyn

It always was. …Or fine, if they insist, at least spell my name right this time.

The room doesn't move. It doesn't have to. Two women just did the work themselves. What's left isn't applause; it's the kind of quiet you take home.

Oprah (V.O.)

You were never just the image. Or the icon. Or the myth.

You were a girl who lost too much too soon and kept giving anyway.

Tonight, you gave again, not for them. For you.

Wherever you are now, if there's justice left in the universe, I hope they're calling you by your real name.

CHAPTER 11

FRED ROGERS – ROBIN WILLIAMS: *THE MAN BEHIND THE LAUGHTER*

ACT III: The Theater of Genius

Fred Rogers (1928–2003)

Ordained Presbyterian minister turned television neighbor, he built *Mister Rogers' Neighborhood* (1968–2001) on patience, imagination, and the dignity of small feelings. He testified before the U.S. Senate in 1969 and saved public broadcasting with a steady voice, not a stunt. Cardigan, sneakers, and direct address weren't kitsch; they were a method for teaching children safety and worth. Off camera he wrote letters, played piano, and guarded gentleness like a craft. Honors include the Presidential Medal of Freedom. Lasting thesis: slow attention is a form of love.

Robin Williams (1951–2014)

Juilliard training, stand-up instincts, and an improvisational engine that never idled. *Mork & Mindy* made him famous; films made him permanent: *Good Morning, Vietnam*, *Dead Poets Society*, Aladdin's Genie, and an Oscar for *Good Will Hunting*. The speed was real; so was the ache underneath. He raised money, visited wards, and gave comedians a bigger permission slip for honesty. His range, club, sitcom, drama, voice booth, proved the same tool can minister or explode. We remember the crackling mind and the tenderness that kept showing up anyway.

Setting

A set built to feel like home: couch, low table, a cardigan folded nearby. A piano waits; the trolley track cuts the floor like a childhood memory. It's theatrical only in the way kindness is: it knows what it's for and doesn't preen. You can almost hear the trolley bell, even when it's parked. The room is designed for small bravery, one honest line, then another, without an audience applauding the effort.

Narrator (V.O.)

Two men who made us laugh. One whispered. The other blew the roof off. One wore a sweater. One wore a thousand faces. Together, they talk about what's behind the curtain.

Gentle piano plays on a record, and Rogers begins with a calm, steady voice.

Rogers

Robin, you've given so much of yourself to others, through laughter, through characters, through the joy you scatter even when it costs you. I'm glad we can sit together here, not as performer and audience, but as neighbors.

Robin grins and speaks with dramatic mockery.

Williams

Careful, Fred. Talk to me like that and I'm going to start crying like a method actor in a yogurt commercial. And trust me, nobody wants to see that footage.

He chuckles, runs a hand through his hair, then forces a smile that doesn't quite hide the weariness in his eyes.

Williams

You know, it's funny. I walked in here thinking, *Okay, Mr. Rogers, cardigan, calm voice, we're gonna sip some tea and talk about feelings,* and suddenly I feel like I'm in therapy with a very polite wizard.

Rogers

Well, Robin, I suppose I do like to help people talk about feelings. But I'm not a wizard. I'm just your neighbor.

Williams

Exactly. And that's what's terrifying. Because neighbors notice when your lawn's overgrown or when your smile looks fake. And you, Fred, you've got this radar. Like you can spot sadness under a Groucho Marx mustache.

Rogers

I think I just learned to listen, Robin. Sometimes when you really listen, you hear what isn't being said.

Williams

Oh boy, then you're hearing a whole Greek chorus up here. Voices everywhere. "Do the genie! Do Mrs. Doubtfire!" and meanwhile, the actual Robin's in the back waving like, *Hey guys, remember me?*

Rogers

When did you first realize that laughter could heal you?

Williams

Oof. Starting deep, huh? You don't want to warm up with a knock-knock joke? Okay. I think it was when I realized I was a little broken. I'd make everyone laugh, the room, the theater, the planet, but inside? Sometimes I was like, *Where's my encore? Where's my laugh?*

But healing… it came in pockets. Little moments. Like when someone told me, "You made me laugh on the worst day of my life." That's when I thought, *Maybe I don't need to be whole to help somebody else feel less broken.*

Rogers

Did you ever feel like you had to be funny, even when you didn't want to be?

Williams

All the time. Comedy was armor. Sometimes titanium, sometimes wet Kleenex. I'd walk into a room, and the expectation hit me like a pie to the face. Except I had to bake it, throw it, and laugh at it too.

He smirks, then shifts tone midstream, voice lowering.

Williams

And once in a while the pie was gluten-free, which made it even more disappointing.

The joy fades. The room feels smaller.

Williams

But sometimes, Fred, I just wanted to whisper. Not scream, not juggle, not explode into twenty different characters. Just sit in the quiet and be held by it. But I was scared silence would make people stop looking.

Rogers

What were you most afraid people would see, if they really looked?

Williams

The stillness. The sadness under the jazz hands. I worried they'd see a guy who didn't always know how to exist without performing. What if the real me was less interesting? Just a quiet, hairy guy with too many voices and not enough mirror? And the fear wasn't that they'd hate me. It was that they'd shrug.

The narrator slips in as the air shifts. Robin's voice trails. Fred doesn't fill the silence too quickly. The weight lingers, like the pause after a child admits something they've never said aloud.

Williams

Sometimes it feels like I carry a crowd in my head, even when the room is quiet.

Rogers

Robin… was there ever a moment when you felt truly seen? No mask. No performance. Just you.

Williams

Once. My son was five. I was wrecked. Burned out. He crawled onto my lap, touched my face and said, "You're sad… but you're still funny."

Robin swallows, blinking faster now.

Williams

That hit me like a freight train hauling teddy bears. He didn't need me to juggle. He just needed me to be there. And broken or not, I was enough.

Rogers

That's a beautiful memory. Thank you for sharing it.

Fred leans forward, his hands folded, eyes wet but steady.

Rogers

Robin, you've given so many people comfort. But I wonder… who comforts you?

Williams

Sometimes… strangers. A nurse before surgery, holding my hand like I wasn't famous, just human. A janitor backstage who whispered, "You saved my life once." But the real comfort? It was small stuff. My daughter's laugh. A buddy texting, "You good?", just that. People think comfort has to be grand, but sometimes it's just someone staying when you expected them to leave.

Rogers

When a child finds the right note, on a cello, in a sketch, in a shy sentence, you can see their whole face change. That's why I always tell school boards the same boring thing: fund the music rooms and the art rooms first; it's cheaper than triage later. And if you're lucky, you'll remember the teacher who looked you in the eye and said, "You're more than noise. Keep going."

Williams

And bless the teachers who got me, and the one who thought discipline was a whistle and a glare. Lovely man. Terrifying whistle. I learned projection out of self-defense.

Narrator (V.O.)

The laugh doesn't erase the ache. It never has. But here in this living room, it's not about erasure. It's about two men letting sorrow and laughter sit on the same couch, finally not competing for space.

Rogers

What kind of child were you, Robin? And what would that little boy think of you now?

Williams

Quiet. You wouldn't expect that, huh? Everyone assumes I was born doing impressions of the doctor in the delivery room, but no, I was shy, small, and mostly alone. My dad was military, mom was elegant, and I was this nervous little guy with toy soldiers. I'd spend hours commanding these carpet-sized empires, entire wars fought between the sofa and the coffee table.

Williams

And that boy... he'd probably go, *"Whoa, we got really hairy."*

He laughs, but it cracks in the middle. He rubs his hands together, thinking.

Williams

I think he'd be proud. He'd see that we made the world our playground, and that people liked it when we played. But he'd also ask, "Why are you so tired?" And I don't know what I'd tell him.

Rogers

Do you think the joy you brought to others was a way of reaching back to that little boy?

Williams

Every single time. Comedy wasn't just a career, it was a message in a bottle, tossed back in time. "Hey kid, you'll be okay. You'll matter. You'll make people laugh." I was always sending rescue notes to that lonely boy.

Rogers

And when you were older, was laughter always rescue? Or was it sometimes escape?

Williams

Both. Rescue and escape, sometimes in the same breath. You get the laugh, and for a second you're Superman. Cape flapping, crowd roaring.

Then you go home, cape's gone, and you're staring at a fridge full of takeout cartons thinking, *Superman never had to do laundry.*

The air in the room shifts. Robin chuckles, but Fred doesn't take the bait for levity. He lets the silence stretch, then eases in.

Rogers

Robin, did you ever find peace in silence?

Williams

Sometimes. Sometimes silence was like a blank stage, waiting for me to bomb. Terrifying. Other times it was sacred, like floating underwater, just heartbeat and breath. Meditation helped, but the silence I really wanted? The one inside my head? That was harder. My brain was like a jazz band that never stopped rehearsing. I was always chasing stillness… some days I got close. Other days, I just ran out of breath.

Rogers

I understand. I used to wonder if people only loved the sweater and the songs, but not the man inside them.

Williams

Oh Fred, invisible? Come on. You could walk into a biker bar in that cardigan and still have the whole place crying into their beer in ten minutes.

Rogers

I'm not sure that's true. But I did feel grief, Robin. Gentle doesn't mean untouched.

Fred lowers his eyes, and for the first time in the conversation his voice trembles slightly. The cardigan softens nothing here.

Rogers

I carried loss too. Friends. Family. And sometimes I wondered if kindness was enough to hold it all.

Williams

Fred... I wish more people admitted that. That you can love and still hurt. That you can preach peace and still feel rage when life sucker punches you. That's the human part. Not the mask.

The cardigan is just cloth. The jokes are only tools. The room is only a room. They sit under its roof and wonder, quietly, whether love is enough when grief keeps walking in.

Rogers

Did the world ever make you feel like you had to be superhuman, and punished you when you weren't?

Williams

Yes. A thousand times yes. People see you on stage, in movies, spitting fire and turning into a Scottish nanny, and they think, *Oh, he IS the magic.* They don't see the crawl-out-of-bed mornings, the days when the joke doesn't land, when you're holding pain behind your back like contraband.

And then when depression hit? People said, "How can you be depressed? You're ROBIN WILLIAMS!" And I thought, *Yeah... I don't get it either, folks.* But depression doesn't check your IMDb. It just sits on your chest and says, *"Do something funny now."*

Rogers

If someone listening feels like the world is too heavy, what would you want them to hear?

Williams

That it's okay to not be okay. That your pain isn't proof you're broken. It's proof you're alive. And that laughter isn't cure, but it can be a rope in the dark. And most of all: you are loved. Even if you can't feel it yet.

Rogers

That was beautiful, Robin. Thank you.

Williams

You're welcome, Fred.

He leans back, suddenly lighter, then bolts upright with a mischievous grin.

Williams

Oh wait, you didn't say *who* loved them. Should I jump in with a genie voice? "You are looooved! Big time! Void where prohibited!"

Rogers

I think they'll know who.

Fred smiles, but his eyes are glistening. Robin notices, softens, then adds in his own quiet voice:

Williams

And I'll say it anyway. Because I wish I'd heard it more myself.

No spectacle. Two men agree to name what hurts, do the next small good thing, and step aside. The silence doesn't demand; it allows.

Rogers

Robin, may I ask about the times when laughter couldn't reach you? Not to pry, only to understand what you carried when the audience went home.

Williams

You may ask. I'll even answer without a funny voice… though the funny voices are in the lobby filing an appeal. There were stretches when the lights went out upstairs. I don't mean a dimmer switch. I mean a blackout. You take the wrong escape route, substances, speed, anything that promises "off" when your head is permanently "on", and suddenly you're juggling chainsaws to feel normal. The crowd cheers, you smile, you go back to the hotel room, and the silence eats the furniture.

Robin rolls a shoulder like he's shaking off a weight, fails, tries again.

Williams

Fred, I'd try to outrun it. Work more. Do stand-up after filming after press after charity, because if you keep moving you don't have to hear the echo. But you always do. Eventually the echo learns parkour.

Rogers

Did anyone ever ask you to be still, and stay?

Williams

A few did. The good ones. My kids, the friends who weren't impressed, the doctors who sounded like mechanics and said, "We can fix some of this if you stop pretending you're a jet engine." Rehab asked me to stay still. God, I hated the stillness. But the body keeps score. The heart too.

Robin flashes a grin, then lets it dissolve.

Williams

I'm not ashamed I needed help. I'm ashamed it took me so long to accept kindness without turning it into a bit.

Rogers

Kindness can be hard to accept when you've survived on applause.

Williams

Say it louder for the balcony where the insecure people sit. I thought applause was love. Spoiler: it is… for about nineteen seconds. Then it turns back into noise and your brain goes, *We should schedule more noise,* which is how you end up chasing sound instead of safety.

Rogers

When you were very young, did anyone ever teach you that you were loved without earning it?

Williams

Not in those words. We had excellence. We had expectations. Love was assumed, wonderful, but achievement translated it into something measurable. You learn to be dazzling because dazzling is the one language every room speaks. The trouble is, love without earning feels like a dialect you never really learned to speak. You understand it when someone else says it. You can't pronounce it for yourself.

Robin attempts a smile, misses by half.

Rogers

Would you try with me? To pronounce it?

Williams

Right now? In this cardigan chapel? Okay. *I am loved without earning.*

He nods once, surprised to find the words still in his mouth afterward.

Williams

Feels like lifting a weight that isn't heavy until you realize you've been carrying it since third grade.

Rogers

Thank you, Robin.

Williams

Don't thank me yet. I'm going to ruin this moment with a joke in three… two—no. No, let it breathe.

The silence lengthens, unbroken. Fred's face softens; there are tears in the corners of his eyes that don't fall. He doesn't hide them.

Rogers

I have wondered, sometimes, whether gentleness was enough. There were days I felt small against the weight of the world, like kindness felt like a teacup at the base of a flood. People wanted big answers. I wanted to sit on the floor with children and make space for their feelings.

Williams

Fred, the sweater didn't make you gentle. You made the sweater brave. You walked into a world that runs on volume and said, *"We can talk softly and still change it."* That's not small. That's subversive. That's punk rock in a cardigan.

Rogers

I don't know about punk rock. But I do know that when you offered your voices to the world, you were also asking for one in return. Someone to speak back to you in the language of presence.

Williams

Showing up doesn't trend. Presence isn't flashy; you kind of stumble your way into it over a lifetime. I think it's the only thing that ever saved me. The days I stayed? Someone sat beside me in the mess and didn't try to clean it up with a broom labeled "positivity."

Rogers

We don't have to clean everything. Sometimes we only have to keep company with what hurts until it learns it isn't alone.

Williams

Put that on a pillow.

Rogers

Robin, may I ask about work that cost you more than people knew?

Williams

Good Will Hunting carved me up. In a good way. People remember the laughter in that film; I remember the listening. That bench speech wasn't performance; it was a man telling another man, "*I see the pain you keep trying to outrun, and it won't work, but I'll sit here while you catch your breath.*" I wanted to be that man more in real life. I was, sometimes. Other times I was the one being saved by a quiet set and a decent cup of coffee.

Rogers

And when the work took more than it gave?

Williams

Then you go home. You pet the dog. You call a friend who knows your voicemail code. You eat something warm that isn't applause. That's the whole list. No magic lamp. Just small, stubborn mercies.

Rogers

Small, stubborn mercies have a way of keeping us here.

Williams

Amen and pass the *c*asseroles.

Rogers

Robin, earlier you said something that stayed with me: that you feared one day the laughter would stop, and you'd learn you were never loved, only… useful. Would you tell me more?

Williams

The terror wasn't silence. It was irrelevance. Not being needed felt like a trap door. My job trained me to measure love in ticket stubs. When the math looked bad, the heart panicked. I'd think, *If I'm not useful, then I'm an imposition. If I'm not dazzling, I'm disposable.* It's not rational. It *is* loud.

Rogers

What would you say to a child who felt that way?

Williams

I'd get on the floor, put the voices away, and say, "*You don't have to earn what's already yours.*" I'd say, "*You can be loved on a day when you do nothing spectacular, and maybe that's the day it sticks.*" I'd say, "*Come here. You're not in trouble for being human.*"

Rogers

Would you say it to yourself?

Williams

I'm trying. Present tense. Some sentences feel like they take a lifetime to conjugate.

Rogers

I'm proud of you for trying.

Williams

Thanks, Fred.

He inhales as if to make a joke and then stops. The slightest mercy.

Rogers

What do you want to be remembered for, not by fans or critics, but by those who knew you?

Williams

That I showed up. That I listened. That I could sit through someone else's storm without turning it into a monologue. That I learned how to be gentle with what I couldn't fix. And that I made space for my kids to be fully themselves, not supporting actors in the movie called Dad.

Rogers

That is a beautiful legacy. Sometimes the bravest thing we can do with our words is not to sharpen them, but to set them down and let someone else go first.

Williams

What about you, Fred? What did *you* want?

Rogers

To give people permission to feel, and not be ashamed of it. To help them know the difficult thing they are carrying is not a disqualification from love. And to remind them that the quiet can be trusted, even when it's frightening.

Williams

Mission accomplished. If you were any more trustworthy, banks would offer you as collateral.

Rogers

I'll settle for being a good neighbor.

Williams

You were, and are.

Fred turns slightly, considering something. He reaches for a small puppet: plain, threadbare, not to perform a skit but to occupy his hands the way people hold a photograph when words are tender. He sets it down between them like a paperweight for the heart.

Rogers

May I say one more thing, Robin?

Williams

Please.

Rogers

There's a quiet child in you. He tried to keep everyone safe. He can rest here now. He doesn't have to perform to be welcome.

Williams

You always do this. You make the room feel like a porch after rain. You talk, and the nervous parts finally set their luggage down.

Rogers

Thank you for trusting me with yours.

Williams

Thank you for asking me to set it down.

Rogers

Joy and sorrow. Do you believe they can live in the same home?

Williams

I think they share a lease. Joy isn't what happens when sorrow moves out. It's the laugh you find while you're still sitting on boxes. It's the "I'm still here" that sneaks out between tears.

Rogers

I believe that too.

Williams

And on the days when you don't, I'll loan you some of mine. Interest-free.

Rogers

And I'll keep the porch light on.

Williams

Deal.

They don't stand. They don't stage a goodbye. They let the ordinary holiness of staying do its work.

Rogers

Before we close… if someone listening is ready to give up, what would you want to leave with them?

Williams

Stay. Just a little longer. Don't confuse sheer exhaustion with emptiness. Have a slice of homemade pie. Call the friend who answers. If you don't have one, call the number on the magnet your doctor gave you. If you threw it away, walk to a place with light and ask a stranger for help. The world is rough, yeah, but it isn't always cruel. And you, whoever you are. You're not a burden. You're a person.

Narrator (V.O.)

You may not need that sentence tonight. Tuck it somewhere anyway: like a number on a fridge magnet, like a hand you haven't taken yet. Minds forget. Bodies remember where the light switches are.

Rogers

Thank you, Robin.

Williams

Thank *you*.

Fred's eyes shine again. He doesn't wipe them. Robin notices and nods. Permission granted.

Narrator (V.O.)

Not saints. Not legends. Just two men who gave their pain a purpose, and their laughter a job besides hiding. They don't fix each other. They don't have to. They sit long enough for the truth to unclench.

Rogers

I'm grateful we were neighbors today.

Williams

We still are.

He stands halfway, then sits again. Leaving too quickly would break the truce. He looks around the little room like it's a place where a person could start over without witnesses.

Williams

Hey, Fred?

Rogers

Yes, Robin?

Williams

Thanks for the porch light.

Rogers

Anytime.

The piano holds its breath. The cardigan does not move. The room returns to ordinary, which is another word for safe.

Williams

Thanks, neighbor.

Chapter 12

Mark Twain – Oscar Wilde: *The Weight of Wit*

ACT III: The Theater of Genius

Mark Twain (1835–1910)

Born Samuel Clemens, riverboat pilot turned writer, he took his pen name from river talk and his conscience from close observation. *Tom Sawyer* (1876) charmed; *Huckleberry Finn* (1884) indicted. He lectured for money, paid back debts after bankruptcy, and made the country laugh its way into self-recognition. The suit got whiter; the jokes got sharper. He loved plain speech, distrusted cant, and used humor like a crowbar, polite enough to get in the door, strong enough to pry it open.

Oscar Wilde (1854–1900)

Dublin-born, Oxford-polished, he turned salons into theaters and theater into confession. *The Importance of Being Earnest* (1895) sparkled; the trial that followed did not. Prison stripped the costume and left a clearer writer. *De Profundis*, then *The Ballad of Reading Gaol*. He believed style could tell the truth and masks could reveal it; he paid for that belief in coin and exile. He died in Paris, broke but quotable, having shown that wit without courage is decoration, and courage without wit is sermon.

Setting

A London club. Leather, lamplight, a decanter half-poured, and chairs angled for a duel conducted with sentences. Gaslight flatters but doesn't lie; the mirror above the mantel knows when to keep its counsel. Books on the walls, coasters like small rules that keep the table honest. It's a room built for sentences that don't need to shout. Two voices, one coal fire, no hurry. The staff hear everything and write nothing.

Narrator (V.O.)

Lamplight is kind; it makes most of us look like we belong. Twain does. Wilde comes in with a small flourish, the kind a man uses when he knows the room will listen. The head waiter pretends not to notice and, to his credit, succeeds. If you've ever stayed too late at a bar or kitchen table while the rest of the world went to bed, you know this air: heavy, honest, and a little drunk on the fact that nobody important is listening.

Twain

When a man gets famous enough, they stop calling him by his name and start calling him by his headlines. I don't mind that—headlines buy the whiskey. But it feels discourteous to meet a man by his headline, so let me begin with the more practical offense: Oscar, your fully assembled name could dam a river. If I repeated it twice, we'd be late for our own funeral.

Wilde

Samuel, I admire your thrift. You folded your name in half and rented out the other half to a river. If economy is a virtue, you are a saint.

Twain

I'm Missouri Methodist enough to blush at that, but not enough to stop you. Sit. If I pour slow, we can pretend we're wise.

Wilde

Pour quickly then, and let us pretend we are young.

Twain

Oscar Fingal O'Flahertie Wills Wilde. I read it twice and felt I owed the air an apology.

Wilde

It's a family heirloom, unwieldy, slightly ridiculous, impossible to insure. Yours is a maritime measurement shouted by men anxious about drowning. Between us, we make one sensible introduction.

Twain

It's true a river taught me to listen before it taught me to write. Names are tools. I kept mine short for ease of use. Yours comes with a velvet case and a small orchestra.

Wilde

And yet both find their way to the same shelf, do they not? The library of men who made a living stabbing pomposity with a fountain pen.

Twain

I can be accused of stabbing, yes. But I mark my target first. You, I suspect, embroider yours.

Wilde

Embroidery is just a wound trying to remember it was art before it hurt.

Twain

There you go again, tying a bow on a gallows. I like it. But I'll ask the rude question early so we don't waste the good whiskey: Was the bow worth the fall?

Wilde

If a man falls for beauty, he at least falls in the correct direction.

Twain

And if he falls for honesty?

Wilde

He is unlikely to be invited to many dinners. Still, one should cultivate the uninvited virtues. They have better company.

Twain

I've always felt we share a kind of employment. People expect us to tidy truth up enough to be seen in public. We smile, tell the joke, and slip a little medicine in under the laugh.

Wilde

The medicine is always bitterness, but the pill can be sugared. My countrymen prefer it that way. Yours?

Twain

Mine say they like it straight, then fill the glass with sweet tea. You write salons; I write riverbanks and parlors like this one. But the business is the same. The joke is a mule. It carries what would otherwise kick us to death.

Wilde

The mule metaphor is good. It implies stubbornness, utility, and a willingness to kick the rider if mishandled. Which is to say: an honest companion.

Twain

I like honest companions. They cost more but break down less. Tell me, companion, did your laughter save you when the room turned from applause to a courtroom?

Wilde

It bought me a few minutes of oxygen. In matters of scandal, oxygen is worth more than dignity.

Twain

I've never found a shop that took dignity at the counter anyhow. They always ask for coin.

Wilde

They do, and then they ask you to prove it wasn't counterfeit. Money has the same problem as morality, everyone pretends to have the highest grade until it's inspected.

Twain

America will sell you a Bible and a lottery ticket at the same window. Britain will give you a sermon and a club. Between them, a man might be convinced he deserves both.

Wilde

Which did you choose?

Twain

The river. It was too busy being a fact to pretend it was anything else. Later I discovered crowds are like rivers with theater tickets. They look solid, then part for the next show.

Across the room a chessboard sits mid-game, but neither man seems in a mood to arrange kings.

Twain

Plain speech is the costume where I come from. It still lies, it just lies without embroidery. Besides, I have my own finery: timing, a slow drawl, a white suit when I feel perverse. You wore a garden. I wore a sidewalk. We met in the same mud.

Wilde

Mud is a democratic substance. Kings and comedians are equal in it.

Twain

That's nearly a sermon. Careful.

Wilde

A sermon is a story that forgot it was supposed to be interesting.

Twain

You wrote sentences that could pass a customs inspection at any border. That's worth something.

Wilde

Perhaps. But a border guard looks for contraband and leaves the man alone. I smuggled style; you smuggled dynamite in a loaf of bread.

Twain

Only because I was hungry.

Wilde

Yes. One writes well when one is hungry for something the crowd takes for a luxury. Dignity. Candor. Mercy. I wanted beauty to be necessary. Society was content with it being decorative.

Twain

Beauty is necessary. It just doesn't announce itself. It stands in a corner with the coats and waits to see who leaves without it.

Wilde

That's very good.

Twain

Don't advertise it. They'll tax me.

Wilde

We are taxed anyway. By expectation first, forgiveness later.

The narrator permits the silence to have a turn. It behaves well.

Twain

Let me be impolite in a polite room. Did the trials break you or clarify you?

Wilde

Both. A man can be a broken mirror and still show a face, though not a flattering one. I asked myself on the coldest nights whether suffering made me wise. It made me precise. Precision isn't wisdom, but on a clear day it shares a border with it.

Twain

America confuses suffering with proof of character. We hold funerals for reputation and call them coronations of the soul. I've never found a reliable conversion rate.

Wilde

The English prefer a dignified silence followed by gossip. Repentance is rarely involved, but the tea is very good.

Twain

You can't repent in public and get the recipe right. The crowd will add sugar until it can't taste the confession.

Wilde

Then we are left with private accounting. How boring and how necessary.

Twain

I'm not bored by the dead that sit at my table. I lost a child. I lost two. There are mornings I still set out three cups by habit and have to put one back. The chair stays where it was. The silence does the talking. The accounting refuses to reconcile.

Narrator (V.O.)

There's a particular stillness that arrives when someone names a loss like that. Even on the page, you might notice your eyes stop skimming and simply sit with the words, the way you'd sit with a friend who finally ran out of ways to pretend they're fine.

Wilde

I am sorry, truly. My grief is of another family, but it knows yours. We nod, pass in doorways, and miss the handshake because our arms are full.

Twain

That's the only fraternity that never checks a card.

Wilde

And never expels a member.

Twain

You used laughter to borrow air. I used it to dig a tunnel. Sometimes we ended up in the same yard.

Wilde

Digging is honest work. Tunnels are honest even when they are illegal.

Twain

We will be quoted for that by men who don't understand it. But that's the cost of language; it gets borrowed by meanings we didn't intend.

Wilde

I have been rented out many times. "Wilde said…" becomes a parasol for someone else's summer. I prefer that to being left in the attic.

Twain

Better a parasol than a cudgel. Though I've been both.

Wilde

We have, and the choice is not always ours.

Twain

Tell me about beauty without the salon listening.

Wilde

Beauty is a promise the world keeps now and then and breaks more often than it admits. It didn't save me. It dignified the parts of me that didn't need saving.

Twain

That's almost religion.

Wilde

Religion is beauty with rules.

Twain

And satire?

Wilde

Satire's beauty with its boots on the table.

Twain

Good. I aspire to rudeness with a conscience.

Wilde

That feels right.

The club has its little rules written in discreet gold letters near the door. No one is reading them at this hour. The rules prefer daylight; at night, custom does the job.

Twain

What would you change if you had the chance to rewrite an hour?

Wilde

Only one hour?

Twain

I would choose a slower anger. Mine comes with hoofbeats. When it leaves, it counts my ribs like a hound.

Wilde

Then our wisdom, such as it is, arrives late and wears the wrong hat.

Twain

That's the only way it knows to travel.

Wilde

I will say this plainly. I am not ashamed of loving what I loved. I am ashamed of not knowing the bill would be itemized in public.

Twain

Public itemizes even what wasn't for sale. Private keeps the receipts for things we swear we never bought. We pay twice, if we're honest.

Wilde

Then let us be honest now, if only to slow the echo.

Twain

Please.

Wilde

I missed my sons' childhoods while practicing wit for strangers. The last picture they sent me had more of their life in it than any review I ever clipped. That is a sin even when it is written well.

Twain

I missed parts of my family while making money out of the country's sense of humor. It was the worst bargain I ever made. I rerouted letters so my wife wouldn't see how much of me was performance. It kept the lights on. It dimmed the room.

Wilde

We agree about the exchange rate.

Twain

And still, if a young writer asked me whether to trade an unquiet life for a full page of honest words, I could not warn him off.

Wilde

Nor could I.

Twain

The tragedy is wanting rightly, and paying anyway.

Wilde

You do have a gift for the second kick.

Twain

It's Missouri schooling. The mule has cousins.

The laughter here is clean; it doesn't show its teeth. The room accepts it and keeps the echo small. It knows better than to send every sound into the hallway.

Wilde

Precision is kindness to the reader. Wit is only honest when it serves that. You have a reputation for insisting upon it.

Twain

There's a difference between the nearly right word and the right one large enough to power a thunderstorm. People think humor is the decoration; it is the wiring.

Narrator (V.O.)

You're feeling the same argument under your fingertips, whether you know it or not. Every page in this book is an argument about the right word versus the nearly right one, and you can taste the difference even if you can't diagram it.

Wilde

We agree. Excess is often a kindness to the writer.

Twain

How many drafts does your kindness require?

Wilde

Enough to embarrass my earlier selves.

Twain

Then you're well brought up.

Wilde

And you?

Twain

I throw the sentence back in the river and let it earn its way to shore. If it doesn't arrive stronger, I let it drown.

Wilde

Cruel and fair.

Twain

That's the motto of the Mississippi.

Wilde

And perhaps of good editing.

Twain

Same river, different banks.

Somewhere beyond the walls, a door latches, a broom whispers along a corridor. The club clears itself gently, like a throat at a funeral.

Wilde

Do you worry about posterity?

Twain

I worry about tomorrow's breakfast. Posterity is a poor tipper and an unreliable guest. But I confess I set a plate for it now and again.

Narrator (V.O.)

Some pages change your mind. A few rare ones change what your mouth is willing to say at breakfast the next morning.

Wilde

I worry less now that I am absent from the seating chart. Time is a better editor than I was. It trimmed brutally and left a few lines I can live with.

Twain

Do you ever think about the moment before the laugh? The small inhale the audience takes, a breath that says they're about to forgive you for telling them something impolite.

Wilde

Yes. It is the gentlest absolution available without paperwork. For a heartbeat you are in a chapel built of lungs.

Narrator (V.O.)

Somewhere outside this chapter, your own room is doing its quiet work, lamp humming, spine of the book warm where your thumb rests. You're the lungs now. They're talking; you're the chapel.

Twain

That's very good, Oscar.

Wilde

Keep it. I am rich in chapels that no longer accept me.

Twain

Now hang on—you may be wrong about that. Chapels forgive productions of themselves more easily than they forgive the original sin. If you'd written your scandal as a play, they might have framed it.

Wilde

I did, in a sense. The court was a theater. My lines were sometimes poor; the staging was magnificent.

Twain

I would have fixed your third act.

Wilde

I would have fixed my second. The first was delightful.

Twain

Your first acts usually are.

Wilde

And yours usually contain a rope with which you propose to pull down a wall.

Twain

Or pull a man to safety. Often the same rope.

Wilde

Rescue and revolt often rely on the same knots; only the direction changes.

Twain

You see, we've come to agreement again. It's troubling. Our readers will be disappointed.

Wilde

Then let us quarrel briefly. It will comfort them.

Twain

Very well. "All art is useless" is a silly axiom.

Wilde

It is a necessary provocation. When art becomes a sermon, it begins to lie. Uselessness guards its truth.

Twain

Art that refuses to work for its supper is a bad guest. It should at least help wash the dishes a little. Show a man his folly in the reflection of a well-polished pan.

Wilde

Then call it beautiful dishwashing and we are reconciled.

The clock makes a small decision and adds a quarter hour to the night. Time is generous when it senses work being done without complaint.

Wilde

What shall we do with the matter of God? It is impolite to invite him and not send a chair.

Twain

Leave him standing. He's used to it. He knows where the door is.

Wilde

You have a reputation.

Twain

I earned it while reading His press clippings. But I will say privately I am not insulted by the possibility of being wrong.

Wilde

That is the beginning of piety.

Twain

Don't accuse me of beginnings. I prefer middles. Beginnings are all optimism; endings are all excuses. The middle is where the work is.

Wilde

Very well. In the middle, I confess I prayed in prison without announcing it. I had no audience, and I did not feel theatrical. There was a scrap of a drawing my boys sent: two crooked figures and a sun that took up half the page. The warder let me keep it because he thought it was nothing. I folded it until the creases nearly met, then unfolded it every night as if that could make up the hours I had already missed.

Twain

Then you might have been closest to telling the truth.

Wilde

I suspected so. On certain mornings, even beauty required a bench to sit on. I had only cold stone. Prayer was a thin blanket with more holes than cloth, and I pulled it up anyway.

Twain

That's the sort of honesty I respect. I swore at the Almighty often enough to qualify as a correspondent. He seldom writes back, which is good manners in a landlord.

Wilde

You keep your tone as if you expect Him to be in the reading room tomorrow.

Twain

I keep my tone as if I expect my own conscience to overhear me. That witness is unavoidable and vindictive.

Wilde

I have been cross-examined by mine. I prefer your jury.

Twain

They're the same. Mine just spills coffee on the transcript.

Wilde

That image pleases me.

Twain

It pleases me to please you. It's cheaper than buying flowers.

Wilde

You always wish for roses with thorns.

Twain

Necessary for discipline.

Wilde

Necessary for art.

Twain

Necessary for not falling asleep before the end.

Narrator (V.O.)

They trade a couple of jokes the way men do when the subject is heavier than they want to admit, and once the air moves again they point the sharp end at themselves. It's not a trick and it's not penance; it's the moment you stop entertaining the table and start telling the truth that might cost you something.

Twain

America is a boy bragging about his muscles and then tripping on the front step. England is an older gentleman who tripped long ago and hired someone to say he meant to. Ireland writes the joke and sends the bill to both.

Wilde

I accept this distribution of labor.

Twain

I prefer to admit my country quickly so I can insult it with affection. The insult is the affection; it presumes the patient might improve.

Wilde

The English prefer to call the surgeon a butler and the blood a spill from the decanter.

Twain

And yet, here you are, gilding their language until it confesses it was hungry all along.

Wilde

Language starves without appetite. I fed it my vanity; it repaid me with clarity when I least deserved it.

Twain

You and I both. I fed it my temper; it repaid me with jokes that read like sermons from the back of the church.

Wilde

The back is the best seat for hearing truth. One is far enough from the pulpit to remember doubt is not treason.

Twain

Put that on a banner, and I'll march behind it.

Wilde

With or without the white suit?

Twain

If I'm marching, it's laundry day.

Wilde

Then I will wear color for both of us.

Twain

You always did.

They drink without ceremony and smile without performing it. The decanter sits lighter, satisfied with the night's employment.

Wilde

I have a last vanity to confess. I loved applause too much to trust silence.

Twain

Then let me give you mine. I trusted silence too much because it never booed. It let me misjudge my best lines.

Wilde

We were both betrayed by accommodating audiences.

Twain

That's why I prefer a room like this. It applauds by not throwing us out.

Wilde

A generous standard.

Twain

A realistic one. The only lasting ovation is the line that returns in a stranger's mouth, improved by use.

Wilde

Then let us give them lines that do not mind being borrowed.

Twain

And do not collapse under their own cleverness. I've written lines that leaned against the wall and tried not to be noticed. They were the ones that got remembered.

Wilde

Humility is the disguise ambition wears when it goes to church.

Narrator (V.O.)

Some conversations don't run out of words. They run out of excuses. This one decides what gets to stay and what needs to be set down, and that choice feels cleaner than wit. They aren't building a thesis or a monument; they're choosing two or three sentences that still work when the room is empty and a reader has to carry them alone.

Wilde

The bill arrives whether or not we eat. I asked the waiter for time; he brought a mirror. But what should we leave them?

Twain

A line each. Nothing gilded for you, nothing rustic for me. Trade masks for a moment and see if we can still breathe.

Wilde

Very well. I will try simplicity and mean it.

Twain

And I will try elegance and not apologize.

Wilde

You first.

Twain

All right. Here's mine: Tell the truth so it doesn't need your defense tomorrow. I learned that one the hard way.

Wilde

Beautiful. Here is mine: Be kind where you are clever; only one of those will be remembered as love.

Twain

That's a fair bargain.

Wilde

So is this whiskey.

The shelves hold. The mirror catches both faces. Inside, two men lift their glasses.

Wilde

To the sentence that survives its author.

Twain

To the laugh that changes its owner.

Narrator (V.O.)

What remains isn't cleverness or posture. It's a line you can use without asking permission and a laugh that still works when no one remembers who said it first. If there's a gift here, it's that usefulness can be honest and humor can be decent, and both can survive outside the room.

CHAPTER 13

GEORGE CARLIN – HUNTER S. THOMPSON: *FEAR AND LAUGHTER IN AMERICA*

ACT III: The Theater of Genius

George Carlin (1937–2008)

Stand-up's precision mechanic, he took a wrench to American euphemism and made language point back at reality. The "seven dirty words" bit became a Supreme Court case; the larger project was clarity. Four decades of specials, books, and cranky sermons disguised as jokes taught audiences to distrust packaging. He hosted the first *SNL*, torched sacred cows, and kept making the messy useful. He didn't hate America; he hated its lies. The punch lines landed because the premises were clean.

Hunter S. Thompson (1937–2005)

Gonzo journalist who put himself in the frame: *Hell's Angels* (1967), *Fear and Loathing in Las Vegas* (1971), and a 1972 campaign book that read like dispatches from a moral hangover. He ran for sheriff, lived like a dare, and typed like he was late for an emergency only he could see. Hyperbole was the flare; reporting was the heat. He wanted the country to stop pretending. When the story lied to itself, he yelled. When it didn't, he still yelled, in case we missed it.

Setting

A Vegas motel room with opinions: balcony cracked to neon, lamp doing its best, curtains the color of old nicotine. On the table, an index card with seven words, a battered typewriter, a chewed pen cap. The TV sells hope and knives on the same channel. The minibar is empty because integrity and impulse have both been thirsty. It's a room that listens once you get loud enough to deserve it.

Narrator (V.O.)

Some conversations start with introductions. This one starts like a bar fight nobody stopped. One man cursed America until it admitted he was right. The other wrote America down like a confession signed in bourbon and bad lighting. Neither came for small talk. Neither believed in clean sentences. They came because truth, when it shows up after midnight, is always a little drunk, a little armed, and not in the mood to be polite.

Carlin

So this is it, huh? The great Hunter S. Thompson—patron saint of bad trips and worse deadlines. Jesus, this room looks like my brain after cable news.

Thompson

And George Carlin, high priest of blasphemy and common sense. Welcome to the kingdom of rotgut and paranoia. Sit down before the carpet crawls away.

Carlin

Carpet's already dead, pal. Smells like Nixon's soul took a dump in here.

Thompson

Nixon didn't have a soul. He had glands. Sweat glands. He leaked like a busted radiator.

Carlin

Yeah, and America kept electing guys like him. That's the real punchline, people voting against their own survival, then wondering why they can't afford dental work.

Thompson

Dental work? Son, most folks would settle for a jaw they can keep. That's why I stopped wondering and started writing like the room was on fire. You call it comedy. I call it triage.

Carlin

Same clinic, different wing. You hit the artery; I hold up the blood and say, "Look, folks. Your country's bleeding and trying to charge you for the mop."

Thompson

Charge you for the mop and bill your grandchildren for the bucket. That's the tab.

Carlin

And the cashier says, "Have a blessed day."

Thompson

Blessed by who? The Chamber of Commerce? The DEA? God fired middle management around '68 and never replaced them.

Carlin

If He did, they'd be in marketing. "New from the makers of guilt, salvation lite. Zero calories, same aftertaste."

Thompson

You know what kills me? People act shocked when the machine eats them. It's a machine. That's the job. You don't buy a wolf and then complain about the howling.

Carlin

I complain when they call the howling "freedom."

Thompson

Freedom has a smell. It's cordite, gasoline, and panic-buy chicken wings.

Carlin

Don't forget plastic. Freedom comes shrink-wrapped and labeled "Family Size" so you feel patriotic while you eat yourself to sleep.

Thompson

That's America: a haunted house with a gift shop.

Carlin

And the gift shop sells flags made in the same countries we lecture about freedom.

Thompson

Buy two, get one war free.

Carlin

You want to talk wars? I watched us bomb a country to teach it not to bomb countries. That's like lighting your kid on fire to show him fire is dangerous.

Thompson

We don't teach, we brand. The lesson is on the skin. And the press calls it "complex."

Carlin

Of course it's complex. There's a lot of invoices.

Thompson

Invoices, kickbacks, prayer breakfasts. The whole pious carnival. You ever notice how a man prays louder when he's laundering something?

Carlin

Money, reputation, a conscience. Take your pick. The louder the sermon, the bigger the offshore account.

Thompson

I tried offshore once. Boat sank. Editors said it was a metaphor.

Carlin

Everything turns into a metaphor when you don't want to admit it's a crime.

Thompson

Here's the crime: they sell hope like a home appliance with a two-year warranty and then act surprised when the motor burns out on Election Day.

Carlin

That's why I stopped selling hope and started selling clarity. It doesn't fix your car, but at least you know the smoke's coming from your own hood. Accuracy over etiquette.

Thompson

Amen. After midnight, that's policy.

Carlin

Policy gets you fired.

Thompson

Or free.

The motel air conditioner rattles like it's in on the joke, coughing dust into a room that hasn't known fresh air since the Bicentennial.

Carlin

You ever get tired, Hunter? Not stage tired. Bone-tired. The kind that sits behind your eyes and watches you sleep.

Thompson

I get tired of pretending words are harmless. People want comedy to be a foot massage. I'm more of a chiropractic adjustment.

Carlin

Crack the spine and hope the patient can still walk to the bar. The tongue's this tiny muscle with a weird kind of power—it can pick somebody up or drop 'em down an elevator shaft. I'm not rubbing feet; I'm checking which way the floor opens.

Thompson

If you're going to drop somebody, at least have the guts to watch them fall. Most people just hire a focus group and call it "a miscommunication."

Carlin

Commercials are lullabies for adults. "Hush now. Daddy bought freedom on layaway."

Thompson

Freedom's late on payments. Repo man's at the door with a tank.

Carlin

He'll leave a pamphlet. "Thank you for your cooperation."

Thompson

Cooperation? I prefer sedition. It scales better.

Carlin

Sedition doesn't need Wi-Fi.

Thompson

It needs whiskey. Which we have.

Carlin

Pour me the truth, then. Two fingers. Three if the news is on.

Thompson

News isn't on. Noise is. The news retired. It sells supplements now.

Carlin

Of course it does. "Try our new anxiety powder. Sprinkle it on your breakfast doom."

Thompson

That's the business model—keep you scared enough to buy, calm enough to work, numb enough to sleep.

Carlin

You forgot guilty enough to tithe.

Thompson

Right. Fear, work, sleep, guilt. Spin it fast and call it culture.

Carlin

Here's what I learned the hard way: culture's mostly the noise the rich make while they drag furniture over your head.

Thompson

I learned the same thing, but with more gunshots.

Carlin

Yeah. You always did prefer punctuation that echoes.

Thompson

Echoes make it real. On paper, a lie can look like a prayer. In a hallway, it sounds like boots.

Carlin

And in a strip mall, it sounds like a sale.

Narrator (V.O.)

The room pauses, not quiet, but charged. Cigarette smoke hangs in layers like unfinished paragraphs. This is where comedy turns forensic, where laughter holds its breath.

Thompson

Tell me about the words, preacher. You made a career out of poking the sacred dictionary.

Carlin

Words are costumes. Everyone acts like they're the body. They're not. They're the suit we put on the thing we don't want to touch. You can tell how rotten a country is by which words you're not allowed to say out loud.

Thompson

You mean the dirty ones.

Carlin

Dirty's a decoy. The filthiest words are the clean ones: "collateral," "enhanced," "predatory," "opportunity." You can bury a village under a white-shirt word and still make your tee time.

Thompson

And we clap. We always clap. Because the microphone is loud and the room is air-conditioned.

Carlin

I did a bit once about the seven words you can't say on TV. The funniest part was watching polite society pretend that syllables were the threat. Meanwhile, actual harm was sponsored by a bank.

Thompson

Banks are the real swear words. We just can't hear the vowels over the lobby carpet.

Carlin

You ever think about quitting?

Thompson

Often. Then I remember what quitting looks like. It's a man in a good tie, nodding into a camera, telling you the graph is headed up and your life is too, as long as you don't ask what they measured.

Carlin

Graphs are how we turn people into furniture, stackable and easy to move.

Thompson

That's tidy. The country loves tidy. Meanwhile the facts are bleeding out behind the billboard.

Carlin

You sound exhausted.

Thompson

I am. You keep screaming, and the void learns your lyrics. After a while it starts singing back.

Carlin

That's when you change keys. Or you throw the microphone.

Thompson

Throw the microphone and they'll sell the dent in the wall on eBay. "Authentic rage, lightly used."

Carlin

Everything's merch now. Even outrage has a SKU.

Thompson

My outrage came without a receipt. Couldn't return it even when I tried.

Carlin

What did you try to return?

Thompson

The fear. The twitch in the hands. The feeling that every knock on the door is either a package or the end.

Carlin

I know that feeling. Mine didn't knock. It sat in the chest and waited. Doctors call it a condition. I call it the bill. You spend years laughing at the country and the country laughs back: "Time's up, pal."

Thompson

Did it scare you?

Carlin

Sure. Then it pissed me off. The body's a landlord with a clipboard. Tenants get evicted for telling the truth.

Thompson

Truth is a lousy roommate. Eats your food, keeps you up, never helps with the dishes.

Carlin

But you miss it when it moves out.

Thompson

Yeah. Then you start buying replacements, God, patriotism, nostalgia. Cheap furniture for a tilted room.

Carlin

Tilt's the right word. The room's been tilted since we drew the first border with a rifle.

Thompson

Borders are just lines you get shot for crossing and bored for living near.

Carlin

And airports are temples where everyone pretends queues are freedom.

Thompson

You do airports; I do highways. Same pilgrimages, different saints. Gas stations are my chapels. You can learn everything about a country from the restroom key.

Carlin

On a cinder block with a chain?

Thompson

Exactly. Nothing says "community" like a padlock on the only door between dignity and a felony.

Carlin

We design humiliation, then call it policy.

Thompson

And we export it. Democracy in a crate, batteries not included.

Carlin

The crate arrives with a manual: "Step 1: Trust the men with the contracts."

Thompson

Step 2: Ignore the screaming. It's the sound of progress.

Carlin

Step 3: Install the gift shop.

Thompson

Always the gift shop.

The ashtray tips slightly under the weight of butts and ash, a miniature landfill of wasted fury balanced on ceramic.

Carlin

You ever love this place, Hunter? Not the postcard. The mess.

Thompson

Sure. I love the speed limit we all break and pretend we didn't. I love the diner at 2 a.m. where the waitress calls you "hon" like it's the last bandage in the drawer. I love a high school gym that smells like victory and disinfectant.

I love a county fair where the Ferris wheel bolts are older than the marriage license. I love the lie that we're decent, because sometimes, for a whole minute, we are.

Carlin

I love a union hall with a coffee pot that tastes like pennies and hope. I love a library where the bored kid finds a sentence that saves him.

I love the sound of a crowd laughing at the wrong part and then realizing it was the right part.

Thompson

There it is. You're a patriot after all, just allergic to flags.

Carlin

I'm allergic to the people who beat other people with flags and call it love of country.

Thompson

They call it love. It smells like fear.

Carlin

Fear sells. "Limited time only. While supplies last. Some restrictions apply. See morality for details."

Thompson

Restrictions always apply. Especially to the wrong people.

Carlin

Speaking of wrong people, what did drugs give you that truth didn't?

Thompson

Speed. Courage. An off-ramp from the polite lanes where liars merge without signaling. And sometimes a trap, let's be honest. You take the shortcut so often it becomes the map. Then you forget where the road was.

Carlin

I stuck to words. They're addictive too. Less hangover, more echo.

Thompson

Words can overdose a crowd. Done it myself. You feel the room go white behind the eyes and you keep going because stopping would mean admitting you're human.

Carlin

I tried admitting it on stage once. Told them I was tired and scared. Best laugh of the night.

Thompson

People like it when the statue sneezes. Reminds them that stone used to be dust.

Carlin

You wrote your fear down. Did it help?

Thompson

Sometimes. Sometimes it just made it legible. Fear's fine print looks like poetry when you're drunk enough.

Carlin

You ever think about the kids reading you in class? Red pen, quiet room, teacher trying to explain why you cursed the way you did.

Thompson

Poor bastards. Tell them I cursed because the clean words were taken. And because the first lie I ever learned came dressed for church.

Carlin

Same. I never hated God. I hated the sales team.

Thompson

Ha. Put that on a billboard between the fireworks outlet and the payday loan. See who salutes.

Carlin

They'll salute anything if you time it with sunset.

Thompson

That's America's magic hour. Everything looks noble for twenty minutes, even strip malls and senators.

Carlin

Senators have great lighting. That's why they never die; they just fade into consultancy.

Thompson

Consultancy is how ambition retires without guilt.

Carlin

So what now? We trade lines until the ashtray fills and call it redemption?

Thompson

Redemption's between a man and whatever keeps him from throwing himself into the pool filter. I'll settle for accuracy. If we can leave this room having described the beast correctly, that's a win.

Carlin

Describe it then.

Thompson

America's a carnival ride run by men counting the cash with one hand and loosening the bolts with the other. It keeps spinning because we like the wind in our faces more than we fear the landing.

Carlin

Not bad. Here's mine: America's a pharmacy that sells sugar pills with names like "Liberty Plus," and the placebo works just long enough to get you through the checkout.

Thompson

Between the two of us, we've got diagnosis and side effects.

Carlin

And a copay.

Thompson

Always a copay.

Carlin

Let me ask something not for the act. For me. Did you pick the chaos, or did it pick you?

Thompson

Both. I had a talent for turning volume up and then blaming the stereo. But the world was loud first. I just matched it. You?

Carlin

I was shy. Honest to God. Then I noticed the room would let me say what they were thinking if I made it funny. Power without a uniform is addictive. I tried to use it to make the right heads hurt.

Thompson

Did it?

Carlin

Sometimes. Sometimes I just made the choir clap. The hard part is making the choir think, without getting evicted mid-hymn.

Thompson

You ever wish you'd been kinder?

Carlin

To people, yes. To systems, no. Kindness to a system is cruelty to whoever it's chewing.

Thompson

I wasn't kind enough. I aimed for truth and hit the furniture.

Carlin

Furniture had it coming. But yeah. We break things. Then we try to fix them with sentences.

Thompson

Sentences hold better than duct tape. Less residue.

Carlin

Unless you print them on bumper stickers. Then they peel in the sun and leave glue.

Thompson

That's politics in July.

Carlin

You ever love anybody enough to stop talking?

Thompson

I tried. The silence made a noise I couldn't stand. I filled it with nouns and bad decisions. Not fair to the people I loved. But it was the only instrument I knew.

Carlin

I understand. I lost someone I couldn't joke around, over, or past. The stage didn't help. It just turned the ache into applause.

His hand drifts toward his back pocket like it remembers carrying a photo there, then stops halfway. Whatever face lived in that space once, he's not about to lay it under this lamp.

Thompson

Applause is a good anesthetic. Wears off fast.

Carlin

And the co-pay is loneliness.

Thompson

You keep coming back to the dentist, George.

Carlin

Because the country's teeth hurt and we keep chewing ice.

Thompson

Fine. Drill me then. What's the cavity?

Carlin

We confuse noise with freedom, choice with meaning, and punishment with order.

We've got a population that's over-marketed and under-loved. And the only institution that still works, more or less, as advertised, is grief.

Thompson

Grief's the only thing that never misses a delivery.

Carlin

No tracking number, though. But it teaches you to lock fewer doors.

Thompson

That's one way to live. Leave the doors open and the liars will steal your television, but they might also drop off a story on the way out.

Carlin

You really are a journalist.

Thompson

Journalist, thief, priest, same toolkit on different days. Confession, record, absolution.

Carlin

I never promised absolution. I promised a mirror.

Thompson

People hate mirrors. That's why every hotel one is lit like a morgue.

Carlin

Or a Senate office.

Thompson

Exactly.

The ice in Thompson's glass clicks once against the rim. Both men look at the static. Neither speaks. The room takes a breath it didn't earn.

Carlin

If we had to say one honest thing to a kid who just found us on a used shelf, what would it be?

Thompson

"Don't wait for permission to name what you see." And keep a notebook. The world runs when you look straight at it. Writing pins the tail on the monster.

Carlin

Mine: "Laugh at the wrong things on purpose until people realize they were the right things." And carry cash. Someone's always going to try to sell you your own reflection; don't finance it.

Thompson

Good. Put them together and you've got survival: name it, laugh at it, pay cash, run.

Carlin

Run where?

Thompson

Toward somebody. That's the trick no one puts on the poster. All this noise, all this fighting, all this holy rage—it's worthless if you don't end up closer to a person you'd trust with your last cigarette.

Carlin

Or your last joke.

Thompson

Or your last night.

Carlin

You think we're cynics.

Thompson

Cynics are just romantics who stuck around long enough to read the footnotes.

Carlin

I like that.

Thompson

I stole it from a better man.

Carlin

We're both thieves. We just return the goods as punchlines.

Thompson

And receipts. Don't forget the receipts.

Carlin

You keep your receipts?

Thompson

Hell no. I feed them to the typewriter. It eats guilt and carbon copy.

Carlin

Typewriter's the only machine that makes honesty louder.

Thompson

A megaphone with ink.

The typewriter looms in the corner, carriage jammed mid-line, like it refused to quit even after its author did. The keys glint under the weak lamp, daring the next confession to land in metal.

Carlin

What scares you most?

Thompson

Silence that feels earned. The kind you get when you've said everything that can be said and the room is still wrong. You?

Carlin

Finding the perfect line and realizing it hurts the wrong person.

Thompson

Collateral damage of the joke.

Carlin

There's that clean word again. "Collateral." The English language should press charges.

Carlin

How?

Thompson

We end where the country begins: a lousy room, two idiots with more opinions than time, and a decision to walk outside and be decent to the first stranger we meet. These days, basic decency is punk rock.

Carlin

Decency with a backbone. None of that "thoughts and prayers" on company letterhead. I'm talking "show up when the car won't start" decency. "Hold a baby so the mom can pee" decency.

Thompson

"Bring soup, no photos" decency.

Carlin

Yeah. The kind you can't monetize.

Thompson

They'll try. God help them.

Carlin

God's middle management is out to lunch.

Thompson

Then we're in charge until they come back. Which means we tip the maid heavy, leave the room better than we found it, and don't shoot the television.

Carlin

That last one's for you.

Thompson

I'm evolving. Slowly. Like a hangover learning manners.

Carlin

Before we go, pick one word to retire.

Thompson

"Normalize." Every time that word shows up, someone's trying to get comfortable with a bruise.

Carlin

Good. I'll retire "respectfully." It's what cowards say before they stab your idea in the kidney.

Thompson

Fair. Add "bipartisan" while you're at it. That just means both sides smell the same money.

Carlin

You're going to get us uninvited from everything.

Thompson

We were never invited. We crashed the party with a notebook and a grin.

Carlin

And a mouth that gets us into rooms our feet can't leave fast enough.

Thompson

Which is why we're good company only after midnight. The day has rules. Night forgives.

Carlin

Night forgets, too. But sometimes in a good way. It forgets the lie you told yourself to get through the afternoon.

Thompson

And remembers the number you should call tomorrow.

Carlin

Call who?

Thompson

Whoever still picks up. Whoever doesn't correct your grammar when you say you're not okay.

Carlin

That's a short list.

Thompson

Then guard it like a revolution.

Carlin

One last thing. We burned through a lot of words. Five of them the kind that get you a letter from a PTA. I don't use them for shock; I use them because they're accurate. Sometimes the only sentence honest enough to fit the world has one in it.

Thompson

Accuracy over etiquette. That's been the policy since we started breathing.

Carlin

Alright, Hunter. Let's leave the minibar to its ghosts and the television to its static.

Thompson

And the gun to the drawer.

Carlin

And the door unlocked.

Thompson

So truth can find its way out. Or in.

Carlin

Either direction's an upgrade.

Thompson

Then we agree. A miracle. Call the editor.

Carlin

Call the maid first. We made a mess, but at least we named it.

Thompson

And we left a tip. In sentences.

Carlin

About the only currency that spends in the morning.

Two men step into the hallway like they're walking onto a small, stubborn stage: no spotlight, no ovation, just a door that doesn't lock behind them and a night that feels a shade less dishonest.

Narrator (V.O.)

Not every conversation changes a country. Some just change the size of the room it has to lie in. The chairs will still be crooked in the morning. The minibar will still be empty. But the air, if you pay attention, will carry one new rule: call things by their names and be decent to the next stranger. The rest is paperwork.

Chapter 14

William Shakespeare – Lin-Manuel Miranda: *The Verse and the Flow*

ACT III: The Theater of Genius

William Shakespeare (1564–1616)

Stratford-born actor and playwright who wrote for a company first and posterity by accident. Comedies, histories, tragedies, and 154 sonnets: built for voice, breath, and box office. He married at 18, raised a family, co-owned a theater, and wrote parts his friends could play. The language dazzles, but the trick is practical: plots that move, motives that ring. He understood crowds, ambition, and the price of power. The Globe burned; the lines didn't.

Lin-Manuel Miranda (1980–)

New York kid with hip-hop in his ear and musical theater in his bones. *In the Heights* won Tonys and put Washington Heights on a Broadway map; *Hamilton* rewired the form with rhyme, scholarship, and swagger, earning a Pulitzer Prize, Tony Awards, and Grammy Awards. He writes parts for working lungs, curates joy, and builds rooms for collaborators to eat. Film songs, activism, and a MacArthur Fellowship followed. Through-lines: story as civic act, virtuosic wordplay in service of feeling, and generosity as process, not PR.

Setting

A black box: ghost light center stage, rehearsal tape on the floor, a boom box and a score on the piano. Seats close enough to hear breath. The room does its job with plywood and echoes, no velour, just whatever the actors can carry to it. Costumes wait on a rack, notebooks on a rail. It's the kind of space where a couplet can test its balance and a 16-bar can learn where to breathe. When the work lands, the air changes before the applause does.

Narrator (V.O.)

Two craftsmen with different tools: ink that stays and sound that won't. They share a small theater, and the work light won't quit. Let's see who blinks first: this moment or us.

The room doesn't care what year it is. The door hangs open; the quiet stretches, not threatening. Just leaving space no one's in a hurry to break.

Shakespeare

Your house has velvet and rush tickets; mine had mud, oranges, and laughter that did not ask permission. The roofs leaked; the nobles complained; the pit spoke with its whole hands. Same math either way. Nobody gets to be bored.

Miranda

And nobody gets to be left out if we can help it. I write for the ninth-row kid who memorized the cast album, the aunt who only came because it's "historical," the usher who hears the show a hundred times and still wants one line to surprise him. If they all lean in, the line is working.

Shakespeare

You cast your audience as carefully as your actors. A useful habit; dangerous if it starts writing for you. We measured by heartbeat. Five steady steps and a turn. Iambic pentameter: da-DUM repeated. Not a cage; a railing. You lean on it when the crowd sways.

Miranda

I count breath too, just on a different grid: sixteen beats to a thought. If a word steals air, it pays rent with meaning. If it can't pay, it moves out.

Narrator (V.O.)

The fifth beat is where actors steal the room: half a step late, half a smile early, and suddenly it means something else.

Shakespeare

Your landlord is strict. We work the same way. I keep the technique quiet. The line should hold without showing the work.

Miranda

And I learned to show the sweat once in a while, so the house trusts the line. A little stumble proves a human wrote it. That matters more than sparkle.

Shakespeare

A small confession: I polished speeches in my head while dodging rotten fruit. Sometimes the fruit improved the play.

Miranda

I've read comment sections that function like fruit. Less vitamin C, more… velocity. Still, point taken. Pressure edits. Deadlines edit like a stern uncle.

Shakespeare

Speaking of uncles: Master of the Revels stood between my page and the stage. Censor, clerk, guardian. I learned to say "king" while speaking "man," to tuck the knife inside the joke.

Miranda

I get it. I have different gatekeepers. Investors, awards voters, people who buy the tickets and the people who tweet about the tickets. No one says "you may not," but the price of "you may" is often quiet. So I say it louder and pray the mic holds.

Shakespeare

And does it?

Miranda

Most nights. Some nights the mic feeds back and I remember I'm still a student. That's probably healthy.

Shakespeare

I envy you, Lin. To speak politics plain, to rhyme on presidents and be cheered for it. My tongue knew chains: royal favor, censors, the risk of Tower cells.

Miranda

And I envy you. No microphones, no critics on Twitter. Just a stage, a candle, and words. You got to test what theater was when it was raw.

Narrator (V.O.)

Two men circling the same old envy. Every artist learns you rarely get both freedom and peace at the same time.

Shakespeare

We should speak of doors. Your work builds them. Mine, at times, only painted the wall and called it an exit.

Miranda

You wrote queens with tongues sharp enough to cut rope. Men spoke them. That wasn't just law; that was habit solidifying into harm.

Shakespeare

A wound I won't prettify. When the law barred the voice, I obeyed and cheated where I could. Boys carried women's sorrow and did it well; it was still theft. If your stage restores the voice I could not legally hire, let my ghost buy a seat and clap until my hands ache.

Miranda

Deal. And I'll own mine. I opened a big door with a show that tried to be a civic party. Then I watched some folks get priced out of the lobby. We built lotteries, rush seats, student shows. It helped; it wasn't enough. The rent in the world keeps finding a way to bill joy.

Shakespeare

The rent keeps a list. I wrote fast because yesterday's bread is not today's guarantee. They say ambition, I say hunger. Both can sharpen a quill.

Miranda

Ambition's just appetite once you put a calendar on it. The risk is becoming a museum plaque before you learn your next scale. I'm forty-something and already reading essays about legacy. That's a strange mirror to shave in.

Shakespeare

Legacy's mostly the stories the living tell about the dead so they can sleep a little easier. Good rumor, sometimes. Dangerous rumor, sometimes. The only legacy worth a candle is the door that remains unlocked when you're gone.

Miranda

Say that again, cleaner.

Shakespeare

If the door you build locks behind you, it was never really a door; it was a showpiece nobody's allowed to touch.

Miranda

That's the thesis I want on the mezzanine wall. And sure, half the time it's just wood and a hinge that squeaks.

Shakespeare

Teach me your cadence without making me your apprentice.

Miranda

Take your heartbeat. Five steady steps. Now tilt one beat so it lands a half-step late: syncopation. Not a gimmick; a small surprise. It tells the ear, "Wake up."

Shakespeare

Like a caesura, a pause that is part of the line, not outside it.

Miranda

Exactly. Also, if you want to make a room exhale, end a sentence on a noun you can see. "Door." "Hand." "Daughter." The eye holds it; the heart keeps it.

Shakespeare

I know that trick. I dressed it in couplets. The crowd hears rhyme like a promise kept.

Miranda

Rhyme is a spice. Use it like salt. If you can taste the handful, you used too much. And yeah, I've oversalted more than once.

Shakespeare

What is your least favorite perfect rhyme?

Miranda

"Fire" and "desire." They should be fined. Also "love" and "above" need a break. We could fund arts education by taxing lazy couplets.

Shakespeare

I admit to crimes of "love" and "dove." Charge me interest and keep my name on the building anyway.

Miranda

We're not taking your name off anything. We're adding names beside it. That's the project.

Shakespeare

Give them form like a doorframe, not a lock. The scene changes tone without shattering, the pause is part of the play.

Miranda

And don't pretend the frame can hold everything. When it groans, we add wood, or we add hands.

Shakespeare

This is the argument I like: strength in service of welcome. Not strength as a guard.

Miranda

Here's where the politics sneaks in. Whose story gets the stage? Whose body gets the mic? I don't want to deliver lectures; I want to deliver scenes that don't lie.

Shakespeare

Scenes that tell the truth and survive the tomatoes.

Miranda

And the subtweets.

Shakespeare

Which are tomatoes thrown from very far away?

Miranda

With less fiber. That… yeah, that sounded better in my head.

Shakespeare

Tell me where you keep your fear, and we'll figure out where to put your courage.

Miranda

Fear—no, let me say it cleaner. Fear: that I become a brand before I become a better writer. Courage: saying no to my own cleverness and yes to the plain sentence that risks sounding small. The small sentence often holds the whole room.

Shakespeare

The plain sentence is a sword without jewels. If it cuts, it was forged well. If it doesn't, no emerald will save it.

Miranda

You're doing it again. Sounds like a quote poster. Pull it back.

Shakespeare

I keep trying to dress the thought up before I let it walk. Try this instead: Say it so the last row hears it, and the first row doesn't feel lectured. That's the line.

Miranda

Better. That one can stay.

Narrator (V.O.)

They do not swap sonnets or sixteen-bar verses. They trade rails: a way to keep balance when the stage tilts. If a line already sings, they stop tuning.

Craft is restraint you can hear. Until it isn't, and then someone coughs and they cut.

Shakespeare

I should say it before we pretend we are only colleagues: your work gave a city to those I let stand outside. I will not praise like a statue; statues are stiff and weather poorly. I will praise like a man who wrote fast to eat and knows the difference between a trick and a tool. You built tools that open doors.

Miranda

I'm grateful. And I'll say what you won't brag about: you put a rough wooden stage in a world that didn't ask for it, and you turned it into a place where a butcher's boy and a baron could cry at the same line. That's democracy, even if the word wasn't ready yet.

Shakespeare

Since we are passing the candor back and forth like a cup. There is another confession. I wrote for men who looked like me and made women partly out of air. The women were not air. They were heavier than my ink could carry under the rules I accepted.

Miranda

And I wrote a show that became a passport for some and a map of missing streets for others. I put faces on money and asked them to sing. It helped some. It hurt some. I keep learning. If I stop learning, shut the house down.

Shakespeare

Look, your mic bows to my quill. They wish to be friends but are shy.

Miranda

Then we help them.

Shakespeare

A ceremony without incense. Good. I distrust smoke.

Miranda

Same. It sets off the fire alarm and ruins the matinee.

Shakespeare

Tell me a word you love too much and wish you did not.

Miranda

"Rise." I use it because it photographs well. I want to write "stand" or "get up" more. Less myth, more muscle. You?

Shakespeare

"Sweet." I used it the way bakers use sugar when the fruit is unripe. I should have trusted the tartness.

Miranda

Then here's a compact: I'll use "rise" only when gravity proves it. You'll use "sweet" only when the tongue can't deny it.

Shakespeare

Agreed. Lines don't earn a stage by looking handsome. They earn it by carrying weight. If they complain, they're not ready.

Miranda

Let's do a small run for the crowd that's not here. Comedy buys us trust, but we get off the exit before we become a bit.

Shakespeare

A bit?

Miranda

Routine. When the joke starts dragging the scene by the ear. One run. Five beats. Ready?

Shakespeare

Begin.

Miranda

Beat one: You rhyme "king" with "thing," and I tell you to upgrade to "ring" and you say...

Shakespeare

—Rings are for promises and prisons, and you cannot tell which until you wear one.

Miranda

Beat two: I try to teach you a hemiola, three against two, and you say...

Shakespeare

—In love and meter, an extra step can save a fall or cause one.

Miranda

Beat three: I warn you not to rhyme "Rome" with "home," you say...

Shakespeare

—I rhymed worse in a draft I burned behind the Globe, lad. Friendship is built on the wrong rhyme that still feels right.

Miranda

Beat four: I pitch a turntable set, you squint...

Shakespeare

—Why should the floor spin when the mind can? I mean, fine. I'll allow your toy if it keeps the drunkard from napping.

Miranda

It's not a toy; it keeps the bored uncle from napping. Let me keep one lazy Susan.

Shakespeare

Keep your lazy Susan. I shall not woo her.

Miranda

Beat five: I ask for your best advice in one line.

Shakespeare

Say the truth close, then say it loud. The order matters.

Miranda

Off ramp.

Shakespeare

We did not crash.

Miranda

We got a laugh and a point. That's the measure.

The bulb hums for a breath.

Miranda

You stopped at fifty-two. I'm in my mid-forties. That's close enough that I count the years between us. Do you ever wonder what else you could have made if you'd had more time?

Shakespeare

Every day. The plays that rot with me are louder than the ones you quote. That's the trick: no man dies finished.

Miranda

So the question is never, "Did you do enough?" It's, "Did you leave the entry cracked so someone else can add the next verse?"

Shakespeare

Then let us write something brief together: fourteen lines and a bridge; not for rhyme, for a vow.

Miranda

Form keeps the promise; the bridge just changes key without breaking it.

Shakespeare

We'll write it in the air: a structure to keep. Let the audience supply the words.

Miranda

Let's speak it like stage directions. Then build.

Shakespeare

Act One: Name the door as a doorframe. Say it out loud.

Miranda

Act Two: Test the hinge with new hands. If it creaks, we fix the wood, not the bodies.

Shakespeare

Act Three: Admit who was left outside and how long they waited. Names help. Sorry helps more when followed by keys.

Miranda

Bridge: Change key without changing pitch; new rhythm, same truth: art belongs to the people who show up and the people who can't get in yet.

Shakespeare

Act Four: Do not flatter your own courage. Courage's a receipt you keep, not a headline you frame.

Miranda

Act Five: Leave the light on. Not as a halo, as a map.

Shakespeare

Couplet: If only friends may speak, you have no city. Only a club.

Miranda

Couplet: If the club becomes a city, it was because someone held the door and didn't ask for a thank-you.

Shakespeare

What do you fear most when you add a new door?

Miranda

That I will build it to my height and call it universal. Your turn.

Shakespeare

That I will bless your new door and secretly prefer the old wall because I recognize its dents. Nostalgia is a poor carpenter.

Miranda

Then the remedy is the same: invite more builders. Not consultants—builders. Put them on the crew and let them argue with the plan.

Shakespeare

I once thought a play ends with a bow. Now I think it ends when the audience can say, "I have work to do," and knows what room to enter to do it.

Miranda

Same for a musical. The measure is whether the song helps you walk different down the steps and into daylight.

Shakespeare

We should speak of the pit and the mezzanine before we go. In my time, the pit was not an insult; it was the engine. The nobility borrowed its heat and called it taste.

Miranda

In my time, the mezzanine is both reward and moat. People save for months to sit there. If they leave feeling scolded, I failed. If they leave feeling seen and the pit leaves feeling heard, we did our jobs.

Shakespeare

Are we not simply naming fairness with different shoes?

Miranda

We are naming fairness and calling it art so we remember to build it beautiful enough to last.

Shakespeare

Beauty is not a soft word. The joint must hold. The line must carry. The step must catch.

Miranda

Say that without the poster gloss.

Shakespeare

Right: Make it well enough that you would let your child stand under it.

Miranda

I've trusted a wobbly beam. Never again.

Lin-Manuel leans forward to adjust the mic, the motion casual, like straightening a picture frame. The cable eases into a softer line.

Shakespeare

We have done what we came to do. We argued without breaking; we laughed without drifting; we named our stains without asking the audience to clap for our honesty.

Miranda

And we put a few tools on the workbench where people can reach them. That's better than a quote.

Shakespeare

No epilogue?

Miranda

Just this: If you want the line to live, give it to the person who needed it before you wrote it.

Shakespeare

This will do.

Miranda

It will. Because it's a rule we can measure. But we must end on generosity. I still owe the crowd a craft swap. One real minute, not a bit. You give me an iambic thought and I'll give you a verse that doesn't show off.

Shakespeare

A bargain. I will not dress it in velvet. Hear it as it comes: I wanted more voices and made excuses. That is the truth. The rest is penmanship.

Miranda

That's clean. Now give it a heartbeat.

Shakespeare

I wanted more voices. I made excuse.

The law said no; I nodded—and refused.

I let boys carry grief that women owned.

I kept the bread and said the seed had sown.

No velvet; just the cost. I should have paid.

Let mouths I stopped now speak what I once made.

Miranda

That lands. Now the verse: same truth, no fireworks. Count the breath, then cut it before it turns into a drum solo.

Shakespeare

I will listen.

Miranda

I wanted more voices and learned too slow.

When the house got rich, the door learned to say "Later."

I built a lottery; some folks still froze outside.

That's on me. We're widening the frame, not shrinking the room.

If a word demands space, it buys the ticket for the person who's waiting.

That's the rule. If it can't, the word leaves. I don't.

Shakespeare

You said it without singing, and I still heard the tune.

Miranda

Because the point sang. We can both live with that.

Narrator (V.O.)

That swap isn't a party trick. It's an audit. Different tools, same brick of truth. It holds. Our backs feel it.

Shakespeare

Now the practicals. Children perform our words in gyms that smell of varnish and hope. What do we owe them beyond a good play?

Miranda

Permission. Cut, swap keys, move scenery like it's theirs. Because it is. Public domain is just the law catching up to the idea the door's already open. When it's my turn to sign the license, I want the drama teacher spending time on kids, not contracts. If you're decoding legalese at midnight instead of running lines with a sixteen-year-old Hamilton, I failed you.

Shakespeare

Then a line for teachers: plain, not poster.

Miranda

Cut what your students can't carry. Keep what their breath can hold. If anyone complains, blame us.

Shakespeare

We will be proud to be blamed.

Miranda

And for community theaters: if the set can turn, let the story spin first. The turntable is dessert. Dinner is the scene.

Shakespeare

The dinner was always the scene.

Miranda

Failure before we leave. Not the pretty kind. The kind that sits in your chair and eats your lunch.

Shakespeare

I wrote kings and youths; some lumber still. A tragedy with a wishbone spine. They taught me this: if the scene argues its cleverness louder than it argues the truth, I am lying politely.

Miranda

I've kept darlings past expiration because I loved the rhyme more than the mouth that had to say it. I've cut others without a funeral.

Shakespeare

Then the test is simple.

Miranda

Kitchen-table test. Two chairs, no music. Say it to someone who owes you nothing. If they tilt their head and say "huh," that's a pass. If they smile at your cleverness, cut it.

Shakespeare

How do you end a night when the house wants more and you know the night has already given the best of itself?

Miranda

You end on generosity. You leave the ghost light on so the next person doesn't trip.

Shakespeare

I will not haunt your carpenters.

Miranda

I will not sand your edges until you disappear.

Shakespeare

Leave a splinter or two. It reminds the hand that wood was once a tree.

Miranda

Leave a backbeat or two. It reminds the foot there's work to be done, but you can move while you do it.

Shakespeare

Then we are settled.

Miranda

We are. Until the next door.

Narrator (V.O.)

They step back: no choreography, just consent. The mic trusts the empty house. The quill dries. The room waits for feet and breath. Someone will come. The door stays unlocked. The ghost light ticks once. I'm leaving it on for you.

CHAPTER 15

FRIDA KAHLO – PABLO PICASSO: *THE DOOR AND THE WALL*
ACT III: The Theater of Genius

Frida Kahlo (1907–1954)

Coyoacán-born, polio at six, bus accident at eighteen. Pain made the room small; painting made it bearable. She married Diego Rivera, loved and fought in both directions, and turned self-portrait into a political, intimate form. The body is central, but the work isn't medical; it's honest. She showed in New York and Paris, held a 1953 Mexico City solo show from a bed, and kept Casa Azul as proof that art can be both shrine and workshop. The gaze is direct; the symbolism is earned.

Pablo Picasso (1881–1973)

Málaga to Barcelona to Paris, he kept changing the rules and proving the change was the point. Blue Period, Rose, Cubism with Braque; *Guernica* as testimony; portraits that argued with faces. Prolific to the point of legend, restless to the point of scandal, he treated style like a tool shed. Lovers, studios, wars. Everything fed the work. He didn't invent modernism alone; he made sure it couldn't be ignored. The argument for him is simple: he kept risking the line.

Setting

A working studio with a blue door, an easel that remembers bad days, tram noise sawing the window frame. Brushes in a jar, a mirror near the canvas for courage and correction. The room isn't tidy. It's alive. Sawdust in the corner, a stool that wobbles, marigold somewhere you'll miss until tomorrow. It's a place where refusal and tenderness share the same table and the city never fully shuts up.

Narrator (V.O.)

She stood in Paris among the Surrealists in 1939, Picasso among them. More glances than souls, there but barely. He sent her off with earrings, but not the argument she wanted. Today is different. For Frida, it is home. A warm Oaxaca afternoon. The easels are sturdy. The canvas is ready to complain.

Kahlo

Before we start. My back's loud. If I make a face, it isn't theater; it's a wire sparking. If I curse, I earned it.

Picasso

Pain shows up on time. Cheapest model I ever hired.

Kahlo

Say another line like that and I'll give you three hands on the canvas. None of them kind.

Picasso

Three would help. I've been short a hand since I was five. Ask the wall my father repainted.

Kahlo

I painted myself because everyone kept correcting me. "Smile less. Hide the brace. Softer colors." No. I kept all of it.

Picasso

I corrected the room. Perspective lies; I broke it. You're welcome.

Kahlo

You hear that tram? That's your ego turning the corner.

Picasso

Better than silence. Modesty is for men who didn't change anything.

Narrator (V.O.)

There will be humor. Not the sketch kind. The survival kind. The kind that keeps a hand moving when the floor lists.

Kahlo

Before you guess my edges, we speak about Diego. People like to make him a mountain I climbed or a storm I survived. That's tidy. He was a country: borders where you don't expect them, parades when you want sleep. I married the country twice and still needed visas. I say it like a joke because jokes keep the air moving, but I mean it. He did what men do when appetite is louder than calendars. I did what stubborn women do when pride is louder than good advice. I'm not proud of the arithmetic. I am proud I painted it ugly, with no makeup on the bruise.

She touches the strap beneath her blouse and waits until the bite lets go.

Picasso

You painted it the way it felt.

Kahlo

There's a version of me who never lets him back in. She smells like ethics and sleeps better. I don't know her. The woman I was loved a mural that kept repainting itself on my wall. You want the clean version for the museum label. No. The true version is that love and stupidity have the same handwriting when you're tired. I was tired. I am tired. And still, I would not trade the color it gave me, even the colors that hurt to use. You can call that dysfunction if it helps you feel smarter than me. I call it another morning I woke up and reached for the wrong door.

She takes a breath that arrives late and lands hard; the cup trembles and settles.

Picasso

Give it to the line that doesn't flatter.

Kahlo

When I painted him, I refused to flatter. Taller where kindness asked for it, smaller where truth asked louder. People accuse me of turning pain into theater. Fine. But the ticket price is mine. If there is one thing I owe him now, it is this: I will not make myself a saint to tidy up his ghost. I was cruel back. I have to live with that, not because a priest scolded me, but because the canvas doesn't lie for anyone. Not even for widows, not even for wives.

Picasso

You don't owe him sainthood. You owe yourself the kind of truth you can sleep beside.

Kahlo

I don't. What I owe is rest I rarely take and a softness I mistrust when the pills work. Diego is not my excuse. He's my weather. I keep painting with the windows open anyway.

Picasso

I understand more than I like. I worked because stopping made me nervous. I could say I worked to survive love, but it would be the pretty version. The ugly version is I liked the power better. I liked finishing better than apologizing. I hurt women. They hurt me. I chose the studio over the conversation that would have taken all night.

Kahlo

Then make the next night longer.

The tram scrapes by. Neither of them looks at it. The room lets the speech settle where dust would and refuses to tidy it up.

Picasso

Middle of a drawing is hell. No one tells you that part. They talk about the beginning when you're brave and the end when you pretend you meant everything you did. The middle looks wrong. It will look worse before it's better. I tell models not to panic; I panic anyway. I chase lines like a jealous husband and a lazy student at the same time. You can't be polite with a face. A face lies unless you corner it.

Kahlo

Corner the dog instead. The metal one. He bites.

Picasso

I'll draw the dog. But I won't make him cute. Cute forgives too quickly. Cute is apology on a postcard.

Kahlo

If you make him cute, I'll haunt your brushes.

Picasso

He'll be small and irritating. That's accurate. Look left. Not heroic. Human. Your mouth carries speeches it didn't ask for. I want the part before the speech.

Kahlo

Person hurts.

Picasso

That's the point.

Kahlo

You and your points. You know… you like them because they're sharp and short. Swords you can wave, not rooms you have to sit in.

Picasso

Rooms bore me unless I'm moving the furniture. I tell myself it's for the painting. Sometimes it's to prove I can.

Kahlo

That's a confession. Keep it.

Picasso

Say it, fine—but if your hand doesn't do the next thing different, it's just talk.

He pulls a pencil from behind his ear, sharpens with a knife, spits the dust into his palm, and draws a quick triangle in the air like he's measuring something no one else can see. He works the page with short, ugly motions. The knife flashes once more; gray dust falls like tired weather.

Picasso

Hold. There. That line near the collarbone. Did you feel it?

~ 255 ~

Kahlo

I felt everything near the collarbone. Try being polite to my nerves.

Picasso

I don't paint politeness.

Kahlo

Good. Neither do I.

Silence comes with the next tram and forgets to leave. She counts to eight and loses the number, then finds it again.

Kahlo

Work's a drug. Half the time you can't tell if you're high or healing.

Picasso

I worked because quiet made the room tilt.

Kahlo

There's taking and there's stealing. You know the difference.

Picasso

Sometimes. After. Not during.

Kahlo

You could have learned sooner.

Picasso

Yes. I didn't.

Kahlo

Careful Pablo, that's almost an apology.

Picasso

Don't get used to it. Turn—no, not so far.

Kahlo

You ever think your women painted you without telling you?

Picasso

I hope not.

Kahlo

You should. Men should.

Picasso

And you, you painted Diego the way you needed him. Taller in some places, small in others.

Kahlo

I painted him true. True is not flattering.

Picasso

True is still a decision.

Kahlo

Everything is. Even telling the truth.

Picasso

People say genius is permission. Wrong. It comes with names attached.

He pauses. He hates the pause and honors it anyway.

Picasso

Men like me pretend appetite is honesty. "I wanted, so I took." It sounds efficient in a studio and monstrous everywhere else. Women stood too close to my work and got blamed for the weather. I called it "muse," like the word could pay rent. Dora should have left less broken. Marie-Thérèse should have slept easier. I worked instead of apologizing. I told myself apology might blunt the edge. Maybe it would have only blunted my pride. I kept the edge. It cut more than canvas.

Kahlo

Don't—don't "might" a woman's wound.

Picasso

Then yes. I will make the painting I owe and show it to no one who sells keychains.

Kahlo

Make this cost. A letter. A check. A studio door you actually leave open.

Picasso

Confessions are useless unless they change what your hand does next. I heard you. Name the thing; I'll sign it and show up.

Kahlo

Good.

Narrator (V.O.)

Policy sounds dry until a room remembers it's a way of saying "you matter" with funds attached. The studio doesn't care for poetry; it cares for weight.

Kahlo

People ask if I pray. I do, but not the way they mean. I pray to paint when the medicine tastes like coins. I pray to the strap to stop pretending it's a friend. I pray to stairs to negotiate a truce. I even pray to a cat who may be real and, if he is, judges me fairly. My prayers are practical. Give me twenty minutes without nausea and I'll paint you a door you can lean on when your own body misbehaves. That's my covenant.

She laughs once, without air.

Kahlo

I am not holy. I'm tired. And I'd like a mango more than I'd like a sermon. If God is bored, mangoes were an apology worth accepting.

Picasso

Mangoes are chaos.

Kahlo

Chaos tastes like summer. Hand me the knife. Slowly.

He does. She doesn't use it yet.

Kahlo

If I go soft on canvas, it's not because I believe angels file paperwork. It's because kindness is a thing I can paint into a room that would otherwise eat someone. If I have a religion left, it's simple: put a time on the kindness and keep the appointment.

Picasso

I'll show up. Put it on my calendar.

Kahlo

Here is what I resent, Pablo. My face is useful to people who would not carry my body up one flight of stairs. They sell me as courage on cotton and forget I still need help with the stool. The store gets paid. The museum roof gets patched. I'm not angry at roofs. I'm angry at pretending a tote bag is a prayer. Sometimes I sign them because the money buys paint. Sometimes I say no and the same people call me difficult, like the spine should apologize for being expensive.

She smiles without enjoying it.

Picasso

Say no whenever you need.

Kahlo

You tell me to say no more. Say no to air? Fame keeps walking after you sit. It repeats the loudest part: the flower crown, the green shawl, the eyebrows like headlines. I don't hate those things. I hate when they're the whole story and the quiet part, the counting to eight so the breath will arrive, gets cut for time. I want the quiet part louder. Not because I am noble. Because I am tired of being a symbol that can be ironed onto a bag.

Picasso

Symbols sell roofs.

Kahlo

Yes. And some roofs keep people dry who would have slept wet. I am not allergic to roofs. I am allergic to being turned into a coupon for bravery while the body that earned it is left carrying groceries alone. If the museum wants my face on the shop wall, put a ramp by the stairs. Put a bench near Las dos Fridas where a woman with a brace can sit without asking. Pay the attendant who brings her water. Let the quiet part be budgeted, not hashtagged. Then print as many bags as you want.

Picasso

You are asking fame to pour concrete.

Kahlo

Yes. If the brand cannot lift a thing, it can at least build a step for someone who must climb. Print that as the poster: blueprints, not hashtags.

She adjusts the strap again, this time without the wince.

Picasso

Guernica bought me a voice; I can spend it on benches and ramps. I'll say so where donors fidget.

Kahlo

You once said fame is lazy. I agree. It repeats the loudest part because it cannot be bothered to learn the rest.

Picasso

Then teach it the quiet part. Start with mine.

Kahlo

You have the power. Your name opens storerooms. Use it to open doors that don't flatter you. That would make me forgive many things I do not forgive.

Picasso

You forgive nothing.

Kahlo

I forgive when someone carries. Even me.

He starts to answer, stops, and for once lets the silence keep the point.

Two cups cooling. The strap finally behaves. A sentence about budgets that will annoy the right donors.

Picasso

Spain is three rooms: hungry, loud, and dead. I learned to paint in the loud one. I learned to be famous in the hungry one. Guernica lives in the dead one. It sits on my chest mornings I pretend I don't believe in ghosts.

The bombs were efficient; I was not. I stretched a scream into a wall and hoped a politician would have to look at it and feel small. Politicians don't like feeling small. They punish a painting for that. So I became a wall they couldn't move. Exhausting, being a wall.

Kahlo

Mexico is color that holds you when the body drops. Also noise. Also heat where it shouldn't be. We live out loud because funerals are expensive and silence never fixed a bone. My country taught me to paint with everything on the table at once: pain next to mangoes, politics next to lipstick, Diego's laugh next to my brace. The priest doesn't love that arrangement; the street does. The street buys what it recognizes. It recognizes stubbornness.

Picasso

The street is a better critic than the salon.

Kahlo

The street is a better neighbor than the board.

Picasso

Good neighbors say no to somebody sooner or later.

Kahlo

Good neighbors do.

Something unclenches in the room. It doesn't last; it doesn't need to.

Kahlo

I keep painting doors. People think it's about escape. It's about leaning. When the body refuses, you need a place to press your forehead that won't lie to you. A door's honest. It either opens or it doesn't, and either way you find out fast. I have stood at many doors that did not love me back. I painted them until one did.

Picasso

I keep building walls. People think it's about control. It's about stopping a charge you can't outrun. The world runs at you with bills; a wall gives you one angle to fight from. I have been cruel from behind my wall. I have been brave there too. You can call it the same thing if you like. I would deserve it.

Kahlo

We need both. A wall you can push against and a door you can open when the room stops pretending to be kind.

Picasso

Doors are dangerous. They imply leaving.

Kahlo

Walls are worse. They imply staying the wrong way.

Picasso

I hate doors.

Kahlo

I hate stairs.

Picasso

…

Kahlo

Enough lists. Hand me the cup.

He passes it. Her hand misses once, then doesn't.

Kahlo

You want my face at rest. I don't know how to rest. I know how to brace. I know how to tell a room I am fine when I am not and then make art rude enough to contradict me. But all right. Face at rest.

She tries. It's not rest. It is closer to human and farther from survival.

Picasso

Better. Less hero. More person.

Kahlo

Person costs.

Picasso

Everything does. What can't you afford?

Kahlo

Fatigue that talks me into lying. Kindness that turns into performance. A dozen steps and a bad rail. Men who call my *no* a suggestion. I can afford mangoes. I can afford one mean joke at the right time.

Picasso

Say it now.

Kahlo

No. I'm saving it for your eulogy.

He snorts despite himself. She doesn't.

Kahlo

Break the body and the story's written on you.

Picasso

Look closer. The frame owns the name.

Kahlo

And your angles? They don't grant consent.

Picasso

Hold. That cheek—there. Stay.

Kahlo

If I pass out, draw that too.

Picasso

I will. Somebody will hang it.

Kahlo

You're disgusting.

Picasso

I'm working. It's the only apology I ever half-learned.

The tram clanks past; the quiet doesn't follow it this time.

Picasso

I used to think if a work was big enough, it canceled the sins attached. People believe that about men like me because they want a clean math.

There isn't any. The work stands. The harm stands. You carry both or you lie. I have lied many times. I am telling fewer now because I can hear myself in rooms like this and the echo is not flattering.

Kahlo

Keep that echo. It's a good teacher.

Picasso

I prefer applause.

Kahlo

Applause feels good for ten minutes. Then the room is the same and my back still yells.

Picasso

Genius is the echo; the person is the ache underneath it. I'm late to answer it.

Kahlo

Then pay.

Picasso

Call it survival.

Kahlo

Call it decent.

He lays the page face down as though it might run.

Kahlo

Let me see.

Picasso

In a minute.

Kahlo

You'll hate it tomorrow.

Picasso

Yes. I… I'd like five minutes of pretending.

Kahlo

Coward.

Picasso

Old habit. I'm trying to break it while you watch.

Kahlo

My turn. Not paint. A line—so I remember this room when the medicine wins.

She pulls a stub of charcoal, tests it on her thumb, and drags a short, stubborn mark across a scrap. It hesitates halfway, then keeps going. She wipes the dust on her skirt without looking.

Picasso

That's it?

Kahlo

Two lines. One for the breath that didn't come. One for the one that did.

Picasso

Enough pretending. Have your look.

She flips the drawing. He leans in. Her mouth opens, then doesn't. She taps once, not at the eyes, not at the lips, but at the small line near the collar where the strap hides. She nods.

Kahlo

You didn't flatter me.

Picasso

I tried not to.

Kahlo

You caught the dog.

Picasso

He bit.

Kahlo

Good.

Picasso

You're not angry?

Kahlo

I am. Just not at the paper.

Picasso

At me?

Kahlo

You assume. I'm mad at the hour. At the stairs. At the part of me that still wants to be pretty when I'm telling the truth.

Picasso

That part never dies.

Kahlo

It can sit in the corner while we work.

Picasso

Give it a stool.

Kahlo

It already took one.

They almost laugh. The tram interrupts, grateful for a job, its wheels keeping a tin-drum rhythm.

Kahlo

Carry my coffee to the sink. I can't stand yet.

Picasso

I'm not your assistant.

Kahlo

I know. Carry it anyway.

He does. He almost drops it, swears in a small voice, sets it down like it's fragile.

Picasso

The cup is heavier than it looks.

Kahlo

Cups lie. People do too. But the weight, you know, that doesn't.

Picasso

You want help with the stool?

Kahlo

Yes.

He steadies it. For a second he looks like a man who has done this before, which he has, which he hasn't, which are both true.

Kahlo

You can go.

Picasso

You always throw people out like this?

Kahlo

Only the famous ones.

Picasso

You're famous.

Kahlo

I have twelve steps and a bad rail.

Picasso

You'll be all right?

Kahlo

No. And yes. I have practice.

Picasso

Then, hasta luego.

Kahlo

Vete. Before I change my mind and ask for help I won't take.

He hesitates, nods, and goes. The room keeps the dents. The tram pulls the city past the window like laundry on a line.

Narrator (V.O.)

Nothing resolved. And that's honest. Two new things exist: a page that won't flatter and a scrap with two lines arguing about breath. Tomorrow someone will sweep and miss the marigold under the stool. The cat under the table, if it exists, blinks like it owns the place. Paint dries where it should and where it shouldn't. If anyone asks what was said, the room shrugs in sawdust and lets the work do the talking.

Chapter 16

Ludwig van Beethoven – Wolfgang Amadeus Mozart:
The Phantom and the Prodigy

ACT III: The Theater of Genius

Ludwig van Beethoven (1770–1827)

Bonn to Vienna, student of Haydn, stubborn from the start. Hearing failed; ambition didn't. He expanded the symphony's job description: *Eroica*, the Ninth, the late quartets, and proved you could weld struggle into the structure, not just the story told about it. He lived untidily, revised like a brawler, and kept composing as if the future were listening. Patronage helped, but willpower did the heavy lifting. His best pages argue that fate is editable if you're relentless enough.

Wolfgang Amadeus Mozart (1756–1791)

Salzburg prodigy playing courts before most boys kept time, he wrote operas that grin and weep: *Figaro, Don Giovanni, Die Zauberflöte*, and chamber music that feels like friends finishing each other's sentences. He hustled for patrons, moved to Vienna, and wrote fast because rent exists. The Requiem stopped with him. The legend is "effortless," but the ledgers show effort and invention under pressure. The miracle isn't perfection, it's humanity singing at speed.

Setting

Not a grand hall. A rehearsal room. An honest piano, a leaning metronome, a chipped tuning fork, high windows letting in city noise. On the stand: a page of *Ave Verum Corpus* beside a stubborn new motif. A cracked hearing trumpet rests on a chair. No applause lives here; the room prefers endurance to myth. When music arrives, it sounds like shift change: work beginning again, not a miracle descending.

Narrator (V.O.)

One hammered the heavens until they gave. The other hid pain in a grin you could hear. Thunder and mischief: two men who bent sound until it told the truth. Not a concert. Not a trial. A confession with a metronome.

Beethoven hovers at the keys, head cocked, a man who no longer trusts his own ears. Mozart leans against the piano, his throne, one shoe tapping, the old street rhythm of a boy outside a tavern. The air is still, but restless. Two men who never shared a stage now forced to share a reckoning.

Beethoven

I was told more than once that I was meant to inherit your greatness. They said it like a blessing, but it felt more like a prison sentence. Your shadow was the whole damn room. Even before I was old enough to drink, people whispered your name as the yardstick against my every bar.

Mozart

They told me you'd be taller.

Beethoven

And they told me you'd be sober.

Mozart leans back with a grin.

Mozart

And I see you brought a storm instead of a comb.

He presses a single key: an A that hangs too long.

Mozart

Hear that? Even my laugh comes with a ghost.

Beethoven

You called it joy, didn't you? Composing with wine on your breath, playing with a carnival's swagger.

Mozart

You think I was drunk on joy? Try writing with your stomach growling loud enough to double as timpani. Try hiding sketches in your coat so the pawnbroker couldn't seize them before they became symphonies. Joy? No, Ludwig. Desperation with a smile slapped on it.

Beethoven

Better a disguise than despair. You flitted through sonatas as though life were a masquerade.

The note, an A, has died out.

Mozart

Masks keep patrons calm. Rage went in the violins where no one could call it vulgar. You know, Vienna keeps a steady beat: the meter of eviction. You learn to syncopate or starve.

The room feels heavier. Nobody claps here.

Beethoven

They never stopped saying it: not "You'll be good" but "You'll inherit Mozart."

It sounded like promotion. It felt like parole with no date on it. Your name was the ceiling and the floor. I couldn't move without hitting you.

Mozart

Ghosts make better company than patrons. At least ghosts don't clap at you in public and sneer over their wine in private. Don't envy me, Ludwig. You Inherited silence; I inherited hunger. Both curses, same song, different tuning.

Beethoven

Silence keeps time with pity. I don't dance to it.

Beethoven's jaw tightens. He strikes a chord. Too hard, too sharp. It clatters in the air and dies without resolution.

Beethoven

They called your music light. I heard the strain in it.

Mozart

Teeth? Charming, Ludwig. You talk like a critic who pays in adjectives instead of rent. The smile was a job. I had a wife with a soft heart and a landlord with a hard ledger. There were nights I ate boiled potatoes and broth so thin it tasted like nothing, and pretended it was a feast because my son was watching. You think I didn't know darkness because I wrote light?

Beethoven

I think you hid it where nobody could call it vulgar. You made rage sound like a waltz.

Mozart

And you made prayer sound like artillery. Which is fine. We were both hiding something. You hid the boy who wanted to be held. I hid the father who couldn't pay the midwife without promising next week's fee. At least I could still hear my creditors banging on the door. That's music, isn't it?

Mozart waits for a laugh that doesn't come.

Mozart

I'll drink the silence, then.

Beethoven

Do you know what silence sounds like, Mozart? It's not peace. It's not rest. It's just this ringing, day after day, and still they wanted more. More symphonies, more noise; they wanted quiet on command. I finished movements and my skull kept humming like a kettle that never boiled down.

Mozart

That's a kettle left on in the next room. No rest in that.

Beethoven

Exactly. And when it screamed, they asked for an encore.

Mozart

I believe you. And I won't pretend I know that pain. But don't pretend yours was the only kind. You lost sound, yes. But I lost my youth in taverns and pawnshops, selling songs for supper. We both got cheated, but differently. I pawned my best coat once and spent the winter pretending I liked cold. Do you know how humiliating it is to choose between ink and bread and still try to make art sound like a festival?

Beethoven

Yes. I know humiliation. I banged the piano so hard a string snapped and whipped my knuckle open. The neighbor below me hit the ceiling with a broom until the plaster fell in polite applause. I used to think if I pummeled the keys long enough, they'd give my hearing back out of mercy. They never did.

Mozart

You hammered the piano like it owed you something.

Beethoven

It did. Silence owed me a voice.

Mozart

And when the voice came?

Beethoven

It came like a storm that forgot which way the window opened. I wrote sound I would never hear and hoped the world wouldn't lie to me about it. Do you understand what that does to a man? You finish a piece and people leap up and you can't tell if it's real or pity. You stand in the middle of thunder and all you get is the vibration under your ribs.

Beethoven swallows; the next words scrape.

Beethoven

And the cruelest part? After a while, I stopped even trusting the vibration. I would watch someone else play my music and feel nothing, as if it belonged to them more than me. The silence wasn't dignified. It was just agony I dragged around to convince myself I still mattered.

Mozart

And you think applause saved me? It didn't. I wrote as if time itself were chasing me, afraid that if I slowed, I'd be forgotten before the ink dried. They called it genius. Half of it was panic. The applause was smoke. By the time I reached for it, it was gone.

Narrator (V.O.)

For once he wasn't the prodigy or the wit, just a boy scribbling to outrun silence. His fear was not death. It was being decoration in someone else's room.

Mozart

I understand the part where you don't trust the room. I lived in that room. I smiled at men who set their wine glasses on my work and told me to keep it cheerful. I hid bitterness in the violins because bitterness with words gets you uninvited. You shouted at God. I... I learned to smile at the ceiling and hope it smiled back.

Beethoven presses a chord that doesn't resolve and leaves it there, mean and unfinished. The candle flame wobbles like it flinched.

Beethoven

Do you know how often I heard your name before mine? Even my praise wore your face. *"He'll be great,"* they said, *"one day."* I wanted to ask which day and who decided. Being celebrated for a future you're not sure you'll survive is its own kind of sentence.

Mozart

I told someone you'd be great and meant it like a toast, not a sentence. We don't get to pilot our compliments once they leave. If the world shackled you with it, blame the world's bad aim, not my mouth. Besides, if I'm the shadow, I'm a very noisy one. You outlived me. You out-thundered me. The museums are full of storms.

Beethoven

Outliving isn't outrunning. I envied your melodies. They look easy until you try to hold them without dropping a single jewel. You found melodies people could carry home. I… didn't. I wrote to get the weight off my chest. Why didn't you ever let your anger touch the surface?

Mozart

Maybe God whispered them. Or maybe I was just lucky enough to hear when others were busy bowing.

Beethoven

That's not an answer.

Mozart

Because it wouldn't have helped. My rage wasn't sacred. It was petty. Rent due. Children hungry. Nobles sneering. So I smiled wider. Played faster. You threw your fists at heaven. I grinned at the ceiling and hoped it grinned back. And when the sneering got too loud, I made a joke, because Vienna forgives a joke faster than it forgives a bruise.

Beethoven

Make one now.

Mozart

What—about your hair? Your temper? The way you glare at audiences like they're late to their own funeral? Fine. Here's one: art is a dinner party where the host starves in the kitchen and the guests compliment the candles. Happy?

Beethoven

No.

Mozart

Relax. I only roast what I can't afford to worship. You didn't come here for jokes anyway. You came here to break furniture and see if anything true falls out.

Beethoven

Honesty is saying what shames you and finding the room still listens. I once wrote a letter I never sent, told the page I was ready to quit. Instead, I kept writing. That wasn't virtue. That was stubbornness with a pulse.

Mozart

Stubbornness saved more art than inspiration ever did. Inspiration's a guest; stubbornness is the idiot who keeps paying the rent.

Beethoven

And kicks the door when the guest is late.

Mozart

Speaking of rent, have I told you about the night I played cards with a count just to delay eviction? He cheated with a smile and pretended it was charm. I let him win because losing was cheaper. I walked home with a stale roll under my arm and lied to Constanze that I wasn't hungry. You see, you had thunder. I had charm. Only one of those gets you invited back to dinner.

Beethoven

They stood and shouted at a wall while I couldn't hear it. Sometimes I wanted to turn and ask whether they were cheering for me or just for the sound of themselves.

Mozart

And sometimes I wanted to ask whether they were clapping for the music or for the mirror it gave them: pretty faces, good taste, no guilt they couldn't afford. They used us to feel good about themselves. I just smiled more while they did it.

A draft sneaks under the door and decides against staying. The piano lid breathes a small, wooden sigh.

Beethoven

Your Requiem in D minor. You were dying when you wrote it.

Mozart

Yes. Coughing between bars. Holding on to rhythm when breath wouldn't. There's a timbre to fear when you know the doctor's eyes are lying. But the Requiem wasn't pity. It was a listening post. For the neglected dead. For the living who walk around like graves with jobs.

Beethoven

And the commission… the mask, the man in the damn cloak. Did all that theater actually help, or just make you sicker?

Mozart

It helped pay for candles. Theater pays better than honesty until the last act. But when the violins entered, I forgot his cloak and remembered the chapel I'd been carrying around in my chest. Paper stuck to my wrist with sweat; the ink smudged like it wanted absolution first. That's where I wrote it. Not Vienna. Not parchment. That chapel that smells like wax and old breath and hope.

Beethoven

When I can't trust the room, I press my palm to the lid to feel what I can't hear. That's my chapel.

Narrator (V.O.)

He listens with his hands. Not for applause, but for proof that the world still answers.

Beethoven

I thought I knew grief. Then I went deaf and discovered cruelty. I couldn't hear a child laugh. Couldn't hear birds. Couldn't hear applause. I wrote symphonies in the dark. You never faced that, but what did you lose?

Mozart

Time. I lost time, Ludwig. I should've lived another forty years. I had symphonies in my chest that never reached my hands. Poverty stole the hours. Illness stole the breath. And the world? The world nearly stole my legacy.

Beethoven

You're kinder to them than I am.

Mozart

No. Just practical. Even cowards want beauty. They paid me in coins and in silence. I hated both, but I took them anyway because they kept the candles lit. Besides, the music never belonged to me once it left my fingers. That's the curse of art: we carry it like a child, and then it goes out into a world that mispronounces its name.

Beethoven

Do you blame them? The aristocrats. The critics.

Mozart

I don't forgive them. But I wrote around them. Rage is a luxury when your debts have faces. You had sponsors who feared you. I had patrons who liked me until the bill. Fear builds walls, sure. But charm isolates too. The smile always costs more to the face that wears it.

Beethoven

Fear built my walls. I lived in one. Only shadows for company.

Mozart

And I lived with creditors pounding and children crying. Either way, the walls closed in. Same ghost, different mask.

Beethoven

Tell me a small thing: something not in your letters. Something mean and ordinary.

Mozart

One afternoon the stew tasted like water and the water tasted like the landlord's hands, because he'd banged on the door so hard the metal left a taste in the air. I told Constanze I wasn't hungry and then ate the ends of the loaf when she put the boy down, telling myself I'd discovered a secret instead of stealing from my own table. Your turn.

Beethoven

I broke a keyboard. Not out of drama. Because the note wouldn't reconcile with the ringing in my head. I thought if I struck it hard enough I could crack the sound the way you crack an egg. I cleaned up the splinters with a dull knife, bled on the felt, and hoped no one noticed either stain.

Mozart

They always notice the wrong stains.

The room smells faintly of tallow and old wood, the way practice rooms do after the hands have left.

Beethoven

You ever miss the stage?

Mozart

Every hour I'm not on it. Not for the clapping. For the moment before the first note, when a room holds its breath and believes in the same thing together. That moment is the closest I've been to prayer without saying a word.

Beethoven

Sometimes I wrote just to force that breath. To make the world stop rattling its cutlery and listen. Not for immortality. Just to be inside that hush a few seconds longer than life normally allows.

Mozart

Then we wanted the same thing. You forced the hush to happen. I waited for it to like me back.

Beethoven

And behind the door?

Mozart

A chapel. Always the chapel. Even in a tavern. Even behind a joke. I once lied about a toothache to dodge a patron's dinner; ate a heel of bread in an alley and called it mercy.

Beethoven

I kept a broken tuning fork in my pocket for years. It never rang right, but it felt like a promise I could touch.

He turns the absent fork between finger and thumb. A question arrives the way a key does: simple, decisive.

Beethoven

You're alive now. One hour left. One piano. What do you play?

Mozart

Ave Verum Corpus. It's short. Modest. But pure. I wrote it when I felt myself breaking. When the silence started sounding like surrender. My body was dying. My breath failing. But in those notes, I heard mercy, not for me, but for the soul I almost let go.

Beethoven

Then play it. Let the world weep again.

Narrator (V.O.)

He closes his eyes. Not to rest, but to listen with what's left. Mozart doesn't pose. He sits like a man who knows the bench better than the throne and lays his hands down. The melody arrives quiet at the door, unassuming, exact. No flourishes. Nothing borrowed. A prayer that forgot to tell you it was one. The room doesn't echo; it absorbs, and in the absorbing you can hear space become kindness.

Beethoven

For a moment, even the ringing kneels.

The last note hangs in the rafters, and the room settles into a single, shared breath.

Beethoven

You told me once that music should be fun. That art should make people smile. Do you think I wanted to carry thunder on my back?

Mozart

No. I think you needed to. Like a priest needs his altar. But don't pretend it didn't thrill you—when the silence shattered and the audience forgot how to breathe.

Beethoven

And you? You played like applause was your heartbeat.

Mozart

Maybe it was. But it never followed me home. They cheered while I unraveled. They clapped while I starved.

Beethoven

I didn't know, Wolfgang. I truly didn't.

Mozart

Nobody did. They wanted magic, not the wound it came from. You… you had the dignity of being feared. I had the convenience of being liked. One keeps doors shut. The other leaves you standing in doorways you can't afford to go through.

Beethoven

People call it genius. I don't even know what that word means. Maybe it's not how loud you echo. Maybe it's just whatever scraps are left on the table when the noise finally dies down.

Mozart

And someone still hums it without knowing why.

Beethoven

Then maybe we did it right.

Mozart

Or maybe we just did it loud enough.

They sit. Not rivals, nor heirs. The piano waits, still holding the ghost of Ave Verum Corpus in its strings. No applause comes. Just stillness: the kind that presses down on your chest and makes you remember something lived here once, and maybe still does.

Narrator (V.O.)

He was mocked. Unpaid. Dismissed. A genius buried in a pauper's grave. The other raged at silence until silence took pity and let him write in thunder. Both filled the world with sound, and yet their fears were the same. For Beethoven, silence was a wound. For Mozart, applause was smoke. Somewhere between wound and smoke, the music lived.

Tonight, through one final request, they are heard again, not by kings or courts, but by the only audience that ever mattered. The room keeps its echo; we keep the work.

ACT IV

THE COST OF CROWNS

What power costs the people who wear it

Crowns look heavy in portraits, but the real weight shows up in the neck and the nightmares. Power sells you pageantry and sends you home with scar tissue you didn't read in the brochure. These chapters stay with rulers and rebels after the parade: when the throne squeaks, the room is smaller than they remember, and the cost stops being theoretical.

Cleopatra and Julius Caesar open the stage, trading glances that redraw borders. Both know how to turn a private room into policy, how a whispered promise can move armies. The real question is whether a bed can hold both love and power without someone waking up to find they've been annexed.

George Washington and King George III meet with only chairs, a table, and the years between them. Independence doesn't play as a tidy victory; it feels like a custody fight where the children are whole continents. Freedom has a cost, and here it sounds a lot like two people realizing they can't go back to calling each other "ours."

Winston Churchill and Sitting Bull stand in grass that remembers hooves and bullets. The empire-builder and the resister, the bulldog of Britain and a leader whose people were nearly written out of the land. Nothing between them cleans history up. It just makes empire choke on the names it once pushed into the dirt and walked away from.

John F. Kennedy and Fidel Castro meet in a ballpark that should echo with cheers and instead just hums with the power lights. Strategy and suspicion pass between them like tossed baseballs: easy, practiced, dangerous if dropped. Underneath is a simpler dread: whether two men who built careers on brinkmanship can leave anything gentler behind than instructions on how to reload.

Each of these encounters scrapes some of the polish off the crown. Power can seduce, can inspire, can scare whole nations into line. But it never comes free. Sometimes the bill is written in blood, sometimes in children's names, sometimes in a history book that finally admits the person in charge was improvising more than anyone knew.

CHAPTER 17

Cleopatra – Julius Caesar: *Love and Conquest*
ACT IV: *The Cost of Crowns*

Cleopatra (c. 69–30 BCE)
Last Pharaoh of Egypt and a working head of state. She spoke several languages, balanced books as well as alliances, and used theater because Rome understood spectacle. She partnered with Caesar, later with Antony, to keep Egypt sovereign; Actium ended that bet. Coins bore her profile; policy bore her signature. Mother to Caesarion, she ruled through famine and invasion and chose her own exit when the math ran out. History argues about the costume; the record shows a competent ruler under it.

Julius Caesar (100–44 BCE)
General, consul, and reformer who gambled a republic and won; until he didn't. He crossed the Rubicon (49 BCE), beat rivals fast, rewrote the calendar, cut through debt and land reforms, and centralized power as "dictator for life." He wrote clear Latin (Commentaries) and preferred decisions to ceremony. Generous after victory, ruthless on the way to it. The Senate answered with knives on the Ides of March. His name became a title; the lesson was simpler: emergencies are addictive.

Setting
In a harbor cabin on the Alexandria pier, the air smells of salt and cedar. A low lamp steadies the room. On the table: a bowl of figs and a rolled sea

chart held by two smooth stones. Outside, the port argues in voices and rope. No velvet, no parade: just a working room where the map waits and the fruit is real. Two people set weapons down and decide which truths can live past the door.

Narrator (V.O.)

History keeps the broad strokes and drops the fingerprints. No trumpets. Just rope, figs, and a room that smells like salt and decisions. A general who built too far ahead. A queen who turned survival into a craft. Tonight they'll talk love and conquest and the messy seam where they meet: ambition, tenderness, fear, and whether power and affection can share a bed without tearing it. We're catching them mid-sentence; the room's been listening longer than we have.

Caesar

You always did make an entrance.

Cleopatra

And you always tried to own the doorway.

Caesar

Owning doors is how men keep their throats. Rome taught me that.

Cleopatra

Rome taught you to call taking a lesson. Egypt taught me to survive it.

They study each other the way veterans look at scars: mapping, not marveling.

Caesar

Do you regret it?

Cleopatra

Which part? Choosing you, choosing Egypt, choosing to live?

Caesar

Choosing me.

Cleopatra

Ask me in a different century.

Caesar

I'm short on those.

Cleopatra

So am I.

She pours for both and slides a cup across. He doesn't drink. Neither does she.

Cleopatra

We can do the public lines if you want. I can say queen, you can say Rome, we can applaud our own restraint.

Caesar

Or we could try the private ones. They cost more, but they spend better.

Narrator (V.O.)

The rumor's always louder than the evidence. Tonight they're trading both, and the room's taking notes.

Cleopatra

Then start with a fact. Why did you really come to Alexandria?

Caesar

Because I was chasing a rival who mistook the world for a board and thought I was a piece he could pin. Because grain keeps armies marching. Because Egypt was a problem that could become an ally. Because I'd heard stories about a girl who refused to disappear.

Cleopatra

And because you wanted to see if the stories would kneel.

Caesar

Sometimes I wanted them to. More often I wanted them to stand and prove I hadn't been lied to.

Cleopatra

I did both, depending on the day.

Caesar

I noticed.

Silence that refuses to be awkward. It isn't peace. It's recognition that they have both run out of room for pretending.

Cleopatra

Do you know what I hated most? Not the envoys who tried to price me. Not the priests who smiled like knives. It was the scribes who wrote me down like I was a rumor with hips.

Caesar

They write what buys attention.

Cleopatra

They write what men will defend to feel powerful. It's not the same thing.

Caesar

No, it isn't.

Cleopatra

And you—what did you hate?

Caesar

The moment I understood Rome would never love me. It would obey me, fear me, use me to tell itself a story about order. Then find a way to keep my name and delete my face. That's what institutions do when a man makes them look in a mirror.

Cleopatra

Then why give yourself to it?

Caesar

Because I couldn't make a world alone.

Cleopatra

Neither could I. That's why we met.

He finally takes the cup. Drinks, winces, not from the wine.

Caesar

They've already painted us. You know that.

Cleopatra

Paintings flake. I prefer voices. Even the lying ones move.

Caesar

Plenty will move after we're gone.

Cleopatra

They already have.

He sets the cup down without looking. The wood catches the sound and sets it gently on the table like it's been trained to.

Caesar

There's a thing I haven't said because it sounds weak, and weak is a word Rome treats like disease.

Cleopatra

Say it anyway. Weakness is honest when it's paid for.

Caesar

Sometimes the hardest words are the ones you finally mean.

I didn't hold him.

Cleopatra

Caesarion.

Caesar

Yes. After the day he was born. I told myself it was for his safety, the optics—gods, I hate that word and I used it long before it existed. I told myself public softness was private ruin. But the truth is simpler. I was afraid the part of me that wanted to melt would betray the part of me I'd taught to be iron.

Cleopatra

He has my eyes and your impatience.

Caesar

That's a dangerous combination.

Cleopatra

So is your name and any child's neck. You think I don't count the hours differently because you didn't hold him? Every step he takes, I hear sand shifting under a building I can't stop from sliding. I loved you. I love him.

Both of those truths are bigger than an army and just as likely to trample me.

Caesar

You always did measure risk like prayer: spoken low, kept close, deadly if ignored.

Cleopatra

And you measured it like tax: owed, exacted, justified.

Caesar

Both keep a city running.

Cleopatra

Neither keeps a child safe.

He flinches in a way only a woman who's shared a bed with him would notice. The room catches the movement and pretends it didn't.

Caesar

Do you ever wish we had met without crowns?

Cleopatra

We would have eaten bread on a stair and argued about the price of olives. I would have thought you arrogant. You would have thought me dangerous. We would have been right and married anyway.

Caesar

I would have built a house by the water. You would have filled it with languages.

Cleopatra

And still the world would have found the door.

Caesar

Yes.

They look at the door like it might answer.

Cleopatra

Do you remember the first night?

Caesar

How could I not.

Cleopatra

The world says it was velvet, brocade, a grand trick. They tell it like a comedy. It wasn't. It was laundry. A thick sack that stank of river and rope. My back hurt for days. I couldn't cough because the sound would sell me. I slid out on your floor like a parcel that had survived shipping, and the man who would end a republic smiled like he'd been handed a poem.

I let them change it to a carpet because it helps them live with what women do to stay alive.

Her voice doesn't break, but it lowers. There's a difference and he hears it.

Caesar

I didn't correct them. I liked the image: bold, impossible, theatrical. It made me look like the kind of man who attracts divinities in wrapping paper.

Cleopatra

You see? We both consented to the lie. It protected us. It trapped me.

Caesar

It protected me too. The truth would have sounded like desperation, not destiny.

Cleopatra

Destiny is what men call it when they plan something ugly and want applause later.

Caesar

Sometimes. And sometimes destiny is just a word people use when they run out of better ones.

Cleopatra

We could use a few better ones.

Caesar

We could.

She reaches for a fig, doesn't eat it, sets it back. The gesture is not dainty; it's restraint with muscle behind it.

Cleopatra

They will say I opened my legs and lost a country.

Caesar

They will be wrong and they will enjoy being wrong.

Cleopatra

Say the rest.

Caesar

They will say I crowned myself on a man's spine. That I bewitched the clearest head in Rome and turned him toward the sun until he forgot the wind.

Cleopatra

And what will they say about you?

Caesar

That I dressed as a king and stole the knife that killed the law. That I built a ladder out of other men's promises. That I wanted to be a god and tripped on my own altar.

Cleopatra

And which part cuts?

Caesar

All of it, when I'm tired. None of it, when I'm marching. They'll say what they need to keep sleeping at night. I've done the same to others. We both have.

Cleopatra

I can live with their lies. I can't live with my son learning them by heart.

Caesar

Then teach him yours.

Cleopatra

I am. But he will hear the other version at the market, in the baths, in the hallways of power. He will have to know which one to survive and which one to outgrow. He will have to know when to smile at a story that protects him and when to break it open with his hands.

Caesar

He will need a spine and a mirror. That's a cruel combination to ask of any child.

Cleopatra

Cruelty preexisted us. I will ask it anyway.

He almost smiles. It fails at the edges and becomes something better: respect.

Caesar

You talk about survival like art. I talk about it like architecture.

Cleopatra

And we built something neither of us could live in for long.

Caesar

We did.

Cleopatra

Do you remember Ptolemy's body?

Caesar

Yes.

Cleopatra

The gift-wrapped corpse, the bows, the calculations. Everyone trying to guess what kind of man you were. They studied your face like a weather sign. I watched you and thought, *He will never be bribed the same way twice.*

Caesar

I tried not to be.

Cleopatra

I tried to be.

Caesar

You were good at it.

Cleopatra

That's not a compliment.

Caesar

It's a fact.

Cleopatra

Facts are worse. Compliments are at least small lies that admit themselves. Facts sit like stones and dare you to move them.

Caesar

Then move this one. Tell me something I won't turn into strategy.

Cleopatra

I sleep badly when the harbor is quiet. I trust cities more when they're loud. Silence makes me think knives are learning to walk.

Caesar

I sleep badly when I don't hear marching. The human foot in numbers is my lullaby and my sentence.

Cleopatra

We chose professions that punish rest.

Caesar

We chose selves that required professions that would.

Cleopatra

Do you blame me for choosing you?

Caesar

I blame you for nothing that kept you alive.

Cleopatra

That's the most Roman absolution I've ever heard.

Caesar

What absolution would you prefer?

Cleopatra

None. Only precision. If I am to be damned, I want the right reason on my headstone.

Caesar

What would that reason be?

Cleopatra

I refused to shrink. That's all. And you?

Caesar

I refused to kneel to men who made themselves small and called it virtue.

Cleopatra

We would have made terrible monks.

Caesar

We would have burned the monastery down because the gates didn't open fast enough.

Cleopatra

And then we would have rebuilt it with better drainage.

Caesar

And a courtyard.

Cleopatra

With lemons.

They almost laugh. The sound is there and not. It knows what it is.

Caesar

Tell me the worst thing you've done that no one will forgive if they hear it clean.

Cleopatra

I used my brother's funeral to set a table for allies and ensure the wine never ran out. I stood beside a child king's cold face and counted votes. Then I went home and threw up until my throat hurt for two days. You?

Caesar

I sent a letter I knew would start a war because I couldn't stand the thought of being ordinary in history's hands. Then I convinced myself it was necessary so I could sleep.

Cleopatra

Ambition is a god that eats and then complains about the seasoning.

Caesar

It got us here.

Cleopatra

It will get us gone.

Caesar

It always does.

Another drink. He doesn't flinch at the taste this time. He's remembering a thousand battlefield mornings when water would have made more sense than wine and wine made more sense than truth.

Cleopatra

What will Rome say about him? Caesarion.

Caesar

That he is inconvenient.

Cleopatra

He is a child.

Caesar

That is usually when men are most inconvenient to empires.

Cleopatra

So we teach him to be a man outside of one?

Caesar

We teach him to speak two languages: power and refusal. And we pray he knows when to use which.

Cleopatra

Prayer is not your trade.

Caesar

It becomes every man's trade when he runs out of road.

Cleopatra

Then you're closer to the temple than you admit.

Caesar

And you're closer to the battlefield than you pretend.

Cleopatra

Pretending is currency. I try not to spend it small.

Caesar

Save it for when knives learn to walk.

Cleopatra

They already have.

She looks at his hands. He looks at hers. Not like lovers telegraphing a scene, but like two mechanics cataloging damage they can no longer repair.

Cleopatra

Say it plainly, Julius. Did you love me or the version of Rome you saw when you looked at me?

Caesar

Both. In different ratios on different days. Some mornings I loved you so much it made me stupid. Some nights I loved the idea that the world could be drawn with a clearer line, and you were the ink that didn't fade in seawater.

Cleopatra

Ink is honest when it dries. People aren't.

Caesar

And yet here we are, still writing.

Cleopatra

On a table no one else will read.

Caesar

That might be the point.

Something in her loosens. It's not surrender. It's breath.

Cleopatra

I wanted you to stand up in Rome and say my name without apology.

Caesar

I should have.

Cleopatra

You didn't.

Caesar

I was building a house that collapses under certain kinds of honesty.

Cleopatra

Then build a better one.

Caesar

I tried. I changed the calendar. I opened the grain. I filled offices with competence instead of the right families. Every improvement made someone richer in resentment. There is no benign surgery on a patient who denies he's sick.

Cleopatra

Egypt is not healthier. I've paid priests to smile at the wrong gods and generals to sneeze at the right time. Sometimes a queen is just a woman who signed more compromises than her hands can wash.

Caesar

Then this is our confession. Not that we loved power. That we loved people enough to use it until it used us back.

Cleopatra

That line will not make it into any book.

Caesar

It doesn't have to. It has to be true in here.

He touches his chest with two fingers, lightly, almost embarrassed by the gesture. She watches and does not mock it.

Cleopatra

When they tell the carpet story, they never mention the smell.

Caesar

What did it smell like?

Cleopatra

Wet flax. River skin. Fear I could swallow but not name. I thought, *If he laughs, I'm dead. If he pities me, I'm dead slower.* I prayed a second look.

Caesar

You got it.

Cleopatra

I did. And the storm is still coming.

Caesar

Mine too.

Cleopatra

Say his name again.

Caesar

Caesarion.

Cleopatra

He will never wear it safely.

Caesar

No one ever wears my name safely.

Cleopatra

I did.

Caesar

You carried it. That's different.

Cleopatra

I'll carry it for him until he can put it down and choose his own.

Caesar

That might be the bravest thing a mother can do.

Cleopatra

It is also the heaviest.

Caesar

I can't lighten it.

Cleopatra

You could say my name in Rome.

Caesar

I will.

Cleopatra

Say it like it belongs.

Caesar

It does.

Cleopatra

Then say it when it costs you.

Caesar

That is the only time it matters.

They are quiet long enough for the boat to remind them it is wood and rope and labor. The sea finds the hull and the hull answers like an old friend knocking from the other side of a door.

Cleopatra

Do you envy men who were content?

Caesar

Sometimes. Then I meet them and remember contentment has a twin named fear that keeps borrowing its clothes.

Cleopatra

I envy women who were invisible and safe.

Caesar

Being invisible and safe is a room. You were a city. Cities burn. And they feed people.

Cleopatra

You always could compliment and warn in the same breath.

Caesar

I've had practice with senators.

Cleopatra

And wives.

Caesar

Also wives.

Cleopatra

I will not be one.

Caesar

You were never only anything.

Cleopatra

Good. Then carry at least that version of me into your Senate.

Caesar

I will carry you into my sentences. It's the only Senate that listens.

Cleopatra

That will have to do.

She stands and crosses to the narrow window. The lighthouse throws its steady eye across the water. She's not praying. She's calibrating.

Cleopatra

If I asked you to stay—

Caesar

I would fail you differently.

Cleopatra

I know.

Caesar

If I asked you to come to Rome—

Cleopatra

I would drown slower.

Caesar

I know.

Cleopatra

Then we drink to what won't happen.

Caesar

To the unreal that kept us alive.

They drink. No toasts, no ceremony. Just two people putting a small boundary around a hurt that could eat a room.

Cleopatra

Tell me a secret about the Rubicon.

Caesar

I hesitated. Not long. Long enough to know I could still turn back and live a quiet life buying olives from men who would never learn my name. I thought of it. I even wanted it for a breath. Then I remembered I'd be lying to myself every morning from then on, and I can't keep that many lies watered.

Cleopatra

I hesitated at the rug—fine, the laundry. I thought, *If he is the wrong man, this is the last light I will see from the inside of a sack.* Then I remembered the rooms where people decided my face before I spoke. I chose a new room. Sometimes bravery is that small. A new room.

Caesar

We chose well and badly in equal measure.

Cleopatra

That sounds like life.

Caesar

It is.

He sets his cup down and stands. Not to leave yet. Just to stand like a man whose body has learned from wars how to carry goodbye without performing it.

Caesar

I would say something noble if I thought it would help.

Cleopatra

Noble is for statues. Say something true.

Caesar

I am afraid they will take my death and make it useful to worse men.

Cleopatra

They will.

Caesar

I am more afraid they will take your life and make it small enough to fit inside their jokes.

Cleopatra

They will try. But jokes get tired and kingdoms get hungry. I feed both until they sleep.

Caesar

You always did.

Cleopatra

If you see him—

Caesar

I won't. That's the point, isn't it?

Cleopatra

Yes.

Caesar

Then if I die before the story corrects itself, remember you were never my scandal. You were my equal and my mirror, and I should have said that with the doors open.

Cleopatra

You just did. Consider the doors open enough.

Caesar

I'll say it again where the knives can hear.

Cleopatra

Good.

Caesar

One last thing. If I had stayed. If the world had been uncharacteristically generous one afternoon. What would you have asked of me?

Cleopatra

To put our son to bed once and not tell anyone. To take off the armor in a room that didn't require it. To say my name without calculating the price. To let me be a woman without the crown for one hour and not be punished for it the next.

Caesar

I could have done two of those.

Cleopatra

Two would have been a revolution. Sometimes a single note changes the song.

Caesar

Your talent was knowing which notes are revolutions.

Cleopatra

Perhaps your talent was believing you could schedule them.

Caesar

Guilty.

Cleopatra

Go. Rome doesn't wait politely.

Caesar

It never has.

Cleopatra

And Julius—

Caesar

Yes.

Cleopatra

When you cross your next river, don't forget the smell. Of wet flax. Of rope. Of fear that decided to move anyway. Say it in Latin if you must. But say it.

Caesar

I will.

He opens the door, and the harbor's breath edges in. He doesn't look back. He doesn't need to.

Narrator (V.O.)

They'll paint it velvet and forget the laundry. Two people set weapons by a bowl of figs and said what history won't use. The future knocks after it enters. Some rooms only close after you've left them twice. The lamp steadies. Cleopatra listens to the water hit the hull and counts to ten, then ten again, until the counting turns into a prayer that doesn't ask for anything and still gets heard.

Chapter 18

George Washington – King George III: *The Crown and the Crossing*

ACT IV: The Cost of Crowns

General George Washington (1732–1799)

General of the Continental Army, first U.S. president, and the man who made restraint a habit. He held starving winters together at Valley Forge, took the oath in New York, and walked away after two terms so the office wouldn't cling to the man. He moved too slowly on slavery and knew it. He favored civilian control of the military, precedent over personality, and home over pomp. Married Martha at 26, kept Mount Vernon as his anchor, and taught a young republic that power is something you borrow and return.

King George III (1738–1820)

A long-reigning monarch who read his papers, counted the shillings, and tried to keep an empire stitched while the fabric changed. To admirers he was dutiful and frugal; to critics, obstinate. He loved agriculture, kept journals in plain prose, and trusted order to outlast disappointment. He lost America, endured European wars, and suffered periods of illness that did not make him comic so much as human under pressure. Married Charlotte at 22, raised a dynasty, and believed the crown's first job was to steady the room when tempers outran judgment.

Setting

New York, July 9, 1776—three days after the Declaration reaches Washington. A narrow room that smells of wax, paper, and rain kept too long in the wood. A rolled Declaration waits on a map table, corners curled from habit. The crown rests on a chair that no one touches. Sand clings to a name that won't dry. A candle steadies itself. A cracked bell outside argues with the hour. The air holds its breath, aware that when the parchment opens, something larger than ink will leave the room changed.

Narrator (V.O.)

Power is loud in public and awkward in private. Here it's a table with fresh ink and a crown pretending to weigh the same as a candle. Two men meet where a country is being midwifed: one learning how to let go with dignity, the other learning how to hold without keeping. The question isn't who wins the century; it's whether power can keep its manners long enough for good laws to outlast good speeches.

Washington unrolls the declaration and lays it flat. The parchment stills, obeying the weight of a man who trusts wood more than ceremony. He brushes a ridge of sand from a wet name and leaves three grains clinging to his sleeve. He doesn't notice; the page does.

Washington

There is no gentle way to say it. We have severed the bond. The paper states it; the cost will teach it.

King George

You announce the sundering like a clerk delivering a ledger, not a subject forsaking allegiance. Sir, you do not break a covenant with a line of ink, nor unmake a crown with a breath.

Washington

We do not unmake your crown. We refuse its claim. The table here understands me. Splinters do not bow to polish.

King George

Nor do splinters sign oaths. Your table understands you; your oath must teach your towns.

Washington

And that's the work.

King George

Continuity is not polish; it is the spine of a realm. Hierarchy preserves the slow blood of nations when appetite demands a quicker feast.

Washington

Appetite has carried too many orders from an ocean away. We asked to be heard. We received dispatches. The ear is nearer than the ship.

King George

You erred in mistaking distance for neglect. Rule requires both circumference and center. Men at the edges like to pretend every circle was meant for their own compass.

Washington

Rule also requires consent. We tried the petition. We burned the candle to the ends. The room remained quiet. So we raised our voices until the quiet cracked.

King George

And called it liberty, like apprentices who confuse unbuttoned coats for mastery. Disorder travels faster than discipline, General. I guard against the spread of fever.

Washington

Your physic made the patient worse. We bleed more from the remedy than the wound. You would bind us with a poultice that hides the rot.

King George

You speak in farms and fevers because they flatter the ear of men who sweat at dawn. Very well. I will stay with that tongue. A field without a hedgerow invites wolves. The crown is a hedgerow.

Washington

A hedgerow planted across another man's bread does not protect him. It cages him. He starves within order.

The candle gutters and returns. A thread of smoke writes its own patient script along the beam.

King George

You dismiss crowns as ornaments. They are obligations hammered into gold. I did not choose the weight; I carried it with ceremony so that storms would not loosen the timbers of the ship.

Washington

I believe you carried weight. I do not believe it was ours to lift. We learned our ship by river first, then by sea. The helms differed. Our hands learned different ropes.

King George

And now your hands presume to redraw my chart. You will find the shoals ancient and the currents unkind to novices.

Washington

We will founder and right ourselves until we learn. I'd rather earn the wreckage than accept a safety you impose.

King George

You are not the first to prefer scars to restraint. Scars look noble in oil and vulgar on a living man. Your posterity will applaud what your contemporaries must bury.

Washington

Let them. I have buried enough already. Duty tastes like ash when spoken too loudly by those far from the fire.

The crown on the chair reflects a troubled halo against the wall, then lets it fade. The map gathers shadow where the coast folds like a kept secret.

King George

You posture as the reluctant rebel. Yet I see ambition under your modest cloth. A soldier who declines to be king is often the most dangerous sovereign of all.

Washington

I have been offered crowns by men with honest hearts and poor judgment. I refused. Not from piety. From discipline. A republic demands more steadiness than a diadem. My pride prefers the quieter trial.

King George

So you exchange a single will, trained, constrained, for a thousand wills quarrelling under borrowed Latin. What you call liberty may be only noise with etiquette.

Washington

It's still better than velvet silence. A noisy table can learn its manners; a quiet one never grows a conscience.

King George

Do you mock ceremony because it steadies hands you want trembling? Or because steadiness exposes your gamble?

Washington

I mock nothing. I distrust polish when the floor is not yet laid. You speak of steadiness from rooms that never sweat.

King George

Rooms sweat differently. Royal labor is not idle; it is invisible by design. The crown must wear composure so the world doesn't smell its fear.

Washington

Composure is easy when the blood isn't yours. A farmer doesn't need a throne to know what the weather means. He just works through it.

Narrator (V.O.)

Some men earn history by signing their names. Others by refusing to. Washington knew which kind he was. The ink belonged to talkers. His proof would be in men who stopped running when the drums started.

King George

Then you have chosen rebellion over loyalty, and call it virtue. You stand before me not as a gentleman, but as a traitor who mistakes conviction for authority.

Washington

If conviction has no authority, Majesty, then every man must wait for permission to breathe.

King George

Empires do not wait.

Washington

No. That's why they forget how.

The bell outside works at its duty: honest, a little cracked, unconcerned with metaphor. The window admits the sound without grace.

King George

Tell me your wound, then. Not the pamphlet version. The one that drags when you stand.

Washington

A winter without boots. Men wrapping their feet in rags and bravery. Fires that carried more smoke than heat. Flesh obeys cold before it obeys speeches. I promised tomorrow; men believed or died. I count both as obedience I did not deserve.

King George

And my wound was a desk buried in petitions signed by grief until my hand trembled to counter-sign them with resignation. I sent ships because the sea at least returns a salt answer. Parliament sent complaints to be read at supper. And the mind—mine—learned a humming you will call illness. It was only the arithmetic of losses sung past comfort.

Washington

We are not enemies in the record, then. We keep different columns; the sums still accuse.

King George

You are cleaner in yours. Mud excuses tears. Velvet forbids them. The world loves the man who weeps in rags and despises the king who does not cry where the portrait might see.

Washington

The world is not present. The men in this room are. I will not spend their blood for a sentence that sounds fine when copied. If the line lives, it must live under candle smoke and splinters.

King George

If the line lives, it must live under law, not sentiment. Law with a lineage, not an improvisation cut to today's coat.

Washington

Then we meet at duty and separate at throne. I choose to be corrected by votes; you choose to be constrained by inheritance. Both are disciplines. One listens wider.

King George

Wider is not necessarily wiser. Noise flatters itself with breadth. Authority remains narrow so the road can be found in fog.

Washington

A narrow path is useful when it leads home. It is cruel when it leads only to a door that never opens.

The candle burns level. The map's rivers glow like veins working toward the sea, faithful to gravity and indifferent to argument.

King George

You accuse me of tyranny. I accuse you of vanity furnished with virtue. We might both bear some truth. What do men do with mixed verdicts, General?

Washington

They keep walking. They make amends where their feet allow. They endure correction without losing their direction.

King George

And when endurance fails?

Washington

They ask for help and learn not to be proud. Or they harden and fail larger. I prefer the first.

King George

You speak of humility and treat it like a tool you keep in your coat. I have found it to be a pain more than a tool. Useful, but never comfortable.

Washington

Tools are seldom comfortable. The handle blisters before it fits.

King George

Say, then, the difference as you see it, without rhetoric. Let the wood hear it and approve.

Washington

Service over crown. Bread first, flourish later. Consent before command. A table where men argue until the ink learns its manners.

King George

Order before appetite. Office before clamor. Continuity before novelty. A throne that forbids the whims of passing moods.

Washington

And here we stand, arm's length, each guarding his furniture.

King George

Not all furniture deserves guarding. Some chairs break the backs that trust them.

Washington

That is why we keep a carpenter close.

The chair with the crown creaks like it's offended by ordinary talk. Neither man reaches for it. Both notice.

King George

We have rehearsed our brave sentences. Permit me one of my allotted questions. Will your republic survive its contradictions?

Washington

Not as written. Only as argued. The argument will be the republic, not the paper.

King George

Then I fear for your patience. People prefer verdicts to trials, especially when hunger sits at table.

Washington

So do armies. Still, I have seen hunger prefer a rough justice to a polite ration.

King George

Bread turns merciless when you slice it with slogans. You will learn mathematics that does not flatter the street.

Washington

We will learn and err. We will err and mend. We will do so without a crown to interrupt the lesson.

The candle coughs once. Washington pinches the wick, then relents and lets it claim its small authority again. Ash blooms and drops, a quiet snowfall on the map's coast.

King George

You grow frustrated when you speak of crowns, like the object itself had injured you. It has not. It merely refused you.

Washington

It refused my neighbors. That is injury enough. My house exists among theirs.

King George

This is the language of a parish warden, not a general aiming at empire.

Washington

We are not aiming at empire. We are aiming at a place where mothers sleep without quartering soldiers. That is enough to occupy a generation.

King George

Your modesty will not survive your victories. Victories remake men while they still imagine themselves unchanged.

Washington

Perhaps. Then let my countrymen dismiss me when my usefulness ends. I will go home. Mount Vernon is patient. The river knows my name better than the city ever will.

King George

You threaten to retire as a flourish, which is a kind of flourish even as it refuses one.

Washington

If I wanted theatre, I would choose a better mouth. The teeth betray me.

King George

I will not exploit a gentleman's dentistry. We have traded enough humiliations.

Washington

Then we may yet be civil.

King George

Civil is cheap in rooms without crowds. The price increases outside.

Narrator (V.O.)

History loves to call this peace, but that's optimism with better lighting. The cannons haven't even cleared their throats. Both men are trying on civility like it might fit, knowing full well it won't survive the season. For a heartbeat, the room pretends rebellion and royalty can share air. Then the moment remembers what year it is.

King George

Posterity will find your touch and call it destiny. Clerks will blame humidity and call it nothing. Both will be wrong. It is merely the fact of a hand at work.

Washington

Work is the only ceremony I trust. It remembers what words forget.

King George

Words have kept my house longer than nails have kept yours. Do not despise their masonry.

Washington

I do not. I insist they carry weight. This page cannot live on posture alone.

King George

Nor can a crown live on myth alone. It requires people who believe in the dignity that restrains their own demands. I have spent a lifetime carrying that cost in weights no one sees.

Washington

And I will spend mine teaching men to bring their demands and then sit to hear why some must wait. It is slower. It is necessary.

King George

You imagine patience available in quantity. It is dearer than gunpowder.

Washington

True. Yet I have seen farmers argue until dusk and still share bread. That gives me courage.

King George

Bread shared today is often bread stolen tomorrow by subtler hands. Beware your merchants and your saints. The former price the table; the latter claim it.

Washington

I will beware both. I will keep my eye on the chair with the wobble, not the chair with the shine. Wobble instructs.

King George

Shine deters rats. Each has its use.

Washington

Then the room requires both, and a man to know which to trust when.

King George

You make governance sound like carpentry. It flatters your trade, not mine.

Washington

Carpentry flatters no one. It either holds or it fails.

Somewhere beyond the shutters, a horse stamps and is quiet. The bell tries again, unashamed of its imperfection.

King George

I will allow you your carpenter's wisdom. Allow me one more question. Who will you trust to braid the rope when your bell frays?

Washington

The hands with splinters. The ones who feel the fibers as duty, not spectacle. In Trenton there is a man who mends a ferry rope in winter. He keeps a nail in his mouth so he doesn't lose it in the snow, and he will not take a coin from a traveler whose hands are already numb. He ties the knot twice, then once again softer, so it will hold and still forgive the pull. He writes no pamphlets. If he ran this city for a month, half our arguments would turn into work.

King George

Your ferryman is a gift, not a policy. Most governments plan for the winter when his tooth aches and he stays home. You'll need a way to keep that rope mended that doesn't rely on finding saints every winter. When you cannot find them, you will be tempted to import a crown by another name.

Washington

I will be tempted. I will ask the people to forbid it. If they fail, I will blame myself before I blame them.

King George

You cultivate a severe conscience. It will be admired in books and abandoned in crises.

Washington

Then let the book keep at least one candle lit. A man's failure should not extinguish an idea's use.

King George

We arrive, then, at our narrow bridge. You place faith in a people learning themselves by debate. I place faith in a curb that made debate safe for generations before your fathers were born.

Washington

Both structures claim mercy. One gives it to office. The other to the governed. We choose differently.

King George

We do. And yet you have spoken without insolence, which I admit is disarming. It complicates my tidy rage.

Washington

I am not interested in your rage. I am interested in your honesty. If you had yielded sooner—what then?

King George

If I had yielded inches, I might have kept coasts. If I had listened with willingness instead of ritual, I might have lost less and understood more. I trained my ear to duty and called the rest noise. Confession lightens a crown after midnight; it returns no coast.

Washington

Thank you for it. I will answer in equal coin. I told men we would prevail when I had doubts I would not say aloud. That lie served a living purpose; it still burdens me.

King George

We both have lied in the name of duty. There is, I suspect, no clean way to carry nations.

Washington

Only cleaner ways than the last time.

King George

You Americans prefer incremental sermons to inherited stability. It is your religion now.

Washington

And yours remains a hymn to office. Both hymns have verses worth keeping.

King George

We agree on fragments and break at the spine.

Washington

The break is the point. It must be clean and without malice. I wish you health. I wish you rest. I wish you a quieter counsel than ministers provide.

I overstep, perhaps.

King George

You do. And yet it lands more as advice than insolence.

And I wish you fortitude without vanity. Your people will love you until they need to hate you. Endure both with the same face.

Washington

I will try.

King George

Try quietly. It becomes you.

The king rises. The chair complains, then forgives. He does not look at the crown. He pauses at the map. He lays his fingertips along a coast he once pronounced with confidence. He does not press. He withdraws the gesture before it becomes claim.

Washington

The door sticks when pulled. Lift, then draw. It honors the stubborn.

King George

Like your country.

Washington

Like your memory.

King George

We will see which proves the heavier anvil.

Washington

Metal is not our measure. Breath is.

King George

You smuggle benediction into politics, General. Priests would applaud if they were not so jealous of new liturgies.

Washington

Let them listen from the stair and decide their homily. We have our own to write.

King George

I do not renounce; I recognize. You have declared. I have heard. That is not peace, but it is not contempt.

Washington

Recognition is a beginning. We will do the rest under weather neither of us commands.

King George

Then I leave you to your drafts—of paper and of wind. Guard both.

Washington

And you to your courts. Guard mercy.

Narrator (V.O.)

Washington's thumb leaves a smudge on the parchment. Small, imperfect, human. Some clerk will curse it, some museum will frame it, and a few centuries later, we'll argue over what it meant. Maybe it meant nothing. Or maybe it meant everything: that freedom, at its birth, was already messy. Empires fall. Monarchs fade. We polish our revolutions later and forget how human they were in the making.

Chapter 19

Winston Churchill – Sitting Bull: *The Land and the Lion*

ACT IV: The Cost of Crowns

Prime Minister Winston Churchill (1874–1965)

Born into privilege, schooled in risk. He rode into gunfire before he ever held office, then led Britain through nights that sounded like endings. Prime Minister during World War II, author of *The Second World War*, and Nobel laureate in Literature. He painted to quiet his mind and wrote to keep order in it. Defender of empire, admirer of liberty, captive of both. His speeches outlasted ration books because he treated language as rations too: measured, necessary, and capable of feeding morale.

Chief Sitting Bull (c. 1831–1890)

Hunkpapa Lakota leader, strategist, and spiritual guide who refused to trade land for safety. He united the plains tribes against U.S. expansion and helped lead them at Little Bighorn, and survived exile in Canada before forced surrender. Briefly toured with Buffalo Bill, learning how spectacle rewrites truth. Shot during an arrest at Standing Rock. Remembered less for defiance than for clarity: a man who knew that a treaty without respect is just another ambush written in ink.

Setting

Night wind combs the prairie and pulls at the edges of a campaign tent pitched near a low fire. Tin cups rest on a crate that passes for a table.

Smoke drifts toward stars that neither empire nor nation can rename. One man studies maps that used to be promises; the other studies the horizon he's trying to keep. The ground is cold, equal, and unconquered. Every crack of the fire sounds like the world rehearsing its next argument.

Narrator (V.O.)

History is an unhelpful roommate: It leaves an empire's dishes in the sink and swears it meant well. Tonight the sink is the prairie, the dishes are two men, and the moonlight does what it can to keep everyone honest.

Churchill

I will not feign a soft entrance, Chief. My life was plotted across atlases with colored pencils and the kind of confidence that pretends to be duty. I spoke for a nation while another century tried to tear itself apart. And you, you spoke for a nation that was told it did not exist unless it learned the conqueror's grammar.

Sitting Bull

Nations come after rivers and before graves. The order matters.

Churchill

We can agree about graves. Must the way to them be of our making as well? We built rails, parliaments, courts. I believed, and too much, that order was kindness in uniform.

Sitting Bull

A uniform is a promise to forget something. Sometimes it's only a button. Sometimes it's a child.

Churchill

And yet you raised warriors. You stood against rifles and governments and factories. Spirit against steel. Why did you believe it could hold?

Sitting Bull

Because steel rusts and the spirit sings even when it is hoarse. Because a child learns a song before it learns a border. Because the buffalo knew the trail without asking a surveyor.

Churchill

A fine picture. And yet history keeps the count. Your people were scattered; the reservations were carved out; treaties were written with generous ink and stingy honor. Was the blood worth the story you kept?

Sitting Bull

A seed looks like a funeral until spring changes its mind. We are still here. Your empire? Does the sun still never set? Or did it only learn to set politely when the papers stopped saying otherwise?

Churchill rubs his thumb along a frayed cuff, hoping the past will polish into symmetry. He is not the caricature of a lion; lions do not carry this much paperwork in their eyes.

Churchill

Progress gives bread, medicine, bridges. Civilization has a smell: coal, ink, bureaucracy—and I confess I learned to love it, the way one loves a flawed aunt who always brings a cake and sometimes brings a sermon.

Sitting Bull

Cakes are sweet. Sermons can be as well. But I have tasted bread that remembered the field and bread that did not. There is a difference.

Churchill

We believed empire could be a schoolmaster; irritating, yes, but at last a tutor in the useful arts. Steam. Law. Letters. I will not pretend there weren't canes and dark corners. There were. But sometimes the lesson saved lives the whip could not reach. We blame history on generals and kings, but most empires rise and fall on what people are willing to say to each other at dinner.

Sitting Bull

A school that washes mouths for speaking to grandmothers is not a school. It is a drought with chalkboards.

Churchill

You speak in riddles. Nations are not governed by drums and metaphors; they are governed by ministries and minutes.

Sitting Bull

The drum is a minute that does not forget it is tied to skin.

Narrator (V.O.)

There is, to be fair, a mismatch of instruments: Churchill is a brass section with a marching score; Sitting Bull is a cedar flute that refuses the key signature. The tune collides and, somehow, harmonizes on certain notes.

Churchill

Your alliances, Sioux with tribes that had once bled against you, those were not prayers; those were politics. Do you not admit that strategy rules even the sacred?

Sitting Bull

When fire crosses fences, neighbors quit counting old offenses. If that is politics, it is the kind that remembers water before speeches.

Churchill

Mind your tone. I carried boys out of a war who died for something larger than property lines and port duties. I will not have their ghosts reduced to an accounting exercise.

Sitting Bull

And I carried boys who died for land that had already remembered their names. If we are trading ghosts, mine are not for sale.

Churchill

Do you hate us: the white man, the Englishman, the American? Name the object and I will label it with the correct flag.

Sitting Bull

I hate forgetting. A man who forgets the word for sky will sell it and brag about the price. Many white men remembered and came with open hands. Many forgot and came with ledgers. Hatred burns quick; it's lazy fuel. Forgetting is the cold wind that keeps blowing long after the fire's done.

Churchill

You will find I am not made entirely of ledgers. I am a painter, a failed one some days, and that is not a metaphor. I know the ache of a line that refuses to become a horizon.

Sitting Bull

Then you know the ache of a line drawn through someone else's home.

Churchill

Touché. I would edit that line if I could, though editors often arrive after the printing press has gone quiet and the damage is bound in cloth.

A moth batters itself once, twice against Churchill's unlit cigar and decides the moon is a kinder addiction.

Churchill

Let us talk of forgiveness. Do you forgive us? It is not a trap; it is a wish disguised as a question.

Sitting Bull

I am a man, not a priest of absolution. Forgiveness is a morning chore that evening undoes. I try again the next morning. Some mornings are longer than others.

Churchill

Then reconciliation—possible? Between the looters of maps and the keepers of circles?

Sitting Bull

Yes. But only when men with microphones learn silence and men with rifles learn to open both hands. Reconciliation isn't a treaty; it's a man with power crying and not looking for the podium.

Churchill

I have wept. Less than I drank, but more than I admitted at the time.

Sitting Bull

Then you have a doorway.

Churchill

I must ask something indelicate. Your life balanced the spiritual and the martial, visions and ambushes. How did you stand at that crossing without tearing yourself in half?

Sitting Bull

I did tear. That is the answer. A hawk does not hunt because it hates, and a holy man is not holy because he never lifted his hand. I lifted mine to protect the circle. Sometimes I lifted too late.

Churchill

Guilt is a uniform the soul cannot take off. Believe me, I have tried to misplace the jacket.

Sitting Bull

Then wear it honestly.

Here the air changes. Not solemn. No, they began solemn.

Sitting Bull

There was a girl. Eight winters old. Barefoot, because winter had a short memory that year. She ran when soldiers came; her doll stayed brave for her. She did not scream when the bullets reached her. She simply sat down in the snow, the way a child sits when told to wait. I buried her because someone had to know the ground still knew its work. I do not know her name now. My people say some names are not meant to be spoken by strangers. But I know her eyes. They ask me each night why I could not stop the wind. Tell me, Mr. Churchill. What do you say to her?

Churchill

I have built speeches like cathedrals and hidden inside them, but a child has no use for architecture. I say: I failed you. Men who looked like me failed you with orders; men who sounded like me failed you with explanations. If I must ask you for anything, I will not call it forgiveness. I will ask you to let your name, unknown to me, sit at tables where decisions are made, so that even the most well-meaning lie has to look you in the eyes before it speaks.

Sitting Bull

The living forget to set a place.

Churchill

Then I will knock glasses off the table until they remember. It is not the most civilized tactic, but civilization has had its turn.

Narrator (V.O.)

Some apologies buy nothing; some open something. Churchill's apology is a crowbar: inelegant, finally useful.

Churchill

If you had the engines of empire: railways, radios, rations—would you have used them? To protect, perhaps to extend?

Sitting Bull

A tool can carve or scar. I would have asked the trails where they wanted the rails, not the other way. I would have sent radios to the grandmothers so no child had to translate grief across a language he was told to forget.

Churchill

You make it sound simple. Power is a hall with doors that only open inward.

Sitting Bull

Then break the hinges. Or leave and meet people in the courtyard. The sky is better there.

Churchill

You are maddeningly persuasive. Were you always?

Sitting Bull

No. I learned to speak because silence was being used against us.

Churchill

I learned to speak because silence was being used by us.

They share a small, surprising laugh. The brief treaty laughter makes when it thinks no one is watching.

Churchill

Progress: do you grant it exists? Has the world improved?

Sitting Bull

You cured plagues and invented new loneliness. You fly in metal birds and forget to look out the window. You taught children to read and to ignore the old people who remember the stories behind the letters. I do not say there is no progress. I say do not call it progress when it is only speed.

Churchill

Then what should be remembered?

Sitting Bull

That the earth is borrowed. That a flag weighs less than a child's laugh. That wealth without balance is a sickness that invents its own doctors.

Churchill

And the bill comes due, yes, interest compounded in regret. I know that ledger. It kept me up at hours when brandy promised eloquence and handed me only sleep.

Sitting Bull

Sleep is an honest negotiator when men finally meet him.

Narrator (V.O.)

That's the real bill: the parts order forgets to remember. Buttons are cheap; children aren't. Empires always swear they'll pay later. Later never has enough chairs.

Churchill

I am tempted to monologue. It is my worst and best habit. Allow me one indulgence, and interrupt me when I deserve it.

Sitting Bull

I will. I believed empire could be steward rather than thief. I believed the British character, its stubborn decency, its fondness for lines and understatement, could chaperone power without gorging on it. I fought one tyranny and found solace in the notion that the bully we stopped forgave the bully we had been. That is not how absolution works. India taught me that. Africa taught me that. Even our own island taught me that when the poor white faces of the East End looked at me with a hunger that did not speak La—no. It spoke hunger. There is more courage in the one you are trying to use now.

Churchill

So this is what it feels like to be interrupted during one's own scheduled monologue. I'll admit: it is both irritating and oddly refreshing.

Sitting Bull

Then perhaps we are even. I have been interrupted by empires for most of my life. You will survive a paragraph.

Churchill

Fair enough. For what it is worth, I hope you're right. I painted. I wrote. I drank. I tried to love my wife properly and my country dangerously. I told jokes in rooms where despair needed a cigarette break. And I failed, and failed again. Half my best lines were dashed off like telegrams and half were sweated over like trenches, and I am not sure which half mattered more.

Sitting Bull

That is craft. The spirits teach it as well: half the visions come in a flash, half in a fever, and a man cannot brag about which is which without lying to himself.

Narrator (V.O.)

This is the part where people *should* lean forward, because the extraordinary men have decided to sound human for five minutes.

Churchill

You ask for remembrance. Here is something small I will remember because you asked: the sound of boots in corridors when news is bad. And the way the corridor smells like dust, even in palaces. And how a single wrong word can wobble a nation. These are not monuments; they are the screws that hold the monuments up. A well-aimed sentence can end a war or a marriage. The universe doesn't label which one you're about to throw.

Sitting Bull

I will remember the way old men clear their throats before council, and how children imitate the sound because they want to borrow importance for a moment. I will remember dogs stretching at doorways to tell us a meeting is over. And the taste of snow when it is still itself.

Churchill

Small truths rescue the large ones from melodrama.

Sitting Bull

Large truths rescue the small ones from being ignored.

Churchill

We are, you see, both romantics of a sort. I, of words and uniforms; you, of circles and names. Perhaps that is why we can speak without drawing swords.

Sitting Bull

We did draw them. We are only tired now.

Churchill

A fair correction.

He accepts it without flinch. If there is growth here, it is not the spectacular kind that wins awards. It is the domestic kind: a man learns to be interrupted and keep listening.

Churchill

If I were a young officer again, saber polished, boots idiotic with shine, convinced I could be both gentleman and conqueror, what would you say to make me hesitate at the village gate?

Sitting Bull

Learn the names of the children before you shout. Remove your hat before you say the word "civilize." Take off your gloves when you shake a hand that has just buried someone. If your orders tell you to forget you are a son, refuse them.

Churchill

Those are inconvenient commandments.

Sitting Bull

A conscience is a poor clerk and an excellent drum. It keeps bad time and saves lives.

Churchill

Then beat it louder. I will try to hear it through the brass.

Sitting Bull

Do not be angry at the brass. Just do not let it march alone.

Churchill

I have said often: some wars are righteous. I will die believing it. But some methods are poison even when the cause is not. We laced our help with humiliation and called it tutoring. We created borders like a bored god with a ruler and said the rivers would cooperate. Rivers are famously bad at cooperating with rulers.

Sitting Bull

They cooperate with stones and patience. Men could copy that but prefer to shout at water.

Churchill

Yes. We prefer to shout at water and then drown theatrically.

Sitting Bull

The spirits are patient with theatrics. They wait until the actor takes off the costume. Then they ask the real questions.

Churchill

Ask them now.

Sitting Bull

Return what can be returned before your children inherit the argument. Teach successors to listen to those who do not vote for them. Plant trees you will never sit under and do not issue a press release about the planting. When you make a mistake, do not package it as a policy. Make it a story you tell until you are tired of hearing your own voice.

Churchill

You will ruin careers with advice like that.

Sitting Bull

Then let better ones grow where the ruined ones stop casting shade.

Churchill

Tell me something foolish. Something you believed and had to repent.

Sitting Bull

That I could protect everyone if I did not sleep. I repented by sleeping and waking to grief anyway.

Churchill

I believed that if I wrote brilliantly enough, the world would forgive the parts of me that commanded poorly. I repented by learning that clarity is not absolution; it is only light. And light is notorious for showing dust.

Sitting Bull

Then keep sweeping. Slowly. The dust is your friend; it tells you where you have been walking.

Churchill

I once said that we shape our buildings and thereafter they shape us. It occurs to me now that we also shape our apologies, and thereafter they shape our future wars.

Sitting Bull

Make your apologies round so they don't have corners to cut people on the way out.

Churchill

You are an excellent tutor, Chief, though I suspect you would decline the title.

Sitting Bull

I am a reminder with a face. That is enough.

Churchill

If you could rewrite one sentence in the story of your people in my century, only one, no magical footnotes, what would you change?

Sitting Bull

I would take the rifles from the hands of the men who were told to protect us and told to fear us in the same breath.

Churchill

I would change the sentence that begins "We meant well…" to "We meant power and sometimes shared its crumbs." Accuracy is the first mercy we owe the dead.

Sitting Bull

Say that at your councils.

Churchill

I will say it here so I cannot pretend I did not think it later.

The moth returns and decides Churchill's ear is not a lighthouse after all. Small progress.

Churchill

Leaders today: what do we tell them, plainly, so the message survives translation into memos?

Sitting Bull

You are not owners of the earth. You are renters with bad habits. The lease is short. Pay in humility and maintenance. Rivers do not care for your borders; grass will grow through your ruins and not mourn. Learn to be quiet where your microphones are loud. If you cannot pray, at least listen to those who can without translating them into policy first.

Churchill

And to the people? The ones who crowd and hope and make a racket of buying and loving?

Sitting Bull

Protect the ones who cannot protect themselves and stop measuring protection only in coins. Feed children before parades. Teach trades that mend rather than only those that speed. Remind boys that bravery is sometimes the refusal to join a loud line.

Churchill

Remind old men that silence is not the same as wisdom; sometimes it is merely tired pride.

Sitting Bull

That too.

Churchill

Well. We have worn the night down with sentences. The moon will send us a bill.

Sitting Bull

The moon has already been paid. Children looked at it today and did not ask for proof.

Churchill

I envy that faith. Mine always came with arguments and a hangover.

Sitting Bull

Drink water. Say fewer words. Listen to one old woman for every three young men. That will cure more than doctors have names for.

Churchill

You have an answer for everything.

Sitting Bull

No. I have a story for many things. Answers are often traps disguised as chairs.

Churchill

Then we'll stand a little longer.

Two silhouettes in a field the maps forgot to label properly. One wrapped in history, the other wrapped in history's consequences.

Churchill

Some wars are never won. Only remembered.

Sitting Bull

And some memories refuse to become peace.

Churchill

May we at least carry them properly?

Sitting Bull

Yes. Two hands. No pockets.

Churchill

Then let us carry them together for a few steps and see whether the load teaches us its own instructions.

Sitting Bull

Walk, then.

Narrator (V.O.)

They walk. No music, no credits, no stapled morals. Two sets of footprints agree for a few yards, then remember their different roads. If you feel a little hope, it might just be your body liking the idea of moving. That's fine. Bodies know things, too.

Chapter 20

John F. Kennedy – Fidel Castro: *The Missile and the Mirror*

ACT IV: The Cost of Crowns

President John F. Kennedy (1917–1963)

Thirty-fifth U.S. president, elected at 43, the first Catholic, one of the youngest ever inaugurated. A war hero with a chronic back injury and a public grace that made television his ally. His administration balanced Cold War brinkmanship in Cuba, Berlin, and Vietnam with New Frontier optimism. He launched the moonshot, stared down Khrushchev, and carried more myth than one life could bear. Assassinated in Dallas after 1,000 days in office, he left a line still quoted because it still works: ask what you can give before asking what you deserve.

Prime Minister Fidel Castro (1926–2016)

Lawyer-turned-revolutionary who toppled Batista in 1959 and outlasted eleven U.S. presidents. He traded Havana's casinos for literacy drives, wealth for ideology, and dependence on sugar for dependence on Moscow. Survived invasion, embargo, and assassination attempts that read like dark comedy. To some he was David with a cigar; to others, a censor in fatigues. He believed history would absolve him, an odd comfort for a man who never stopped writing it himself.

Setting

In Estadio Latinoamericano after hours, Havana air hangs sweet over infield dirt that remembers a dive no one filmed. A scuffed baseball waits in the grass; a transistor radio mutters Spanish through static; two bulbs on the scoreboard refuse to agree. The dugout bench is honest pine, paint on the rail keeping its stories underneath. Beyond center field a taxi argues with a dog and loses. A groundskeeper's rake leans teeth-down at the fence; a gate rattles once and chooses quiet. The PA clicks, thinks better of it, and lets silence take the last at-bat.

Narrator (V.O.)

Baseball pretends time is measured in outs; tonight it's measured in restraint. Two men, one island, and a ball no one's hiding behind.

Kennedy

I picked a stadium because games have rules and governments pretend to. Thought it might keep us honest.

Castro

Games end. Power doesn't. But fine—home or away?

Kennedy

Neutral ground. No crowd for either of us.

Castro

There is always a crowd. They simply cannot afford the ticket.

The infield swallows a small breeze. The ball doesn't move.

Kennedy

Let's not decorate the first question. Bay of Pigs was on me the day I signed. I inherited the plan and still owned the failure. Men went in with hope and came home with new names. That's on me.

Castro

Good. We begin where the bodies begin. Your failure fed our certainty. It told my island the empire still bleeds. We hung their rifles in museums and I gave speeches without mercy.

Kennedy

And firing squads?

Castro

Revolutions are surgeries, not parades.

Kennedy

Surgery should leave the patient alive.

Castro

So many of mine were not allowed to live at all. How clean would you like me to remember it?

Kennedy

Clean isn't the goal. True is.

The radio tower blinks again, like it refuses to miss a beat that isn't music.

Kennedy

Missiles then. The crisis swallowed October and half my sleep. I chose a blockade because an airstrike sounded like bravery and smelled like a funeral. We walked a thin rail between war and humiliation.

Castro

You call it a blockade. I call it a noose tied with law. We were prepared to die rather than kneel.

Kennedy

I read your letter to Khrushchev. The one that said if we were invaded you'd consider the unthinkable.

Castro

I did not write it to be framed.

Kennedy

Neither did he. We answered the softer letter because it left room for daylight. We all pretended there was only one.

Castro

Backchannels. Your favorite theater. Men with notes in their pockets pretending to be history's hands.

Kennedy

Backchannels kept children alive. That is not theater. That is plumbing.

Castro

Plumbing that flooded my island for decades after your ships turned back.

Kennedy

Then call it what you want. It worked.

Narrator (V.O.)

History doesn't clap for plumbers, but leaks drown cities. Call it plumbing if that keeps kids alive.

Castro

You speak of children. Mine learned to read under a roof that would not have existed without a revolution. A poor country stood up. Clinics where there were none. Fields that fed more than owners. You call it propaganda. I call it a ledger.

Kennedy

And in that ledger: prisons, UMAP camps, the poet who cannot read his poem without permission.

Castro

Poets have survived jailers with less poetry than mine.

Kennedy

That sentence sounds good in a room without bars.

Castro

And yours—sounds good in a room without bombs. We both have rooms.

Kennedy

I won't argue that. I will argue this: a free press is how a country learns it is lying to itself.

Castro

A free press is how a rich country launders power and calls the paper trail a virtue.

Kennedy

Sometimes. Often. And yet, it gives the poor a page to write on without asking permission.

The lights hum louder for a breath, then settle like they heard something they remember.

Castro

Tell me the weight, John. Not the policy. The weight.

Kennedy

All right. You want the weight? It's waking up knowing one phrase misheard on a cable could turn cities into ash. The weight is deciding whether the next plane is a warning or the first shot. The weight is Jackie asking what time I'll be home and me saying "soon" without knowing if soon exists.

Castro

I carried other weights. A country that wanted miracles and a sea that wanted me drowned. I slept with a gun and a dictionary. I learned to preach in numbers and hide in statistics. Loneliness makes loud men louder. I became a statue before I died and then had to live with it.

Kennedy

Statues are bad listeners.

Castro

So are presidents.

Kennedy

Touché.

Somewhere behind left field, a dog barks twice and gives up.

Kennedy

Let's talk about the thing that would've saved lives if we'd been better men. We could have met. Quietly. Let Bobby carry a message that wasn't a dare.

Castro

I would have come. But you sent other visitors. Your intelligence officers treated my island like a puzzle that made them feel clever. Assassinations disguised as bad luck.

Kennedy

I'm not going to pretend I didn't know. Some of that happened while I wore the suit. Some of it before. Some after. I don't forgive it by calling it complicated. I name it ugly and keep going.

Castro

Good. I prefer ugly I can see. It wastes less time.

Kennedy

We almost did something decent anyway. Prisoner exchanges. Doctors. Baseball teams touring both ways. Do you know how many fights a nine-inning conversation can prevent?

Castro

Baseball is not neutral in Havana. It is a hymn. But yes. A shortstop can change a flag faster than a speech on a bad day.

Kennedy

Then why didn't we try harder?

Castro

Because you loved your exiles and I loved my certainty. That is an honest pair of chains.

Kennedy

You're not wrong.

The ball on the plate looks smaller the longer they talk, the way guilt does when you finally name it.

Castro

Your country taught me something cruel: humiliation explains more of your policy than any official philosophy ever did. We were humiliated for a century. We chose a story that let us look in the mirror.

Kennedy

Humiliation writes bad laws in my country too. We call it security and pass a budget.

Castro

And I call it vigilance and pass a sentence.

Kennedy

Here is the fear I never said into a microphone: I worried about my generals almost as much as I worried about yours. Men who wanted to trade boys for posture.

Castro

I worried about my own purity police: the ones who preferred hunger with pride over bread with concession. Pride is a cheap cook. It fills the room with smell and still leaves you empty anyway.

Kennedy

That's a good line.

Castro

It is a true one. Keep it if you like.

Kennedy

I'll pay you with a confession. I thought about 1964 as a second chance to do the slow work: diplomacy that doesn't make the poster. I did not get the year.

Castro

You died before your contradictions did. That is a kind of mercy.

Kennedy

Sometimes I think so.

The scoreboard's one live bulb blinks again, patient as a heartbeat that refuses to be poetic.

Castro

Your turn to accuse. You've circled the cage long enough.

Kennedy

All right. You jailed dissent you called counterrevolutionary when you meant inconvenient. You told the world it was necessary and sometimes it was just safer.

Castro

Yes.

Kennedy

You ran camps that broke men and called it work.

Castro

Yes.

Kennedy

You let the revolution swallow people it promised to feed.

Castro

Yes. Do you want a speech or an answer?

Kennedy

Just the yes. It's heavy enough.

Castro

Your turn.

Kennedy

I starved families with policy and called it leverage. I green-lit plans I would not have admitted in a debate. I learned how fast a principle makes room for an exception once the brief gets thick enough. And I smiled for cameras so no one had to see the cost.

Castro

We have very fine mirrors tonight.

Kennedy

We do.

The fan in the press box finally stops. The quiet that follows is less noble than expected, more useful.

Kennedy

If we had met, really met, perhaps we could have written rules for leaving each other alone without pretending it was love.

Castro

Perhaps. But you would have needed to disappoint Miami, and I would have needed to disappoint men who thought they were the revolution simply because they were angry.

Kennedy

I disappointed many. Not enough of the right ones.

Castro

Same.

Kennedy

There is one more reckoning neither of us can avoid. Your people who fled. Their grief is a hard country. It sits in my cities and asks me to explain you. I do not do it well.

Castro

Exile's a tax nations levy on themselves when they can't keep their own promises. I cannot ask their forgiveness in a stadium. I can say their names out loud and stop pretending they do not exist. I did not do that enough.

Kennedy

Say one now.

Castro

There are too many. Choosing would be theater. I will say this instead: I have signed papers that taste like metal in my mouth years later. That is how I remember them.

Wind finally moves across the infield and does nothing helpful.

Kennedy

We should leave one thing small and practical behind. Not a doctrine. A rule a human can use.

Castro

Very well. Mine: Do not let humiliation write your policy. It is a poet with a knife.

Kennedy

Mine? If your plan only works after you erase people, it doesn't work.

Castro

Those rules will never shake hands, but they can at least nod.

Kennedy

I'll take it.

They sit without language for a stretch that feels like medicine doing its slow job.

Castro

Before you go, tell me something I cannot get from your tapes.

Kennedy

My back hurt all the time. It made me patient with other people's pain and impatient with their excuses. I do not recommend the method.

Castro

And I slept better on a cot than in a palace. The cot did not expect a speech.

Kennedy

The palace always does.

Castro

One more thing. Baseball. You brought it for a reason.

Kennedy

Because someone has to pick up the ball. Otherwise we stare at it and call that history.

Castro

Pick it up, then.

Kennedy

You sure?

Castro

If you throw it, I won't pretend it is a treaty.

Kennedy

Fair.

He walks to the plate, bends like it costs him, and lifts the scuffed ball. The leather is tired; the seams hold.

Kennedy

Fast one or slow?

Castro

Slow. Let the island see it coming.

Kennedy

All right.

He lobs. It arcs, honest and unambitious. Castro catches it clean and does not smile.

Kennedy

Back home they'd boo me out of Fenway for that pitch.

Castro

Again?

Kennedy

No. Once is mercy.

Castro

Agreed.

Narrator (V.O.)

This is the kind of moment power keeps private: too human for speeches, too quiet for monuments. Outside, a car horn coughs twice. The night crew hoses down a block no one will notice in the morning. Somewhere, a girl practices scales and a neighbor files a complaint. Both are right enough for their rooms.

Castro

You want more than rules and confessions. You want a story your country can live with.

Kennedy

I want a story that leaves fewer names off the credits.

Castro

Then listen. Isabel and Raúl. Sister and brother. She left on an afternoon that tasted like salt. He stayed because leaving felt like failing the dead. She teaches in Miami. He manages a warehouse that used to be a church. They talk on the phone when the lines behave.

She sends photos of her boy in a uniform that is not a uniform. He sends a picture of bread that does not need a ration card. They both say "home" and both mean two rooms.

Kennedy

I know that family. Different names. Same ache.

Castro

I told myself I was building a place where they would not need the other room. I told myself exile was a fever that would break. I kept telling it while the thermometer broke in my hand. I should have said their names more. Out loud. In speeches that didn't need them, so that I would.

Kennedy

I should have visited her classroom instead of her headline. The way we build policy around silhouettes and call that empathy. There's a sin there we don't bother to name because it doesn't smoke.

Castro

Name it now.

Kennedy

Cowardice with paperwork.

Castro

Good. Keep the words cheap and the cost high. That is the only exchange rate that ever stays honest.

The scoreboard bulb blinks, then finally burns out. The darkness is even, which is not the same as kind.

Kennedy

What would you have me tell your people who left?

Castro

Tell them I did not love them less for leaving. Tell them I loved my story more than I should have. Tell them I learned too late that a revolution cannot ask people to be a chorus forever. Some want a chair and a quiet dinner. That is not treason; it is Tuesday.

Kennedy

And your people who stayed? What do I tell them about me?

Castro

Tell them you were a man who tried to keep his country from choosing panic. Tell them you failed and you tried again. They will understand the second part better than the first.

Kennedy

I can live with that.

Castro

You cannot. But it will live without you.

Kennedy

Touché again.

The outfield holds its shape just long enough to be remembered correctly.

Kennedy

There's a smaller thing I never asked in public because it would have sounded like flirting. What do you love about your island when no one is looking?

Castro

Street baseball at dusk when the ball is taped and the bat is a broom handle and no one keeps a score that can ruin a boy's night. A guava sold slightly underripe because the vendor trusts time to finish the job. A grandmother who lies about how long her recipe takes because she wants you to stay. You?

Kennedy

The same things in other places. A dock hand who knows the weight of a coil without looking. A cop who forgives a broken taillight because the kid's tie is wrong in a way that means he tried. A choir that hits the harmony on accident and pretends it didn't.

Castro

You want to be ordinary.

Kennedy

Sometimes. The country keeps interrupting.

Castro

Mine too.

Kennedy

We're drifting. It's not a sin. It's a sign we are human again for a minute.

Castro

Then drift once more. Ask the question you asked yourself in Dallas before the crowds, before the flowers and the banners and the last corner you turned.

Kennedy

Did the job make me a better man or just a better liar?

Castro

Answer it.

Kennedy

Both. I learned truth at a speed that bruised me, and I learned concealment to keep the room from panicking. I do not know if the averages favor me.

Castro

The averages do not save anyone. But they let widows buy bread while they wait for the monument. That has to count for something even if we don't like what.

Kennedy

And you? What question rises when the guards are tired and the speech is over and the hallway is empty?

Castro

Did I use the people to build the revolution or use the revolution to serve the people?

Kennedy

And the answer?

Castro

On the best days the second. Too many days the first. I trust the ones who will read our names to do the math more honestly than we did.

Kennedy

They'll still get it wrong.

Castro

Of course. The living always insult the dead by tidying them up.

Kennedy

Try not to laugh when they do it to you.

Castro

I will fail at that too.

The taxi beyond center field coughs back to life, rolls forward, and stops again like a thought that changed its mind.

Kennedy

One last exchange before the lights forget us. If you could return one thing you took, what would it be?

Castro

Time. That is impossible. So the second-best answer is voice. I would return voices I filed away under security. Some would sing against me; some would sing past me. A nation needs that noise. What would you return?

Kennedy

A year. 1964. Not for the election. For the after. I wanted to learn how to be patient without being slow. There is a difference my office didn't teach quickly enough.

Castro

If you had the year, what would you have done first?

Kennedy

I would have asked for a small trade. Doctors for prisoners. A scholarship fund named for no one. Quiet money to keep families together while the loud men argued. All the unphotographed things that build trust because they lack a ribbon to cut.

Castro

That's how real doors open—with keys nobody claps for.

Kennedy

Write that down for them. They will forget otherwise.

Castro

They will forget anyway. Forgetting is how nations sleep. Waking up is how they earn their breakfast.

Kennedy

You are more of a poet than you pretend.

Castro

Do not punish me with that label. Poets remember too much.

Kennedy

We need a finish that is not a bow. Just an agreed truth we can walk out beside.

Castro

Truth: I will always fear humiliation. It stains worse than blood. I will build too many walls to avoid it if I am not watched.

Kennedy

Truth: I will always be tempted by elegant solutions that break real people. I will call them strategic because the word is clean.

Castro

Then let them watch me for the first and you for the second. Let them write it down. Let them bring it to the stadium at night and see if it still sounds brave when the seats are empty.

Kennedy

And let them pick up the ball.

Castro

Yes. Once is mercy. Twice is habit.

Kennedy

We'll leave it at once, then.

Castro

We will.

They do not shake hands. They do not pose. The lights cut one bank at a time until the stadium becomes a rumor with chairs. The radio tower keeps blinking because that is its job.

Narrator (V.O.)

Games end; governments pretend not to. The ball stays where it is, waiting for whoever shows up next with rules and a conscience. One blink at a time, the tower keeps watch. So should we.

ACT V

FIRE AND MEMORY

Where the fight never ended

If power builds monuments, resistance scratches its name into the stone. This section belongs to people the world tried to shove off the page and failed. Their words don't pretty the wound up. They drag it into the light and dare us not to flinch.

Maya Angelou and Harriet Tubman share a stage, poetry and footsteps woven together. One carried words that lifted, the other carried bodies through the night toward freedom. Together they make it clear survival isn't luck; it's a route you lay down one dangerous trip at a time.

Abraham Lincoln and Martin Luther King Jr. sit centuries apart chasing the same promise. One signed proclamations, the other stood under Lincoln's stone gaze and described a country that didn't exist yet. The line between them doesn't bend on its own; people drag it forward, often knowing they won't live long enough to walk it.

Malcolm X collides with Nathan Bedford Forrest, flint meeting steel. It doesn't sound like a debate; it sounds like the country shouting in two different directions at once. One man insists on dignity, the other on domination. Sparks fly because only one of those can survive in the same country.

James Baldwin and Anne Frank compare notes across silence, both writing in rooms the world would have preferred not to see. Their pairing shouldn't work, yet it does, because the same kind of cruelty won't stop coming back in different coats and titles. In their pages, grief stops being private and starts pointing at what happened.

And finally, Nelson Mandela and Princess Diana. A statesman who survived a cell, a princess who survived a camera. Both marked by power, both still stubborn enough to answer with care. Put their voices together and you start to suspect that tenderness, used right, can move more than rage ever does.

Resistance isn't always loud. Sometimes it's a sentence, a path, or a remembered life that refuses to disappear. The mark it leaves outlives most monuments, especially the ones built to pretend the memory never mattered.

Chapter 21

Maya Angelou – Harriet Tubman: *Still I Rise—Still We Run*

ACT V: Fire and Memory

Dr. Maya Angelou (1928–2014)

Poet, memoirist, performer, and teacher who turned private trauma into public strength. From *Caged Bird* to an inaugural podium, she built sentences that carried steel and sunlight in the same line. She acted, organized, recorded albums, and gave crowds a language that could hold them without lying. Honors piled up; the point stayed simple: dignity for the bruised parts of America, practiced aloud. Her signature wasn't inspiration. It was craft: make room, make rhythm, make the hard feel sayable. People stood taller because the words fit their backs.

Harriet Tubman (c. 1822–1913)

Conductor on the Underground Railroad, Union scout and spy, and stubborn builder of other people's mornings. Born enslaved, she freed herself, then kept returning, dozens guided north under stars, passwords, and nerve. "Moses" wasn't myth. It was logistics, prayer, and maps in the sky. She helped lead the Combahee River Raid and later fought for veterans and women's rights. Small in frame, immense in courage, she treated freedom as a route you carry, not a room you hide in. The legend says fearless; she says fear rode with her, and she kept the reins.

Setting

In a church basement that doubles as a station, folding chairs face a slate dusted with last week's lesson. Lanterns wait on a scarred table; a county map glows where fingers traced the same route too often. Worn boots and a shawl stand by the stairs like a period you can't argue with. A hymnbook lies open, corners smudged. The back door opens to a lane that keeps secrets. Down here courage is practical: knocked rhythms, quick answers, and coffee that forgives being burned.

Narrator (V.O.)

This is a conversation between a woman who turned breath into trumpet and a woman who turned breath into running. One built a staircase of syllables out of a brutal childhood silence. The other learned the forest's grammar: bark, water, starlight. Because maps were for people who already had names. If they are saints in your mind, sand them back down. Saints don't sweat. These two did.

Angelou

Sister Harriet, I owe my every breath to the one you took running. You made the air taste different for all of us. Tell me, when you first stood on free ground, what did your soul say?

Tubman

It said, *breathe, girl.* And for the first time, the air didn't belong to anybody else. I looked down at my hands, these same hands that once fed another woman's table, and I told 'em, *You're mine now.* But I didn't sit long with the feeling. Too many still chained behind me. Freedom that only fits one body is a blessing half-spent.

Angelou

And you went back. Again and again. Most folks touch light and never risk the shadows again. What did you know that the rest of us keep forgetting?

Tubman A

That freedom ain't a place you hide in; it's a road you carry. If I was alone with it, then I was just comfortable, not free. I heard people prayin' into quilts, sighin' to keep the hounds from hearin'. I had visions, call 'em seizures, call 'em God, I followed what I was shown. I swore to the Lord I wouldn't leave a soul that I could carry. If strength ran out, I asked for a bigger spoon.

Angelou

Some days the work isn't sprinting. It's balance. The world shakes the beam and calls it natural law, and still you breathe, set your heel, and stick the landing. Not for judges. For the children who need to cross after you. Sister Harriet, the legend says fearless. What did fear teach you?

Tubman

How to shut my mouth and open my ears. Trees tell you things if you don't argue. Water has opinions about crossing. Stars will talk if you stop naming them and start listening. Fear pointed, not away, but through. Don't pretend it's not in the room; seat it by the door, keep it where you can see it. That's how I stayed alive, and how I kept others alive.

Narrator (V.O.)

When she says "fear," she delivers it without perfume. Not as a dragon to be slayed but as a fussy uncle you seat by the exit. The room loosens. Angelou's shoulders drop a quarter inch, the way a singer drops her jaw to hit the note without cracking.

Angelou

Sister, I wrote about cages because silence was a kind of bar. But chains can be soft. They come dressed in salaries, in policies, in a voice that says wait just a little while longer. When you say "freedom," what are you pointing at?

Tubman

The right to tell your own body what to do. The right to rest when you tired. To love who you love without a map hung 'round your neck. Papers don't mean nothin' if a man still owns your time. You can be outside the plantation and still be plowin' for somebody else's harvest. Freedom ain't a fence or a deed. It's authority.

Angelou

Authority. I like the taste of that word today. Tell me what you see when you stare across this century from where you came from. Does it look like progress, or practice laps?

Tubman

Both. I seen a Black man in a White House; I also seen Black boys on the ground with cameras pointing at 'em like witnesses that forgot how to speak. You got buses that run without horses and phones that pull voices out of the air, but a law can still be a whip if the hand holdin' it is the same. Some days I think we traded iron for paper. Folks keep tryin' to spell "free" with somebody else's tongue.

Angelou

I am a woman who once chose silence so the world would feel the weight of what it had done to me. I did not speak for years because I believed my voice had killed a man. Later, I learned survival is a louder instrument. But there are days I want to close the piano and go home. What do we say to the young who are tired before they've even had their coffee?

Tubman

Tell 'em the coffee ain't the point. You scream, you vote, you march, you do every soft and every loud thing you can. And then, if none of that works, you do it again. People say patience to you like it's a prayer. Sometimes patience is a lullaby for the jailer. I ain't say be reckless. I'm sayin' don't mistake quiet for holy. If I had stopped when I was hungry, you and me wouldn't be sittin' here company.

Angelou

You will forgive me if I push, Sister Harriet. I am a woman who has had words used as a weapon and as bread. There is a risk to heat, too. One broken window becomes a chorus for people who never wanted to listen in the first place. Where is the line between holy fire and house fire?

Tubman

The line is in the why. Burnin' to be seen ain't the same as burnin' a path. You ain't got to torch your own kitchen to prove the food is hot. But I know this: folks who fret about windows usually forgot who's inside. I got no patience for a sermon on decorum while a mama is buryin' her baby. Forgive me if that sounds hard; life made me that way. I bent so the ones behind me could stand up straight.

Narrator (V.O.)

There it is. Not a schism, exactly, but a clash of cymbals. The poet has spent a lifetime massaging thunder into something that can be sung in a church and taught in a school. The conductor of night trains is not much interested in curriculum. You can hear the difference in their verbs: Maya wants to speak and to gather; Harriet wants to move and to take.

Angelou

I hear you. And I know the cost of the soft methods, because soft does not mean painless. I wrote and organized and watched leaders I loved die in April and February. Some nights, I resented God's calendar. There is a calendar in me—every square a funeral with a speech, and sometimes the speech felt obscene. I do not wear patience like a blister. Does that count?

Tubman

It counts. You ain't got to apologize for livin' through the way you were given. Your pen might be a lantern; mine was a pistol when it had to be, and a hymn when even a pistol begged mercy. Sometimes I wish I could've talked more and shot less. But I didn't live in a time that asked. I lived in a time that demanded. And even then I was scared. People write me like I was granite. Honey, granite don't wake up to gunfire and keep walkin'. Fear rode with me. I just kept the reins.

Angelou

Thank you for admitting fear. The statues we build refuse to sweat. I sweated over lines you think rolled out of me like thunder. Half my poems I dashed off out of a wound that wouldn't close; the other half I polished until the floor beneath my desk knew the shape of my pacing. I missed as often as I hit. I once tried to compare hope to a coat rack—it did not hang right.

Tubman

A coat rack? That's a poor man's ladder. But I get it. I once told a girl to walk like a leaf and she near fell in a creek tryin' to be poetic about it. Walk like yourself, I told her. She still got away. Sometimes God asks for poetry; sometimes He asks for shoes that don't squeak.

Narrator (V.O.)

They laugh, and it doesn't erase anything, but it sands an edge. The air itself seems to steady, as if the room has chosen a key and decided to hold it. Nothing interrupts. You don't stop thunder to rearrange the furniture.

Angelou

Sister Harriet, we have not talked of your wound: the blow to your head as a child, the visions, the lost time. People paper that over like wallpaper, pretty but dishonest. What did it mean to move through the world with lightning on your brain?

Tubman

It meant the day had cracks in it. I could fall into sleep with my eyes open, like God cut the cord to the lamp and said hush. I saw things: rivers in places there weren't any, faces where the woods should be alone. Doctors would've called it one thing; I called it instruction when it kept us alive. I ain't say every vision was holy. But some nights the path lit itself, like the stars had lowered an inch to help me see. If you got a wound that sings, you learn the tune.

Angelou

And you composed with it. I am thinking of the Combahee River, of you leading that raid: boats, rice fields, a quiet night torn open. Those men followed a woman who had already carried the night on her back for years. Did the army understand who you were?

Tubman

The army understood what I could do. Men understand utility before they understand miracles. I was a scout, a nurse, a cook—whatever the day demanded. That night at Combahee, the water smelled like a promise and a swamp at the same time. We freed over seven hundred souls. Lord, if I had been made of marble, I would've sunk. I was made of bone and prayer; we floated.

Angelou

When I was a girl, I did not speak for years. A man hurt me and then died, and I thought my words had killed him. Silence felt like a law I'd signed with my blood. Later, I decided that if my voice could kill, it ought to be strong enough to resurrect. But the silence is still in there. It returns on bad weather days and in hotel rooms. Do you have ghosts that keep your schedule for you?

Tubman

I got names I couldn't carry. Nights I turned back because a baby's cry would've fed a hound an address. I can tell you the shape of a tree I left somebody under while we waited for the moon to move. We did not lose all of 'em. But I hear every one we did. I ain't ask God to take the guilt; I asked Him to lend me shoulders big enough to walk under it.

Angelou

That is the bravest sentence I've heard in years. And now I will be impolite: I want you to challenge me. I want you to say the thing about art I don't want to hear.

Tubman

Since you asked: sometimes poems get framed while people get buried. Sometimes a speech is a dress rehearsal for a march that shouldn't need a dress at all. I ain't down on art. You've held more people together with a stanza than a congressman ever did with a handshake. But promise me this: when you see a law masqueradin' as a mercy, tear it off the wall, not just the corner. Words can be a knife. Don't be afraid to cut.

Angelou

I receive that. Now I will be impolite in return: sometimes war becomes a muscle, and when the enemy leaves, the arm keeps swinging. Violence breeds an appetite that lies. It says there is always one more link to break, and then we will rest. But it forgets the appetite is part of the chain.

Promise me this: when the door opens, don't kick the next one just because your foot learned joy the hard way.

Tubman

I promise to set the foot down when the door truly opens. But I ain't apologizin' for kickin' doors that pretend to be a sky. We don't owe courtesy to a lock.

Narrator (V.O.)

They are not bickering. They are testing the fence: where it's wired, where it's rotten, which sections need a bolt cutter and which need a ladder. If you came for a tidy debate with polished lines, you misread the sign on the door. The sign says: bring shoes.

Angelou

Let's talk about faith without hymns for a moment. Not the Sunday kind, but the Wednesday night kind when the car won't start and the deadline is a rumor. What did faith look like when it was twelve degrees and your feet were wet?

Tubman

Like a blanket that's too small but still warm where it touches. Like sayin' a Psalm with your mouth closed so the snow don't carry it to a deputy. Like tellin' a boy that the stars are friendly even when you know clouds are comin'. I ain't sellin' a pretty faith. Mine was a faith with blisters. But it moved. And it made fear sit down for a while so hope could run point.

Angelou

You will have noticed by now the faint hum in the room. It's nervous—so am I. I have watched people need a happy ending like oxygen. They clap at the bow even when the play dies on the floor. We both know endings are usually just corners. How do you end a night that started two hundred years ago and hasn't slept?

Tubman

You don't. You tuck it in and take the next watch. You tell the ones after you where the dogs like to drink and where the fences lean. You say the password. Not the fancy one, the true one: keep goin'.

Angelou

Keep going. I've sold that as a benediction and also muttered it like a swear word into a motel pillow. Here is a thing I never say on stage: I wrote some lines because I was lonely and I wanted a stranger to nod at me. The revolution is needy sometimes. It asks to be seen too. If the work is a prayer, it is also a plea.

Tubman

A plea ain't a sin. The Psalms are full of 'em. You think God don't know when you are bargaining? He's heard better lawyers. I bargained every time I went back. Lord, one more trip and I'll rest. I lied to Him; He knew. He let me lie so I could keep movin'. Truth is a destination as much as a command.

Narrator (V.O.)

If you require your heroes to be tidy, you have misfiled your heroes with your towels. These two confess, and the floor does not open. It holds. The chair creaks like an amen. The hum, inexplicably, softens. Probably the board operator fixed it, but the story prefers to think the room decided to listen.

Angelou

Sister Harriet, I want you to speak to a child listening on a cracked phone in a bedroom that isn't quiet. She is twelve. She is brilliant. She is told her fury makes her unlovable. What do you say to save her from a softness that would smother?

Tubman

Baby, you were born free. Don't let nothin' convince you otherwise. Your blood has survived ships and whips and men who thought your voice was a curtain they could draw. You ain't broken. You forged. If they build a wall and say be grateful for the shade, you take a spoon to its foot or climb where the bricks forgot their mortar. You hear me? Don't you stay in chains they painted gold.

Angelou

To the same child, I add this: people will teach you to fold yourself like a napkin and call it manners. You may fold for dinner. Do not fold for history. The world is sloppy; be exacting anyway. Some mornings your courage will smell like coffee, and some nights it will smell like cold sweat. Either way, drink it. And when your voice shakes, let it. Trembling does not disqualify truth.

Tubman

Tell her, too, that friends matter. I walked alone sometimes, but I was never alone. There were conductors and station masters and women who sewed secrets into hems. Ask for help before pride makes the request smaller than it needs to be. Pride is a poor lock; it keeps allies out and lets enemies in.

Angelou

We have asked a great deal of the listener. Let us pay them with honesty about regret. If regret were a country, I would have two citizenships. Is there a night you would take back if time weren't so stubborn?

Tubman

I'd take back a night near Poplar Neck when a man turned his whole body into fear, and I had to decide between hushin' him and losin' a dozen others. I chose the dozen. He made it, but I can still hear what almost happened. Regret is a teacher who likes to assign homework no one can finish. I bring it apples; it still gives me work.

Angelou

I regret not calling a friend the day before he died. I regret pretending to be fine so well that the people who loved me believed me. I regret metaphors that became pretty lies. But I do not regret the poem that embarrassed me into becoming better. Sometimes your worst draft is the floor you stand on tomorrow. If the sentence is humble, it will let you climb it.

Tubman

You talk like a woman who has carried shame and knows its weight. Shame is a sack with a hole; you pour your life into it and it still never fills. I don't carry it now. I carry memory. Memory hurts cleaner.

Narrator (V.O.)

If you have been waiting for the moment when they break, it is here, except breaking is wrong. They don't break; they deepen. The trick of television is to pretend depth can be measured with a stopwatch. The trick of lives like these is that time is a sloppy archivist and a pretty bad therapist. You learn to keep the good pages.

Angelou

Sister Harriet, I am feeling impertinent. Do you ever get angry with God?

Tubman

Oh, baby. Not the polite kind of angry neither. I told Him He sent me out without enough light; He told me He'd given me stars. I told Him I was tired of bein' brave; He told me brave didn't mean not scared. It meant keep goin' scared. We fussed. He won. I got what I needed, not what I asked.

Angelou

I have shouted at God, too. Then I wrote Him letters and mailed them to people who needed them more. I have found Him in the oddest places: hotel ice machines, Greyhound terminals, a smile on a janitor's face that could hold a city. If He is not everywhere, He is at least not picky. He shows up to bad metaphors and forgives them.

Tubman

Then He'll forgive mine. I once told a boy the river was a door. He looked at me like I'd grown moss. I said, doors ain't always wood. Sometimes they're water that's too cold but still passable. He said, I can't swim. I said, baby, neither can fear. And then we walked.

Angelou

If the world needs a benediction, give it one; if it needs a dare, give it that. We have given them both tonight, I think. Will you leave us with a sentence that knows it is not the last word?

Tubman

Take who you can and go. If you can't take 'em, teach 'em the trail. If you can't teach 'em, leave bread crumbs your enemies think are nothin'. They'll be somethin' in the right hands. And when you reach a place that feels like breath you own, don't build a fence before you've built a door.

Angelou

I will leave you with a repetition, because repetition is how we stitch wounds shut enough to walk: still I rise is not a boast. It is an inventory. It is me counting what's left after the fire: the spoon, the song, the stubborn. If I rise tomorrow with less, I will count again. If I rise with more, I will share the excess like bread at the back door.

Narrator (V.O.)

Two women sit with all their centuries, and for a second they are only women: one with a brain that learned to carry lightning without burning down the house, the other with a throat that learned to turn lightning into music. If you want a curtain line, you may have this: holiness is not a removal of dirt; it is the decision to keep walking with the dirt and still make something worth touching.

Angelou

Sister Harriet, are we closer?

Tubman

Closer ain't there. The chains ain't iron, but they still try to catch your mind. The laws changed their names; some hearts ain't learned new language yet. Work remains. But look at the road behind us, and then tell me you don't know how to keep steppin'.

Angelou

Then we keep stepping. I will call it a march when the streets are crowded and an errand when they are not. I will call it a poem when it sings and a list when it doesn't. Either way, it is movement. Either way, it is breath.

Tubman

Either way, child, it's ours.

Narrator (V.O.)

The handshake passes weight like movers trading corners of a piano. Outside, the air is the same as before, which is the point and the problem. Inside, two chairs sit, warm where they were, cooling at the pace of honest wood.

And still—like dust—we rise. And still, like breath, we run.

Chapter 22

Martin Luther King Jr. – Abraham Lincoln: *The Long Arc*

ACT V: Fire and Memory

Dr. Martin Luther King Jr. (1929–1968)

Baptist pastor who turned nonviolence into strategy and sermons into marching orders. Boycotts, bridges, jailhouse letters. He made a nation hear itself and then answer. Nobel at thirty-five; murdered at thirty-nine. Not a saint in marble, a planner in motion: coalition, discipline, and moral clarity under fatigue. His dream wasn't a bedtime story; it was a civic schedule. He asked the country to love with its laws, not just its language, and kept asking when danger made that request sound unreasonable. The arc didn't bend by accident. He pushed.

President Abraham Lincoln (1809–1865)

Self-taught lawyer who carried a fractured republic through civil war and toward emancipation. He wrote prose that sounded like scripture because it served policy, not performance. Melancholy without self-pity, patient without paralysis, he chose cadence when swagger was cheap and mercy when victory could have been mean. Days after Appomattox, he was shot and became both martyr and mirror. His sentences still work because they hold power without vanity and sorrow without pose: government as duty, paid for by ordinary people who would live with the bill.

Setting

In a small hall with borrowed dignity, pews remember weight and the lectern remembers spit and grace. A quill waits in a glass case like work at rest; a nave candle guttered, then steadied, the wax keeping score. If you listen, a train passes. Two chairs face the aisle, not the altar. The flag stands because leaving it out would have been louder. Programs from some old event pretend it's still today. The air carries dust and hymn. This room is ready for sentences that mean it.

Narrator (V.O.)

History tells itself with clean edges; people do not. The nineteenth century gave us a lawyer who kept a nation from splitting by cutting something rotted out of its center. The twentieth gave us a preacher who refused to let that nation pretend the cutting was complete. Both men paid in the same currency. Bullets don't care for eras. They care for impact. Tonight, in this made-up slice of eternity, two chairs and a candle try to hold more truth than a monument.

King

President Lincoln, I don't think of you as a guest. I think of you as a man who still sits at the table of our unfinished work. You carried a war that tore the skin of this nation. I carried marches that showed the wound still open. Tonight, maybe we can speak plain about both.

Lincoln bows slightly. His large hands fold with a farm boy's awkwardness.

Lincoln

Dr. King, I'm honored. And humbled. I have wondered whether I belong at this table. Not in your century. Not in your struggle.

King

Belonging is measured in burdens carried, not calendars kept. You carried yours across fields where cotton and blood shared soil. You belong. Let's start where the schoolbooks start. They call you the Great Emancipator. Be plain with me: did you always believe slavery must end, or did the war force your hand?

Lincoln

I believed it must end, though I did not always believe I was the instrument appointed to end it. My first duty, as I understood it, was to keep the Union whole. A house with a cracked foundation is still a house to the people inside it. But as the war lengthened and the casualty lists built a second river across my desk, I realized the Union was not worth saving unless the rot was cut out. The war did not create my conviction; it dragged it into daylight where even I could not ignore it.

King

Conviction revealed is not the same as justice delivered. But you did deliver something real, and that matters. Let's talk about cost. What did freedom mean to you? Not in statute, but in marrow.

Lincoln

Freedom is dignity made lawful. The right to rise, yes, and the right to be left alone by the boot. Yet I feared we would call a man free and then leave him starving, hated, hunted. A proclamation can unfasten shackles; it cannot untie hatred. The law can reach a wrist quicker than it can reach a heart.

King

Still true. We changed the script, but left the stage tilted. When you signed that paper, did you believe it would work, or was it a signal flare to re-aim the war's meaning?

Lincoln

Both sword and signal. It freed no one in the loyal states, but it changed the war's core. It told Union soldiers they bled for more than borders. It told enslaved men and women that the tide had turned and their flight could be toward a cause, not merely away from a lash. It told foreign governments there was a moral here that cost public dignity to betray.

King

Symbols ignite. But absent reconstruction of law, purse, and spirit, they sputter. What frightened you more: division or silence?

Lincoln

Silence. A nation can survive disagreement; it cannot survive indifference. Division I could meet with arguments and armies. Silence is rot that turns beams to dust before a cannon ever fires. I feared a country that would stare at chains and whisper, this is fine.

King

Then you feared rightly. Apathy isn't silence. It's the choir singing while nothing changes. Tell me plain: what truth about race in America did you grasp that most white men in power did not?

Lincoln

That it was not a matter of policy but of wound: deep, generational, aching beneath every sermon and statute. My peers thought a neat stack of laws could tidy it away like tariffs. But wounds do not heal by statute. They require repentance and repair. Men in power rarely repent; they manage.

King

May they hear you now. May they do better than both of us.

Narrator (V.O.)

Textbook versions of these two are bronze men with polished edges. Useful for parades and bad documentaries. These aren't those men. One sat with Frederick Douglass, who could slice pretense clean in two. The other wrote from a jail cell to clergymen who feared disorder more than injustice. The subtext in both rooms was the same: polite people often ask the oppressed to be patient; this is a little like asking a man to wait for his lungs while he drowns.

Lincoln

Dr. King—

He clears his throat with a small smile that looks borrowed.

—if I may ask some questions?

Martin grins, honored by the gravity of the request.

King

Please. You once said we cannot escape history. Tonight, we hold it by the lapels.

Lincoln

You spoke your dream on a hot day in the capital and the air carried it farther than either of us can measure. Did you fear it would be misused, taken as a shield by those unwilling to look at the nightmare?

King

Every day. People quote my words about character over color like a magic spell to end complexity. Meanwhile, the machines grind: housing, wages, schools, prisons, steady as factory belts. A dream is not a lullaby; it's a demand letter. Quoting a man's dream while burying his demands is theft, sung in four-part harmony.

Lincoln

You said the moral arc bends toward justice. I have wondered: what bends it?

King

Pressure. Persistence. Pain. That arc isn't a rainbow in the sky; it's a trench dug by people who march, sit, bleed, and get up the next day. It bends because hands insist it does. Sometimes it snaps back and smacks your knuckles. You keep pulling.

Lincoln

In my time I sent men toward cannon fire because I believed a terrible calculus served a necessary cause. You preached love to men who spit on you. Tell me, was there never a day you wished to answer hate with hate?

King

Every morning. I am not marble. I am a man who buried friends and preached in sanctuaries that had just been bombed. Rage sat beside me, close enough to nudge my ribs. But I chose love not because I lacked rage, but because I feared what my rage would build. Violence feels righteous for a minute. Then it leaves nothing righteous standing.

Lincoln's eyes lower; a long pause.

Lincoln

I admire that discipline. I'm not certain I possessed it. I spoke as if I did. But privately, my hands shook.

King

We all tremble. We just don't print it on handbills.

Lincoln

You were called communist, radical, enemy to the peace of good citizens. Were you ever afraid the country would never be ready to hear you?

King

Readiness is a way people hide from responsibility. I didn't speak because they were ready; I spoke because silence would have killed me—and others. If people were ready, that was mercy. If not, the truth was. That had to be enough.

Lincoln

Then courage is measured not by applause, but by the thickness of the silence after you speak.

King

And by whether you keep going while it's still thick.

The candle gutters, throws a taller shadow, then steadies. There's a faint metallic smell old buildings exhale when the talk turns to war. The quill in the glass case seems to lean a fraction, like it's listening for verbs.

King

I'm going to be impolite, sir. Early in your presidency you entertained colonization: sending Black Americans elsewhere. Your thinking evolved, yes. But hear how that landed: to my people, it was eviction from the only home we've known, a home built by stolen hands.

Lincoln winces, then nods, unvarnished.

Lincoln

I did consider it. In the arithmetic of that hour, terrified that the whole machine might snap its axle, I reached for the wrong lever. Douglass rebuked me without ceremony. War makes men desperate; desperation makes fools of them. I learned, too slowly for the wounded, too late for many, but I learned.

King

Thank you for saying it plain. We get apologies so polished they slide off. Sometimes a man has to say, I was wrong, and let the words sit until the floor stops creaking.

Lincoln

Then let me be equally impolite. The movement you led, brave, just, walked into places where anger lit fires. Often it was outsiders who resented your presence; sometimes it was our own feverish country. Either way, streets burned. How did you weigh the cost for the shopkeeper whose livelihood vanished overnight?

King

I thought about that shopkeeper constantly. The line between righteous anger and destructive frenzy isn't painted on the pavement where you can see it coming. We taught nonviolence because it was moral and strategic. Because it saved lives in the long count and forced injustice into the light without letting the oppressor pick the terrain. Nonviolence isn't passivity; it's disciplined pain. Sometimes we failed. A spark in one alley could undo months of work. I grieved that, and I kept preaching because grief doesn't repair a roof.

Lincoln leans back; the chair complains in a wooden squeal.

Lincoln

Forgive the noise. This chair was built in a decade that hated comfort.

King

We do our best work in uncomfortable chairs.

Lincoln

Tell me about that day in Washington. The dream day. Did you know it would ring for decades?

King

No. I knew the crowd felt like the Mississippi put on shoes and came walking. I knew Mahalia's look that says, "tell them about the dream," and when a woman like that tells you to sing, you sing. I didn't know the words would be clipped into buttons, stripped of their demands, and sold back to schoolchildren as a bedtime story. So we keep waking them gently, again and again.

Lincoln

You carry it kindly. I wasn't always generous with my speeches. I rewrote until the ink looked tired. I keep thinking about that quill in the corner. Lately it scratches like a crow in my ear. Before a cemetery address I once felt I'd drafted a grocery list where a eulogy should be. Half my sentences sat like fence rails I'd hammered crooked. The next day those same sentences behaved like soldiers at inspection. The craft mocks you, then rescues you.

King

Half my sermons were like that. I dashed some off and people wept. I sweated over others and people smiled politely, the way you do at a painting of a ship you've never sailed. The craft keeps you honest; the crowd keeps you humble.

Narrator (V.O.)

Writers live in houses they built from sentences that sometimes won't hold a roof. The weight of a sentence isn't in its syllables, but in whether you can still look someone in the eyes after you let it fall. Between these two men stand dates and places: a boy in a White House bedroom growing suddenly still; four little girls in a church basement who never made it up the stairs; a theater balcony; a motel balcony. These are not metaphors. They are rooms where breath ended and history kept talking anyway.

King

Let's talk aftermath. You didn't live to see Reconstruction through. The nation had a chance to finish the work: citizenship, protection, land, and we traded it for a smaller peace. If you'd had more time, what would you have done?

Lincoln

I can't speak omnisciently across the river. But I'll be concrete: federal guarantees not bartered in smoke-filled rooms: protection of the person, protection of the vote, and something like land or credit and schooling so a man could stand upright in his own yard. I trusted too long in gentlemen who kept their honor in separate drawers. I would have governed more like your marchers: eyes forward, feet disciplined, pace steady—even when stones found the windows.

King

Stones keep finding windows. After we changed the laws, the map changed back. Poll taxes put on new clothes. School lines were drawn with bus routes instead of ropes. The water fountains lost their signs and kept their inequality. A man could vote in the morning and be priced out of housing by evening. When I turned toward poverty, toward wages and the war chewing our spirit, some who once cheered me began to mutter. Loving me was easier when I was an idea than when I was a budget line.

Lincoln

Metaphors limp when they must carry too many bodies.

King

That one lands. Keep it.

Lincoln

Tell me bluntly: did you resent the people who loved you loudly but listened softly? The ones who came for the dream and left before the debt collector knocked?

King

Sometimes. A pastor isn't supposed to say it, but yes, sometimes I walked off a stage and felt alone in a sea of amens. I wanted the amen to linger long enough to patch a school roof, to fix a courthouse ramp, to fund a clinic. I wanted them to stay for the budget meeting after the benediction. That's not poetic—just weary. Forgive it.

Lincoln

I won't. It needs no forgiveness. I know that loneliness. Crowds cheered like revival and I went home to newspapers that carved me with tidy paragraphs. I grew suspicious of boos and huzzahs both. Neither builds a bridge. Votes do. Appropriations do. Signatures at midnight do. There, I've slipped into the unromantic field of process. It lacks music, but it moves the plow.

King

We needed both plow and pulpit. Your pen and our feet. Some nights I worried I asked your successors for too much. Then I'd see a mother in the first pew holding a photograph of a son, swept into a cell like litter, and I'd know I'd asked for too little.

Narrator (V.O.)

We like to narrate history as blocks of stone: clean stacks, sharp corners. It's more like patchwork. Eras stitched by people who were late to dinner and early to funerals. Reconstruction didn't fail in a drumroll; it leaked. White sheets appeared. Polling places moved. The law blinked. Jim Crow arrived dressed in paperwork and municipal smiles.

Lincoln

Tell me about that letter from your jail. Not the lines schoolchildren memorize. The man writing them. What did the cell smell like?

King

Damp and ink and the breath of men who learned to sleep on hope because the mattresses were thin. I wrote because good clergymen told me to wait. They loved order more than justice. I don't insult them without remainder; I recognize the reflex in myself, the wish for clean calendars over clean consciences. But a man in a cell sees what the free refuse to notice. I wrote in the margins because the margins were what we were given.

Lincoln

I wish I could say I never loved order more than justice. I can't. I often loved quiet: the quiet of a room before decisions, the quiet of postponement. I mistook postponement for prudence. Prudence has backbone. Postponement wears slippers.

King laughs, then sobers.

King

Keep that line. It's not marble; it's human enough to squeak.

Lincoln

If you take my slippers, I must borrow your boots. We both know their weight.

King

On the heaviest days, my boots felt filled with stones and names. Names of children. Names of small towns where the sheriff's smile was cellar-cold. I'd preach about love, go home to a phone that wouldn't stop ringing—each ring an accusation from the world: do more, do better, do it now. Pastors aren't supposed to say this either, but some nights I wanted to hide in an empty church and let the dust preach to the pews.

Lincoln

And I wanted to bolt the White House door and crawl into bed with a book of jokes. Mary thought I read to distract myself, and I did, but sometimes laughter is the hinge that keeps a door from ripping off its frame.

King

Humor keeps us off the edge. I hope God laughs; otherwise the universe would creak itself to pieces.

Lincoln

If He does, I ask He laugh gently at me. I gave Him plenty of material.

The candle throws a thin ribbon of smoke. It looks like writing that forgot the alphabet. The quill in the case seems to tilt again; maybe a trick of light, maybe an editorial suggestion from a feathered ghost. The room has the intimacy of confession without a screen, of a bar where the bartender knows when not to wipe the counter.

King

People call me saint and traitor with the same mouth. They did then; they do now. It's strange to be mythologized by those who wouldn't have marched with me when it cost anything. How did you endure the way history wears your name?

Lincoln

Poorly, some days. I felt like a coat men put on when convenient and hung in a damp closet when the weather turned. If those who speak my name would practice one discipline, it'd be this: wash your hands first. Memory isn't a garment. It's a trust.

King

Amen. Memory as trust. Not marble you polish: story you keep honest.

Lincoln

Do you forgive the man who killed you?

King

I practice forgiveness like breathing: some days easy, some days tight. I forgive because I won't let a stranger's hatred be landlord of my spirit. I don't confuse forgiveness with forgetting. The people who loved me do not owe my timeline.

Lincoln

For me it was immediate and not. I didn't want to carry that man's rage into whatever comes after. And yet sometimes, if "after" has hours, I woke to a tilt in the room and forgave again. Not because he earned it, but because I needed it.

King

Then we agree forgiveness frees the forgiver first.

Lincoln

We do.

King

One more hard turn. Did you ever envy an ordinary life: someone who came home dusty from good work, ate supper without imagining troop positions between the peas and potatoes?

Lincoln

Every day. I envied the man who could finish a fence and see that it was good, who slept with the house quiet. I would have been restless in his bed. A calling is a neighbor who knocks at unreasonable hours.

King

Mine never stopped knocking. I'd be on the phone with a councilman whose patience retired in 1957 and hear a child in the background asking for water. I loved both voices. I couldn't serve them both to fullness. That failure followed me like a friendly dog that didn't know where home was.

Lincoln

We were husbands who made widows of our hours. Not poetic. Arithmetic. I owe Mary more evenings than exist. I suspect Coretta kept a list with the same tally.

King

She did. She still does, though the numbers sing now. Those who loved us also loved the work, even when it stole their quiet. That's a grace I don't deserve and gladly accept.

Lincoln

Then accept another: may your people remember you as a man who loved them more than his speeches, and may your speeches keep doing good after the applause goes home.

King

And may your people remember that practicality without conscience is just cowardice with a briefcase.

Lincoln laughs, really laughs, then dabs at one eye.

Lincoln

I accept the rebuke and the briefcase.

King

Before we close, a simple dare. What do you want said of you in one sentence?

Lincoln

He kept the house from falling and made room for those left on the porch.

King

He taught the house what love requires and kept knocking when they pretended not to be home.

Lincoln

That will do.

King

That will do.

Narrator (V.O.)

You want a thesis that ties up the cruel threads and leaves them looking like a braid. Sorry. The best we can do is watch two men breathe the same careful air and admit what they got wrong and what they'd still fight for. The nation they loved lurches forward: two steps, a trip, a hand on the rail, another step. The room isn't magic. The candle is only a candle. But they sat together. Sometimes the miracle isn't the speech. It's the sitting.

King

Before we let the candle go, a closing hope. Mine is simple: that those who have lost faith remember the promise was never perfection; it was possibility. We don't worship the nation; we test it. We don't abandon it; we rebuild it. And we teach our children that a dream isn't a spell that changes the world while they sleep. It's a chore list they inherit with love.

Lincoln

And mine: that the nation learns to weep before it wounds; that it counts citizens dearer than symbols; that freedom is kept as a trust, not flaunted as a trophy; that it finally becomes what it promised on parchment.

King

Then may they inherit good tools.

Lincoln

And a sturdy table that doesn't wobble when a hard subject leans on it.

King

We'll fold a tract under the bad leg. Just this once.

Lincoln

Just this once.

Narrator (V.O.)

If you insist on a moral, here's one stitched from what they left: laws matter, love matters, persistence matters, and the work will not be finished by the people who begin it. The rest is up to whoever finds the room after them. There will be a quill in the corner. It will scratch like an old hinge that needs oil. That sound is the sound of history asking for another page.

Chapter 23

Malcolm X – Nathan Bedford Forrest: *The Rifle and the Resolve*

ACT V: Fire and Memory

Malcolm X (1925–1965)

Street survivor turned minister who demanded Black dignity without apology and sharpened America's ear to the costs of respectability. He preached separation, then widened his vision after pilgrimage without softening its spine. His cadence was surgical, his anger disciplined. Assassinated at 39, he left behind an evolution as doctrine, proof that changing your mind in public is its own form of courage. He taught that the point of truth isn't comfort; it's clarity. His legacy still startles because it names what comfort forgets to see.

General Nathan Bedford Forrest (1821–1877)

Cavalry strategist who rose from slave trader to Confederate legend, then fell into infamy as the Klan's first Grand Wizard. Gifted tactician, catastrophic conscience. He proved that skill without morality becomes machinery for evil. He later claimed repentance, but the ledger stayed written in blood. History remembers him not for victories but for invention: of terror as policy. His name endures as warning, not honor, evidence that brilliance without decency builds nothing worth defending.

Setting

In a courthouse that promised neutrality but can't remember how, marble stairs shine from the wrong feet. A statue points nowhere useful; a Confederate flag hangs level behind glass. The air hums like a jury that hasn't decided. Rope stanchions draw polite lines around evidence pretending to be heritage. A folding chair sits uneven beside a pew someone miscounted. Scuffs on the floor keep returning no matter who scrubs. When voices rise, the dome returns them unedited, the way truth sometimes does.

Narrator (V.O.)

Put two Americas in one room and they argue the room's name. Heritage points at a monument; evidence points at a scar. They won't fix a century tonight. They're here because every time we "end" this argument, we only pause it. The most dangerous stories are not the ones we ban, but the ones we repeat so often they stop sounding like choices.

Malcolm looks at the empty chair across from him.

Malcolm X (V.O.)

When I was small, people in my town learned to lower their voices around dark corners. I learned early that you can tell the truth and still end up on the wrong side of a rope. They said my father fell under a streetcar. They said it like gravity had a motive. Funny thing: gravity didn't scribble the threats on our door. Gravity didn't burn our house. And when my mother began to bend under the weight of that kind of silence, the state called it guardianship. I call it what happens when a country mistakes trauma for policy. I'm not here to win a debate. I'm here to hold a mirror, and God help him if he mistakes it for a window.

He looks up. Door latch clicks.

Narrator (V.O.)

The door opens like a slow verdict. Nathan Bedford Forrest walks in with the calm of a man who assumes the deed is in his pocket. Boots with a cavalry memory. A coat easy on shoulders that once carried a saber and a sermon. He doesn't scan the room; he expects the room to have scanned him. He sits without a hand offered. The empty chair tilts at an old sound. Malcolm leans in.

Malcolm X

Nathan Bedford Forrest. Slave trader. Confederate general. Founder of men who turned hoods into sacraments. You didn't just fight a war. You franchised fear. I didn't ask you here to reminisce. I asked you to answer.

Forrest's smile reads as proof. Then he speaks with a strong southern drawl.

Forrest

Now you hold on, boy. I don't answer to a preacher with a mouth full of sermons. I fought for my people and my land. Not for hate. For order.

Malcolm

Order?

Forrest nods once.

Forrest

Before streets turned to jungles and boys started mistaking noise for courage. Before the flag got shamed by people who forgot who cut this country out of trees and swamp.

Malcolm

You didn't cut it. You chained it. You raped it. You branded it. You called it civilization because theft sounds so small.

Forrest

We brought civilization. Your kind was chasing spears in the bush. We gave you God. We gave you language.

Malcolm

You gave us chains and a Bible and told us to say grace for the gift.

Forrest

You're welcome.

The silence after that line steps forward and stands between them. It doesn't shout. It chooses its place and begins to press. Forrest smirks and finally sits in the empty chair.

Malcolm

You ordered Black men hanged without trial. You lit fires under bedroom windows. You taught boys to tie knots before they learned to write. Don't tell me war. Don't tell me law. Tell me the truth: you industrialized terror.

Forrest

War ain't polite. You want to win, you use what God gave you. We had land. We had law. We had the right to defend both.

Malcolm

The law said we were fractions. When you put a rope around a neck, how much of a man did you count?

Forrest

I counted threat. I counted rebellion where obedience was due. Natural order, son. That's what keeps a country from eating itself.

Malcolm

Your "natural order" was a whip with a Sunday schedule.

Forrest

And you'd trade order for chaos fast as a match. You want revolution. I wanted peace.

Malcolm

Peace built on submission isn't peace. That's terror wearing manners.

Forrest tilts his head with casual contempt.

Forrest

Men like you wouldn't have sat across from me in my time. You'd have known better. Or you'd have vanished.

Malcolm

I'm not across from you, General. I'm standing on the ashes you tried to sweep under history's rug.

Forrest

Ashes? All I see is a country chewing its own tongue. Statues toppled. Streets on fire. And men like me—legend.

Malcolm

No. You're curriculum. A case study in how power mistakes itself for virtue.

The air shortens its sentences. The room itself seems to lean closer, like a witness who can't pretend not to see anymore. Forrest sits easy, but it's the ease of a duelist confident at twenty paces. Malcolm's stillness is a different instrument. Less sword, more scalpel.

Forrest

You talk like you built this country. Tell me, preacher: what did your kind actually build?

Malcolm laughs once, then lets it die.

Malcolm

Everything you're terrified of losing. We picked your cotton until the fields knew our names. We laid the rails that carried your ore and your war. We shaped a market you later baptized as "free" but kept chained in practice. Wall Street's bones know the traffic you called commerce. The house you live in is framed with our backs. You bought our bodies and then congratulated yourself for having a head for numbers.

Forrest

I was born poor. Dirt poor. No family silver, no Harvard. I made a fortune because I knew value when I saw it and had the spine to seize it. That's America—was, anyhow. A man takes what's his by wit and will.

Malcolm

You didn't discover value. You priced human beings. The inventory screamed. You called it "overhead." You want applause for arithmetic done on other men's lives?

Forrest

It was legal. It was commerce. New York bankers shook my hand and counted too. Don't pretend your precious North didn't hold the ledger.

Malcolm

Oh, I won't pretend. I'll name it. Cotton kings and clip-cloth clerks took communion together every payday. The whole country cashed the checks. But you, Nathan, you built your house so close to the screams you stopped hearing them. That's not self-made, Nathan. That's just you teaching yourself not to hear.

Forrest

Listen here, son. I knew men who bled for the ground under their boots. I kept women safe, kept towns quiet. We had codes. We had honor.

Malcolm

Honor? Is that what you call a rope when the preacher blesses it? Is that what you call burning a schoolhouse and telling yourself you "kept the peace"? You didn't keep women safe. You kept them ignorant and used their fear as a leash. Your chivalry was a curtain. Behind it, the stagehands were busy with torches.

Forrest

You talk pretty. That's what you people do now: talk. I led cavalry. I moved faster than the enemy could think. I broke their lines. That's who I am: a man who wins.

Malcolm

You outran men. You never outran justice. You brag about speed while history walks you down on foot.

There's a small sound in the room, not quite a creak, not quite a sigh. Maybe the building itself has heard this argument before and remembered it ended badly for furniture. Forrest's confidence has the lacquer of habit. Malcolm's precision has the mercy of aim.

Forrest

Tell me something plain. You say the system's rigged. If it's so rotten, why not leave it? You preached separation once. Pack your people and go. Start your own country, see how you like the mess.

Malcolm

Leaving is strategy, not surrender. Sometimes you step back from a rabid dog to live another day. But don't mistake my pivot for retreat. This is my land, too. My people tilled it without pay. We prayed on it without sanctuary. We buried on it without tombstones.

You think I'm going to hand you the deed because you came dressed like a statue? No, General. I don't run from smoke. I walk through it. You burned crosses. We carried them. A cross burns fast. A deed lasts longer. Who signed yours?

Forrest

You sound proud to hurt. Pride don't pay wages. Pride don't pave streets. Order does. We kept order when the world went sideways.

Malcolm

Order is a word men like you use when you mean obedience. And that road ends at the record. I brought names and dates. You want a quiet built out of muzzles. The only thing you ever paved was a road back to the auction block.

Forrest's eyes narrow; he tastes the word before spitting it out and then chooses not to, swapping to a cleaner insult that still stinks.

Forrest

You boys got uppity once folks let you vote. You mistake permission for power.

Malcolm

And you mistake costume for courage. Put a mask on a coward, you get a committee. Give him a badge, you get policy.

Forrest

We wore the hoods because the night was full of cowards with matches. We answered in kind.

Malcolm

You wore hoods because faces tell the truth. Men who think God is on their side don't hide from their neighbors.

Forrest

You think you scare me? You think you can erase who I was?

Malcolm

I don't need to erase you. Time sandblasts better than I do. Your statues are already cracking from the inside. Your flag fades in the sun it once claimed. Kids learn your name in footnotes now, not hymns. You don't live in America anymore, Nathan. You live in its shadow, and even that is shrinking.

For a heartbeat, they're both quiet. It isn't a truce. It's a shared breath before the next plunge. Somewhere a pipe knocks. Somewhere a memory surfaces with wet hair and worse news.

Forrest

You think this is all about hate. You're wrong. I feared what would come when our order fell. Not just for me. For women behind doors. For towns that needed men to stand up straight. You tear it down, what takes its place? Chaos. Vengeance. I wore the uniform because someone had to hold the line.

Malcolm

Say the quiet part, General. You feared the day we stood up and asked for the bill. You feared the day we said our names out loud. You feared your sons having to meet our eyes without a rope in their hands. You didn't hold a line. You braided one. And you taught boys to smile while they pulled it.

Forrest

I did my duty. I didn't blush when it asked me to be hard.

Malcolm

Cruelty makes a fine uniform. It never looks wrinkled.

Forrest

You're talking poetry. Men live on facts. The fact was, my side lost. But we kept something worth keeping: pride. Bloodlines. The old ways.

Malcolm

The "old ways" required auctions at dawn and funerals at midnight. Bloodlines? Just fences with a nicer name. And pride without conscience is just hunger dressed up in a tuxedo.

Forrest rests two fingers on the chair's iron arm like he's considering whether to bend it. Malcolm's hands remain flat on his knees; calm is part of his aim. The silence hums. It isn't electrical, it's historical.

Forrest

Fine. Brag on your building. Name it. Not music and swagger—stone, timber, law. What did you build that stands when the wind blows?

Malcolm

Start with the fields. Then the rail lines you called arteries when you wanted glory and called expenses when we wanted wages. Add the mills that fed your bank accounts. The docks where the sugar stuck to the boards and the blood never quite washed out. The houses your wives cried in and told themselves were sanctuaries while the kitchen hands learned to pray without sound.

You want law? We built courtrooms with our bodies, test cases with our broken families. You want stone? Read the foundations. The mortar's got our names in it if you listen before the tour guide starts.

Forrest

You think history will give you a receipt?

Malcolm

It already has. Every census that counted us like cattle and then used the numbers to draw districts; every bank record that called a man collateral; every deed that said a woman couldn't own the ground her children were born on. If receipts are what you want, go find the iron shackle fit for a child's ankle and ask the rust who paid.

Forrest

You people always come with tears and theater. You want me to kneel in front of your grievance like it's God.

Malcolm

I want you to recognize that your "self-made" story was scaffolded by screams. You can call it grievance if it makes your breakfast sit quieter. I call it the file the country mislaid on purpose.

Some arguments run like rivers: meandering, muddy, never stopping. This one comes in waves. You can feel the next swell gathering in the room: religion, chivalry, the economy itself, like thunder far off, counting down the seconds to the strike.

Forrest

You're a clever man. I'll give you that. But clever men get people hurt. They say pretty things and poor folks pay the bill. That's what your speeches do. Stir boys up, send 'em out to march, then go home to your desk and write about justice while the mothers wash blood out the cuffs.

Malcolm

You're confusing incitement with sight. I describe the fire. You lit it. And spare me the lecture on mothers. Your kind ran rope like laundry between trees and called the stain "God's will."

Forrest

Watch your mouth.

Malcolm

Or what? Will you pray me quiet?

Narrator (V.O.)

And there it is. The chord both men were circling: not just law or land, but heaven. One of them learned to weaponize the name of God. The other learned to strip a lie of its halo.

Forrest's smile returns, thinner. He inhales like a man about to bring God into the room as a character witness.

Forrest

We believed in God. That wasn't theater. That was bedrock. He made the races separate, gave us order. Genesis said it plain: the sons of Ham were cursed. Paul wrote it clear: "Servants, obey your masters." Even Christ said render unto Caesar. We rendered unto God by keeping order in His house. You call it chains. I call it scripture.

Malcolm

Your God was a plantation overseer. A God who wore boots and cracked whips. Don't preach to me about order when you turned scripture into paperwork for chains, with a hymn scrawled in the margin. The same Bible says, "let the oppressed go free." The same Christ flipped tables when the temple turned into a market. My God didn't curse Ham. Your preacher did. My God doesn't anoint slave drivers. He drowns Pharaohs.

Forrest

We carried crosses into battle, son. Rode with them stitched on our flags. We sang hymns while we rode down rebels and kept the Almighty with us in smoke and charge.

Malcolm

The Almighty doesn't ride with night riders, Nathan. He doesn't bless ropes on oak trees. You burned His cross into our lawns and called it holy. My God split seas for slaves. Yours guarded auction blocks. Don't confuse the two. Numbers scratched into wood do not fade. They only darken with hands.

Forrest

You twisting words. God gave us duty, families to protect, towns to defend. We drew lines hard because someone had to.

Malcolm

You drew lines like a man carving up a carcass. You called them boundaries. We called them graves.

The word "God" fills the room like incense no one agreed to light. Forrest wields it like iron. Malcolm cuts through it like smoke. Each invocation a duel, not a prayer.

Forrest

Say what you want, but we kept our women safe. That was our code. Our honor. Call it chivalry if you want. I call it duty.

Malcolm

Chivalry? You locked women in parlors and called it virtue. You put them on pedestals so you wouldn't have to put them at the table. And behind the curtain you dragged Black women into fields and cabins. Don't talk to me about protection. You weren't guarding women. You were guarding bloodlines and property lines.

Forrest

We feared mongrels. That was the danger: bloodlines fouled, our daughters defiled. We rode to keep them pure.

Malcolm

Pure? You used purity like a sword. You told white women we were beasts so they'd beg you to ride, and then you turned around and forced yourself into Black women's beds. Spare me the fairy tale of "protecting women." You didn't shield them. You weaponized them.

Forrest

That's slander.

Malcolm

That's birth records. Generations of children with your features, born in cabins you wouldn't enter by the front door. History doesn't hide them, Nathan. You do.

For a second, Forrest's jaw works like a hinge grinding. He exhales, smirks again, but the smirk feels forced this time, like a mask cracked down the middle.

Forrest

You want to moralize, but money don't lie. Cotton built the South. Cotton fed the North. Cotton clothed the world. And I turned a dollar into ten. That's why they called me a genius.

Malcolm

Genius? You trafficked lives and called it arithmetic. Wall Street's first skyscraper stands on the backs you broke. The dollar you praise was minted in skin.

Forrest

It was legal. Commerce, pure and simple.

Malcolm

So was genocide, once. So was child labor. Half the time, law is nothing but power's handwriting. And don't think it ended when your fields went fallow. You swapped the auction block for the booking desk, but the math hasn't changed. You want praise for selling a man like corn? Then hang your medal on a shackle and see if it shines.

Forrest

You think industry runs on sermons? It runs on steel and fields. Without our system this country would've starved.

Malcolm

Without your system it might've been honest. You built a house out of blood and then bragged about how straight it stood. Every empire calls its cruelty necessary. Yours just had better cotton gins.

Forrest

I didn't fear you. I was a man. A soldier. A fighter. Men hold ground. You boys hide behind speeches.

Malcolm

Real men don't need hoods to prove it. Real men don't rape, don't hang, don't burn children and call it discipline. You confused brutality with manhood.

Forrest

You confuse noise with power. You rile boys up, send them to march, and leave mothers to wash their blood out of cotton cuffs.

Malcolm

And you confuse silence with safety. You thought if we bowed our heads, you'd never have to meet our eyes. My father died because men like you called murder protection. I grew up learning that dignity was a man's armor. Not a sword. Not a rope. Dignity. A Black man walking upright in America was revolution enough to scare you. That's manhood, not the swagger you wore with your saber.

Both men pause. Forrest's breathing is heavier now, his hand twitching on the chair arm.

Narrator (V.O.)

The word "man" echoes between them like a hammer dropped in a narrow stairwell. For Forrest, it means dominance. For Malcolm, dignity. The definitions do not touch. They glare across the gulf like strangers.

Malcolm sits still, eyes fixed, letting the silence swell. When he finally speaks, his voice has the weight of someone who knows how to turn a pause into a sermon.

Malcolm

You ask what I *want*. Not revenge. Not chaos. Justice. I want my daughter to grow up without learning fear in her marrow. I want my sons to walk streets without memorizing exits. That's not prophecy. It's a bill past due. You called yourself a guardian. But you guarded nothing. You built cages and convinced yourself they were walls.

The room holds still. Forrest's lip curls, then his rage slams a fist on the armrest.

Forrest

Ungrateful! We gave you this country and you spit on its flag—

Malcolm jumps out of his seat and cuts him off.

Malcolm

You gave us ropes. Rape. Stolen names. Four centuries of backs broken. And when we stood up, you lit crosses and hid your faces like cowards. Don't talk to me about flags.

Forrest rises; his voice hoarse with fury.

Forrest

This land was ours! The Founders built it for our posterity!

Malcolm

And we built it with blood—for free! You didn't found a nation. You shackled one to your fear!

Forrest

You want revenge! You want white boys hanging from trees!

Malcolm

I want justice! And if that feels like revenge to you, then maybe you finally know what it felt like to be us for four hundred years!

Forrest

You're no liberator. Just another Negro chasing martyrdom.

Malcolm

No, Nathan. I'm the voice your grandchildren will study when they ask why your statues came down. I'm the headline. You're the warning label.

Forrest suddenly knocks over his chair. Metal crashes on concrete. He lunges forward, but Malcolm doesn't move. His posture is unflinching, his stillness harder than any blade.

Malcolm

Run if you want. Hide in marble and myth. Burn your ghost stories across the night sky. But the truth doesn't need your permission anymore. Not today, Nathan. Not tomorrow. You're the margin. And I'm the headline.

Door slams. Forrest gone. The air holds the echo like a fuse still burning.

Malcolm stays standing, the toppled chair lying on its side like a casualty. He exhales once, long, quiet, almost a prayer. The silence clings to him, not empty but alive; the room seems to take an oath. Somewhere outside, a flag hangs limp against its pole. For the first time, the room feels bigger without the general in it.

Narrator (V.O.)

When the door slammed, the room didn't go quiet. It told the truth louder. Malcolm didn't beg. He didn't bargain. He demanded. And Nathan Bedford Forrest, like every bully who baptizes fear in the name of God, left the room exposed, angry, running from the very fire he swore was holy. What lingered after wasn't hymn, wasn't march. It was just truth refusing to shut its mouth.

Chapter 24

James Baldwin – Anne Frank: *Echoes in the Silence*
ACT V: Fire and Memory

James Baldwin (1924–1987)

Novelist, essayist, and witness who loved America enough to tell it the truth slowly and precisely. From Harlem to Paris, he wrote about race, sex, faith, and belonging with sentences that cut and then held. He refused simplifications, debated on television, consoled on the page, and modeled the discipline of facing what hurts. His work shows rage can serve love when guided by care, and that clarity is a kind of mercy: language tuned to responsibility, not applause.

Anne Frank (1929–1945)

Teen diarist whose hidden attic became the world's window into the Holocaust. Her pages hold fear, wit, boredom, and hope, the ordinary life tyranny tries to erase. Arrested and killed at fifteen; her voice outlived the rooms that tried to silence it. Published by her father, the diary restores scale: one girl, one family, one hope, so numbers stop numbing and the word human means a person again. She wrote so the future would have no excuse to forget.

Setting

In an attic that breathes like an instrument, a checkered notebook lies open with a pencil tucked in; a lamp throws a long beam where dust performs and forgets its audience. The window latch is smooth from learning discretion. Down in the canal, a boat sighs against its rope and stays. On the shelf, a typewriter case sits closed, less silence than discipline. Two chairs face each other at a distance that forgives. If a page turns here, the room will hear it and make the sound bigger.

Narrator (V.O.)

They were never supposed to meet. One was hunted. The other haunted. One wrote in hiding. The other wrote to expose. But somewhere between history and heartbreak, they found each other: in the space where silence remembers everything.

Baldwin

When I first read your words, I was ashamed of how little I understood. Not because I hadn't lived pain. God knows I had. But your voice... it was too clean, too brave. You weren't just surviving. You were witnessing. And you were only a child.

Anne

That word. *Only.* People always say it like I was too young to understand. But hiding doesn't wait for adulthood. Hunger doesn't check your birthday. When you're in danger, you grow up inside. Quietly, like the walls are listening.

Baldwin

And were they?

Anne

Always. You could hear footsteps on the stairs and feel your chest lock up. You could hear the creak of wood and wonder if it would be the last sound before everything ended. Every noise meant something. Every silence meant more.

Baldwin

That silence. It's something I've known, too. Different walls. Different reasons. But same echo. In America, silence is what follows your voice when people decide not to listen. It's not peace. It's punishment.

Anne

I kept writing because I thought it might save me. Not save my life, exactly. I knew that wasn't promised. But save something *of* me. My words, maybe. My hopes. The girl I was before the attic swallowed everything else.

Baldwin

And it did. It swallowed your laughter. Your first love. Your rhythm. You didn't just lose freedom. You lost time.

Anne

Yes. Two years inside that hiding place. Two years of being careful not to drop a spoon, not to flush a toilet at the wrong hour, and not to scream when the nightmares came. I learned how to hold my breath for entire days.

She touches the edge of the diary but doesn't open it.

Anne

I wrote what I couldn't say. About missing the sun. About wondering if my friends remembered me. About feeling ugly and afraid and sometimes... hopeful, for no reason. Hope felt like rebellion.

Baldwin

It is. Hope gets dangerous when they insist you stay afraid.

Anne

Did you ever feel guilty... for surviving?

Baldwin

Yes. Especially when my brothers didn't. When my country asked me to fight for freedoms I couldn't even claim back home. I lived in exile without leaving Harlem. And when I left America, I still carried it inside me like a wound that wouldn't clot.

Anne

So even freedom... wasn't free?

Baldwin

Freedom's this thing white men wrap in flags and forget how to share. What I learned was that survival isn't the same as freedom. And silence, yours, mine, our people's—is never empty. It's full of the things we're not allowed to say.

He sits across from her. Not above. Not below. Equal.

Anne

I've imagined what it would've been like… to grow up. To be twenty. Thirty. To kiss someone without fear. To sleep with the window open. But I never let myself stay in those dreams too long. They felt too warm. Like stepping into a sunbeam you're not allowed to touch.

Baldwin

And still you wrote. You knew the odds. Wrote anyway, even as it closed in.

Anne

Writing was the only thing that felt real. The war changed everything: my school, my friends, my home. Even my name. I wasn't Anne anymore. I was "the girl in hiding." "The Jew." But in my diary, I was just… me.

She finally opens the book. It doesn't glow. It doesn't cry. It just waits.

Anne

I didn't write to be remembered. I wrote to feel less alone.

Baldwin

Now the world has to listen.

Anne

Do they? Or do they just quote me?

Baldwin

You're right to ask. They love quoting the dead. It costs less than changing the world that killed them. But your voice still breaks through. It reminds us that fear can't erase imagination. That walls don't stop words.

He leans forward. The air shifts: gentle, but charged.

Baldwin

Do you know what hit me hardest when I read you? It wasn't your suffering. It was your clarity. You saw the world for what it was: cruel, absurd, unfair, and still found something worth loving.

Anne

That's what childhood gave me. Not innocence… just being stubborn about hope. I insisted that people were still good. Not because I was naïve. But because I had to believe it. Otherwise, what was the point of hiding?

Baldwin

You wrote about the chestnut tree. About beauty in the middle of terror. I saw that, too, in my own way. Music played on busted radios. Church ladies humming over burning buildings. It wasn't peace, but it was proof.

Anne

Proof of what?

Baldwin

That the soul doesn't die easy. You know the first thing I bought in Paris wasn't a coat. It was a secondhand typewriter. The ribbon stained my fingers like I'd shaken hands with ink. In Harlem I wrote to be heard over sirens. In Paris I wrote to hear myself at all.

Anne

We were afraid of the kind of noise that proves you exist. A dropped spoon could be a disaster. A flushed toilet could be a knock on the door.

Baldwin

And yet the page makes its own noise, doesn't it? That soft drag of paper. The little bite of the keys. It says, *I'm here, and I didn't ask to be let in.*

Anne

I learned to trust sounds that didn't betray me. Pencil on paper. Breath in the dark. The boat rope on the canal when the wind remembered us.

Narrator (V.O.)

The light drops a notch. Shadow does what shadow does: tightens the room. The diary stays open but still. The quiet isn't grief now; it's attention. What's left is the weight of truth, and it asks the same thing of anyone listening: don't look away.

Anne

They called us "vermin." "Parasites." "Untermenschen." Words meant to make you forget you were human. They printed them in newspapers. Painted them on walls. Whispered them like prayers. And after a while, you start wondering if the mirror believes them too. The Nazis didn't just try to kill us. They tried to erase us.

Baldwin

They called us "boy." No matter how old you got. "Savage." "Monkey." N*****. And when that didn't break us, they came for the rest. "Faggot." "Pervert." "Abomination." You don't survive a world like that without losing pieces. But I kept writing. Even when the publishers slammed the door. *Giovanni's Room* sat untouched because I'd told the truth about love that didn't fit their version of dignity. I wasn't Black enough for some, not straight enough for others. But the pen didn't care. The page took it all.

Anne

Was it worth it? Telling that truth?

Baldwin

The week the manuscript came back, I owed rent. My editor took me to lunch and called it "ill-timed, indelicate." I smiled like it didn't cut. On the way home I carried the pages against my chest because I didn't have a bag and I didn't have a country either. Friends warned me I'd be shelved as a warning label. They were right for a while. But the book was the first honest room I ever lived in. I cooked in it. I slept in it. When the world refused the key, I kept the door.

Anne

I get that. They wanted me to be a poster: pretty edges, easy quotes. But the real room was smaller, with dark corners. It was still home.

Baldwin

Say your name.

Anne

Some nights I wrote my name across a whole page—ANNE, ANNE, ANNE—until the letters looked like a little city. If they erased the address, maybe the city would still be there.

Baldwin

I used to sign forms "J. Baldwin" to take up less room. Later I started writing "James" slow, every letter claiming a chair. At customs, at hotels, anywhere somebody needed to shrink me to fit a box. I filled the box and then breathed in it.

Anne

It sounds small, but it isn't.

Baldwin

It never is. They rename you so they can forget you. You write your whole name so you can remember yourself.

Anne

I started to hate hearing my own name. Not because of what it meant to me, but because of how it echoed in whispers. "Anne's father is Jewish." "Anne might be next." I became a rumor. A burden. A countdown.

Baldwin

I used to think that if I spoke well enough, if I was eloquent enough, sharp enough, careful enough, they'd stop seeing the color of my skin. But all it did was make me more frightening. A smart Black man wasn't a victory. It was a threat. A smart queer Black man? That was a target. And yet, I still spoke.

Anne

I envy how fiercely you fought back. I tried so hard to stay hopeful, to be soft. But there were days I wanted to scream. Not because I was angry. Because staying quiet started to feel like helping the bad guys.

Baldwin

It was. But not yours. The world betrayed you. And then it had the audacity to sanctify you. They made you a symbol because it hurt less than admitting you were real.

Anne

Yes. Exactly. I became "the diary." The girl who smiled through horror. People act like my hope was magic. It was just how I kept it together. But I wasn't a saint. I was terrified. I was confused. I was alive.

Baldwin

And that's what makes you dangerous. Not what you endured, but the fact that you kept writing anyway. They can control what's said about you. But not what *you* said. Your words are permanent rebellion.

He picks up her diary gently. Doesn't open it. Just holds it like something holy and unfinished.

Baldwin

People ask me why I write so much about pain. Why not joy? Why not beauty? And I tell them: I *do*. But joy without context is decoration, and I'm not decorating a house built on graves.

Anne

That's what scared me most: that we were dying quietly. That no one would know we were real people, not just a number. That I'd vanish into ash and be remembered as one of six million, instead of me.

Baldwin

They did that to us too. Lynched bodies without names. Burned churches with no headlines. Whole cities erased because someone decided we didn't matter. And then they asked us to "move on."

Anne

But how do you move on when everything still spins on the same axis?

Baldwin

I didn't. I carried it. I built on top of it. I whispered the names. I told the stories. Sometimes that's the best we get, not justice, but memory. History forgets loudly. People remember quietly.

Anne

Do you think I'd be different if I'd lived? Not just older. But colder?

Baldwin

I think the world would've tried to make you colder. But I also think you would've resisted. You had too much fire in you to freeze.

Anne

Maybe. But fire without a place to burn just becomes smoke.

She looks at him now, fully. Not as a host, not as a student. As a witness.

Anne

When you first read my diary… did you cry?

Baldwin

No, not at first. I got angry. Angry I didn't learn you sooner, angry they teach your story like a parable instead of a warning. But as the hours went on and the house went quiet, the anger cooled and grief came. I was in a borrowed kitchen *in the middle of the night,* the refrigerator humming like a stubborn choir. I told myself I was only revisiting a few pages; then the sun had the nerve to show up, anyway. I wept. Not just for you. For the world that let you die.

Anne

That means more than you know. Not because I wanted tears. But because so many read me and never *feel* me. They nod. They quote. But they don't sit with the silence I left behind.

Baldwin

Then maybe that's why I'm here, not to interview you or console you; just to sit with the silence and not look away.

The lamp flickers slightly. Baldwin doesn't move. Anne places her hand on her diary, then closes it slowly, like a door she can open again when she's ready.

Narrator (V.O.)

The attic is nearly swallowed by dusk now. Only a weak bulb overhead hums, casting a halo over Baldwin and Anne. They don't move quickly. No more debates, no more confessions. Just presence. Two people sitting in the same small room, separated by time, joined by truth.

Anne

Sometimes I imagine what it would've felt like to grow old. Not just survive, but *live*. To write my second book. To fall in love with someone who didn't need to hide it. To walk through Amsterdam with no fear. Maybe I would've gotten married. Maybe not. I think I would've been loud though—older, braver, louder. I like to think I would've made a mess.

Baldwin

You already did. You made a mess of silence. That's why they still quote you. Because you didn't die quietly.

Anne

But I didn't scream either. I didn't fight back. I didn't protest. I just… wrote. I tried to hold on to something beautiful. I wrote about the chestnut tree outside, its branches my only proof the world was still alive. And that feels so small compared to what others did.

Baldwin

You were a teenage girl hiding in an attic while the world tried to pretend it didn't know. The way you wrote wasn't performative protest; writing at all was defiance.

Anne

You think I would've been published?

Baldwin

You were. You still are. Most writers never get that—being felt.

Anne smiles. Small, but real. She picks up her diary again, but doesn't open it. Just runs her thumb along the edge like it might still be growing.

Baldwin

You know, I used to believe in God. Deeply. Church was fire and light and rhythm and fear. Then it became guilt. Shame. A leash. I walked away, but part of me still lights candles sometimes. Not because I believe someone's listening. But because I want to believe I'm not alone.

Anne

I used to pray too. Sometimes I still do, though I don't know who I'm praying to. Maybe the stars. Maybe just to the room. I just wanted the world to stay beautiful. Even when it was ugly.

They sit with that. Not as theologians. Not as converts. Just two souls with splinters of faith still lodged in their ribs.

Baldwin

I once stood at Oxford in a room full of polished gentlemen and said the American dream was built on my people's broken backs. They called it a debate. I called it truth. But after I spoke, they clapped politely and went home. It felt almost worse than silence.

Anne

They did that with me too. Read my diary. Cried. Then forgot. Or worse: acted like hope was the whole point. Like if you smile enough in the face of horror, it becomes poetry.

Baldwin

It wasn't poetry to us. It was a survival manual.

Anne

Exactly.

She stands now, walking back to the small window. There's no view, just an echo of one. But she presses her hand to the glass anyway.

Anne

I never saw the stars again, James. Not after we went into hiding. I used to make them up. Imagine them. Pretend they were still out there. But some nights… some nights I wasn't sure if they were.

Baldwin

You and me both.

He joins her. The attic isn't wide, but the silence stretches. The kind that only comes after truth has been told.

Anne

Do you ever worry we'll be forgotten?

Baldwin

All the time. But that's not why we wrote, is it?

Anne

No. I think… I wrote because I was scared. And I wanted proof that I was here. Even if nobody found it.

Baldwin

Then we weren't writing for eternity; we were just writing for the next breath. For the kid hiding in a library. For the girl shaking on a subway. For the boy who's not sure if he'll make it through the week. That's enough.

Anne

And if they stop listening?

Baldwin

Then we write louder.

Anne

Can we try something? One minute. No words. Just… let the room remember us.

Baldwin

Alright.

They sit. A bicycle clacks over cobbles outside. The attic timber settles. Somewhere below, a glass meets a sink. No one asks the silence to perform.

Anne

I heard all of it.

Baldwin

Me too. Still here.

Anne

Thank you for hearing me. Really hearing me.

Baldwin

Thank you for never shutting up.

She chuckles. It's the softest sound in the room, but it hits hard.

Anne

I hope someone's reading your books in an attic right now. Hiding. Trying. Writing. I hope they know they're not alone.

Baldwin

And if they don't yet… maybe they will tomorrow.

Narrator (V.O.)

Hope isn't an alibi here; it's a duty you carry in a small hand and one careful sentence. They didn't survive the war. Or the hatred. Or the emptiness that came after. But their words did. Scribbled on stolen pages. Spoken from pulpits and podiums. Not just memories. Not just warnings. But declarations that even when the world forgets your name. A diary, a sermon, a voice refuses to be silenced.

The attic fades into darkness. No exit music. Just the faint sound of paper turning. And breath. Still breathing.

Chapter 25

Nelson Mandela – Princess Diana: *The Prison and the Palace*

ACT V: Fire and Memory

President Nelson Mandela (1918–2013)

Prisoner turned president who proved forgiveness could be strategy, not surrender. Twenty-seven years in a cell taught him patience that looked like grace; the new South Africa learned it by watching. Nobel Peace Prize (1993), earned not by forgetting but by refusing to live by grievance. He negotiated without flattery, reconciled without forgetting, and governed with dignity under impossible expectations. The miracle was not amnesia but refusal to live by grievance. He treated mercy as endurance training until a nation could lift itself. History remembers his smile; he earned it the slow way, by refusing to hate efficiently.

Princess Diana (1961–1997)

A royal who dismantled distance through touch and candor. She turned cameras meant to judge into light for what mattered: AIDS wards, minefields, children who'd stopped being seen. The marriage collapsed; the myth didn't. Her life rewrote compassion as something that can still sweat, stumble, and show up. She made kindness visible without polishing it. When the world watched her break, she offered it honesty instead of vengeance. Gone at thirty-six, she left a template: empathy as resistance.

Setting

In a garden that keeps the afternoon without pretense, sunlight filters through broad leaves and paints restless shapes across the grass. Children argue over a ball beyond the hedge; their laughter folds into birdsong. Two chairs rest under an old tree, a chipped teacup between them catching the last of the light. The flowers are tolerated more than arranged. It isn't a palace yard or a prison yard, just a patch of calm where the world can stop pretending for a while, and the air feels practiced at listening.

Mandela (V.O.)

Before the headlines, before the flashbulbs, there was a young woman trying to love and be loved, inside a machine built for silence. In 1997, I met her for half an hour in Cape Town: handshake, cameras, a few careful compliments. Not the talk either of us needed. I've met presidents, rebels, poets. But never someone who lived behind palace walls and still found the courage to step outside them. She was called many things. Today, I hope she can be the one we were rarely allowed to see. Herself.

Nelson Mandela sits with calm certainty, patient eyes, legs crossed, hands resting gently. Princess Diana enters the garden quietly, hesitant but composed. She wears no crown, no headlines. Just a simple blouse. He smiles as she walks to him. They begin like old friends who've only just met.

Mandela

Welcome, Princess. Or may I call you Diana?

Diana

Diana is fine. I was never very good at the titles.

Mandela

Nor was I. They called me many things before they settled on President. But none of those names knew my heart.

Diana

Then we have that in common.

Mandela

More than that, I think. And if I may. When grace crosses a room, don't wait for permission. Ask her to dance. Policies can build a nation, yes. But invitations… those are what build lives. One steadies the world. The other steadies the heart.

Mandela motions for her to sit. She does, smoothing her skirt with a small nervous habit. Their eyes meet, not as strangers, but as survivors sensing something familiar.

Mandela

You know, I've spoken with men who led revolutions, with those who built empires… but I've never spoken with a woman who had to survive a crown.

Diana

It's not as heavy as it looks. Not at first. It's hollow. Light enough to float through the fairy tale. But once it settles, it presses down in places no one can see.

Mandela

And no one removes it when the weight becomes unbearable.

Diana

No. They just tell you to stand up straighter.

She offers a half-smile. Not bitter, just tired. Mandela doesn't speak right away. He lets her words hang. She notices, and it slows her. Softens her shoulders.

Mandela

Tell me, if you don't mind. When was the last time someone asked how you were, without needing the answer to be palatable?

Diana

I… can't remember. I suppose people usually ask because they want a soundbite, or because they're hoping I'll crack.

Mandela

I'm not here for either.

Diana

Then I don't quite know what to do.

Mandela

You breathe. You speak. You tell the truth, even if it trembles.

There's a long pause. She leans back. For a second, she looks younger, closer to the schoolgirl in photographs, before the gowns, the tabloids, the walls of photographers.

Diana

Alright then. It's been… hard. Not in the way people think. Not just the divorce or the press or the Camilla of it all. That was just the public part. The real difficulty was trying to be loved by a place that never intended to love me back.

Mandela

The institution?

Diana

The family. The Firm. Whatever name you want to give it. It wasn't cruelty, not exactly. It was coldness. Procedure. If I cried, I was being oversensitive. If I smiled too brightly, I was courting attention. There was no way to be enough… unless I disappeared.

Mandela

And did you?

Diana

I tried. At first. I played the part. The wave, the smile, the perfect young bride. But I was nineteen. I didn't even know who I was yet. How could I perform her convincingly?

Mandela

They wanted the image, not the woman.

Diana

Exactly. The moment I started to show pain, I became a problem. But Nelson, you were locked away for twenty-seven years. How did you not lose yourself?

Mandela

Oh, I did. In pieces. In waves. There were years when I forgot the sound of my daughter's voice. Days I couldn't remember if I was more than a cause. But you learn… if not to hold on, then at least to not let go completely. Even if it's just by a thread.

Diana

And if you don't have the thread?

Mandela

Then you borrow one from someone who sees you. Even if just for a moment.

They sit quietly. No music. No dramatic cue. Just the quiet understanding that something real is starting, not grand, not loud, but undeniable.

Diana

They never saw me, Nelson. They saw a dress. A silhouette. A headline. But not the woman. Not the girl who still felt invisible, even as cameras followed her into the bathroom.

Mandela

Then let them see you now. Not the ghost of their fantasy. But the woman who lived anyway.

She nods, eyes glassing just slightly. Not tears yet, but the kind of breath before truth starts to hurt. And heal.

Diana

People think I was raised in luxury. That being born into an aristocratic family meant a life of comfort. But no one talks about what it's like to be a little girl crying in a forty-room house while your parents scream in opposite wings.

My mother left when I was six. Just… left. I remember the car pulling away. I stood at the window and waited hours for her to come back. She didn't. Not that day. Not the next. That kind of absence becomes a mirror: you keep looking into it, hoping to find something warm. All I saw was emptiness.

Mandela

That pain does not belong to class. I know it well. I was nine when my mother died. No warning. No goodbyes. Just the silence afterward. I was sent away soon after: to another village, another life. They said it was tradition, but it felt like exile. I was too young to understand it was meant to shape me. I only knew it hurt.

Diana

Yes. That. Being sent away without explanation. I went to boarding school, and for a while, it was the only place I felt real. I wasn't very academic, but I was good with people. Still, even there, I had this ache, like everyone else had been given a map and I was just... wandering.

Mandela

And yet, you learned how to connect. That is not taught in books. That is earned in pain.

Diana

I tried to be kind to everyone. The teachers said I was too emotional. I cried easily. I felt everything too much. But they never asked why. They just told me to smile more. Be less complicated.

Mandela

People fear what they do not understand. Especially softness. Especially in women.

Diana

It's strange. I was told I was too soft. Then later, too manipulative. Too needy, too cold, too wild, too reserved. I've been all the opposites they accused me of. But never enough to be safe. Or loved without condition.

Mandela

Did you marry hoping to find that safety?

Diana

Yes. I was nineteen. Charles was thirty-two. I didn't even know what love really was. I just knew I needed it. And he... he was the prince. The one they said would make it all right. I thought if I smiled big enough, behaved well enough, gave him beautiful sons… it would earn something back.

She glances down. Not ashamed. Just reckoning.

Mandela

And did it?

Diana

It earned me silence. And expectation. I was a success in the press, but a failure in the family. I became what they needed, but not what I was.

Mandela

That is not failure. That is sacrifice.

Diana

It didn't feel noble. It felt like disappearing in plain sight.

Mandela watches her. Not probing. Holding space. A slight breath before she speaks.

Diana

I remember one moment. Very early in the marriage. I was pregnant with William. Morning sickness, pressure, the press hounding me even in the hospital. I overheard a staff member say, "She should be grateful. She's set for life." And all I could think was: *Set for what? To be silent forever? To wave while bleeding?*

Mandela

People assume pain stops at privilege. That because the world sees gold, it must not bruise. But pain does not check bank balances. And loneliness is louder in a crowd.

Diana

Exactly. The first time I made myself sick, it was after a dinner with the Queen. I'd eaten too much, and someone made a joke about me putting on weight. I was twenty years old and five months pregnant. That night, I went to the bathroom and taught myself how to disappear. I thought it would give me control. It didn't. But it gave me something that felt like it.

Mandela

Bulimia is not weakness. It is grief made physical. A body screaming what the heart has been forbidden to say.

Diana

I didn't want to die, Nelson. I just wanted to be heard. And every time I tried, they turned the volume down.

Mandela

They made you the face of fairy tales, and never asked if you liked the story.

Diana

They gave me a script. But never the pen.

Mandela

Then let this be your pen. Tonight. With no cameras but these. With no duty but truth.

Diana

Alright then. Let's start with the lies they told. And the ones I believed.

The garden stays still, but the air has changed. Diana's voice no longer wavers. Mandela's presence feels heavier now, less symbolic, more human. There's no applause waiting. Just truth, unvarnished and unpaid for.

Mandela

You said they gave you a script. May I ask, when did you begin to rewrite it?

Diana

The night I realized he would never love me. Not really. Charles was kind, once. Measured, polished. But his heart… it was never mine. I thought it was the pressure. The duty. The cameras. I told myself, "It'll come in time." But love doesn't arrive on a schedule. It either grows or withers. And I was watering dead soil.

Mandela

Were you honest with him?

Diana

I tried to be. But even honesty became ammunition. If I cried, I was unstable. If I confronted him, I was dramatic. He once told me I was too emotional to be Queen. That I embarrassed him. But the real embarrassment was the lie we both lived: me, pretending to be adored; him, pretending I didn't exist unless the cameras were rolling.

Mandela

And Camilla?

Diana

She was always there. Even before the wedding. They were still in love, and everyone in the palace knew it. I wasn't the beginning of a new chapter, I was a detour. And the Firm wanted the photo, not the marriage. So I smiled. I smiled through the affair, through the distance, through the moments I could feel myself disappearing.

Mandela

You deserved more than endurance.

Diana

I didn't want perfection. I just wanted partnership. But what I got was protocol. Cold hands and colder glances. I'd walk into a room and be measured before I was greeted. Even when I gave them heirs, William and Harry, they saw it as duty fulfilled. Not life created. Not love extended.

Mandela

And the Queen?

Diana

She wasn't cruel. She was… steel. Polite, reserved, impenetrable. I remember crying after Charles left one night. He'd walked out mid-argument, said I was being childish. I went to her, hoping for something. What, I don't know. A mother figure, maybe. She listened, then said, "There are things better not discussed." That was the end of it. Silence, perfectly curtained.

Mandela

That kind of silence is not peace. It is erasure with good manners.

Diana

Yes. And when I tried to raise my voice and speak to the press, to give interviews, I became the villain. A woman with feelings, speaking plainly, was unacceptable. But a grieving widow? That, they could use. They didn't mind if I was broken, as long as I bled quietly.

Mandela

When I was imprisoned, the guards tried to strip us of identity. We were referred to by number. We were not allowed to mourn family deaths. We were made invisible to break our will. I see the same machinery in your story. Just with better lighting.

Diana

That's the cruel part. I was on the front page, every day. And still, I was invisible. I once said in an interview that I had bulimia. That it was a secret I'd carried for years. Do you know what the palace said? They were "disappointed." That I had revealed private matters. But it was never private. It was killing me in public.

I would eat until I felt full, then purge until I felt empty. It was the only thing I could control. My weight, my appetite, my body… those were mine. Until even they turned on me.

Mandela

Pain you bury turns into illness sooner or later. Pain you say out loud… that's where strength begins.

Diana

That's what I learned. Eventually. But the journey to that lesson nearly killed me. The night after my divorce was finalized, I sat on the bathroom floor and cried harder than I ever had. Not because it was over, but because I didn't know who I was without being the one left behind. The one who wasn't enough.

Mandela

And who are you now?

Diana

Someone who survived. Someone who feels too much and hides less of it. Someone who knows that kindness isn't weakness, and that silence, while noble in royalty, is often fatal in women.

Mandela

I was not a perfect man. I was angry for many years. I believed suffering made me righteous. But then I realized… it only made me quiet. I missed my children grow. I missed my wife's pain. I lost decades I can never return to. So now, I do not sit across from you as a moral symbol. I sit here as a man who also had to learn how to be whole after being hollowed out.

Diana

Then maybe we both stopped being symbols the day we started speaking plainly.

Mandela

And in doing so, became something far more dangerous. Real.

Narrator (V.O.)

There's a moment after pain where the world isn't fixed, just steady enough to talk. That's when a symbol remembers she's a person, and the room remembers how to listen.

Mandela

Diana, you said you survived. Not everyone in your position did. Not with their soul intact. What changed?

Diana

A shift. Not all at once, but enough to stop waiting for rescue. I remember it clearly. The BBC interview. I knew it would cause trouble. I knew they'd say I was unstable or bitter or manipulative. But I didn't care. For the first time, I wanted to tell the truth without asking permission. When I said, "There were three of us in this marriage," it wasn't just a quote. It was a reclamation. I stopped being the performance. I became the narrator.

Mandela

The moment the prisoner writes his own sentence, he becomes free.

Diana

Exactly. And I began to find a new kind of purpose. Not the one they handed me, but one I carved out myself. Visiting hospitals, hugging children with AIDS when no one else would. Walking minefields, knowing the risk. I did those things not because they were safe, but because they were real. And because those people, those who were forgotten or feared, they didn't see me as a princess. They saw me as a person.

Mandela

They saw what the world refused to.

Diana

They didn't need me to be perfect. They just needed me to be there.

Mandela

After I was released from prison, I was told I had become a symbol. I walked out expecting to find my family. Instead, I found a nation that saw me as its father. And I was proud, but also terrified. Because I knew what I had missed. My daughter was grown. My grandchildren didn't know my voice. Winnie had become a different woman. I stood for freedom, but I had lost years I could never earn back.

Diana

That… that's it, isn't it? You do the right thing, the noble thing, the brave thing, and it still costs everything.

Mandela

Yes. I loved my country. But I was not always kind to those closest to me. And no revolution absolves you of personal absence. When you give yourself to the world, you must learn how to reclaim the fragments of the man, or woman, you left behind.

Diana

I never thought of myself as brave. Just loud. Just open. But maybe there's courage in that, too.

Mandela

There is. When a woman speaks in a room that prefers her silent, she changes it. Even if no one claps.

Diana

I used to think kindness was my weakness. That being soft made me disposable. But the people I sat with: the sick, the lonely, the unloved, showed me something. They didn't want a speech. They wanted a hand. They wanted presence. And I could give that. Even when I had nothing else left.

Mandela

Sometimes compassion is the only resistance we're allowed. And the only one they can't punish forever.

Diana

Do you regret it?

Mandela

What?

Diana

Becoming the symbol. The father. The legend.

Mandcla

I regret the rooms I never reentered. The birthdays I missed. The time I couldn't hold my children when they wept. But I do not regret the fight. Because my freedom was never just mine. And neither was yours.

Diana

I suppose we both became what others needed… while trying to remember who we were.

Mandela

And perhaps tonight, that remembering becomes enough.

The light softens as the sun shifts behind the clouds. Diana rests her hands in her lap. Mandela sits back, but his eyes stay locked on her: gentle, steady, unafraid of silence. The weight on her shoulders is no longer about grief. It's what remains after the masks fall away.

Mandela

May I ask you something difficult?

Diana

You've earned that.

Mandela

Do you forgive them?

Diana

Which "them"? The family? The palace? The tabloids? The public? Myself?

Mandela

All of them. Or none. Start where you can.

Diana

The men… I'm still working on that. Charles didn't love me the way I needed. And Camilla didn't care what that cost. But I don't hate them anymore. I pity them, in a way. Because love built on convenience always rots. As for the system, the Firm, it doesn't ask for forgiveness. It just continues.

Mandela

And yourself?

Diana

That's the hardest. I forgave myself for being young. For wanting love too badly. But I still struggle with the things I let slide. The moments I chose silence to survive. And the moments I screamed so loud, I didn't recognize my own voice. I've hurt people too. People who needed more of me than I had left.

Mandela

Then let me say this: you were not too much. They were too small. You were not fragile. You were simply told that your cracks made you unworthy, when they were proof you felt deeply. And you did not fail. You lived.

Diana

That means more than I can say. Especially from you.

Mandela

I am no judge, Diana. I am only a man who's made peace with his own shadow. And I know this: forgiveness isn't forgetting. It's refusing to let the pain own the rest of your story.

The right words don't fix the past. They just keep your grandchildren from getting handed the same script with a prettier cover.

Diana

Then maybe I'm almost there.

She looks toward the clouds. The garden sways softly in the breeze. She turns back, eyes glimmering, not from sadness, but from presence.

You know what I'd do if I had one more day?

Mandela

Tell me.

Diana

I'd walk into Kensington Gardens without security. I'd find a bench near the lake. No cameras. No schedule. Just… stillness. I'd watch the swans. I'd eat something indulgent. I'd call my boys, not for duty, not for formality, but to tell them they turned out better than I ever dreamed. And then I'd sit there and think, "Maybe that's enough."

Mandela

And it would be. Your boys carry your light. Not the one made for flashbulbs. The one that reaches the forgotten corners. The warmth that tells a child, "I see you." That is your legacy. Not headlines. Not scandals. But the way your absence taught the world to listen.

Diana

Thank you. I've never been able to hear that without a crowd before.

She reaches across the small table. Mandela doesn't hesitate. Their hands meet, not ceremoniously. Just real. Human. Steady.

Do you believe in peace, Nelson? Not the political kind. The personal kind. The kind that stays after the applause fades.

Mandela

I do. Because I've seen what comes after survival. I've seen the power of a voice returned to its owner. And I've seen what happens when the world's cruelty is met with grace, not surrender, but grace. That... is peace.

Diana

Then maybe tonight is the closest I've ever come to it.

Narrator (V.O.)

No trumpets. No farewell parade. Just a quiet room, and a woman who once lost everything finding something again. Not fame. Not forgiveness. Just herself. Mandela watches her go. No need for final words. The silence she leaves behind isn't absence. It's presence, finally unburdened. And somewhere in the garden, the breeze carries no headlines. Only peace.

Mandela (V.O.)

I've spoken with world leaders. Shared prison cells with revolutionaries. Buried friends and raised nations. But this conversation... it moved something quieter in me. She didn't come here seeking pity. She came to speak what had long been denied. And in doing so, reminded me: *The hardest battles aren't always fought in the streets. Sometimes, they're fought behind smiles. And sometimes... surviving them is its own kind of victory.*

Albert Einstein

Closing Thoughts

Upon reading this book

I did not expect to feel this way.

I have spent my life chasing the structure of the universe: stars, atoms, and the music between them. But this… this is a different kind of structure. One made not of matter, but of meaning.

You have taken voices from across centuries and placed them into conversation. That is a miracle, not of physics, but of imagination. It reminds us that space and time are not barriers, but threads we can weave.

This, too, is relativity. You've collapsed centuries of thought into a single point: the past has not passed. It sits in your hands, still asking questions.

A book like this does not strike the intellect first. It stiffens the shoulders, tightens the jaw, and makes the fingers hold the page as if they're bracing for something they've felt before but never named.

I was never much of a politician or a theologian. But I cared deeply for justice, and for curiosity's survival. I see both here. I see an attempt to understand the minds that shaped us—and sometimes shattered us. I admire it, and I offer a warning:

We too often confuse schooling with education. The former trains recall; the latter cultivates judgment. When history collapses into dates and proper nouns, examinations may be passed while understanding is never earned.

Let students interrogate the past, what the room smelled like and why the letter was written, until knowledge becomes discernment.

Knowledge without empathy becomes calculation.

Empathy without action becomes sentiment.

Action without reflection becomes disaster.

Think. Feel. Then act.

Imagination is not a toy; it is a tool.

History is not finished. It depends on how well we listen.

You imagined a better conversation here. Now try one out there.

The future is not inevitable. It is shaped by what we dare to change.

– A. Einstein

Postscript

The conversation is finally over, but the questions remain. This book wasn't written to fill the void of history; it was written because the voices wouldn't leave me alone.

One sleepless night I found myself wondering: what would Jesus say to Judas if they met again? What would the Dalai Lama ask a man like Hitler?

It wasn't a plan for a book. It was a question that kept returning. Soon voices from across centuries were arguing in my head, and I didn't want to leave the room.

History too often shrinks into dates and names when what we really need are voices and choices. Silence is unbearable once you realize who isn't being heard.

If it made you smile, or think, or argue with the dead, then it did what it was built to do.

You don't clap here. You just sit with the book a little heavier in your hands. Feeling some old script in you, some private audition you didn't realize you'd been performing. Start to loosen its grip.

To my wife, Sommar: none of this happens without you. Your patience, your strength, your love kept me upright when I was lost in ghosts. You are the soul behind every page, whether your name is printed on it or not.

And if there's someone in your life you might lose, don't wait. Sit with them now. Ask the question while you still can. Once they're gone, only memory answers back. Until perhaps, someday, they do.

If that line catches in your throat, you're not done. Some words ask your lungs to make room for a version of you that doesn't have to audition for its right to stay.

Stay kind. Stay stubborn. Stay curious.

– Jon

About the Author

Jon Nelson writes to bring history's most fascinating voices back to life, not as distant legends, but as people with humor, fear, brilliance, and flaws. *The Weight of Conversation* is his debut work, a blend of character-driven storytelling and philosophical dialogue that reimagines how we meet the minds who shaped our world. He believes the right conversation can bridge centuries, spark curiosity, and make the past feel vividly human.

Jon lives in Phoenix, Arizona, with his wife and four children. He can be reached at Jon@NelsheimPress.com, especially if you bring strong opinions or better questions.